G

IN THE OLD WORLD, NAPOLEON'S EMPIRE IS IN FLAMES BUT IN THE NEW WORLD, ADVENTURERS FIGHT TO THE DEATH TO CLAIM THE VIRGIN WILDERNESS.

John Cooper Baines—The restless young American frontiersman whose search for freedom results in his building one of the largest ranches in Texas.

Catarina Baines—The tempestuous, aristocratic and passionate wife of John Cooper—she could not deny her proud Castilian family heritage, or her husband's savage code.

Don Felipe de Aranguez—A ruthless soldier of fortune, he lived by the sword, lusted for power—and would betray the devil himself for his share of the richest prize in the New World.

Kinotatay—An Apache warrior, his vengeance was the only law in a cruel, hostile land where every man was an enemy—and mercy was a swift death.

Bess Callendar—Captured by the Comanche, she was fated to be sold as a white slave.

Carlos and Weesayo—Two young lovers, their plans for perfect happiness were shattered by the turbulent events in the New World.

A Saga of the Southwest by Leigh Franklin James
Ask your bookseller for the books your have missed

THE HAWK AND THE DOVE—Book I
WINGS OF THE HAWK—Book II
REVENGE OF THE HAWK—Book III
FLIGHT OF THE HAWK—Book IV

A Saga of the Southwest
Book II

WINGS
OF
THE HAWK

LEIGH FRANKLIN JAMES

Created by the producers of
Wagons West, White Indian,
Children of the Lion, and
The Kent Family Chronicles Series.
Executive Producer: Lyle Kenyon Engel

BANTAM BOOKS
TORONTO · NEW YORK · LONDON · SYDNEY

Like *The Hawk and the Dove*,
this book is lovingly dedicated
to the memory of Helen M. Little

WINGS OF THE HAWK

*A Bantam Book / published by arrangement with
Book Creations, Inc.*

Bantam edition / May 1981
2nd printing .... November 1981

*Produced by Book Creations, Inc.
Executive Producer: Lyle Kenyon Engel*

ISBN 0-553-20635-4

Published simultaneously in the United States and Canada

---

*Bantam Books are published by Bantam Books, Inc. Its trade-
mark, consisting of the words "Bantam Books" and the por-
trayal of a rooster, is Registered in U.S. Patent and Trademark
Office and in other countries. Marca Registrada. Bantam
Books, Inc., 666 Fifth Avenue, New York, New York 10103.*

PRINTED IN THE UNITED STATES OF AMERICA

11 10 9 8 7 6 5 4 3

ACKNOWLEDGMENTS

The author wishes to express his gratitude to the Book Creations, Inc. team of Marla and Lyle Engel and Leslie and Philip Rich, whose painstaking aid and encouragement immeasurably helped bring *The Hawk and the Dove* and this book to gratifying fruition. Also to Fay Bergstrom, who has no peer as a transcriber-typist with the ability to detect a fault an author may well overlook in the heat of creation; thanks to her timeless and far too often overtime work, both volumes in this new series began with cohesive and fault-free manuscripts.

PRINCIPAL CHARACTERS
IN
WINGS OF THE HAWK

John Cooper Baines
Catarina (née de Escobar), his wife

The de Escobars

Don Diego, Catarina's father, intendant of Taos
Doña Inez, formerly his sister-in-law, now his wife
Carlos, Don Diego's son
Weesayo, wife of Carlos, daughter of the Apache, Descontarti

The de Pladeros

Don Sancho, mayor of Taos
Doña Elena, his wife
Tomás, their son
Conchita Seragos, former serving maid, his wife

Staff of the de Escobar hacienda

Miguel Sandarbal, foreman of the ranch
Esteban Morales, assistant foreman
Concepción, his wife
Teofilo Rosas, sheepherder
Margarita Ortiz (Tía Margarita), the cook

The Americans

Amy Prentice	Bess Callendar	The six Texans
Tom Prentice	Frank Corland	Matthew Robisard and
		Ernest Henson

The Jicarilla Apache

Descontarti, chief of the Jicarilla Apache
Namantay, his wife
Pastanari, his son
Kinotatay, Apache brave
Pirontikay, his son

Padre Juan Moraga

Other Characters

José Ramirez, bandit

Jorge Santomaro, bandit

Don Esteban de Rivarola,
rival ranch owner

Louis Saltareno, a merchant

Sarpento, Comanche chief

Ortimway, Ute chief
Lieutenant Jaime Dondero

Don Ramón de Costilla,
horse breeder

General Felix Maria Calleja
del Rey, viceroy of New Spain

Don Felipe de Aranguez,
viceroy's aide

Josef Manrique, governor of
New Mexico

Prologue

A warm sun bathed the plaza of the little city of Taos on this May morning in the year of our Lord 1813. A platoon of Spanish soldiers who had ridden in from Santa Fe the day before stood at attention before the scowling sergeant as he read them their orders of the day. They were to patrol the town, making sure that none of the Pueblo Indians were illegally trafficking in tobacco, since that would deny the province the tithes and taxes due it. As the sergeant continued to rasp out the orders, the soldiers were also instructed to be extremely vigilant to detect signs of insurrection among the peones, and even among the rich hacendados. A revolutionary fervor was spreading through the land, and any indication of tithes or other monies being withheld, any instances of illegal trading, any presence of Yankee traders, were to be checked, with force if necessary. As the sergeant read on in his hoarse monotone, the attention of the soldiers wandered. Several of them covertly glanced at the handsome Indian women who walked by with baskets on their heads, while others surreptitiously unfastened the top buttons of their tunics to allay the fierce warmth of the sun.

In June of last year, President James Madison had approved the declaration of war against Great Britain. The British blockade of the seas extended from New Orleans to New York, though the young United States Navy had already won some signal victories. What this meant for Spain and for New Spain—the great Spanish territory in the New World —was that the United States was becoming a formidable nation whose southern and western boundaries were continuously expanding, right up and into Spanish territory. Ever since the United States had bought Louisiana for fifteen million dollars, the Spanish were aware that the young nation was getting closer and closer and that there would be border struggles, maybe even war. Thus, as bold and adventurous Americans in pursuit of their destiny infiltrated the regions of Texas and New Mexico, the Spanish proceeded to act decisively and quickly before losing control of their territories. Any Yankee gringos found in New Spain were to be dealt with severely, even with death. The expansion of the American Southwest must come to a halt.

The citizens of Taos felt removed and isolated from all these events going on in the world, and indeed even from their own capital in New Spain, Mexico City. This sense of isolation only increased when the Corsican usurper, Napoleon, imprisoned the rightful Spanish king, Charles IV, and his rebellious son, Ferdinand VII. New Spain seemed to be slipping away from the mother country, and there was the feeling that an era of unrest and agitation might occur in the New World. The exiles from Spain who dwelt in Taos, like the alcalde, Don Sancho de Pladero, and the intendente, Don Diego de Escobar, the father-in-law of young John Cooper Baines, were beginning to find the conditions intolerable. The only encouragement for Don Sancho and Don Diego—men who had remained loyal to the Spanish crown—was the belated news that the Grande Armée of the until now invincible Napoleon had been forced to retreat from Moscow last October. Napoleon had gone back to Paris to form a new army, but would face the new coalition of Russia, Prussia, England, and Sweden. Now there was the hope that soon the rightful king would sit upon the Spanish throne and that Spain would resume its rightful place as a world power. Then, perhaps, the affairs in New Spain would return to the serenity that had been known for generations.

Yet, despite this enthusiastic outlook, those Spanish citizens who took their orders from the viceroy in lieu of Charles IV remained cautious. The seeds of rebellion had been planted three years ago by the country priest, Miguel Hidalgo, and there was the lingering fear of a revolution for an independent Mexico. What was more, officials and administrators, claiming to withhold their monies until the rightful king was on the Spanish throne, were actually using the money for their own selfish gain. The land was filled with greedy and power-hungry men who were taking advantage of the chaotic times to fill their own pockets. So, to put an *end to the corruption and insurrection that were becoming widespread, Viceroy Francisco Venegas had been replaced two months ago by General Felix Maria Calleja del Rey— "the butcher." His military prowess, the aristocracy believed, would strengthen the imperial troops against any further corruption and rebellion, even if it meant further oppression and even bloodshed.*

One

John Cooper Baines eased himself out of the four-poster bed, careful not to waken his sleeping wife, Catarina, and swiftly donned his breeches. Just over six feet tall, he was towheaded and wiry, and his sturdy, amiable features were sun-bronzed from his long years outdoors. Yet for the past two months, since his marriage to Catarina de Escobar, he had lived in the *hacienda* of his father-in-law, helping with the spring shearing and adapting himself to the monotonous, if pleasant, life of a rancher.

Until his marriage, John Cooper had not slept in a bed for nearly six years, since the night before that tragic September day when he and his Irish wolfhound, Lije, had helplessly witnessed from their hiding place in a cornfield the murder of his father, mother, and his two sisters by drunken renegades. The fifteen-year-old boy had buried them, and then, taking his father's rifle and provisions, with Lije as his only companion, left his boyhood home forever.

He had lived with the Ayuhwa Sioux, where he had shared in the hunt and had learned the signs and the words of the Indian tribe. With his father's Lancaster rifle, "Long Girl," he had won acclaim from the friendly Ayuhwa for his prowess as a hunter. He was then only sixteen, and it would have been easy to have settled with these gracious people, with plenty of buffalo to hunt and a simple life to enjoy; he might even have taken one of the many admiring young maidens of the village as his squaw. But John Cooper Baines had bidden farewell to the Ayuhwa and moved westward, in search of a new and satisfying life that would overcome the terrible anguish of that never-to-be-forgotten massacre in Shawneetown.

He had lived and hunted with the Skidi Pawnee, and he and Lije had stayed for a time with the Dakota Sioux. He was nineteen by the time he had arrived in the great southwestern region of the continent, which had been claimed by the Spanish as New Spain. There he had lived high in the mountains in an Apache village, where he had become blood brother to the chief, Descontarti.

Yet fate had decreed that the orphaned John Cooper Baines should become united with the family of a proud Spanish *hidalgo*, Don Diego de Escobar. At about the same time that the young boy had watched in horror as his family was massacred, the middle-aged nobleman had been summoned to the Escorial to answer to a trumped-up charge of treason. Don Diego, with his son, Carlos, his daughter, Catarina, and his sister-in-law, Doña Inez, was banished from Madrid and sent to Nueva España, where he was appointed intendant of the province of Taos in Nuevo Mexico. It was there, in the Jicarilla Mountains, that John Cooper Baines had saved the life of Don Diego's son, Carlos, and had been invited to visit the family's *hacienda*, where he met and fell in love with Catarina, Don Diego's pampered and temperamental daughter. After a stormy courtship, Catarina had come to realize that she loved the young mountain man as much as he loved her.

John Cooper turned to look down at Catarina, still asleep, lying on her side, her cheek cradled against the rumpled pillow, her burnished black hair setting off the creaminess of her soft skin. He smiled gently; she was making such a great effort to forget all her selfish habits and prove herself truly a worthy mate, devoted and passionately in love with her husband.

The Apache, whom Catarina had come to know, had named her *La Paloma*, the dove, as they had named John Cooper *El Halcón*, the hawk. Catarina had understood at the outset of their marriage that there would be times when her husband would seek his freedom; that, unlike her cockatoo, Pepito, whom she kept in a silver cage, he could not be caged forever, even out of the deepest love for her. Now, on this beautiful May day, restlessness stirred within John Cooper, a yearning to ride the trail into the mountains with Lobo racing beside him. A cockatoo could be caged; a hawk, never.

He could glimpse the glint of the sun edging through the

shutters of their bedroom windows, and all at once a nostalgic yearning for the pure air and the mountains assailed him. Faintly to his ears came the mournful baying of Lobo, the eighteen-month-old whelp of a timber wolf and Lije, John Cooper's Irish wolfhound. Now five feet long and weighing just over a hundred pounds, Lobo's larger head and elongated tail proclaimed the heritage of his sire, but his yellow eyes and sharp fangs were the inheritance of his dam. He chuckled softly to himself: Lobo was fretting, too, over the leisure he had been obliged to spend in the shed, leashed and impatient to be off hunting with his master.

Yes, it was high time they took the trail together into the mountains. There was a distant peak, beyond the Sangre de Cristo range, a strange, towering, and isolated peak which he had long wanted to explore. It was spring now in the mountains, and the flowers and the trees would be blooming, and beyond would be the barren patches still whitened by the winter's snow.

Catarina would surely understand: she had agreed to his freedom, and she had already proven herself to be a loyal, loving wife. He had not dreamed that he could be at such oneness with another person. Yet there was a difference here, a difference between two persons whose divergent backgrounds denied their union, and yet subtly made it all the more enduring and exciting. But now it was time for John Cooper to discover how much freedom his marriage with beautiful, tempestuous Catarina would really grant him.

Donning his buckskins and boots, John Cooper hurried to the kitchen where fat, jovial Tía Margarita was already scolding the young maids of the household into wakefulness and attention for the morning chores. Seeing him, she cried out, "Oh, Señor Baines, we did not expect you to be up so early. Not a *marido joven, ciertamente*. I was about to tell Leonora to bring breakfast for both you and your sweet *esposa!*"

"I will take it to her, Tía Margarita." John Cooper grinned. "Just some chocolate and your fine biscuits with honey—that will be enough for us. It's a beautiful, warm morning."

The fat cook bustled about the kitchen getting the breakfast tray together. "There now, Señor Baines," she smiled warmly, "all is in order as it should be." Then she herself, observing his infectious grin, asked, *"Es muy romántico, ¿no es verdad?"*

"Gracias, Tía Margarita." John Cooper set down the tray on the kitchen table and, moving quickly to her, kissed her on the cheek. "What would this household do without you?"

"Get along with you, Señor Baines!" Margarita was crimson as a beet and turned away to hide her blushes. "Do not waste kisses on an old woman like me. Waken your *esposa* with such a kiss—now be off with you so that I can prepare *el desayuno* for Don Diego and—oh, how happy it makes me to think of it!—his future *esposa*, Doña Inez. I did not know the first wife of *mi patrón*—she died before he left the Old World—but if she was anything like her sister, Doña Inez, then she was a saint. Now go on, go on. Why do you tarry? Your *esposa* waits for you!"

As he walked back down the narrow hallway to their bedroom, John Cooper wryly reflected that being a husband added curious new obligations to his way of life. He remembered how, before they were married, he had tricked Catarina into riding along with him so that they might ultimately visit the Apache stronghold and she could thus discover the joys of his way of life. She had turned up her nose at the pemmican he offered her for supper, and then, after Lobo had caught a rabbit, she had been dismayed when he blithely suggested that she skin and cook it. Now he was carrying her breakfast tray much as might a *caballero*.

Deftly shifting the silver tray to his left hand, he turned the knob of the door and entered. Catarina, still drowsy with sleep, stared at him, her green eyes questioning. Then she sent him a dazzling smile: "How thoughtful, how sweet you are to me, my dear one!" Suddenly, her eyes narrowed. "But you are wearing your buckskins—"

"Yes, Catarina." He crossed over to the bed and carefully set down the tray before her. "Don't let the chocolate get cold. Tía Margarita gave me orders about it, you see."

"But why are you wearing your buckskins? You only wear them when you go hunting or off to the mountains with your Indians." She spoke petulantly as she sat up, pushing away the thick sheaf of her black hair, but she was exquisite in her lace-trimmed white shift. He stared at her admiringly, a little smile playing about his lips. "And now you are teasing me, you are making fun of me!" she declared. "I shan't eat a bite of this breakfast until you tell me what you're going to do."

He seated himself on the edge of the bed, leaned over, and playfully kissed the tip of her nose. "You always look more beautiful when you're angry. I should know, because you always used to be that way with me before we were married."

"Yes, and I shall be angry again, very angry indeed, if you don't tell me what it is you are going to do."

"But I told you, my darling, that there would be times when I'd want to go back to the mountains, when I'd want to breathe the free air and to hunt with Lobo. And it doesn't mean that I love you any the less—surely you've no right to say such a thing after the happiness we've known."

Catarina blushed and lowered her eyes as she made a great show of inspecting the tray. "I do love you, I love you more than I ever thought I could. But why are you so restless, so dissatisfied after such a short time? Does it mean you want to be away from me?" She took a sip of chocolate, then another. "Isn't having a *desayuno* like this ever so much better than that awful dried meat you tried to feed me when you took me to the mountains that time?"

"It depends on what a person's used to, Catarina darling," he patiently explained. He took one of her hands and brought it to his lips, then turned it over, kissed her palm, and closed her fingers over the kiss.

"But, dear Coop," she said as she made an enchanting moue at him, "Carlos and his wife live here at the *hacienda*, and they are quite happy."

"That's only natural for Carlos, since he's your father's son, just as you're his daughter, Catarina," John Cooper explained. "But Weesayo is the daughter of the Apache chief, and she's already asked Carlos to let her go back now and again to the stronghold. And he'll let her do it. Because if he kept her here all the time, the Apache in her would be sure to rebel."

"Oh, I see! And I suppose you're going to tell me next that you have Indian blood in you too."

"But I have, *mi corazón*," he laughingly assented. "I'm Descontarti's blood brother, and before that I exchanged blood with the Ayuhwa and the Dakota as a blood brother."

"Oh, you are just impossible!" Catarina declared as she

flashed him a sultry look, then popped a piece of honey-dipped biscuit into her mouth and washed it down with a sip of chocolate.

"Catarina, don't be angry with me," he said softly. "You know you're welcome to go with me. I'd love to have you with me in the mountains, and you did agree that you'd come with me now and again."

"Yes, I know, my dearest one." She gave him a wistful look. "But right now it is still our honeymoon, and I'll confess I am a little selfish about the comforts here at the *hacienda*. And it's so good to have you here with me. You know I love you—haven't I proved it to you?"

She set the tray to one side of the bed, beckoning to him, drawing back the covers. "Please love me. You know, I want a child by you, my sweet savage, my *querida* Coop."

"Yes, Catarina, I want our child, too. But you mustn't ever use that as a trap to hold me, as a cage the way you keep Pepito. The hawk must always be free to soar when he will. Yet the hawk comes back—and all I'm asking now is just a few days. There's a mountain I want to explore, Lobo and I."

There were tears in her eyes as she turned away from him and flung herself down on her side, covering her face with her hands. "You really don't love me after all, in spite of all you've said and done," she groaned in a self-pitying tone.

John Cooper shrugged and bit his lip. There was just no reasoning with women. And yet, seeing the black of her tumbled hair and the creamy whiteness of her shoulders, he couldn't just turn his back on her as she'd done on him and walk out of the room and go hunting, not until there was peace between them. With a sigh that bespoke the unpredictability of women in general and Catarina in particular, he eased himself back onto the bed, turned to her, and, taking her in his arms, kissed her on the nape of her neck. "Please don't be angry with me, dearest Catarina. It's just that—well, I've worked so hard here at the *hacienda* trying to please your father, and I'm beginning to feel lazy. It isn't right for me." He kissed her again, then spoke quietly. "Someday we'll have lots of children, and a home of our own, too."

Instantly, she was all contrition, felinely twisting to him, her arms linking round his neck as she drew him toward her for a kiss. "Oh, darling, forgive me, I am just a hateful *muchachita,* but I love you, and it's still all so new and so wonderful to have *mi esposo* here with me all alone in this big, comfortable bed. Don't go just now, dear Coop. Stay and love me."

She began to whisper endearments, and as her fingers slipped down to caress him, he began to kiss his wife's neck and mouth. He had never known such happiness with another woman, and he wondered why he had to feel torn between the woman he loved and the freedom he craved. Only after they had abandoned themselves in passionate lovemaking and then had rested for a time in each other's embrace did John Cooper kiss his wife gently and rise from the bed. He buttoned his breeches and his jacket, then bent over her.

"I am going now, my dearest," he whispered, his hand caressing her hair.

After a moment she turned her head toward him, and there were tears in her eyes. "Very well then, go," she said. "I certainly can't stop you." She turned over with her back to him, her little fists clenched.

John Cooper sighed and in a low voice, said, "I'll be back before you know it." He bent to kiss her neck, but this time Catarina was unyielding. There was a faint sniff of disapproval from her, but she did not respond to his endearment. With another sigh, John Cooper left the room and went to the stable to saddle his horse and let Lobo out of the shed.

John Cooper filled his leather canteen with water and wheedled from Tía Margarita slices of mutton from the roast which had been served the night before. These he salted down and packed into a deerskin pouch.

As he saddled his mustang, Miguel Sandarbal, the *capataz* of the sheep ranch, joined him. "Is there any service I can render you, *amigo?*" he asked. John Cooper respected the candor, honesty, and dedication of the mature foreman, who had accompanied Don Diego and his family from Spain. John Cooper particularly admired his way with horses, and there was no difference in status between them, so far as John Cooper was concerned. To Miguel's suggestion, he shook his head and countered, "There's a mountain I've wanted to explore for a long time, Miguel. It's a beautiful day, and it's as good a time as any."

"I think I know which one you've in mind, *mi compañe-*

ro." For Miguel, this was the highest compliment he could pay to a man who was neither his employer nor his master. "It is the one the *indios* call *La Montaña de las Pumas*, the Mountain of the Lions."

"Is it called that because of the mountain lions there? Well, so much the worse for them, as I'm taking 'Long Girl' and plenty of ammunition," John Cooper replied as he tightened the cinch straps of the saddle.

"No, it isn't that. There is a legend about that mountain. No one goes there any more, though I don't really know why. But the story, as I heard it from some of the *trabajadores*, is that many years ago there were lions in the area and many ghosts of the Indian dead, so it was shunned."

"Miguel, don't tell the others. I'll take Lobo along, and if there are any mountain lions there, he'll flush them out. So you needn't worry."

Miguel grinned. "Oh, I will not worry, *mi amigo*. You are a very brave man. How well I remember how you fought off the evil bandit, Santomaro, when he and his men attacked the *hacienda* last winter. I pray to God he never returns. Well, don't be gone too long," Miguel warned. *"Mi patrón* will be getting married in eight days' time"

Lobo had heard John Cooper's voice and was already scratching furiously at the door of the shed, his excited growls proclaiming his impatience to rejoin his master. As soon as the door was opened, the young wolf-dog rubbed his muzzle against John Cooper's leg, uttering soft growls, his yellow eyes blazing with excitement. John Cooper playfully twisted his fingers in Lobo's thick, gray hair, then rubbed his knuckles over the powerful head. Lobo closed his eyes and emitted what almost seemed like a contented purring.

"Ah, so you've missed me, you rascal!" John Cooper affectionately exclaimed as he squatted down and rubbed the knuckles of both fists against Lobo's shaggy head. "Well, this time I'm going to make it up to you for keeping you a prisoner so long. But you'll just have to get used to it, because things are different with me now, you know. I've a wife to look after, not just you." At this, the animal stared intently at John Cooper, uttering a low growl and showing his fangs. They were strong, with the front incisors capable of piercing the jugular vein of an enemy. A shadow passed over John Cooper's freckled, suntanned face as he remembered how Lije, Lobo's father, had died to save his master. With an arrow in his side, the Irish wolfhound had leapt across a ten-foot chasm to go for the throat of the vengeful Sioux brave who had intended to kill John Cooper with that arrow.

Lobo barked and wagged his tail with anticipation as he watched John Cooper mount the mustang. Then, glancing back over his shoulder, Lobo raced on ahead as if to affirm his desire to take the lead, exulting in his freedom.

Miguel raised his hand in salutation: "*¡Vaya con Dios, mi compañero!*" he called.

"*¡El mismo usted, amigo!*" John Cooper called back as he returned the salute. Then, his face alert, his lungs drawing in the pure, mountain air of Taos, he rode after the galloping wolf-dog.

It would take at least three or four days to reach the mysterious mountain, and that would mean a week of glorious freedom, living outdoors, sleeping under the stars, a kinsman to nature which, unlike people, had no hypocrisy, no deception for those who understood its eternal secrets. Already John Cooper could feel the constraints of life at the placid *hacienda* slipping away from him, but with this difference: deeply in love with his young wife, he intended to inculcate within her his feelings for nature. He hoped that she could share his love of adventure and self-sufficiency. If Catarina was truly of worth, and he was certain that she was, she would understand the priceless gift of sharing life on equal terms.

As he rode the familiar trail, he saw the bursts of yellow in the cottonwoods along the stream, and as he looked up at the towering mountains, he saw the brilliance of snow which still lingered on the peaks. At the middle point of the range, he could perceive golden aspens merging with the evergreen forests of spruce, pine, and fir. The mountain he sought was obscured by this range, the Sangre de Cristo, and was some forty miles beyond it, in the direction of Texas.

There was a sudden cawing overhead, and John Cooper reined in his mustang to look upward, in time to see a large black raven fly from the branch of a distant spruce tree over the wooded trail, dip once over Lobo, and then disappear again with a mocking caw. John Cooper recollected how the Apache considered a raven a sign of bad luck, an evil omen.

As the sun began to set, John Cooper made camp on a

ledge midway up the mountains, in a small cave sheltered by
thick, towering trees. Here he shared part of his salted
mutton with Lobo and washed it down with the cool water of
his canteen. Then, making a bed for himself by gathering
together fallen leaves just outside the cave, he fell into
dreamless sleep.

Lobo wakened him by nuzzling at his cheek with an
eager low whine, wanting to be off. Thus far, they had come
across no game, but once John Cooper had spied a young
buck racing toward a stream far above them. The provisions
he had taken with him would last for a few days. After that,
he and Lobo would forage on the land as was his wont.

The trees and the wildflowers diminished the heat of the
bright May sun, and the journey was pleasantly cool. The
trail was one which Indians had taken and then sheepherders
as well. It was well worn and easy to follow. And when they
turned northeast at the end of the mountain range by tomorrow noon, the mysterious mountain would be at last visible.

John Cooper had calculated well. On the third morning
of their outing, they left the mountain range and came to a
plateau which led into a rich, fertile valley. Beyond in the
distance was the mysterious mountain whose peak he could
now see in the clear air and bright sunlight.

John Cooper decided this would be a good place to rest,
and he dismounted and set to work making a fire. Lobo had
chased a rabbit earlier that morning and had killed it with a
single crunch of his powerful jaws, then had brought back the
carcass. It was a reminder of those distant days when Lije
was all that stood between him and the vast, unknown
wilderness.

When the rabbit was cooked, John Cooper cut it into
sections and, as he ate, fed chunks of the meat to Lobo, who
gobbled them down noisily. He was a man at peace, and his
only regret was that Catarina was not here to enjoy the
beauty, the serenity, and the sense of freedom.

As he looked out at the valley and the towering mountain peak in the distance, he thought about the day he would
build a new house for himself and Catarina and the children
they would have. Perhaps even someday, in the rich, fertile
country of Texas which lay beyond that distant mountain, he
and his father-in-law, Don Diego, would start a new ranch,
free from the interference of the governments of Santa Fe
and Mexico City.

Don Diego was not a rebel, and it was his fervent wish that Napoleon be defeated and the true king of Spain be returned to his throne so that Spain could once again take her place among the foremost nations of the world. But until that time, he would attempt to hold back revenues from the greedy administrators of Neuva España, despite the danger that he might be condemned as a traitor.

John Cooper had had little book learning, but he remembered well how his mother had explained the importance of knowing about history and world affairs. And John Cooper, giving much thought to what Don Diego had told him, wondered if the Spaniard was being unrealistic. The world was changing and would continue to change, and would things really be any better in New Spain even if the rightful king were restored to power? So long as avaricious, power-hungry administrators ruled, there would be injustice and evil in the world.

John Cooper believed there should be no restrictions, no prohibitions on foreigners or strangers entering any lands. Free trade meant free enterprise, and free enterprise meant the very quintessence of freedom. His own father had told him that, when he had related the struggle of the Irish peasants against the insolent tariffs of the ruling British. That was why his father, Andrew Baines, had come to this new world to become his own master.

But the beauty of the landscape turned his mind from such philosophical thoughts to the pure, sensual enjoyment of the valley and the distant, snowcapped mountain. He and Lobo continued through the valley, and the towering mountain was nearer now. It was at least six thousand feet above the valley floor, but steep and precipitous. He would have to leave his mustang about midway and ascend by hand and foot. It was much too dangerous even for an expert rider like himself to hazard.

By midafternoon, having climbed a winding, tortuous trail, he dismounted and tethered the mustang to the branch of a huge oak tree. There was grass for grazing, and already the mustang dipped its head and began to eat. John Cooper took his father's Lancaster rifle out of its leather case, primed and loaded it, thrust extra balls and the powder pouch into the pocket of his buckskin jacket, and now began the ascent.

About two hundred yards from where he had left the

mustang, he found a trail, nearly obliterated by bushes, wildflowers, and the inevitable erosion of time. Here it wound directly up the mountain, and he climbed it until, panting and nearly exhausted as the sun began to set, he found himself on a plateau some four hundred feet from the mountain top itself.

He had filled the canteen from one of the mountain streams before he had begun the laborious ascent, and there was still enough of the salted mutton to make a meal for Lobo and himself. He fell asleep, but this time not until after a serene hour of awareness of his isolation. He had seen, before the sun set, the nearby peaks which ended the Sangre de Cristo range, and they hid the village of Taos from his view. Now he was truly isolated, far even from the stronghold of his blood brothers, the Jicarilla Apache.

He was awakened at dawn by Lobo's low growls. Instantly, he seized his father's rifle, remembering what Miguel Sandarbal had told him of the legend of this forsaken mountain. Yet all the way up this steep climb, there had been neither the paw marks nor other spoor of any mountain lion. Once, he had seen a wild ram, and again a jackrabbit, but the mountain was as still as if only he and Lobo dwelt upon it. The sun was bright, and the air cool and still. No wind blew, and there was an eerie silence to all this plateau. After taking a swig from his canteen, he shared the last bites of salted mutton with the wolf-dog and then straightened to look up at the mountain top.

There was almost no way to ascend it. It would take ropes and axes to hew a dangerous footing out of those massive boulders. But at least he had satisfied himself thus far that there were no legends, no ghosts, and certainly no mountain lions.

He shrugged and sighed aloud. "Well, at least we've had our exercise to make sure we don't grow soft and fat, eh, Lobo?"

But the animal was regarding him with its glowing yellow eyes and uttering short little barks, then turning to trot back toward the northheasternmost edge of this plateau which formed a kind of circle at the base of the precipitous peak.

"What's the matter, Lobo? Have you heard something or seen something? Oh, all right, I'll come with you," he said with exasperated good nature. Holding his rifle at the ready, he moved round the perimeter of this circular plateau and then stopped short in his tracks where Lobo stood. With the thick fur at the ruff of his neck rising, the wolf-dog backed away a moment, growling uneasily, and then turned to stare at his master.

"My God!" John Cooper exclaimed, scarcely believing what he saw.

A few feet ahead was a rocky ledge framed by two massive fir trees. The ledge was perhaps four feet above John Cooper's head, and from where he stood, he could see skeletons lying upon the ground. He hastened forward, and carefully reaching up to grip the rocks and then finding a foothold, he drew himself up to the ledge. On the ground below, Lobo barked frantically as his master disappeared from sight, and John Cooper looked over the ledge and said, "It's all right, Lobo boy, it's all right. I'll be down soon." The wolf-dog stood rigidly, his ears alert, his barks now becoming low growls, and John Cooper turned to gaze down at the grisly spectacle.

There were six skeletons lying close together, skeletons on whose skulls were rusted metal morions, and whose bony fingers clutched ancient arquebuses and muskets. Near them, still solidly planted in the gritty earth, were two rusted metal tripods used to support the heavy, ancient weapons. And just beyond these were other skeletons. He moved toward them and saw tiny bits of brown cloth and rotted cords. He instinctively crossed himself; these were the skeletons of monks. The others were those of Spanish soldiers.

There were flint arrowheads and the barbs of lances, whose wooden hafts had long since become rotted. Indians must have surprised these monks and soldiers before they could defend themselves. And it must have been many long years ago, for the bones were clean and the weapons old and unfamiliar looking.

Lobo, smelling something he wasn't sure of and frantic for his master's safety, had leaped up to the ledge, scrabbling with hind paws to find footing till he reached the top, and now stood growling, softly over these grisly remains of a tragedy which had taken place long before his young master had been born. Then he warily eyed John Cooper, and once again his hackles rose. Now he seemed to be staring toward the south and John Cooper instinctively turned to determine what had caught the wolf-dog's attention. At the base of this totally inaccessible mountain top, he could see a huge slab of rock, weatherbeaten and with faded, curious markings upon it. They had been etched out of the stone by chisels, but he could not decipher their meaning. He moved closer to the slab. He realized it concealed the entrance to a cave, and he could feel the cool air pouring out. He paused a moment, puzzled.

He had taken his tinderbox with him, and now he broke off a long dry branch from one of the huge fir trees, wrapped moss about the top, and kindled a fire to make a torch. When it blazed, he sidled against the opening, holding his breath so that he could squeeze through the narrow opening. Lobo barked angrily, reluctant to follow. "Hush, Lobo! I'll be out in a jiffy. I just want to see what's inside," John Cooper reassured him.

Holding the torch out ahead of him and easing himself in carefully, he just managed to squeeze through the narrow opening. When his eyes cleared and accustomed themselves to the weirdly flickering glow of the torch, he caught his breath and his eyes widened in disbelief.

He was in a large cave, and in the center was a broad wooden table. Seated on benches around it were the perfectly preserved bodies of thirty or forty dead Indians. Their hands were bound behind their backs with rawhide thongs, and they were wearing only breechclouts and moccasins.

Spellbound, he moved forward, holding the torch high, staring at the stolid and impassive mummified faces, some of them still contorted in the agonies of death with eyes bulging and glassy.

They had died, very likely, about the same time as the soldiers and the monks outside. Yet the altitude and the dry mountain air and this sealed cavern had kept their bodies intact.

There were no signs of food or water on the table, but on the rough-hewn boards lay four ingots of pure silver, bars about eighteen inches long and two inches thick and three inches wide. Wonderstruck, John Cooper turned to his right and saw the opening of a crude mine shaft. Moving toward it, he found old mining tools, and saw along the farthermost wall stacks of silver ingots like those upon the table.

How could all this have happened? Padre Moraga had told him something of the history of Nuevo Mexico; how nearly one hundred fifty years ago, the Indians under their mystic leader Popé had revolted against the Spanish rulers and very nearly driven them out of the territory. Undoubtedly, the monks and soldiers had brought Indians from distant villages to mine this silver, and enslaved them here so that they could tell no one about its vast wealth. Very likely, they had been given only the meagerest food and drink to keep them alive.

He moved back to the main room and the grim table. Shuddering and again crossing himself, he approached one of the mummified workers and saw how the rawhide thongs had dug pitilessly into the thin wrists of the victims. Their captors had fettered them with dampened rawhide thongs which dug into the flesh as they dried.

The crackling of the torch and his own hoarse breathing were the only sounds. He wondered how it was that these slave workers had been left to die. Perhaps the monks, having taken out enough silver for their immediate needs, had decided to keep the mine secret and so had left these enslaved workers to die in slow agony. Or perhaps again, as the monks and soldiers prepared to leave, a band of Apache had surprised and killed them. And the Apache, whom he knew to be greatly superstitious, had not gone inside this narrow cave opening, but left it there to guard its secret for all eternity. Thus the legend had grown that this was the Mountain of Lions—and of ghosts as well. Indeed, there were ghosts, uneasy ghosts who had died in slavery and in terror.

As he moved again toward the mine shaft, he saw an opening to the left, much lower, about chest high. Holding the wavering torch out ahead of him, he entered. It was a workroom filled with a wealth of church relics: silver crucifixes, exquisite silver rosaries, and a huge cross with the figure of Christ crucified upon it and set upon a massive stand of gleaming silver. The workmanship was of incredible beauty and intricacy. Obviously these Indian slaves had been carefully taught and had been forced to labor hard for mere survival. Their reward had been this lingering, atrocious death from starvation and thirst.

He pocketed several of the rosaries and crucifixes, then returned to the cavernous room where the dead Indians were seated. He took two of the silver ingots from the table, and hearing Lobo's impatient barking and scrabbling attempts to force himself through the hole, he called, "I'm coming, Lobo!

We'll go back now!" He was momentarily startled by the sonorous reverberations which his voice made in this abandoned, isolated tomb.

When he emerged into the pure air of the full day, he stood trembling for a long moment, shaken by the enormity of his discovery. Endless wealth. With the silver bars he had taken, he would be able to buy for himself fine horses and breed them. He would be able to buy weapons to use to defend the *hacienda* from thieves and jealous enemies. Indeed, with all the untold wealth in the ghostly mine, he, his wife, and his in-laws would be able to build a new ranch in the Texas country. Don Diego would be free from the onerous demands placed upon him as intendant by a government which had taken everything from him, including his homeland. The de Escobars and the Baineses would build their ranch and be able to defend it from all manner of thieves—those that roamed the countryside and those that ruled the country. And with these riches, there would be enough for Padre Juan Moraga to use to help the poor.

John Cooper's mind was swimming with the possibilities, and he decided to go to the Padre himself and get his advice. For the time being he would tell no one else, not even his wife or his father-in-law. In case there was any trouble—and it seemed there was always some kind of trouble in these unstable times—it was best that his loved ones knew nothing.

Two

‡‡————————————————————————————————‡‡

At four o'clock on the afternoon of May 16, 1813, Padre Juan Moraga celebrated the marriage of Don Diego de Escobar to Doña Inez de Castillana in the little chapel of the former's *hacienda*. Now fifty-three, Don Diego wore the uniform of a grandee of Spain, with blue coat and silver epaulettes and fawn-colored breeches. Underneath the doublet was a courtly white waistcoat on which he had pinned the order of the Infanta, awarded to his father by the father of the very monarch who had exiled him to Nuevo Mexico. His goatee and mustache were of silver gray, and he wore no wig. His leonine head, proudly held, showed hair that, though as gray as his goatee and his mustache, was thick and full and showed no sign of thinning with his mature age. Of medium height, he seemed taller because of his proud bearing, and he glanced fondly at the handsome dark-brown-haired spinster who, in a white silk dress with full-flowing skirt and train supported by two of the younger maids of the household, displayed the splendor of her mature figure.

Though ten years younger than her husband, Doña Inez looked fully twenty years his junior: the warmth and radiance of her handsome face, the enchanting smile which curved her full, red lips, and the almost adoring look which she cast upon him as they stood before the priest bespoke her ecstatic joy. For on this day he wed her, not because she was the sister of his dead, deeply mourned wife, but because he had found her indispensable in his new life.

Catarina and Weesayo, the beautiful young Apache wife of Carlos, had helped Doña Inez dress for the ceremony. Carlos and John Cooper, embarrassed and out of place, had

21

been ordered by Catarina herself to leave the *hacienda* until it was nearly time for the ceremony. They sought refuge in the bunkhouse, where they could talk with men like Miguel Sandarbal and the Corrado brothers, as well as Teofilo Rosas, the jovial sheepshearer whom Miguel had hired in Chihuahua.

John Cooper had returned to the *hacienda* just that very morning, after his eight-day sojourn to the mysterious mountain. His first act upon dismounting had been to take his saddlebags and hurry with Lobo to the wolf-dog's shed. Once inside the shed, he quickly buried the two silver bars and then rubbed the back of the shovel over the filled in hole until there was no sign that it had been freshly dug.

There had been no time to talk with Padre Moraga that morning, since the priest would be performing the marriage ceremonies and, in fact, had already arrived at the little chapel in the *hacienda*. It would have to wait until the following morning. In the meantime, he would keep the crucifixes and rosaries hidden in a little deerskin pouch.

Now John Cooper and Carlos, both husbands in their own right, although only of a short duration, sought not to show their embarrassment at being routed by the distaff side of the household. They talked jovially with the foreman and the *trabajadores* as they waited for the ceremonies to begin.

John Cooper had been obliged to wear the formal dress of a *caballero,* and he felt most uncomfortable in it. He would have given a great deal to shuck the tight frockcoat and waistcoat beneath, the gleaming breeches and the buckled shoes in favor of buckskin jacket, moccasins or deerskin boots, and comfortably fitting riding breeches. Carlos eyed him and chuckled softly: "I do not think Catarina would ever call you a savage, not looking at you today, *amigo.*"

"No, I suppose not," John Cooper ruefully retorted. "But then, I daresay Weesayo will hardly recognize you in that frockcoat and those tight trousers. How in the world you could ever ride a mustang is beyond me—"

"Oh, you think not?" Carlos heartily laughed. "If there is time enough before the ceremony, I'll challenge you to a race, my Valor against your mustang."

"There isn't time, señores," Miguel put in with a knowing wink. "I see Tía Margarita coming out to look for all of us *trabajadores.* That is a sure sign they're ready to start inside. You had best go in, young gentlemen."

"So be it," Carlos said as he threw an arm around John

Cooper's shoulders. "I am really happy for my father. And I love Doña Inez almost as much as I did my own mother."

"So you should. She's a wonderful woman. And she'll make him very happy. Well, let's go in so we can be the first to congratulate them," John Cooper urged with a smile.

In the little chapel of the *hacienda,* most of the congregation had already assembled. Padre Moraga stood at the altar, and John Cooper went to the side of his wife. They had not spoken all day, Catarina always seeming to be too busy with some preparation for the wedding, and even now as he joined her, she seemed to ignore him completely. Realizing she was angry at him for leaving her for over a week, he sighed as he watched Carlos and Weesayo across the aisle holding hands throughout the ceremony. He also noticed the de Pladero family sneak into the chapel quietly during the middle of the ceremony, and he was amused to see, as always, the harried look on Don Sancho's face. The mayor of Taos and good friend of Don Diego, Don Sancho de Pladero, along with his son, Tomás, was continually harassed by his shrewish wife, Doña Elena; and John Cooper wondered what domestic crisis it was this time that had made the family almost miss the ceremony.

After Padre Juan Moraga had pronounced the words that united the former grandee of Spain and the sister of his dead wife, Don Diego turned to the handsome spinster.

"How beautiful you are today, *mi corazón,*" Don Diego murmured. "What a fool I was to waste so many years in realizing how much I needed you—and how grateful I am for all you have done for Carlos and Catarina."

"I wanted to. And you don't know how happy I am, Diego—oh, how good it is to drop titles and to speak as woman to man, perhaps for the first time between us, " Doña Inez whispered to him. Then, closing her eyes, she eagerly surrendered herself to his first conjugal kiss. Tears stung her eyes as it ended, and she murmured back, "I have already made my confession to Padre Moraga, and I promised to be a very good wife to you. And then, too, I can tell you now, without shame or concealment—I have always loved you. But I am happiest that you were the one who chose to ask me to share your life. There were times, I'll confess it—as I did to the good father—when I almost asked you to ease my loneliness and to let me help with this burden of your new life, Diego."

"My darling one. My Inez," whispered Don Diego. "God has been very good to both of us." Once again, they kissed, and there was a sigh of gratification and then applause from Carlos, John Cooper, Weesayo, and Catarina.

Radiantly, Doña Inez turned to them, holding the bouquet of spring flowers which Catarina herself had picked early this morning along the mountain range. "It is the custom to throw the bouquet to a bride's maid," she said, her eyes shining half with joy and half with tears, "but since both of you are married, it would have no real meaning. Let me keep this bouquet, then, my dearest niece, because it came from you. I shall cherish it, and tonight it will be on the stand beside our bed and remind me how loving you have been—like a daughter indeed."

Catarina burst into tears and flung herself into her aunt's arms, while Don Diego coughed and politely turned aside. He was distracted, to his own great gratitude, by his son, Carlos, who embraced him and then shook hands vigorously. *"Mi padre,* I wish you long years and only happiness!"

"Mi hijo, may the good God bless you. This truly is a day I shall never forget—*el Señor Dios* has given me the bounty of a second life, and I mean to enjoy it for as long as He allows. But to have a son and a daughter like you and Catarina, and you, John Cooper, a son-in-law as dear to me as my own Carlos—well, that is even more blessing than a man like myself deserves."

It was John Cooper who stepped forward now and exclaimed, "I want to congratulate you both—and especially you, dear Doña Inez, to wish you all the happiness you deserve."

With a happy laugh, the radiant bride let go of her husband's arm and hugged John Cooper, who kissed her on the cheek with gusto. Then he whispered to her, "Remember, dear Doña Inez, how I said that one day I'd call you mother-in-law? Well, now that day has come, and I'm grateful to you for your advice and your help with my sweet Catarina. I'm even happier that you're now really related to me!"

"What a lovely thing to say to me, dear John Cooper." Doña Inez hugged him again and kissed him back on the cheek. "And what a happy day it is for this household to have all of you here at such a wonderful moment, to know that you, John Cooper, and you, Carlos, are as happy as I am. God is very good to all of us."

"Amen to that, my beloved wife," Don Diego gently added as he claimed Doña Inez's arm. "Ah, my good friends, Don Sancho and Doña Elena, and Tomás! It distressed me that you were not here when the ceremony started. But as you see, I was so eager to claim my beautiful bride that I did not wait—do forgive me!" At this, Doña Inez squeezed his hand and gave him an adoring look, then blushed again as she saw Catarina smile and teasingly wink at her.

"It grieves me that we could not get here any sooner, dear Don Diego, my old friend," Don Sancho de Pladero anxiously exclaimed. "Unhappily, there was a domestic crisis at our *hacienda* which delayed us." He gave his wife a quick, vexed glance. "One of the new maids, a young girl new to the household, you understand, was helping the cook in the kitchen and had the misfortune to drop a dinner plate."

"One of our very best, too," Doña Elena spitefully exclaimed, her lips tightening with disapproval. "And I was much too lenient with her, scolding her when what she really deserved was a whipping. But of course, since my son is foreman now, he doesn't believe in such discipline for the maids."

It was young Tomás de Pladero who now acted as peacemaker, gently interposing, "That's true, Mother, because flogging servants is barbarous and has no place in our modern way of life. People will work harder if you're tolerant and forgiving—and besides, she was trying her best to please and was just frightened."

"I know, my son. I seem to remember—" Doña Elena began, but this time her husband cut her short, his face reddening: "Please, my beloved wife, have the kindness to remember that we are here to wish our good friends joy in their marriage and not to disconcert them with our domestic trivialities." Then he extended his hand to Don Diego, who warmly shook it, and the two men embraced. Doña Elena, a faint smile of condescension on her face, turned to Doña Inez and extended her own good wishes.

Catarina moved to one side to engage Tomás in whispered conversation. Before she had married John Cooper, it had been the hope of Don Diego and Don Sancho that their children would marry, but Catarina had fallen in love with the young American, and Tomás had fallen in love with one of the maids in their household, much to his mother's distress. "I do hope, Tomás," she told him, "that your mother's little speech doesn't mean she's going to change her mind about your marrying Conchita."

"Never in this world, Catarina! It's decided. And Conchita would be overjoyed if you would be her matron of honor."

"I'd adore that, Tomás! I am so happy for you."

"Well now, at least you have not missed the real festivities," Don Diego proudly exclaimed. "Tía Margarita has promised us a wonderful feast, and all our *trabajadores* will share in it with us. Come outside and let us see what they have prepared for us!"

Two days earlier, Miguel had sent his men to work on building the outdoor oven, the *horno,* to cook the mutton and to bake the bread and pies made with dried fruits, as well as to roast *piñones,* corn in the husk, and green chili peppers. It was made with a platform of mud and stones over four feet square and a foot high, on the surface of which hunks of broken adobe brick and stones were laid round and round in rising layers, mortared with mud and tapering gradually inward to form a dome four or five feet high. An arched opening was left on one side to serve as door, with a small hole made near the top for the smoke to escape, and another at the base as an air intake. The hollow inside was plastered with fire-resistant clay, leaving a smooth flat surface as the floor of the oven.

As Don Diego and Doña Inez stepped outside, a cheer went up from the assembled *trabajadores: "¡Viva Don Diego y Doña Inez, salud y longevidad!"*

There was music provided by the flute of young Esteban Morales, Concepción's husband, the violin of Juan Ortiz, Margarita's genial husband, and the old accordion of Benito Romigar, the carpenter of the *hacienda,* whose two boys and two girls, in their early teens, came out in costume to dance at this joyous *fiesta.*

Seated beside her husband, Doña Inez repeatedly squeezed his hand, her eyes starry with joy at being a part of this merrymaking, so spontaneously proffered by the *trabajadores* of the *hacienda* as a proof of their regard for their master and mistress.

Her ineffable joy lasted throughout the festivities and into the night, when most of the guests had departed and everything had become still. Having first visited the little chapel to pray, Doña Inez now prepared for bed, her husband having thoughtfully gone outside for a last brandy with Don Sancho. She donned her delicate, lace-trimmed nightshift and ascended the Jacob's ladder into the canopied four-poster bed which had been brought all the way from Mexico City by *carreta* and mule train. As Doña Inez waited in the darkness, she blushed and trembled, for she was a virgin, and yet with all her soul and all her flesh she longed for this night. In the chapel, she had prayed to the Holy Mother, "I wish to be all things to him, blessed *Madre*. I know that I am old in years, but if you who bore our dear Savior could see fit to grant me a child by him, I would ask for nothing more in all this life. That would be the surest sign of the love I have always had for him, the respect and the admiration for the kind, good man he has been to me and to my dead sister, Dolores. Forgive me if I am selfish in this, oh, Immaculate One!"

She heard his footsteps and she trembled, and there were tears in her eyes when he took her in his arms. His kiss was gentle, almost benign. His hands held her, and she felt ecstasy grow in her until it was almost too much to bear. And at the moment of union, her cry was not of pain, but of delight in the wonder of their oneness. She clung to him, kissing him ardently, chaste yet eager to show her self-effacing love.

On the morning after the marriage of Don Diego de Escobar to Doña Inez, John Cooper Baines mounted his mustang and rode into Taos to the church of Padre Juan Moraga. The old church stood at the southern end of the plaza, a quarter of a mile from Taos Creek which divided the Indian pueblo into two sections. It was the largest edifice of the entire plaza, built of adobe, and the Indian and *peón* artisans had constructed a spire at the very top.

Inside, there was majestic contrast between the stark wooden pews for the parishioners and the brilliant *retablos,* holy pictures by native artists painted on flat tablets or boards. These craftsmen used gypsum to make a smooth, white painting ground, and this was mixed with natural mineral colors and egg. Slabs of seasoned pine or cottonwood were hewn into rectangular shapes, with the edges carefully squared, and the top part of the back thinned so that the board would hang flat when suspended by a leather thong.

John Cooper knelt and crossed himself as he entered the church, his eyes moving to the pictures which these primitive yet devout *santeros* made. There were the pictures of the

Holy Virgin and the Child, and one depicting the Nativity
with the animals, the shepherds, and the Wise Men. The altar
piece was carved from several large pieces of limestone
assembled to form a unit some twenty-eight feet high and
sixteen wide, with panels of religious portraits in bas relief,
each surrounded by florid stone moldings. Finally, atop the
altar piece, stood a statue of the *Cristo* on the cross, one in
which the artisan had achieved stark realism by using human
hair and eyes of mica. The wounded side had a sponge and
wick so that it might drip red liquid, and there was a little
carved angel hovering by the wound and bearing a cup to
catch the precious blood, the symbol of Holy Communion.

"Good morning, my son." John Cooper started as he
heard the soft voice of Padre Juan Moraga, who had emerged
from a door at the left side of the altar. "You come early to
pray, as I do."

"I—I wanted to see you before anyone else came here,
Father," the young man explained as he rose and approached
the priest. From the little deerskin pouch, he took the
crucifixes and rosaries which he had found in the cavern at
the top of the mysterious mountain. "These are for you, for
the church."

"My son, these are old and of beautiful workmanship,
and the purest silver!" Juan Moraga, who was sixty-two and
soft of voice and frail of physique, still possessed an intense
strength in the firmness of his features and the candor of his
dark-brown eyes. He kissed the relics then stared wonderingly at John Cooper. "But where did you find these?"

"That's what I wanted to tell you. And you must keep
the secret. It—it's like a miracle—" John Cooper strove to
find words to tell the story of his expedition to the mountain
and explain how he had found the treasure.

"It *is* truly a miracle," Padre Moraga breathed when he
had finished. "And yet it is not so strange when one remem-
bers the history of the *Conquistadores*, John Cooper. I once
told you how *Popé* led the *indios* in a revolt against the
Spaniards and might easily have driven them out of all Nuevo
Mexico, except that the Indian tribes began to fight one
another and so weakened themselves and allowed their own
defeat. But after them came other Spaniards who were
determined that the *indios* would not exterminate them, and
who themselves were cruel and made slaves of the gentle
Pueblo people. Now very likely, some of these military men

discovered that mountain and its silver mine, and forced the Pueblo people to act as slaves, and guarded the secret carefully."

"That is what I thought, too, Father."

Juan Moraga stroked his chin and reflected a moment. "And all these years the secret has remained guarded by those unfortunate dead—the slaves who were never allowed to betray the secret, and their captors who kept it greedily to themselves for their own gain. For certain, it did not aid the poor. And now you have discovered it. What do you plan to do with this great wealth, my son?"

"To be honest with you, Father," John Cooper said smiling awkwardly, "I wanted to keep a few bars so that I could buy fine horses and breed them. And I'd like to buy weapons so that if bandits attack the *hacienda* again, we can defend ourselves without losing the lives of our people. But I don't know about the rest of the silver, Father. That's why I came to you. There's so much there. I could give it to Don Diego for the ranch—perhaps even to start a new ranch. Or I could turn it over to charity, to the poor, just as you say."

"One must be cautious, my son. If the government in Mexico City were to learn of this, I can foresee that there would be many opportunistic, greedy men in power who would try to seize it for their own gains. The soldiers of the new viceroy come frequently into Santa Fe and Taos now, always looking for larger and larger revenues. It is said that, across the seas, Napoleon's star is dimming and the rightful Spanish king will return to the throne. But it may be when that happens the Spanish monopoly on trade and the high tariffs will become even greater. The crown will be eager to strengthen its power and make the provinces of New Spain even more dependent. There might be bloodshed, and the poor would be worse off than they are now. What you offer is a wonderful thing and proof of your greatness of heart, my son. But I must think about this. Perhaps the time is not yet ready to distribute the treasure among the poor."

"I understand what you are saying, Father, and it is for these very reasons I thought Don Diego could use the silver, to start a new life, free from all the restrictions he faces as intendant."

"That is for you and your father-in-law to decide, John Cooper. I can only advise you to proceed cautiously. There are not only men in power who would be hungry for the silver. There are also the other enemies of you and your father-in-law."

John Cooper knew that Padre Moraga was referring to treacherous men like Jorge Santomaro and José Ramirez. Santomaro, having taken a blood oath of vengeance against both the *intendente* and the *alcalde* of Taos for the execution of his brother, had attacked their *haciendas* with his gang of bandits early in that year. Santomaro and his men had been repulsed by the efforts of John Cooper Baines and the loyal *trabajadores*, but the threat of another attack was a very real one. José Ramirez, at one time the foreman on the ranch of Don Sancho de Pladero, had poisoned the sheep not only of his employer but of Don Diego as well. As punishment for this crime, members of the mysterious brotherhood of the Penitentes had bound him to a cross, flogged him, and left him in the woods. John Cooper, taking pity on the man, had freed him and given him another chance to live.

"Do you know, my son," the priest said in a lighter mood, "I sensed somehow that you understood the faith, though I did not ask you when I married you to the Señorita Catarina de Escobar."

"Well, Father," John Cooper self-consciously explained, "my father was an Irishman, and we settled in old Shawneetown on the banks of the Ohio. There wasn't a church there then, but about once or twice a year a priest came, stopping at our little town and going on to visit other settlers. When that happened, we had services. The rest of the time, Pa had his prayer book from the church back in Ireland, and he or Ma would read to us of a Sunday."

"That accounts for the naturalness with which you accept the Spanish version of the faith, my son." Juan Moraga smiled. "I think you know that I am head of *Los Hermanos Penitentes*, the Penitent Brothers. I will tell you, we of the Penitentes are derived from a lay order of St. Francis of Assisi—if you remember, my son, he was a profligate young son of a rich father who gave up all his wealth to the poor and who preached a sermon to the birds. Just so, we serve the poor and the downtrodden, but we mortify our flesh during Holy Week, and we enact the story of the passion of our beloved Savior. At times, when we are guilty of vanity or pettiness, we flagellate ourselves with whips of cactus or yucca, carry heavy crosses, and thus imitate the agony of Christ's last hours. This is to remind us that He died for our sins, and that we must not expect His miracle to purge us whenever we desire it. Ours is not an easy faith, my son, and there are some who call us fanatics—I have seen to it, however, that we do not inflict our own fervent faith upon the simple Indians, as often, alas, those embattled priests who followed the *Conquistadores* tried to do. So now you understand me better, perhaps."

"I do, Father. Thank you for telling me."

"Rest assured, my son," the old priest continued, "one such as you need never fear the Penitentes. You carry within your heart a decency and truthfulness which will quickly enough reveal to you when you have gone astray. Men call that the voice of conscience—it is in reality the voice of God."

Padre Moraga turned to the altar, knelt, and clasped his hands in prayer. When he rose, his face was serene. "Let the treasure be our secret, until it is time, John Cooper, my son. It will be safe in the meantime. It has been so for nearly a hundred years, until you were led to it—and who is not to say that our dear Lord did not guide you along the way?" Here the priest crossed himself, and John Cooper emulated him. "Even in your own household," the priest continued, "I think it would be wise not to say too much, because the servants might overhear and spread rumors that would lead to questions by the military—"

"I understand, Father. I shan't even tell Don Diego or my Catarina, at least for the time being. If I do take those silver bars to buy horses with, and I'm asked where I got them, I can always say I found them in a cave or in some abandoned house or something like that—I'll think of something."

"Of course you will, my son. Bless you for coming to me first and for offering all this wealth without thought of yourself. Most men would have kept the secret to themselves and greedily begun to work at transferring the silver to a personal hiding place. I daresay you will do much to allay the evil and greed in the world. Bless you, my son, and be sure that your secret will be safe with me. If God wills, we both may turn this secret into restitution to the poor, the needy, and the oppressed among us."

Three

Shortly after the wedding of Don Diego de Escobar to Doña Inez de Castillana, the unseasonably cool spring weather at last gave way to brilliant sun and almost summertime warmth. Miguel Sandarbal, exhorting his workers to the task of shearing, had by now completed this springtime task. The bales of wool had been stored in sheds not far from the bunkhouse, ready for shipment by burros back to Chihuahua and thence to Mexico City.

But on the ranch of Don Sancho de Pladero, mostly because the *alcalde* owned a far larger flock than did his neighbor, Don Diego de Escobar, the shearing had not yet been completed. Moreover, five of the ranch's best shearers had fallen ill about two weeks earlier and had only now recovered. Consequently, the conscientious Tomás de Pladero, in his new role as *capataz,* was working with them, with a humility that distressed his mother but secretly delighted his henpecked father. Remembering how his brutal predecessor, José Ramirez, had manipulated the workers by threats and bluff and wheedling promises of rewards that he had no intention of keeping, Don Sancho's son sought by his own honest example to inspire his *trabajadores.* One of them, Ramón Cortilla, who was still weakened from his illness, had made the blunder of seizing a ram by the neck and forcing it down upon the ground, discovering too late that he was unable to control its frenzied kicks and bleatings.

"No, no, Ramón, you give yourself too much work. Watch, *amigo,* and I'll show you how it is done," Tomás said. Moving to one of the older rams, he squatted down, then gripped the ram by the neck and flung it on its side across his lap. His knees pressing against the ram's lungs halted the

32

feverish breathing and thus rendered the ram docile. Maintaining his grip around the ram with his left arm, Tomás seized a pair of shears and began to snip the fine merino wool. "See, Ramón? I'll wager this ram weighs more than I do, *amigo*, but the way I am holding him, he can't struggle and get loose. You can take your time shearing, and you'll get the full quota of wool."

Ramón Cortilla turned and winked at his older neighbor, Paco Maduro. "He is a *rico*, Paco, but I like him much better than that accursed Ramirez. He is not too proud, even if he is the only son of the *patrón*. You know, I am going to work harder for him than I ever did for Ramirez."

"I, too, Ramón," Paco nodded eagerly. "He doesn't talk down to you, like all these fine *caballeros* of Taos. And don't forget, even if he looks weak, he thrashed that demon Ramirez and drove him away from our *rancho!*"

"*Sí, es verdad.* What I like best about him, *hombre*," Ramón muttered as he emulated the young *capataz* by grasping a ewe and forcing her down across his knees as he grasped the shears, "is that he is going to marry a *criatura*, that sweet *muchachita*, Conchita Seragos. Do you know, I wonder that his mother has come around to agreeing to it. She has given our good *patrón* Don Sancho a very hard time."

"That one!" Paco contemptuously sniffed. "D'you know what I'd do if she were my *esposa*, Ramón? I'd take a stick to her backside, that's what, and she wouldn't give herself such airs."

"*¡Silencio*, Paco!" Ramón hissed. "Speak of the devil, or the devil's daughter, here she comes. And there is our sweet *muchachita*, Conchita, watching her *novio*. Ah, even an angel couldn't have a sweeter smile than Conchita, and it is certain they're both in love. I like that very much."

"Let us see how Doña Elena treats her daughter-in-law to be," Paco chuckled as he returned to his work.

Conchita, in white blouse and red-dyed cotton skirt, stood outside with folded arms across her bosom, her dark eyes radiant with affection for the young *capataz* who worked among his men and who tried—though he was certainly conscious of her presence—to pretend that she was not even there. She sighed deeply, for she could still not believe her good fortune.

At this moment, Doña Elena de Pladero emerged from

the *hacienda*, frowning her disapproval. She was now forty-six, her black hair tinged with much gray and coiled in an imposing mass at the back of her head. The *trabajadores* eyed her fearfully, for she was known to have the temper of a Tartar. She wore a black silk gown with the chain of a gold crucifix around her thin neck; her prim face and disapproving, thin-lipped mouth seemed to rebuke the men for the simple reason of being alive.

She scanned Tomás, who wore a peasant's breeches, a red waistcoat which he had unbuttoned halfway down, and the black boots of the *capataz*.

"Tomás, aren't you forgetting yourself?" she called out in a shrill, critical voice, her green eyes narrowed with anger.

"Why, no, *mi madre*," he called back with a genial smile, "this is my work. You have forgotten that I took Ramirez's place as *capataz*. I am just showing the *trabajadores* how it is done."

"I should think by now, since they have shorn sheep for years on this *hacienda*, they'd know what to do without your telling them," she fired back at him. Then, turning, she scowled at Conchita. "And you, my daughter, it is not seemly that the *novia* of my son be out exposing herself in that gaudy *criatura*'s costume to all these lowly *peones*."

"I—I'm sorry—I was watching Tomás—" Conchita faltered, turning crimson with discomfiture.

"That is very evident. But it is not proper. You would do better to go into the kitchen and listen to our cook instruct you how I wish my son's meals to be prepared—that is to say, *if* you become his wife."

At these harsh words, Conchita burst into tears and covered her face with her hands.

Biting his lips with vexation, Tomás de Pladero finished the shearing of the ram, then let it run away bleating, and straightened, his face dark with anger. "*Mi madre*, that wasn't at all called for!"

"Do you dare to contradict your own mother? By all the saints, Tomás de Pladero, I do not recognize you any longer. Ever since you declared your infatuation for this orphaned girl, I do not recognize you at all." Doña Elena drew herself up in all her aristocratic bearing.

"Excuse me, *amigo*," Tomás muttered to Paco, whom he

had made assistant *capataz.* "Carry on just as you have seen me do. It's going very well. I'll take care of this myself."

The young *capataz* walked toward his mother and, keeping his voice low so that the eagerly listening workers could not overhear him, murmured, *"Mi madre,* I respect you, and I have always shown you the honor that a son owes his mother. But now you go too far. There is no need to talk to Conchita like that. My father has already given his consent, and you gave yours. Now, all of a sudden, you begin to throw it into her face that she is only a servant and an orphan. I will not have this, *mi madre!"*

"I think I shall faint—oh, you ungrateful wretch, how can you speak to your poor mother in this fashion!" Doña Elena exclaimed, covering her face with her hands and bowing her head in histrionic anguish.

At this very moment, Don Sancho de Pladero emerged from the *hacienda.* Seeing at once the tension between his wife and his son, he scowled and demanded. *"¿Que pasa?* Why are the two of you in such a black mood on such a beautiful day?"

"It is your son, Don Sancho," Doña Elena sobbed. "He no longer shows respect for his mother. I have borne this for years, ever since I came with you from my beautiful Madrid to this dusty place in the mountains, forsaken by all. Now, in my declining years, my own son defies me."

"Come now, Doña Elena, surely you exaggerate. Tomás, tell me what has gone on here. And there is Conchita—the poor girl is crying—what the devil has taken place? Why, I see the *trabajadores* are hard at work, and they are doing very well. We shall have more wool this year than ever Ramirez brought me—and that is your doing, Tomás. I am proud of you, my son."

"Oh, yes, now you too are forsaking me, Don Sancho!" Doña Elena wailed.

"It's only that Conchita was watching, *mi padre,"* Tomás quietly explained. "And Mother came out, and she didn't like the fact that I was working side by side with our *trabajadores.* Then she told Conchita she'd best go to the kitchen and learn how to cook my meals."

"I understand. I think, my son, it is time for me to assert myself. I have waited far too long. And in a sense, I am glad this happened before your marriage. I welcome you and your wife-to-be. I respect you both. As for you, Doña Elena, I have something to say to you. And it can't be said out here in view of all the others—come along with me, woman!"

With this, he grasped his wife by the wrist and, ignoring her shrill cries of rebuke, led her back into the *hacienda*. Don Sancho himself was unrecognizable. All these years, he had kowtowed to his haughty wife, suffering her constant carping over the poor servants, the discomforts of Taos as against her illustrious and luxurious home in Madrid. He had effaced himself here in Nuevo Mexico in catering to her foibles because of the guilt he felt for forcing her to leave Spain for this abandoned little town in the mountain range, months away even from the comparatively lesser glories of New Spain. But now, perhaps because the warm spring air and the sun had revived him, or perhaps because he had secretly exulted in his hitherto placid young son's defiance, he paid her plaints no heed as he drew her stumbling down the hallway, past several of the scandalized maids who gasped and crossed themselves, until he had reached their bedroom. Then, shoving her inside and bolting the door, he glowered, "This time, you have really gone too far, Doña Elena! As *el Señor Dios* is my witness, I have done everything in this world a man could do to make you happy, to make it up to you for having taken you away from your *bailes* and your *fiestas* and all your far more handsome and eligible suitors in Madrid. But now, after all these years of marriage, Doña Elena, I want you to understand that you would try the patience of a saint himself. And you have tried mine for the very last time, woman. I have wanted to do this for years, and now, thanks to your treatment of my son and this fine young girl whom I shall be proud to accept as my daughter-in-law, I am going to try to teach you a lesson—I only pray it is not too late in life for you to profit from it!"

"What in the world are you talking about? Have you taken leave of your very senses, Don Sancho de Pladero? Let me up at once—oh, not my skirt and petticoats—oh, heavens, I shall die of very shame—"

His tall, mature wife uttered cry upon cry of indignation and disbelief as, seating himself on their wide bed, Don Sancho de Pladero flung Doña Elena across his lap, and hoisting her skirt and petticoats and tucking them up above her waist, he delivered a resounding smack upon her svelte posterior.

"Oh, no—I am not a child—how dare you assault me in this humiliating fashion?" Doña Elena howled. "Don Sancho de Pladero, I warn you, I shall leave you—I shall—*ayudame!* No, you are hurting me—good heavens, I can't bear it—stop it—will you let me up—I implore you—oh, it is too much, please, you are hurting me—you truly are—oh, please, I beg your pardon—I'll do anything you want—only stop, stop, my beloved husband, the pain is dreadful—I'll be good—I won't ever criticize Conchita again, nor my son, either—only stop, I implore you!"

Despite all her entreaties, her husband remained impassive. Controlling her frantic squirmings, with a strength she had not believed possible in a man of fifty-five years of age, he continued to spank her with increasing vigor until she dissolved into tears and lay abject across his lap.

His face crimson from the exertion and also from a sudden access of sensuality, Don Sancho demanded, "Well now, woman, do you promise never to interfere in the affairs of my son and Conchita again?" He punctuated this query with another emphatic open-handed blow of his right palm which drew a shrill, "*¡Sí, sí, mi esposo!* I will do anything you say, if you will only stop! I swear it by all the saints!"

"Very well, then. I have your oath, and you had best not try to get out of it, or I'll use something stronger than my hand the next time!"

He drew her up, and suddenly Doña Elena de Pladero flung her arms around her husband's neck and hid her face against his chest as she sobbed out her repentance.

But there was still another surprise in store for the former virago of the de Pladero household. Her husband began kissing her passionately as he deftly slipped down her drawers, and Doña Elena found herself in the conjugal posture of submission to her husband's ardent yearnings.

"Oh, *Dios*—how can you—oh, in broad daylight, too—oh, my husband—ohh—oh, *Dios*—oh, yes, please, oh, I'll be so good!" she groaned; and with this, Doña Elena's transformation from shrew into contritely humble and adoring wife and mother was complete.

It had been several months since José Ramirez, *capataz* for Don Sancho de Pladero, had vanished from Taos. The squat, coarse-featured, thickly-mustachioed foreman had, ever since he had ingratiated himself into the post of foreman for the *alcalde,* used his authority to coerce the attractive maids of the de Pladero household to cater to his depraved lusts. Early during his tenure, he had compelled the young Consuela Viola to become his concubine, and to spy on the other *criadas* of the household. Because of his tyranny and sadism, many of these helpless young girls had acquiesced to his carnal demands. Tomás de Pladero had seen José Ramirez's attempt to fondle Conchita, his beloved, and had of his own accord thrashed the scoundrel and discharged him from the *ranchero.*

José Ramirez, brooding over this dismissal by a young man whom he had considered a total weakling, had taken his revenge. To pay back the de Pladeros, he had killed many of the young lambs by injecting them with dried rattlesnake venom. But the Penitentes had discovered his crime and had taken Ramirez out to the mountains and there, tying him to a wooden cross, stripped and flogged him, and left him to atone for his sins.

John Cooper, while walking Lobo, had found the *capataz* and, cutting him free, had given him water from his canteen and then told him to go back to Mexico and never return.

José Ramirez had indeed gone back to Mexico, to his home province of Durango, which he hadn't seen for nineteen years. He knew the province well, having spent the first part of his life there, and it was easy for him to earn his livelihood here by working as an assistant to *hacendados.*

He had shaved off his mustache to change his appearance, and had dyed his black hair gray to further his disguise. In addition, he had adopted the name of Calderón, which had been that of his mother's uncle. These were precautionary acts to protect himself in the event that he might be still wanted for a murder he had committed here nineteen years earlier. Though he now knew himself to be in no danger from the authorities, it suited him to retain the name and keep his disguise.

He changed jobs twice within this time, to test the strength of his disguise and to make certain that the past had been completely forgotten. Also, he was careful not to become involved with any woman. His brutal, *macho* vitality had, to be sure, attracted several *criadas* on the two *rancheros* where he had spent the last several months, but he studiously

avoided them. What consumed him all this while was his
hatred for the de Pladeros, as well as for the sanctimonious
Penitentes who had whipped him like the lowliest of *peones*
and left him tied to that cross to die. He had no love, either,
for the young mountain man who had saved him from death
and given him another chance to redeem himself. If anything,
his hatred for John Cooper Baines was all the more intense
for the latter's having been witness to his ignominious punishment. Someday, he promised himself, he would return to
Taos and pay back that accursed Tomás de Pladero, as well
as the blond *gringo*.

Yet he couldn't do it alone, he knew. Somehow, he must
find someone to become his ally, someone with friends who
enjoyed a good fight with plenty of tequila and *mujeres* and
even *dinero* as payment for their sport. He had gone without
a woman now for nearly a year—to be sure, that didn't count
the times he'd visited the *casa de putas* in the little border town
of Ceballos. But of course, it wasn't the same thing. Not the
way it had been back in Taos, when he had been *capataz* and
had the power of the whip over these frightened young
criadas whom he could teach to gratify his lusts simply by the
threat of a good flogging. This new job of his, working as a
sheepherder for a nearly blind old *hacendado* whose wife was
nearly as old as he was and whose *criadas* were all stupid
indios, fat and smelly and not a one among the lot to tempt
him, wouldn't last much longer, anyway. Old Sebastian Gal-
vez had told him just the other day that he and his wife were
planning to sell the *ranchero* and go back to Mexico City to
spend their last years in retirement.

So, on this Friday in May, when he received his wages,
José Ramirez mounted his horse and rode into Ceballos in a
glum mood. It would be like every other week: a bottle of
very bad tequila which would cost him double what it was
worth, and then an hour with one of the stupid *putas* at
Señora Madriaga's house. There were five of them: he'd had
all of them, and he knew in advance how they'd act. If it
wasn't that his *cojones* told him that he needed release, he
wouldn't even bother with them.

Tonight, the little *posada* on the outskirts of the town
was nearly empty. Ramirez mouthed a curt greeting to the
gaunt bartender, fished out two silver *pesos*, and received a
bottle of tequila. He waved away the glass offered to him, for

it was certain to be fly-specked and even chipped. What a wretched place for a man of his stature and abilities, he thought to himself.

There was only one other customer in the *posada* this evening, a coarse-featured, stocky man with a huge mustache and thick black stubble on his fat jowls. He wore a dirty sombrero pulled down over one side of his face, and thick *calzoneras*. Ramirez observed that a nearly empty bottle stood beside him on the table and that his glass was empty. Out of a need for companionship, he accosted the stranger: "*Amigo*, will you drink a glass of tequila to my health? I have a fresh bottle here, and I don't like to drink alone."

The man at the table turned slowly, pulled his sombrero back, and squinted at José Ramirez. Then he shrugged, "*Gracias, hombre.* For want of anything better to do in this stinking little town. But since you want me to drink to your health, I should at least know your name," the fat-jowled man proposed.

"It is José Ramirez." He was reassured enough to give his real name. "And you?"

"Jorge Santomaro, *servidor de usted.*"

Ramirez started and nearly dropped the bottle to the floor, his eyes widening. "*¡Jesus María!*" he blurted out. Then he crosesd himself.

His companion uttered a dry chuckle. "I see you have heard of me, *mi compañero.*"

Ramirez leaned across the table, his face suddenly eager, his dark eyes glittering with excitement.

"Señor Santomaro, I hope you won't take offense at what I'm about to say to you, but the fact is, I had to fight against you last winter—oh, believe me, Señor Santomaro, it was only because I was the *capataz* and was ordered by my *patrón* to defend his *hacienda.*" Ramirez, with an ingratiating smile, spread out his hands with the gesture of a man who could hardly be held responsible for what he had done.

"*¡Caramba!* Now you begin to interest me, *mi compañero.*" Jorge Santomaro put the glass to his lips and downed a hearty gulp of the raw tequila, then he leaned toward his companion. "Then you must have been the *capataz* for that swine of an *alcalde*, Don Sancho de Pladero, who had my poor brother, Manuel, hanged eight years ago."

"That's right. But I swear to you, by the memory of my mother and by all the saints in heaven, Señor Santomaro, that

I personally had nothing against you—it was only my duty to have my men ready for the attack of your *bandidos!*"

"Keep your voice down, *hombre*. Luis there is a friend of mine, but there is no sense in letting his long ears take in more than he needs to know about me, ¿*comprende?* Well, now, we have a good deal in common, I'd say. You know, then, that after we were beaten off at Don Sancho de Pladero's *hacienda*, we turned to attack that of the *intendente*. And there was a *gringo*, a tall young *rubio* with a savage wolf he'd trained to kill men—a *diablo gringo*."

"I know whom you mean, Señor Santomaro. His name is John Cooper Baines. I have no love for him, either, any more than for that *patrón* of mine and his son, Tomás," José Ramirez eagerly confided. "I was later told that it was he who planned the counterattack against you and your men, Señor Santomaro."

"Well, then, I have a score to settle with him, as well as with your accursed *patrón*, it appears. But how is it that a young *gringo* should live at the *hacienda* of the *intendente* of Taos?"

"Because he married Don Diego's daughter, Catarina, that's why." Ramirez was anxious to enlighten the man whom he now regarded as his heaven-sent avenger. "That one! I saw her riding on her mare, and she gave herself the airs of a *duquesa*. To tame such a spoiled hellcat as that one, this accursed *gringo* must surely have used the whip!"

Santomaro grinned crookedly, baring discolored, rotting teeth. "And it would please you, *mi amigo*, to do that to her, I'm guessing."

"With the greatest pleasure in the world, Señor Santomaro!" Ramirez agreed.

"You can be useful to me, Ramirez. Now listen to me. I've been a *jefe* of *bandidos* for eleven years. It began when my companions and I worked from dawn to sunset for a few *centavos* in the silver mines of a *rico* in the province of Cohuahila. And one day, our *patrón*, to teach us all a lesson of obedience, as he told us, had one of my friends whipped to death because he'd been caught stealing some of the ore from the mine."

"*¡Muerto a los ricos!*" Ramirez muttered, as he took another swig from the bottle, then filled the bandit's glass to the brim. He made a sign to the gaunt bartender to bring another bottle and, with a flourish, counted out two more silver *pesos.* Then, turning back to Santomaro, he excitedly asked, "But you paid that *patrón,* back, didn't you?"

A cruel smile twisted Santomaro's lips as he nodded. "Yes, you can say that. We tied him to the table in his kitchen, and we cut him with our knives, slowly, so that he wouldn't die too quickly. And after that, we took his wife and daughter until they were exhausted from servicing us. Then we cut their throats. And those *peones* and I became *bandidos,* and no royalist troops sent to pursue us ever found us."

"How I envy you, *mi compañero!*" Ramirez breathed.

"My brother, Manuel, five years younger than I, wanted to be *jefe.* I warned him that to raid Santa Fe and even Taos was madness, because of all the *soldados* there, but he took fifteen men with him. Only three survived, and they were hanged, and it was Don Sancho de Pladero who pronounced the sentence on my brother." Santomaro shrugged. "Last year, when I had assembled another band, I sought to pay back that murderer. My men were dispersed, but all that is in the past. Now, I am recruiting loyal men who will follow me."

"And you are thinking of going back to Taos?" Ramirez hazarded.

"In time, *amigo,* in good time." Santomaro reached for his glass and finished it in a single gulp, then set it down with a loud clatter on the table. "First, there are *mujeres* and *mucho dinero* to be had for the taking. There is much unrest in Nueva España nowadays. Why, in the province of Chihuahua, and in San Luis Potosí, there have been revolts of the *peones.* The *soldados* are busy, and they are scattered. Now, with my band of strong, well-armed men, I can raid the towns in the provinces of Sonora and in the northern border of Chihuahua. Horses, weapons, women, and gold are there for the taking."

"And then?" Ramirez whispered, trembling with excitement.

"Why, *mi compañero,* and then, when we are strong, when we are more than a match for those cowardly royalist *soldados,* we can go back to Taos and settle the scores—yours, as well as mine."

"I'll join you! I ask only a chance of avenging the injustices done me in Taos, Señor Santomaro."

Santomaro smiled. "From what you say to me, I know

that you will be loyal. And you will help me win my own vengeance. Tomorrow, I ride to Allende, where I have two good friends. They will be the beginning of my new band. And you shall be my lieutenant, José Ramirez. But understand this"—the bandit's eyes suddenly narrowed and grew cold—"you will take orders from me, and you will follow them. I shall be the *jefe* in all things. Understand that, and we shall do well together, *mi compañero*. Otherwise—"

"*¡Comprendo, mi jefe!*" José Ramirez babbled, as he extended his hand in token of their pact.

Four

It seemed to Carlos de Escobar, now approaching his twenty-second birthday, that life could be no more beautiful and rewarding than what he was now enjoying. True, he still did not have any clear-cut goals for the future. He knew that he didn't enjoy the prospect of becoming a sheep rancher like his father, and, indeed, it continued to distress Don Diego that his handsome and exuberant young son, though married, had not yet decided what to do with his life. Still, there was great consolation in that the young man was supremely happy. Many times, since his marriage to the lovely seventeen-year-old Weesayo, daughter of the Jicarilla Apache chief, Descontarti, Carlos had gone into the little chapel to thank the good God for granting him such happiness with this enchanting, gentle girl. Also, he had said prayers for the well-being of his good friend, John Cooper Baines, married to his sister, Catarina.

As for Weesayo herself, she had been overjoyed by the gracious and warmhearted reception extended to her by Carlos's father, Don Diego, and by the sympathetic Doña Inez. She remembered how both of them had kissed her and wished her long years of joy after her second wedding in the chapel by Padre Moraga. To be sure, the Apache wedding performed by the shaman was what most counted for her; but because she understood that it was Don Diego's wish to see his only son married by a priest, she had eagerly consented— particularly when Carlos had told her that this would be his pledge to love and respect and adore her all their lives together. She was happy that Don Diego and Doña Inez were married now: they seemed so kind, so concerned with every-

44

one else's welfare, that it was high time their own lives were happily merged.

To please Don Diego, Weesayo had left off dressing in her usual light-colored deerskin, though she still wore the turquoise necklace which her father had given her. Her blue-black hair was plaited into a single braid which fell to the right and nearly to the middle of her back, but she no longer placed the white eagle's feather in it, a sign that she was now married. Doña Inez had given her a pretty, white silk blouse and a blue skirt, and both she and Don Diego had exclaimed how well this new attire enhanced Weesayo's loveliness.

What pleased her greatly, though it also embarrassed her a good deal, was the respect and consideration shown to her by the maids of the household. The wife of Andrés Barceló, Louisita, had been assigned to her as personal maid. Weesayo could not quite get used to the ceremonial bringing in of the breakfast tray by this jovial young woman, and had blushingly told Carlos that she was not used to having anyone wait on her.

This evening, the very day after Doña Elena de Pladero had discovered that she did not know quite everything about her husband after more than twenty years of marriage, Weesayo lay beside Carlos in the quiet darkness of their comfortable chamber. Her hands grasping his, she murmured, "Would you be angry with me, my husband, if I asked you to take me back to the village of my father? I know he would like to see us both and be certain that all goes well with us."

"Light of the Mountain, dearest light of my life, whenever you wish it," Carlos tenderly responded as he held her close to him.

Weesayo uttered a heartfelt sigh as she reached up with her soft palm to touch his face. *"Mi esposo,* do you, can you know how happy you have made me?"

"It is rather I who would say this to you, my Weesayo," the young Spaniard whispered back. "All my life, even when I am very old and even if I should be blind—though I pray *Dios* to let me have my sight to the very last so I may see your lovely face—I shall remember how you looked when you came out of your father's lodge and John Cooper and I were there. It was then I fell in love with you, *mi corazón!"*

"And I also with you, *mi* Carlos," she whispered. Her palm caressed his cheek and then brushed the short Vandyke beard, and suddenly she giggled. "You could never pass for one of my people, *mi querido*," she teased him. "All the men of our tribe pluck out the hairs of the beard, or scrape them off with the side of a knife or the head of a lance."

"That sounds very painful, my dearest one," he laughed softly. "My people use a razor, made of the finest Damascus or Toledo steel. Ah, that's right, you have not seen me shave yet. Tomorrow morning I'll show you how it is done. And although I love your people and their ways, I do not think I should care to give up my razor for either plucking out the thick hairs I have in my beard or scraping them off."

Weesayo laughed happily. "I thank the Great Spirit that He brought you to me to be my man, and that I am now your *esposa*—oh, how I love that word in your language! And Carlos, *mi esposo querido*, I must tell you something. I— Carlos, *mi esposo*, I am with child."

"Weesayo, how wonderful! Oh, my darling, a child of our love; surely *el Señor Dios* will bless our child!"

"I pray so, too, and to my Great Spirit, *mi* Carlos," she whispered back, her face turned from him now and her eyes wet with tears she could no longer suppress. "But by our laws, once an Apache squaw is with child, she may not share the blanket with her husband until the child is weaned. Oh, Carlos, I have known squaws in our village who must wait two years before they may again lie with their men. And yet—and I know I am wicked and shameless, and you must forgive me because I love you so much—I do not think I could bear it to be without you all that time!"

He leaned over her now, cupping her face in his hands, murmuring endearments as he kissed the tears away and then took her lips. Hoarsely he murmured, "You know that I respect you and your people and your laws, *querida*."

"Oh, Carlos, Carlos," she sobbed as she flung her arms around him. "It is our law, not my wish—please know that, but I love you so much, even more than life itself!"

"Hush, my dear one, my Light of the Mountains!" He, too, was close to tears now. Lying back, he drew her to him and held her close against him, with her head cradled against his chest. He stroked her cheek and her hair, and then whispered, "My darling one, my Weesayo, it is true that we were married by the shaman. But don't forget, we came to the chapel of my father's *hacienda* and Padre Moraga solemnized our union in the faith of the people you and your father call white-eyes. Now, if that is so, then isn't it true that we now belong to both worlds, yours as well as mine? And in our faith, Weesayo, our Great Spirit bids us cleave unto each other and give each other joy and comfort throughout our lives."

She stared at him wide-eyed. "Is that true, *mi corazón?* Your Great Spirit will not rebuke us both if—if we lie together when I am strong again and after our child is born?"

"Of course He won't, my darling. He will know that we love each other dearly and that we obey His holy commandment."

"I am so glad!" she whispered as she hugged him and kissed him ardently. "And let us visit my father at once. I must tell him about our child, and I will explain to him just what you have said, how we come from two different worlds that are now one. And I think he will understand, because he knows that you care for me and will protect me."

"To my dying breath," he said in a voice that trembled with ardor. And then later, when she cried out in her ecstasy, he held her close to him and whispered, "All my life I will remember how I saw you that first time, and how I knew that there could never, will never, be any other woman in the world for me. I pray that even your shaman will know that here with me you will be truly my beloved woman as you were in your father's stronghold."

Early the next morning, before leaving for the Apache stronghold, Carlos and his wife went into the chapel where they had been married. As they knelt down before the altar, Carlos, crossing himself, murmured to Weesayo, "Look carefully, my darling, at the statue of the *Cristo.*"

Weesayo, kneeling beside him, her hands clasped in prayer, lifted her face and then uttered a startled gasp. "But, *mi* Carlos, it is the face of an *indio* on the *Cristo!* How is that possible?"

He turned to smile at her, his eyes admiring her slim grace, her softly rounded face with its almost ethereal beauty, the large, dark, eagerly questioning eyes. "Five years ago, *mi dulce,* when my father came to Taos as *intendente,* Don Sancho de Pladero asked him to sit in judgment on Luis Saltareno, a merchant who had ordered a religious statue for his chapel from one of the Pueblo Indians. Now, this *rico* claimed that the statue of the *Cristo* was of poor artistic

quality, and so he paid the old, crippled *indio* only half of
what he had promised him. And when my father asked this
Luis Saltareno how he could say that it lacked artistry, the
rico complained that the face of the *Cristo* was ugly. And do
you know what my father said, *mi corazón?*"

She shook her head, glancing again at the statue. It was
a three-foot carving of Jesus dying on the cross, a figure
which old Castamaguey had whittled from the soft root of the
cottonwood tree, then coated with plaster made from gypsum
and animal glue. He had painted it with yellows and greens
made from plants and roots, the browns taken from iron ore,
and the blacks from charcoal. It was, contrary to what the
merchant, Luis Saltareno, had said, masterful workmanship,
and its creation had consumed more than a month.

"He said, my sweet one, that we are taught that *Dios*
made man in His own image. Well now, the Pueblo *indio*
conceived of our *Cristo* with the features of an *indio*. It is
truly logical that an *indio* would see our blessed Savior as like
unto him and his own people. And I myself devoutly believe,
Weesayo, that though there are many races and nationalities
of people, there is but one God for all the people of this
world, and this is why I think that your father will accept our
shared way of life."

She blushed, her face radiant, then reached for his hand
and squeezed it. As she gazed intently at the statue, she said
aloud, "Hear my prayer, oh, Great Spirit. He of my people,
as well as You, who are truly the one and the same for us. I
love my *esposo*, and I pray to You to give us a child who will
be blessed with Your love for those You have made like unto
Yourself. And I, Weesayo of the Jicarilla Apache, will pray
to You as always I have done to the Great Spirit of my
people, knowing that You will hear me just as He has always
done." With this she crossed herself, and then turned and
kissed Carlos tenderly as they rose and left the chapel.

Then, since it was only a little after dawn, they went to
the kitchen of the *hacienda*, where, somewhat to Margarita
Ortiz's dismay, Weesayo insisted on preparing her husband's
breakfast. After they had had their melon, chocolate, and
some of Tía Margarita's mouthwatering cornbread, they
thanked and praised the cook for such indulgence. Carlos
added, putting his arm around the cook's waist, "It is much
too early for my father and stepmother to be up, dear Tía
Margarita. So I entreat you to tell them, when their breakfast

is served, that Weesayo and I are going to visit her father and that we will be back before a fortnight."

"I don't know what to make of you, Señor Carlos," Tía Margarita groaned, shaking her head and then making the sign of the cross. "But of course you'll have your own way. I shall pray to all the saints that the two of you will have a safe journey to and from those mountains. But you, young master, I warn you, take very good care of this sweet *esposa* of yours, because if any harm befalls her, even though I am only a poor *criada*, I swear I'll take a stick to your shoulders—and you are not too old for that yet, don't forget it!"

At this, Carlos straightened, then made a courtly low bow and gravely replied, "I swear it on my honor as a *caballero*, Tía Margarita." Then, approaching her, he quickly whispered, "You see, she's with child. So I shall surely look after her with greater care than ever. And if your prayers are heard, I promise you'll be there for the christening of our *niño*." At this news, the cook gasped, quite forgetting her dignity, and hugged both Weesayo and Carlos. "*Vaya con Dios,* young master and mistress!" she exclaimed.

It was a journey of four days, but for Carlos and Weesayo it was a time of absorbed delight in each other. The balmy weather of the day and the cool night air exhilarated them. And over their little campfire at night, Carlos enchanted Weesayo by telling her stories of his boyhood and the sights and happenings of old Madrid. She, in turn, told him many of the legends of her people, handed down from generation to generation. By now he had learned to speak the Apache tongue fluently, and he marveled at the instant understanding of his thoughts and words which this gentle young girl achieved. Not even with his own father or with John Cooper had he ever revealed so candidly his dreams and hopes for a life that concerned itself not at all with ceremonials and aristocracy and wealth.

He had brought presents, too, in his saddlebags for Descontarti and for Namantay, Descontarti's first wife who was Weesayo's mother. And again he had delighted Weesayo by explaining to her, "I know it is not permitted to look upon or talk to one's mother-in-law, and I shall respect this law. Yet I do not think Namantay will object if you give her this present and say that I wished you to give it to her because you are her loving daughter. I think she will guess that I have love in my heart for her—though I may not say it—if only because she gave you birth and thus brought the Light of the Mountain into my life forever."

Carlos had commissioned Miguel Sandarbal a few months earlier to purchase in Santa Fe a superb handwrought razor of the finest Toledo steel in a velvet-lined case, as a gift for Descontarti. In addition, the faithful *capataz*, at Carlos's suggestion, had been able to buy a fine Spanish *pistola* with filigree silver ornaments around the polished wooden butt. Moreover, the Santa Fe gunsmith had added a silver "D" in the center of the butt. And for Namantay, Miguel had been able to obtain from a silversmith an elegant hand mirror backed in silver and a necklace of silver links, as well.

Late in the afternoon of the fourth day of their journey, Carlos and Weesayo rode into the stronghold. The sentries had already heralded their coming, and Descontarti and Pastanari, his eleven-year-old son by his second wife, Nadikotay, had ridden down the trail to meet them. The Apache chief rode Lanza, the magnificent white stallion that he had stolen on one of his raids against the Mexicans several years ago. In his early forties, he was wiry and powerful, though short of stature. His black hair was drawn into two sheaves which fell at each side of his head and was decorated by a red headband through which an eagle's feather was thrust.

Pastanari, tall for his age and as wiry as his father, suddenly exclaimed, "I see my sister now, father." He lifted his hand in salute and kicked his moccasined heels against his mustang's belly to quicken its gait.

"I, too. And I see my white-eyes blood brother who is her man," Descontarti declared. He lifted his lance in salute, then reined in the great white stallion as Carlos and Weesayo rode up to meet him and Pastanari. "Welcome, my daughter. And to you, Señor Carlos. It is good to see you. You have brought her safely back to visit our people. Already many of them have asked me how Weesayo fares in the *hacienda* of the white-eyes."

"All goes well with us, *mi padre*," Weesayo said in her sweet voice, with an adoring glance at Carlos who rode beside her. "Indeed, it was Carlos's wish to bring me back to you so that you would see what happiness we have already known in the short time since the shaman made us one person."

"I rejoice, my daughter. And I am grateful to you, my blood brother. The Light of the Mountains, our beloved woman, is dear to all of us."

"She is even dearer to me, Descontarti," Carlos said. "Before we ride into the stronghold, I have gifts for you. And Weesayo has brought a gift for her mother." With this, Carlos drew out the Spanish *pistola* and handed it to the Apache chief, and then the razor case and the mirror and necklace.

Descontarti took the pistol with an enthusiastic nod. "I welcome you to our stronghold, and tonight there will be a great feast and a dance in your honor, Señor Carlos."

Then, opening the velvet razor case, he frowned, and asked, "But what is this? Is it a knife for the cutting of meat or rawhide thongs?"

"No, my father," Weesayo quickly interposed, suppressing a delighted little laugh. "You see that *mi esposo* has a beard on his chin, unlike the men of our tribe. And he has shown me how he shaves off the hairs on his face and trims his beard with this. I will show you, too, my father. He says that it will be much less painful with this instead of the plucking or the scraping that Apache braves must do."

"So, my daughter," Descontarti smiled, "you try to teach the chief of the Jicarilla Apache a *gringo* way, do you not? Well, I am not too old to learn a new way." And then, his eyes fond and gentle upon her, he said, "Not when I see with my own eyes that her *esposo gringo* has made her happy with him away from our stronghold. But come now, we shall talk while the feast is prepared."

That night, after a lavish feast, the braves and the young women assembled for a ritual dance of welcome. Carlos rose from his place beside Descontarti and, taking Weesayo by the hand as if she were a princess, led her into the center. There, he kissed her hand and then bowed to her like a true *caballero*. And then, to the murmured approval of the onlookers, he began the dance. During their journey to the stronghold, Weesayo had taught him the intricate steps and gestures of this ceremonial, and to her delight as well as that of her father and the people of the tribe who gathered to watch, the young Spaniard acquitted himself commendably.

And when the dancing was done and Carlos led Weesayo back to sit at the left side of her father and settled himself on Descontarti's right, the chief of the Jicarilla Apache turned to him gravely and said, "Now truly is there joy in my heart and peace to the years of my old age, for I know that my daughter is truly beloved by you who are my blood brother."

Five

Exactly a week from the day on which John Cooper Baines revealed the secret of the silver mines to Padre Moraga, there took place a revelation of momentous proportions for the young mountain man.

Since his return to the *hacienda* after his eight-day sojourn, John Cooper had devoted himself to making up to Catarina for his absence. Like the most dutiful of husbands, he had brought her breakfast on a tray each morning, wakening her with a kiss and assuring her that he loved her deeply. And, though admittedly he found it far more comfortable to wear the hunter's garb that he had always worn during his life with the Indians, he resolutely hid away the buckskin jacket and the moccasins lest they renew Catarina's annoyance with him.

Catarina found her husband's attentions and endearments totally winning, and she soon got over her annoyance. She was as determined as he to be a good and loving mate, to be sensitive to his needs, and to understand that there was a time for being together and a time to be apart. She vowed she would make every attempt not to be selfish and moody, but rather responsible and grown-up.

It was nightfall, and there was a warm silence in the house of Don Diego de Escobar. A full moon shone down from the cloudless sky, dappling the tall peaks of the Sangre de Cristo with a burnished silver. Through the shutters of the window in the room where John Cooper and Catarina communed, there was a faint twittering of birds seeking their nests. The warming air wafted the scents of oleander, jasmine, and hyacinth.

His arm under her shoulders, his right hand stroking her

glossy black hair, John Cooper whispered, "How different it is between us now, *querida*, now that we're together for the rest of our lives!"

"*Mi corazón*," she whispered back as, feline and supple, she turned to face him, her arms drawing him to her. "I think I loved you from the very first day, even though I was so cruel to you."

"Have you thought about what I said before I left for the mountain, about our having a house all to ourselves, dearest Catarina?" John Cooper asked gently.

"Oh, yes. But—but would it be far away from Father and Doña Inez and Carlos, do you think?" she doubtfully countered, arching away from him, her fingers pressing into his shoulders as she stared questioningly into his sun-bronzed face.

"Not really, Catarina. I've thought about it a lot, lately, and I'm hoping that one day your father and I can start a new ranch, in a place where we can be free from restrictions and intolerance. I was thinking we could get some land in Texas, wonderful land for grazing cattle as well as sheep, for raising horses, for growing crops and such. We'd all live together in a grand *hacienda*, just as we do here, and someday we could have our own house, and your father and Doña Inez, and Carlos and Weesayo, could be in others close by. We'd be just like neighbors, but all of us free and to ourselves. Right here in Taos, your father and Don Sancho get along wonderfully, and they handle the affairs of the town so that everyone's friendly and the Indians are treated as they should be. But I'm not sure what will happen in the future—only let's not talk about things we can't control, only what we can do for ourselves."

"I agree," she said, moving back to him with a happy little sigh and nestling her head on the crook of his shoulder.

They lay together contentedly, and John Cooper thought again of the enormous discovery he had made in the mountains. He wanted very much to share the news of the silver mine with Catarina, but he remembered Padre Moraga's warnings. Perhaps he would tell her when it was clear to him where and when they would move, and when he knew himself what he would do with the treasure.

"Coop," Catarina began demurely, after they had rested in silence for a while.

"Yes, *querida?*"

"I have something very important to tell you—but I don't want you to think—I mean, it won't change your mind about me, will it?"

"You silly goose, how can I tell unless you tell me what it is?" He laughed as he kissed her mouth again and held her tightly to him. "What is it, my sweetheart, Catarina?"

"Well, it—" she blushed now and turned her face away in a sudden excess of modesty. "It happened last month, and I wasn't sure. But just before you came back from the mountain, it happened again, and now I *am* sure. *Mis tiempos de la luna*—Coop, can you guess what I want to tell you?"

He started, then gasped. "You mean—is it really true, Catarina?"

"*Sí, mi corazón, mi esposo.*" Again, she burned her face against his chest and held him tightly, and he could feel the trembling of her body against his own.

"Our child," he murmured, profoundly shaken by her revelation.

"Yes, dearest Coop. Our child. Oh, please, don't think I am telling you because I want to hold you and keep you a captive—but I love you so much I wouldn't mind if you never left me, not when we are like this. Can you understand that? I am yours so completely now. There is no one else in the world for me—of course, Father and dear Doña Inez—but it is not the same thing at all—do you understand me?"

"Of course I do, my dearest sweetheart, my wife," he breathed. "I love you. *Te quiero.*"

From behind the covered cage of the white cockatoo, they heard the ruffle of wings and an almost indignant squawk. John Cooper half-sat up, then burst into laughter. "He's jealous, Pepito is. All this time he's been saying '*Te quiero,* Catarina,' and now he hears someone else taking his place."

"I know. But surely you are not jealous of him, my darling?" She reached up to draw him back down to her, laughing softly, eager for him.

"No. He's in a cage and his life is easy and he's looked after. I've tasted a freedom he's never known and never will know." He fervently kissed her eyelids and then her mouth. "If we have a son, I'd like to name him after my father, Andrew. And I'd like to have new adventures and new places to seek out, so that I can teach him to enjoy all the things that freedom means. Can you understand what I'm trying to say,

Catarina? I swear to you it doesn't mean I don't love you with all my heart and soul—because you know I do."

"Yes, I know that. That is why I am yours. Oh, Coop! I—I'll have to learn, as I am learning now with such great happiness, *mi corazón,* to accept you for what you are and as you are. You will be patient with me, won't you?"

"To the very end of our time together, Catarina. I love you so!" He held her close, and with a happy little sigh, she drew him to her. Their rapture sought and found fulfillment. In his cage, Pepito again uttered his plaintive call, shut out and neglected by his young mistress.

From the very moment when Catarina had revealed that she would bear his child, John Cooper had realized the necessity for training Lobo to accept their first-born. Even now, he admitted to himself, there was much to be desired in the way Lobo grudgingly allowed Catarina to walk along beside him when he had the wolf-dog on the leash.

John Cooper had lived with Indian tribes and seen how they regarded their dogs not as pets but rather as workers, and he was ready to take on the challenge of training this crossing of Irish wolfhound and timberwolf.

John Cooper had seen already that Lobo was a superb hunter and a vigilant watchdog. But Lobo's primary strength was in his ability to attack, to kill, and to maim enemies as well as game. Lobo could kill a man with a single compression of his powerful jaws. He fully realized that the young wolf-dog possessed even more stamina and endurance than Lije.

Every day since he had come to Don Diego's *hacienda,* John Cooper had gone to the shed, put Lobo on his leash, and disciplined him into walking a given distance back and forth, just as one might walk a dog for exercise. Lobo really never cared for this, John Cooper knew, but now it was even more important than ever: to make him unhesitatingly obey would be the very first step. If he could not be trained, then it would be dangerous to have him around the baby which Catarina would bear in December.

During all of the week, John Cooper experimented with Lobo's training. Gradually Lije's whelp began to respond until he obeyed almost all the time. And then it was time to teach Lobo how to get along with other people and especially children.

With this in mind, John Cooper sought out the young sheepherder, Esteban Morales. Esteban's lovely young wife, Concepción, helped Tía Margarita in the kitchen, and was in her own right a superb cook as well as seamstress. Last year, John Cooper had saved Concepción's little son, Bernardo, from a scorpion, and Esteban Morales had sworn that he would be John Cooper's man for life and would pay back the debt. Now the young mountain man knew exactly how Esteban could do that. The sheepherder had a special skill for making wooden flutes and whittling toys for his little son as well as for the children of the other *trabajadores*. John Cooper commissioned him to fashion a kind of rag doll that would look like a baby, and he would use this to train Lobo. In that way, by the time Catarina's baby was born, Lobo would be more likely to accept it as part of John Cooper's family.

Early one morning, John Cooper led Lobo to a large grassy knoll flanked by towering spruce trees about a mile east of the *hacienda*. Removing Lobo's collar and leash, John Cooper took the rag doll that Esteban had made and cradled it in his arms, pretending to croon over it and rubbing his cheek against it. Lobo watched him intently, his keen yellow eyes unwaveringly fixed on the young mountain man's face. He showed his teeth for an instant, and John Cooper quickly reached down and cuffed him on the side of the jaw. "No! Bad boy! Here is baby, friend. Lobo will not growl or show his teeth!" Then, putting out his right hand with the palm upward, he made a gesture that signified that Lobo should lie down and punctuated this with a sharp command. Lobo made a purring kind of grumble, and then slowly lowered himself to the ground and lay, panting, his pink tongue rolling out as he watched. "Good boy!" Instantly, John Cooper reached into his leather pouch and drew out a piece of salted mutton which he held out as he squatted down to face Lobo.

Now rocking the rag doll back and forth in his arms, John Cooper continued: "This is my baby. Lobo will love my baby as he loves me. Good boy. Lobo will not show his teeth or growl at the baby, *¿comprende?*" And when the wolf-dog remained motionless, his bright eyes intently studying his young master's gestures, John Cooper again reached into the pouch to pull out a tidbit as Lobo's reward.

All that week, the young mountain man and Lobo practiced this same kind of ritual. There were times when the wolf-dog seemed impatient, eager to go bounding off in search of game. Once or twice he did, and John Cooper punished him by rapping him across the snout with his knuckles as hard as he could, shaking his head and saying, his face clouded with annoyance, "Bad boy! No. No meat for Lobo. When Lobo disobeys, no meat, *¿comprende?*"

And by the time the week was over, Lobo had gone so far as to come up to the squatting young mountain man and run his pink tongue over the face of the rag doll, the symbol of a child that John Cooper and Catarina would have at the year's end.

Six

The settlement of Taos had been established in the early 1600s and had been named after its founder, Don Fernando de Taos. In the year 1723, the first official annual Taos trade fair was held, and the Pueblo Indians of the little hamlet bartered with the Apache, Ute, Navaho, Comanche, and Pawnee. From Chihuahua, the crafty merchants of Mexico rode, bringing with them imported goods from Spain and great silver dollars prized as ornaments among the Navaho. The fair often lasted through August, and all roads led to Taos in these summer weeks—Taos, high on the chilly peaks of the Sangre de Cristo, amid its green meadows watered by icy streams. At one time there would have been American mountain trappers with their rich stores of beaver, mountain men very much like John Cooper himself, men who had lived much of their lives with friendly Indian tribes and had taken squaws to solidify this alliance. But now the fair was closed to all American traders as the troops of New Spain jealously guarded the Spanish monopoly on trade.

Now that the shearing was done and the warm, sunny weeks of June moved swiftly toward July, both Don Sancho de Pladero and Don Diego de Escobar prepared for the Taos fair. It would be a time for trading, for meeting old friends and neighbors, for marveling at the truce between crowds of usually warring Indians who, settling their differences for this one time each year, traveled from great distances to sell their wares and to acquire horses and—though it was strictly forbidden by edict of the viceroy—weapons, whiskey, and *aguardiente*.

Both Weesayo and Catarina were with child, yet the Apache girl, who had returned from the stronghold with

58

Carlos, seemed to have more stamina and suffered fewer ill effects from the early months of pregnancy. Catarina, however, took to her bed from nausea and weakness, and the thought of accompanying her husband to the mountains was quite forgotten. Gravely concerned for her well-being, he attended her with such solicitude that Tía Margarita remarked to one of the maids, "Never before have I seen an *esposo* so attentive, so fearful over the slightest change in his wife's feelings! *Dios,* one would think it was Señor John Cooper who was going to have the *niño* himself, the way he frets and asks questions of me."

Little news from Europe had come to Taos of late, but there was news about the war between the young United States and Great Britain. Early this month, the British ship *Shannon* captured the *Chesapeake,* and in the battle, the *Chesapeake*'s heroic young captain, James Lawrence, was killed. His dying words were to be an inspiration to all American combatants: "Don't give up the ship!"

Both Don Sancho and Don Diego expressed some little concern over the coming fair, particularly since the Indians would want to buy not only strong drink but also guns. Knives, to be sure, were permitted by the Mexican authorities, but not firearms. "We have greedy merchants here in Taos who will certainly circumvent the law, Don Diego," Don Sancho worriedly explained, as the two men sat sipping their brandy in Don Sancho's study one Saturday evening at the end of June. "I am also concerned about the viceroy's determination to keep out all American traders. He and his aides are afraid that the *gringos* will come here to turn over a very quick and certainly very handsome profit."

"That indeed is a problem, Don Sancho. As for myself, I have no wish to keep a monopoly, and I am sure that the *gringo* goods are often of better quality than we could import through Mexico City."

"That is my opinion, also, though you understand it is the opinion of a private citizen, and certainly not that of the *alcalde* of Taos," Don Sancho quickly interposed. "In the past, I have had many memoranda from either the viceroy or the governor in Santa Fe stipulating in the very strictest terms that any *gringo* who dares to enter Taos for the purpose of trading shall be imprisoned by me and sent under military escort to Santa Fe, where he will be very severely dealt with. Indeed, there have been a few instances where *gringos* have not only been imprisoned for long periods of time, but actually shot by a military firing squad."

"But that is barbarous!" Don Diego protested.

"Yes," Don Sancho sighed as he reached for the brandy decanter again, "I agree. But I am only a minor official and sworn to do my duty. I feel as you do, that we are so isolated here in Taos and so much at the mercy of the long transports of goods from Mexico City to our little town that it would be a very wholesome thing to open Taos to the *gringos*. But I am afraid I shall not see this in my lifetime, Don Diego. Well now, another glass of brandy before you leave me. It has been a most delightful evening, and I am reluctant to end such enjoyable discussion. Your very good health!"

Two days before the opening of the great fair, John Cooper, out of curiosity to see the varied traders en route to Taos, decided to saddle his mustang and ride out along the trail which the Indians would take from the Rocky Mountains and the great plains. He had resolved to do no buying for himself at the fair. The silver bars he had secreted in Lobo's shed he would use at a later time—it would be too conspicuous to bring the silver to the fair. Perhaps after the excitement of the fair had abated he would buy those fine breeding horses. But for now he would content himself with what he already had—including his weapons.

Part of the impulse to ride out on the trail was motivated by his surprise on being told that Pawnee would come to the fair. One of Don Sancho's *trabajadores* had told him that during the past several years not many braves of that tribe had come to trade. But John Cooper well remembered that, a little more than two years ago, he had saved the daughter of the Dakota Sioux chief from sacrifice to Morning Star by the Skidi Pawnee. And if, by chance, he should go to the fair and walk unguardedly about the displays of Indian merchandise, he might be recognized by a member of that village where he had lived and against whose sacrificial cult he had committed the most sacrilegious of crimes. Yes, it would be well to anticipate any such danger by riding out, well-armed, to see if there were Pawnee and if, indeed, any of these might recognize him.

At Don Diego's suggestion, Miguel had commissioned two of his best workers, Luis Delgado and Salvador Bernardós, to go to last January's fair in Chihuahua and to buy some pieces of furniture, rugs, coffee, and some cases of French wines, as well as perfume for Doña Inez and Catarina. In addition, Miguel had urged them to purchase several pistols and rifles, if they saw any articles of outstanding workmanship offered at this great annual fair. Indeed, once the Taos fair ended, many of the merchants of Taos, as well as the traders who had come to them, journeyed on to Chihuahua for the Mexican counterpart, which was held on an even more lavish scale. Luis and Salvador had brought back three excellent Belgian rifles, even superior to the one which Carlos himself was fond of using, as well as half a dozen pistols with silver mountings on the butts and quicker trigger action than was customary with handguns of this species, these latter being designed by an elderly and gifted gunsmith in Mexico City.

John Cooper had wanted to try one of the Belgian rifles, and Miguel, at Don Diego's order, had presented him with one for his own use, as well as two of the fine new pistols. He took these three weapons along with him as he saddled his mustang. He had dressed in his buckskin garments so that those Indians he should meet along the trail would recognize him as one who knew their ways. Finally, around his neck he adjusted the rawhide thong that held the leather sheath of his slim knife of Spanish steel.

He decided not to take Lobo with him. If he met other riders on the trail and they proved unfriendly, they might goad the dog into attacking. Besides, if by bad luck any of the Skidi Pawnee from the village where he had lived were coming to Taos, the presence of Lobo would very quickly remind them of the young *wasichu* and his wolfhound. In those days, his hair had grown down past his shoulders and he had even had a beard. Now, at Catarina's urging, he had allowed her, just two mornings ago, to take scissors to his hair and to shave away his beard.

John Cooper rode off northward along the twisting trail at the base of the Sangre de Cristo mountains. It was warm, and the sun was brilliant in the cloudless sky; he breathed in and sweet, pure air and grinned with almost boyish delight at this brief excursion back to the freedom he had known for so many years. The trail was wide, and there was room enough for travelers in both directions. First to pass him was a group of four Comanche, riding on small but marvelously swift gray mustangs. He lifted his hand in salutation to them and they gravely and silently returned the greeting.

A quarter of an hour later, six Pawnee rode past him. Again he saluted them, and breathed a secret sigh of relief when he saw that their tribal markings were not those of the Skidi. He would have greeted them in their own tongue, but he thought it wiser not to do so. They might wonder how it was that a *wasichu* could speak their language, and perhaps when they returned to their village, they would spread the news; then it would be known that the young white-eyes who had blasphemed against Morning Star still lived.

By noon, he had counted at least thirty groups of Indians heading for Taos with their wares, many of them Apache and Comanche, some Navaho, and three different groups of Pawnee.

Then, as he guided his mustang toward the east, he heard a sobbing cry, and then the unmistakable smacking noise of a leather strap against flesh. He reined in his mustang and waited; a moment later, around the bend, a young white boy and a girl stumbled forward, wrists bound behind their backs with rawhide thongs. Behind them, mocking them, rode two Ute, or *Yuuttaa,* as they called themselves. One, who brandished a long rawhide thong which he slashed across the girl's shoulders, wore a bright red headband through which an eagle's feather had been thrust, designating him as chief of the tribe. The brave beside him, stocky, with scowling features, a quiver of arrows strapped to his back, brandished a long bow. With an imprecation in his own tongue, he reached out and slashed one end of the bow across the boy's shoulders, drawing a yelp of pain.

At the sight of the young mountain man, the Ute chief halted his mustang and gestured to his companion to do the same. He was taller, sturdy, his head bald except for a broad middle swatch of greasy black hair which extended to the nape of his neck. *"Buenos días,"* he grunted.

The two white captives had stopped and fought for breath, their heads bowed, as John Cooper quickly glanced at them. The girl was pretty, with a heart-shaped face and long light-brown hair. She wore a homespun dress, badly tattered, and her feet were encased in worn moccasins. The boy was black-haired, slim and tall, his face haggard and sweating from the enforced march.

"Buenos días," John Cooper quickly responded, lifting his right hand with the palm turned upward, then made the sign of respect to a chief, a sign understood by virtually every Indian tribe. A faint smile creased the cruel, thin mouth of the Ute chief, and leaning back in his saddle, he gestured toward the two white captives, declaring in Spanish, "I bring these *gringos* to the fair for sale."

The two captives raised their heads and stared wonderingly at John Cooper. Adopting a noncommittal attitude, the mountain man averred, "They are young; they will bring a good price."

"That is what I, Ortimwoy, chief of the *Yuuttaa*, believe. Perhaps you would buy them from me? They have given me much trouble, and I would be rid of them—if you pay well for them. Then Tiowa, who is my war lieutenant, and I will have time to see what we need for our village at the fair."

"Will the great chief of the Ute allow me to speak to your slaves?" John Cooper politely demanded. "I live with the great *hacendado* who is the *intendente* of Taos, for I have wed his daughter."

"That is good." Ortimwoy permitted himself a grin. "Then you are *rico* and you can pay well for these slaves. Yes, speak to them, and you there, girl, answer this young *hacendado* with a straight tongue, or you will feel the thong many times before we reach Taos." With this, leaning forward and raising the rawhide thong, he slashed the young girl across the middle of her back. She uttered a sobbing cry, twisted and writhed under the stinging pain of the blow, and John Cooper saw tears trickle down her flushed cheeks. Her hazel eyes fixed on him with an imploring look.

"What's your name, girl?" he said in English.

"It—it's Amy Prentice. I—I'm nearly sixteen. This here's my brother Tom; he's seventeen."

"How is it that you are the slaves of a Ute chief, Amy?" John Cooper inquired.

"Our folks were killed in a wagon heading for Wyoming country, mister." Amy Prentice's voice quavered. "They were going out there because my uncle was a fur trader with the Shoshoni, and he wrote us that they were friendly and that we would love the country." She glanced back nervously at the two Ute, and Tiowa scowled and brandished his bow at her.

"These Indians, were they the ones who captured you, Amy?" John Cooper pursued.

The young girl nodded, then burst into tears and covered her eyes with a trembling hand. "Yes, sir, it—it was that one, Tiowa, who tomahawked my mother and father. That's why he's so nasty now; he—he wants me to be his squaw and I won't—I just won't, mister!"

"I understand," John Cooper soothed her. "And your brother, Tom?"

"They've worked us like slaves; we had to do everything, carry water, make fires, even skin buffalo. But that wouldn't be so bad for Tom, he likes outdoors and hard work, 'cause he did that on the farm we had back in Illinois—"

"Illinois?" John Cooper echoed as he leaned forward to stare down at the girl. "Where did you come from back there?"

"It was near Cairo, mister."

"I see. I—I came from Illinois myself, from Shawnee-town. Anyhow, if Tiowa wants to marry you, why is Ortimwoy ready to sell you both now at the fair?"

"Because I told the chief I just wouldn't marry any Indian, not ever!" Amy staunchly declared, raising her face and fixing John Cooper with an anguished look. "Tiowa said he would make me, and he—well, he whipped me a couple of times till Ortimwoy stopped him. And then Ortimwoy said that he could get more for us in Taos than he could by working us."

"Amy, I'm going to try to buy you both—now don't look so scared! I don't want slaves, but I can take you back to my *hacienda* and maybe get you both jobs there."

"Oh, mister, if you only could, I'd pray God to bless you every night of my life!" Amy Prentice passionately burst out. "I can cook and sew just fine, and Tom, he did fine on the farm. He likes animals, and he knows how to take care of them."

"That's good. I'm going to talk to Ortimwoy now." He gave her a friendly smile and an encouraging nod, then turned to the Ute chief. "What will you take for your two slaves, great chief of the Ute?" he asked.

Ortimwoy scowled, pondering the question. "I see you have two fine new *pistolas, gringo*. I will take those. Is there ammunition for them?"

"Yes, in a pouch tied to my saddle. And I will show you how to load and fire them if you wish."

"I have old *pistolas,* I am chief of the Ute, and no *gringo* needs to teach me how to use such weapons," Ortimwoy declared with an indignant snort.

"I ask pardon of the great chief of the Ute; I did not mean to offend him. And what more does he desire for these slaves?"

"The squaws of my village have asked Ortimwoy to bring back necklaces of beads. My squaw asked me to find her a Spanish comb. Squaws are stupid, as all men know, but it is wise for a man to keep them at peace in his tepee."

"I will ride back to my *hacienda* and meet you back here on the trail, great chief of the Ute. I will bring necklaces of beads and several Spanish combs."

"And two jugs of *aguardiente,* also," Ortimwoy craftily added, glancing at Tiowa, who was glowering at the young captives and muttering to himself. "And for Tiowa here, who counted coup over the father and mother of these two salves, he, too, must have something so that he will not be angry. Perhaps a fine gun like the one you carry in a sling at your saddle, *gringo.*"

"I will bring the *aguardiente* and a gun, as well."

"So be it. These white slaves are sickly and weak. We will halt here for our noonday meal and give them some water so they can walk back with you when you return."

John Cooper nodded, made the sign of respect to the chief, and then quickly muttered to Amy, "You'll be free soon, you and your brother, Tom."

"Oh, God bless you, God bless you!" Amy sobbed.

Turning his mustang, John Cooper galloped back along the trail to the *hacienda* of Don Diego and sought out Miguel Sandarbal. The *capataz* frowned and shook his head. "It is risky business, young master, giving *aguardiente* and a rifle and *pistolas* to *los indios,* and you know it is against the law."

"That's true enough, Miguel, but I couldn't bear to see that girl and her brother treated like that. I'm guessing they've had to walk, bound the way they are, all the way from Ute territory."

"I understand you, *mi compañero.*" Miguel's features softened. "But be very careful."

"Don't worry, I will be. Neither the pistols nor the rifle will be loaded. Besides, I'm going to take two horses along so Amy and Tom Prentice can ride back with me. That way, there won't be any skullduggery, especially from that Tiowa. I don't like his looks, and he's hankering after little Amy."

"I'll say prayers for you, *mi compañero*. Go now."

John Cooper rode back along the trail, the two mustangs behind him docilely carrying in their saddlebags the jugs of brandy, the trinkets, and the rifle with balls and powder. He had unloaded the two new pistols and put these into the saddlebags also, along with powder and balls. In their place, he strapped a third pistol to his belt, already primed and loaded, as was his Belgian rifle.

He found Ortimwoy and Tiowa, their horses tethered to a spruce tree off the trail, squatting on a little grassy knoll. Amy and Tom Prentice knelt nearby. John Cooper dismounted and approached, holding out his hands with palms upward. "I have kept my promise, great chief of the Ute," he announced. "I have added many more necklaces and Spanish combs than you asked for."

"That is good, *gringo*. And you have brought two horses also? That is even better."

"No, Ortimwoy, these horses are for your white slaves to ride back. They are exhausted. You have marched them a long way from your village."

"That is true, *gringo*. But they deserve this treatment. The girl is rebellious; she will choose no brave, not even Tiowa who took her. And the boy is of no use to us. He works well enough, but I know there is hatred in his heart because he saw Tiowa kill his mother and father. And one day he might grow strong enough with that hate to try to kill my war lieutenant. Yes, it is best that I rid myself of these two."

John Cooper opened the saddlebags and handed the rifle, the two pistols, the pouches of balls and powder, and the one containing the necklaces and combs to Ortimwoy, who grunted with satisfaction as he examined them. Then he gestured with his right hand. "Take them." And, as any good trader might do by way of afterthought, he wheedlingly added, "Perhaps one of the horses?"

"A bargain is a bargain, great chief of the Ute. But perhaps I shall see you at the fair and we may barter for something else that takes your fancy," John Cooper answered in Spanish.

Then he approached Tom and Amy, drew out the sharp Spanish dagger from its sheath around his neck, and cut the rawhide thongs binding their wrists. "Get on the horses as quick as you can. We're going to ride back to my *hacienda*," he told them. "I don't like the looks of Tiowa one little bit, so let's put distance between him and us."

Amy had begun to cry again, but her brother put his arm around her shoulders and led her to the horses. He helped her onto the first horse, took the second himself, and the two of them trotted off down the trail.

Tiowa's face was black as night, his anger visible in the glaring looks he shot the young mountain man and then his chief. But the latter impassively shook his head. "It is as the *gringo* says, Tiowa: a bargain is a bargain."

Mounting his mustang, John Cooper turned back to Ortimwoy and lifted his right hand. "Till we meet in Taos, *¡vaya con Dios!*" he called with a friendly grin. Then, fighting the instinct to gallop down the trail after the Prentices, he slowly trotted after them.

Once the two Ute were out of sight, John Cooper spurred his mustang to catch up with Tom and Amy. They had halted their horses and were waiting for him. Amy was crying, but this time in gratitude. "Oh, m—mister," she sobbed, "I'll make it up to you, I swear I will! I thought I was going to die back with those awful Indians. And poor Tom, they worked him like an ox, and even the squaws whipped him with branches and straps to break his spirit. And all the time, we had to try to keep alive, remembering how that brute Tiowa had killed my poor father and mother and then laughed at me when I started to cry because I saw it!"

"Best not to think about that now, Amy. The main thing is, you and Tom are free. I'll bet those Ute didn't give you anything to eat today, did they?" John Cooper asked. And when both of them simultaneously shook their heads, he continued, "Well, once you're back at the *hacienda,* I'll have Tía Margarita fix you a real fine meal. By the way, I'd best be telling you my name. It's John Cooper Baines."

"We're both mighty beholden to you, Mr. Baines," Tom Prentice soberly declared, his young face taut with strain and fatigue.

"You'll both have a chance for a new life now," John Cooper declared. "Tom, your sister tells me you're good with animals. I'll bet Miguel Sandarbal—he's the foreman of our sheep ranch—can give you a good job. It's easy work, and you'll get your keep and some money, too. After a bit, when you fatten up and get your strength back, you can decide what you want to do. And you, Amy, if you can cook and sew the way you say you can, there'll be plenty of work for you at the *hacienda*."

"Is it your *hacienda*, Mr. Baines?" Amy asked.

"Oh, no, not hardly," John Cooper laughed. "You see, I married the daughter of the man who owns it, Don Diego de Escobar. He's the intendant of Taos, and that's a very important job. Well, we ought to be back at the *hacienda* before an hour, I'd say. I'd feel a mite safer if we didn't dawdle any, though." He glanced back over his shoulder at the trail behind him.

Soon they had reached another sharp bend in the road along the mountain range, and suddenly John Cooper heard a sinister buzzing sound which he recognized all too well. At the same moment, his mustang reared with a frantic whinny, and he saw the rattlesnake uncoil itself from a flat rock at the side of the trail and draw back its ugly head. Instinctively jerking at the reins, he forced his mustang to the right and away from the reptile, just as an arrow whizzed by his head.

Amy uttered a cry of alarm. "It's Tiowa, Mr. Baines. For God's sake, he's after us—"

John Cooper drew the Belgian rifle out of the sling, forced his protesting mustang to turn, and saw the squat Ute brave in the act of notching a second arrow to the string of his long bow. Controlling the mustang with his left hand, he forced the butt of his rifle against his shoulder and, squinting down the sight, pulled the trigger in a snap shot. The recoil was greater than he had expected, and it bruised him, but he saw Tiowa jerk back in his saddle, then drop the bow and slide down from his horse onto the trail where he lay face down without movement.

"Gosh, Mr. Baines," Tom gasped, "that sure was some shot!"

"What do we do now, Mr. Baines?" Amy said, her voice faltering, her widened eyes fixed on the inert body of the Ute brave.

"It's all right, Amy. You heard the chief say I'd bought you fair and square, so what Tiowa did went against his orders. I had every right to defend myself, and it was Tiowa or us—that's the only way you can look at it."

Suddenly Amy began to sob, covering her eyes with her hands. John Cooper heard the thunder of a horse's hooves, and a moment later the Ute chief galloped up to them. He turned to look down at the body of his war lieutenant, then grunted, "Tiowa was a fool. I told him I had made the trade. You brought the rifle for him, and that was more than fair."

"I am glad the great, wise chief of the Ute sees that I mean his people no harm. I knew that you had given him the order to obey you, and that was why, when he tried to kill me, I had to kill him to save my life."

"Ho, that is so. Well, then, I will keep Tiowa's rifle. He will not need it where he goes to explain to the Great Spirit why he disobeyed his chief." With this, Ortimwoy dismounted, rolled Tiowa's body over, and unstrapped the belt which contained the pouch of balls and powder. Then he drew the rifle out of the dead Ute's saddle sling. He straightened, tightening the belt around his own waist, then nodded to John Cooper. "Perhaps you and I will meet at the fair, *gringo*. Perhaps you will bring more pretty things for the squaws when you come there. Then perhaps I will trade you back the rifle that you meant for Tiowa, who does not need it any longer."

"If you like, Ortimwoy. ¡*Vaya con Dios!*" John Cooper grinned. Then, lifting his rifle in salute to the Ute chief, he turned his mustang back toward the *hacienda*.

It was Doña Inez who welcomed the orphaned brother and sister when John Cooper brought them back to the *hacienda*, and she immediately made them feel at home by her sympathetic kindness. She hurried at once to Amy Prentice, took the trembling girl into her arms as a mother might do, and, stroking Amy's head, soothingly reassured her in English (for in Madrid Doña Inez had studied several languages and spoke them passably well). "There now, my dear one. You are safe, nothing will harm you here. How tired you must be—but come with me, and I'll see that you have a good warm bath and something to eat and then all the sleep you will need to recover your strength."

As Doña Inez led Amy away, the latter turned to give

John Cooper a look of the most infinite gratitude, and Tom
Prentice hesitantly approached him. "Mister—Mister J—
John Cooper, sir, I'll never be able to thank you enough. I'll
work for you for the rest of my days for what you've done
for Amy. Here's my hand on it."

"You won't have to work for me, Tom boy. There's no
slavery here. Now I'll get you fixed up with Miguel—here he
comes now! Holá, Miguel, aquí!" And when the capataz
hurried forward, John Cooper quickly introduced Tom Prentice and explained the boy's story. Then he addressed Tom
again. "You're in good hands with Miguel. And I'll bet
before long you'll be one of the best hands on the hacienda!"
John Cooper laughed, then, taking the reins of the three
horses, he led them back to the corral.

It did not take the compassionate Doña Inez long to find
out all about Amy's tragic bereavement and the girl's abilities
as both seamstress and cook. After she had taken Amy to the
kitchen and urged Tía Margarita to prepare a bounteous
lunch, she saw to it that Amy had a bath. Then, giving the
pretty young girl one of her robes, she led her to one of the
guest chambers and, with mock sternness, ordered her to
sleep as long as she wished. This done, she went back to the
kitchen to explain to Tía Margarita the girl's plight.

"May the saints preserve us all!" The fat cook crossed
herself and shook her head, blanching with horror. "But it's
no wonder the young master came to her rescue, Doña Inez!
He has such a good heart, mucho corazón!" Tía Margarita
beamed and nodded as if this was still another proof of her
initial judgment of the young mountain man.

"Now, then, Tía Margarita, I have had a nice long talk
with her, and she is sleeping, the poor lamb. She cooked for
her parents back on the farm before they came out west, you
see. And she can sew very well. Now, I was thinking, Tía
Margarita, you are the best cook for miles around, and I do
not want to offend you, but perhaps you could see your way
clear to letting Amy help you?"

"Of course!" The plump cook closed her arms across her
bosom and tilted back her head in an attitude of prideful
understanding. "I would have suggested that myself, with all
due respect, Doña Inez. ¡Pobrecita! I will let her try the little
things, you understand, like sauces and helping make some of
the tortillas."

Once again, Tía Margarita was overcome with emotion,

and dabbed at her eyes with the hem of her apron. "Oh, Señora de Escobar, it is such a joy to serve you and Don Diego and everyone in this household—everyone is so appreciative—oh, dear, now you see what you have done? You have made me cry, a fat, old woman like me—"

"You are not fat, and you are not old, but you are wonderful. And here is what I think of you," Doña Inez softly interrupted as she took Tía Margarita in her arms and kissed her soundly on each cheek, then left the kitchen.

Seven

Don Sancho de Pladero was a busy but happy man. Preparations not only for his son's wedding but also for the annual Taos fair, at which he would preside, had been going on for weeks, and there was never a moment's rest. Even in the evening, when the *alcalde* looked forward to collapsing into his bed, he was kept busy, making up for lost time with the now-devoted Doña Elena, whose sexual appetite was prodigious. But he was happy. He was in love once again with his wife; the wedding of Tomás to Conchita Seragos was a joyous event; and the fair of Taos promised to be one of the most successful ever.

Don Sancho, in his capacity as *alcalde* of Taos, formally opened the fair by welcoming all those who came to it. He spoke of the great example of peace and friendship which this coming together of Indian tribes and Mexicans and Spaniards and French symbolized. And he alluded to the terrible war afflicting their beloved Spain, at the mercy of Napoleon, and even to the newer, if not so well-known, conflict between the Americans and the British which, to be sure, did not seem to concern the inhabitants of Taos in the slightest degree.

The trading was brisk, even more so than in past years. The superb weather and the excitement for the people of Taos at this welcome break in the monotony of their lives made the fair take on the aspect of a gala fiesta. Later this evening, indeed, there would be dancing: various Indians would stage their ceremonial dances, a shrewd way of interesting the spectators in buying more of their wares. And with the profits thereby derived, they could stealthily buy the whiskey and *aguardiente*, the knives and guns and ammunition, and the blankets and the horses which they coveted.

It was a strange spectacle to see, assembled in this beautiful valley at the foot of the majestic mountain range, with the little village of Taos in the background, Indians in their multicolored blankets and headdresses; French trappers who wore beaver caps and animal skins and who seemed different from their Indian competitors only in their florid beards and the equally florid oaths they swore as to the prime quality of their wares; Spanish grandees who still dressed as they might have at the Escorial; foremen like Miguel Sandarbal in boots, britches, and rough jackets; Mexican merchants whose faces were obscured by the huge sombreros they wore and whose colorful serapes made the local *caballeros* envious of such dazzling bright hues. Yet it was not precisely a Tower of Babel, since Spanish was the communal language spoken at this fair, and for those French trappers who knew not a word of the Castillian tongue, the sign language they had learned in dealing with Indians stood them in good stead.

A few ladies came as well, the wives of the *hacendados* who would not trust their maids to shop for them, and who were intrigued and secretly thrilled to see the fierce Comanche, the wily Apache, the dour Pawnee and Arapahoe, and the sullen Ute, and even the powerful Kiowa, almost side by side, and all of them extolling their wares in guttural, hardly intelligible Spanish accompanied by impressive gesticulations. And there were the more placid Navaho, stocky and sturdy, patient and silent, their wares displayed in beautifully woven baskets—blankets with exotic pigmentations, beaded belts and necklaces so dear to the women of Taos.

Don Diego de Escobar had decided to attend the fair himself, with Miguel representing his interests. "You see, *amigo*," he genially pointed out, "if these merchants and *indios* see that it is the *intendente* who wants something, they are certain to raise the price. Whereas you, as a *capataz*, can haggle with them and get what we need for the *hacienda* and for your *trabajadores* and their *mujeres* without becoming impoverished in the process."

"That is very wise, *patrón*," Miguel nodded. "Do you think there will be more Mexican merchants this year than last?"

"I am sure of it, Miguel. And I tell you, I am going to send a dispatch to the viceroy himself about this shrewd little accounting scheme they have. They come to Taos, mind you, and they buy a few things for themselves, say at two *reales* to the dollar. But when we want to buy things from them in Chihuahua, we suddenly find their dollar means four or six or even eight *reales*. By this ingenious method every year, they drain Nuevo Mexico and especially our little province of Taos of the greater portion of our wealth. Now, Miguel, mingle with the crowd, try to see what the Mexican merchants are asking, and find out who is the worst offender in buying with the cheaper dollars and selling for the expensive ones. Perhaps I can devise a way to keep these unscrupulous wretches from selling their goods to our poorer citizens."

"*Sí, patrón.* I'll keep my eyes open, you can be sure of that."

Miguel and two of his men, bringing along a *carreta* harnessed to a docile burro, went to the fair shortly before noon, and the capable *capataz* proved himself to be a shrewd trader. Just as Don Diego had foreseen, in his *trabajador* attire and with his forthright demeanor and speech, he was able to buy all those things on his master's list of requirements at the most reasonable prices. He was able to overcome the greed of some of the merchants by shrugging and depreciating their wares, by pretending to walk away with total indifference, and some of them called him back and almost angrily offered him what he sought at the price he originally intended to pay.

Just before he had left for the fair, Teofilo Rosas had mournfully remarked, "*Mi amigo* Miguel, how it would please me if, when you go to the fair today, you would buy me a wife. Did I not tell you, when you engaged me after I had had my freedom from my old *patrón,* the Señor Corbazon, that beside the higher wages you would pay me, you would find me a nice *novia?*"

Miguel had laughed and clapped Teofilo on the back, replying, "*Hombre,* you have been in Taos five years, and if you haven't yet found a *novia* or an *esposa* for yourself, there is little I can do to help you. Why, you see yourself that I am still without one. But that is because my work comes first, Teofilo, and my master's welfare. When the time comes, there will be a *mujer* for you."

But this conversation had planted a seed in Miguel Sandarbal's mind. Now that his purchases were completed and he could evaluate the displays of merchandise and the personalities of those who offered them, he found himself suddenly remembering the one romance of his life and how it had been thwarted. While Teofilo Rosas was only thirty-eight, he, Miguel, was in his late forties, only a few years away from the age of fifty when he would surely be considered an old man who should have nothing to do with *mujeres lindas*. He had inherited a celebrated fencing school in Madrid from his father, who had given lessons to Don Diego himself when the latter had been a boy. And then he had fallen in love with a convent-bred girl, whose aunt, detesting him as a commoner, had arranged to have him imprisoned on a trumped-up charge and sent to labor on a penal farm. While he had been in prison, she had married his sweetheart off very quickly to an elderly nobleman. Then he had gone to work for Don Diego as assistant to the head gardener and replaced the gardener after the latter's death. Now he was *capataz* to his beloved master here in Taos, and for these last five years he had devoted himself with all his energies and will to his master's happiness.

Yes, he thought somberly to himself, *it's all very well for Teofilo to hanker after a woman, but perhaps it is time I thought about myself. Alas, I am probably too old now, too set in my ways, to have anyone care for me. Oh, well, at least I can take joy in the knowledge that I have faithfully served Don Diego. Go along with you, Miguel, you are an old fool and you know it. You weren't meant to marry Luisa, even though she loved you very much. Be content with your memories, then, and with your work.*

Having purchased some cases of El Paso wine from an affable Mexican merchant, he came back to the latter's stall, intent on relaxing and enjoying himself. Don Diego and Doña Inez would be along shortly, he knew. The two *trabajadores* had already gone back with the *carreta* and the burro to unload the purchases at the *hacienda*, and he'd told them to come back and that he'd stand them treat for wine and chili con carne and *tartas* as a reward for their diligence.

"Ah, it is you again, Señor Sandarbal!" the short, thickly mustachioed wine vendor greeted him. "*Amigo,* it is my pleasure to offer you a flask of this excellent wine, which you have shown such good judgment in buying from me this day. Drink to my health and to your own, *hombre!*"

"*Muchas gracias, amigo.*" Miguel smiled as he accepted the leather flask. Uncapping it, he took a hearty swig and smacked his lips. "Yes, that is the finest I've tasted in this province."

"Or likely to taste anywhere else, ¿no es verdad? You have brought me luck, Señor Sandarbal. I have sold nearly all my wine, because once the other capatazes of Taos saw the great Señor Sandarbal selecting my wine for his patrón, they flocked to my stand. I shall go back to Chihuahua very rich."

"Very likely," Miguel chuckled, "and when my men and I visit you in January, doubtless the price will be doubled or even trebled."

The Mexican's jovial face took on an expression of desolate grief. "Ayudame, how is it possible you would think that I would be so greedy, esteemed Señor Sandarbal? I seek only a little profit for my labors, just as you do yourself. Are we not trabajadores together?"

"Not exactly so, amigo, but let us have no unfriendly words on so beautiful a day. I thank you for the wine, and I wish you good fortune in Chihuahua."

"And to you, the same in Taos, Señor Sandarbal." The little Mexican took off his sombrero and bowed low.

Miguel chuckled with amusement, his somber mood dissipated, and he took another swig of wine, capped the flask, and moved on to see the sights.

Suddenly, a faint cry of, "Oh, pl-please don't!" made him turn his head as he was contemplating a display of Navaho pottery and blankets. Over to his right, standing beside a pile of buffalo and deer skins, was a tall Comanche, naked to the waist, his chest painted with intricate tribal signs in yellow, black, and red, with a red headband and an eagle's feather to denote his status as tribal chief. In his left hand, he held a rawhide leash which was fixed to a collar around the neck of a bedraggled, yellow-haired white woman, whose wrists were bound with a rawhide thong in front of her. Her gingham dress was badly ripped at one side and over one shoulder, exposing pale, pink skin. Her face was flushed with shame and tears trickled down her cheeks. Before her stood a white-haired hacendado whom Miguel recognized as Don Felipe de Cortomar, twice a widower and one of the most dissolute womanizers in all Taos. It was rumored that his first wife had taken her own life when he had shown preferential attention to her teenage maids.

Miguel, his sun-bronzed, bearded face clouded with compassion, pushed his way toward the Comanche and his white captive. The Comanche eyed him narrowly, then continued his harangue: "Me sell this *gringa* very cheap, ¿comprende? How much you give, señor?"

Don Felipe de Cortomar coughed, then stroked his double chin, his beady dark-brown eyes avidly scanning the shrinking young woman. When she turned her face away and uttered a sob, the Comanche chief raised the strap in his right hand and dealt her a vicious cut across the hips. "You smile at *hacendado, puta gringa!*" he angrily commanded. Then again, wheedlingly, to Don Felipe, "How much! How many *pesos* you give for white squaw?"

"Two hundred," the portly, white-haired *hacendado* replied.

"How much you give, *hombre?*" The Comanche turned to Miguel, trying to calculate the interest of the *capataz* so that he could force up the price to his own profit.

Miguel bit his lip, embarrassed at being caught up in this human auction, yet greatly distressed to see the plight of the young blond woman. "Two hundred fifty," he impulsively exclaimed, after a swift estimate of the savings he had managed to put by for himself.

"I, Sarpento, chief of Penateka Comanche, say it not enough. You, señor, how much you give for *gringa?*" He turned back to Don Felipe.

The white-haired widower shot Miguel a contemptuous glance and then, with a great show of ostentation, cleared his throat and loudly called, "Three hundred *pesos!*"

Miguel suppressed a sigh of extreme chagrin. That was more than he could afford, and it would do no good to ask the Comanche to hold up the sale till he could borrow from the friendly *trabajadores* who would surely accommodate him. Reading his decision in his downcast look, Sarpento turned back to Don Felipe: "Three hundred not enough for fine white squaw like this. She bear you many sons. She not take Comanche to her blanket, but a *hacendado* like you, señor, she will obey. If she does not, I give you this strap to use on her." With this, Sarpento maliciously sent the rawhide thong thwacking across the young woman's shoulders, but this time, though she winced at the pain, she compressed her lips and refused to cry out.

"I'll give three hundred fifty, not a *centavo* more!" Don Felipe hoarsely declared. He came closer, evidently wanting to inspect his prize at closer range. Miguel dug his fingernails into his palms and was about to turn away, detesting Don Felipe with all his soul.

"I bid four hundred!" came a clear, strong voice from behind him. Miguel turned, astonished, to see Don Diego de Escobar and Doña Inez, holding onto her husband's arm.

"That much better!" Sarpento grinned. "What you say to that, *hacendado?*"

"Four hundred fifty, but I won't go beyond that, I warn you!" Obviously nettled by this opposition, Don Felipe de Cortomar gave Don Diego de Escobar a furious look.

"Five hundred, then," Don Diego calmly rejoined.

"That very good, señor!" Sarpento grinned. "Your last chance, *hacendado*. Five hundred, this wise, good señor has offered Sarpento."

"Let him take her, then!" Don Felipe de Cortomar snapped as, with a great show of indignation, he jostled gaping passersby out of his way and strode off.

"Patrón," Miguel hoarsely muttered, "it was good of you! I wanted to set her free—that poor woman—"

"I know, I saw," Don Diego whispered back and patted Miguel on the shoulder. "I could not let her go to Don Felipe, that despicable lecher, any more than you could. We'll find a place for her in the *hacienda.*"

"Gracias, patrón. You have done a wonderful thing today, and *el Señor Dios* will bless you for it," Miguel fervently responded.

Don Diego approached the Comanche and paid him in silver *pesos.* "You take white squaw now," Sarpento said. "Here is strap, you beat her if she not obey, señor."

"No, Sarpento. Throw away the strap or keep it for your other women. And take the leash and collar off her," Don Diego ordered.

Grumbling, the Comanche took his hunting knife and cut the thongs binding the blond woman's wrists, then the leash, inserting his stubby fingers inside the collar. Not without a vindictive little tug that made her gasp, he sawed away at the rawhide collar till it dropped to the ground.

"Come along, señorita, you are free now." Don Diego offered her his arm as he would to a lady of quality.

"May God bless you, señor!" the young woman sobbed. Solicitously, Doña Inez came forward now and put an arm protectively around her shoulders. "It is all over now. We'll find work for you at our *hacienda*. I am Doña Inez de Escobar and this is my husband, Don Diego," she said gently.

"I—I'm Bess Callendar, Señor de Escobar. That Indian captured me when my husband and I were traveling from San Antonio, where his brother lived, to the north. They attacked our wagon train and he—Sarpento—killed my husband."

"How terrible—and what courage you must have had to survive," Doña Inez murmured.

"He—he wanted to make me his squaw, but—but I wouldn't. I prayed God would take me so I could be with my husband, Edward, again—but Sarpento made me a slave instead. He said that if I wouldn't m—marry him, I would have to do the work of a slave, and I did. And I guess—well, he got tired of me after I kept saying I would not marry him—so he brought me here to sell me. Oh, God bless you, thank you, for saving me—I don't know how much longer I could have gone on like that!" Bess Callendar burst into hysterical sobs while Doña Inez held her tightly and murmured soothing words.

"My husband," she said, turning to Don Diego, "let us go back to the *hacienda*. I shall take charge of Bess myself. You know my maid, Dolores Costilla, is with child, and it may just be that Bess could take her place until we can find something more fitting for her."

By the end of July of this year of 1813, Miguel Sandarbal's ennui with the industrious monotony of his days in Taos had been replaced by an uncommon zest for what each new day would bring. To some extent, this was the doing of young Tom Prentice. At John Cooper's suggestion, Miguel had taken the youth out to the corral and, giving him a lariat, indulgently proposed that he try his skill at roping some of the more restive mustangs which had been penned off in one section. So ably did the youth acquit himself that Miguel excitedly declared, "A feeling for *los caballos* such as you have, Señor Tom, is a gift the good God gives to men. It is rarely come by with even very hard work—as I well should know from my own days on a farm in Spain. They respond to you, they understand you, they know you are *muy simpático*. There is no need to waste your talents on the sheep. They are placid, stupid creatures, easily led. But it takes a *vaquero muy grande* to know how to make horses do his bidding. You and I will be good friends, Señor Tom!"

As for Amy, the pretty young girl rapidly regained her strength and coloring, thanks to the lavish meals that Tía Margarita forced her to eat, and the care and concern shown to her not only by the servants, but also by Doña Inez, Catarina, and Weesayo. She had, too, a delightful sense of humor, and had begun to blossom under the kindly aura which prevailed in the de Escobar *hacienda*. It did not take long for her to show how expert she was as a seamstress. Hence Catarina, now engrossed in her pregnancy and concerned that her husband continue to find her attractive, virtually monopolized Amy's services. The two young women became fast friends, and Amy was put to work creating new dresses which would conceal Catarina's approaching maternity, yet at the same time accentuate the loveliness of her bosom and shoulders.

John Cooper was happy to see Catarina find a new friend and interest in Amy, since it was certain to lessen her fits of pique in not being able to accompany him on the occasional hunting and exploring expeditions he planned to make with Lobo. Meanwhile, he continued to train the wolf-dog to accept the members of the household and the ranch.

One morning, at the end of July, as he went out to saddle his mustang, he met Miguel talking to Teofilo Rosas near the corral. After the latter had ingratiatingly bowed himself away, John Cooper chuckled and turned to Miguel. "Well, *compañero*, how goes it with you?"

"Very well, young master, very well, indeed." Miguel grinned and drew in a deep breath. "I think that summer is the loveliest time in Taos. It reminds me a little of the suburbs of Madrid, when all the flowers are blooming and the sky is blue and clear."

"But you don't miss Madrid any more, do you, Miguel?"

"No, young master. Not in the least! My life is here now. My master, Don Diego, and his beautiful señora are happy, and his daughter, Catarina, is happy with you, Señor Baines, and Carlos and his wife show such tenderness as makes me wish I was twenty years younger. *¡Ayudame!*" Miguel uttered a long, nostalgic sigh.

"I've a notion that you've several reasons to be in such

good spirits, and that you're not really complaining about the past, even excepting the way you just sighed," John Cooper teased him.

The middle-aged *capataz* grinned and winked. "Then you have guessed my secret, master." Miguel glanced around nervously. "But is it so obvious as that?"

"No, except that I suppose because I'm in love, I can' feel when someone else has the same idea."

"She is a very beautiful woman, but the trouble is, I am twice her age, Señor Baines. Worst of all, my master, Don Diego, bought her away from Sarpento, though I was ready to do it, except that—well, to tell you the truth, I didn't have so many *pesos* saved up."

"I know, *compañero*. You've spent a great deal out of your own pocket to give presents to Carlos and Catarina, and to do things for your *trabajadores*. You've a good heart, *mi capataz*."

"Promise that you will not breathe a word of this to anyone," Miguel anxiously insisted.

"Of course I won't. But I'd remind you that, if Don Diego paid what he did to free Bess Callendar, it wasn't to make a *criada* out of her. She's working as a maid for Doña Inez just till Don Diego can think of a proper place for her. When the right time comes, and you want to talk to her about marrying you—"

"*Por todos los santos,* who in the world said I was going to do a thing like that? I, who am near fifty, homely, and with a skin tough as leather?" Miguel protested.

"You're not yet fifty, and you're a fine figure of a man. I only hope I'll be in the shape you're in when I reach your age, Miguel. And out here, age doesn't mean anything at all. If you love her and she loves you, you'll both find a way to overcome that nonsense," John Cooper stoutly declared as he grinned and clapped the *capataz* on the back and then strode off to the corral to saddle his mustang.

The next day Miguel Sandarbal chanced to see Bess and Doña Inez working in the little garden which Don Diego's wife had planted in the patio. His jaw dropped and he stood there staring like a bemused schoolboy, for he scarcely recognized this beautiful, young, golden-haired woman as the bedraggled captive whom he had first seen at the Taos fair, collared and leashed like an animal. Her golden hair tumbled below her shoulder blades, and her face was round and sweet, with large, soft blue eyes and a dainty, slightly turned-up nose. She was speaking to Doña Inez in a soft voice. As Don Diego's wife said something which made her laugh, Miguel raptly perceived the dimples at the corners of her full mouth. Feeling guilty for his eavesdropping, he hurried off, but his heart was pounding and for the rest of the day he could scarcely keep his mind on his duties.

At sundown, when Doña Inez came out alone to water the flowers, he pretended to have an errand in the *hacienda* and accosted her. "A good evening to you and Don Diego, Doña Inez," he stammered.

"And to you also, Miguel. The garden is flourishing, don't you think?"

"Oh, to be sure, but then, it's because it is so well tended."

"What a nice compliment! And I think I'll pass it along to the Señora Callendar—after all, she has been helping me with it."

"I know—that is to say, I—I—" Miguel floundered and a flush spread over his cheeks. "I have some news for Don Diego. I was just going into the *hacienda*—"

Doña Inez laughed softly. "Why are you in such a hurry, Miguel? I am perfectly aware of the fact that you find the Señora Callendar most attractive. She is a lovely young woman."

"I—I am sure of that, Señora de Escobar." He nervously twisted his sombrero to and fro, looked down at the ground, and damned himself for his sheepishness. "She is half my age—*Dios*, what am I saying!" he blurted out, then shook his head in exasperation.

"I understand you, Miguel." Doña Inez came to him and put a hand on his shoulder. "There is no need for pretense between us; we are old friends, aren't we, Miguel?"

"But, Señora de Escobar, I have only just met her—and besides, there is the matter of the difference in our ages—and I am an old *capataz* and she is a *gringa*—"

"Hush now, Miguel, that is silly, and you know it is. Weesayo is the daughter of an Apache chief, and yet I couldn't be happier for Carlos in the wife he has chosen."

"But she would laugh at me if I tried to tell her that I care for her—she would think that I was just—you know—"

"No, she would not." Doña Inez shook her head. "She will have occasion to watch you working with the *traba-*

jadores and with the horses and the sheep. She will soon see that you are a fine man, a man of dignity and honor. I'll certainly further your suit so far as telling her what a fine man you are."

"Señora de Escobar, you are an angel from *paraíso!*" His face shone with an incredulous joy. "I was thinking—no, it is too early to mention such a thing—"

"No, go ahead, tell me what it is you're thinking, Miguel," Doña Inez urged.

"Well, Señora de Escobar, has she spoken to you at all about what she wants to do? I mean, does she have any folks or friends she might be thinking of going back to in Texas?"

"There I can ease your mind completely, Miguel. No, she and her husband had moved from Virginia to start a little ranch in Texas, and her parents died a year before she was married."

"*¡Pobrecita!*" Miguel sympathetically murmured. "What bad luck she has had for one so young and so *linda!*" Miguel sighed.

"Courage, *hombre!*" Doña Inez laughed and patted him on the shoulder again. "You can see that the field is open for you. Only my advice is, don't overwhelm her. Go gently for a time, let her get used to you."

"I swear, Doña Inez—I mean, Señora de Escobar—that there is no kinder, no more understanding woman than you in all the world!"

"You are an arch-flatterer, Miguel Sandarbal." Doña Inez uttered a merry little laugh. "But save your flowery speeches for the *gringa linda* when the time comes. Now, a moment ago, you were about to say something—what is it?"

"Well," Miguel said, taking his courage from Doña Inez's unexpected camaraderie with him, "what I was thinking was that she might like to have her own little cottage. We have plenty of time now, the *trabajadores* and myself, because the shearing is over and the men could use a little work to keep them in shape—as I could myself." Seeing her meditatively frown, he hastened to amend, "Oh, no, Señora de Escobar, I wasn't thinking of an arrangement such as that *cobarde* José Ramirez had with the *criadas* of Don Sancho! Never in the world, I assure you—"

"But you didn't have to tell me that, Miguel. You are the

very soul of honor. I see what you are driving at. You think that, if she had her own little place to live, she would feel less dependent on us, and that we were not taking her into our *hacienda* out of simple charity. I see no reason why it shouldn't be done, Miguel. I am sure she would like that very much. Indeed, only this morning, she was saying she wanted to know what she could do to—earn her keep, I think that was the phrase she used. Do you know, the Señora Callendar taught school before her husband married her. She reads and writes, and she is really quite intelligent. I myself have been trying to think how we could keep her busy and happy while she stays here."

"Maybe I could make a suggestion there, Señora de Escobar," Miguel ventured. "You know, I have been writing up the reports every month for Don Diego about our flock, and keeping the inventory of supplies. Now perhaps the Señora Callendar could do that, and much more neatly, for you know that my handwriting is atrociously bad."

"Why, I think that is a simply marvelous idea, Miguel!" Doña Inez smiled at him. "I will propose it to her tomorrow, and then we'll see. And now I think you said you had something to say to my husband?"

"*Sí, sí*, I had almost forgotten—thank you for reminding me. *Buenas noches*, Señora de Escobar!" Clapping his sombrero on his head and whistling a jaunty tune, Miguel Sandarbal strode off toward the *hacienda*, and the look on his face was that of a man who has been told he may enter the Garden of Eden.

Eight

Frank Corland's undoing was that he came late to the fair at Taos, arriving to sell his packloads of beaver skins about the middle of August, just a week before the end. Yet he was fortunate that he had bypassed Santa Fe, or he might have found himself languishing in a dungeon in Mexico City or Chihuahua.

Governor Joaquín de Real Alencaster had left office as *gubernador* of Nuevo Mexico in the year 1808, and Alberto Maynez had temporarily filled the post until the appointment of Josef Manrique who now presided at Santa Fe. All three autocratic heads of this Spanish-dominated land north of the Rio Grande were inimically disposed toward Americans. Not only was it felt that the advent of American traders into Santa Fe and Taos would undermine the profitable monopolies imposed by the viceroy, but also the government in Mexico City greatly feared that such an invasion would mean war with the young, upstart nation. The purchase of Louisiana from France in 1803 had brought the young nation closer to her Spanish neighbor, and, indeed, the earlier border struggle between Spain and France was now between Spain and the United States. Thus, adventurers and trappers who wandered into New Mexico during these formative years at the turn of the century aroused suspicion as to their motives in crossing into Spanish-dominated territory and, worse than that, risked severe and even cruel reprisals.

Frank Corland had heard some of these accounts, but an accident on the trail turned his footsteps toward New Mexico. He was just twenty-six, affable, industrious, and, not unlike John Cooper Baines, had been an orphan since he was fifteen. He had lived with his father and mother in a little

85

Louisiana hamlet on the bank of the Mississippi. When his parents had been murdered by river renegades, he had moved downriver toward New Orleans and there gone to work for a Creole trapper who had been like a foster father to him.

Now, a decade later, when the Creole died from river fever, Frank found himself a prosperous trapper and trader in beaver skins, with six men working for him. The preceding winter had been extraordinarily successful, and he had many beaver skins of prime quality to sell. Also, he had just been jilted by a flirtatious, black-haired Creole girl to whom he had believed himself engaged. Being a romantic idealist, he resolved to drive her fickleness from his mind by heading an arduous trading expedition which would take him to Texas. There was, he knew, a considerable demand for beaver skins among the settlers there, and they would pay excellent prices. He even envisaged the possibility of trading some of his skins for the long-horned cattle, whose meat was much in demand in New Orleans.

Accordingly, he had set out in January with four of his men and six burros, the cured beaver skins packed in bulging saddlebags. But near San Antonio, he and his men were warned by a lone rider that a war party of Comanche was in the vicinity. Frank quickly decided to go farther southwest and to hug the winding Nueces River to escape the hostile Indians.

What he had no way of knowing, to be sure, was that the rider was one of a band of renegades who intended to divert him and his men in exactly that direction so that they could be ambushed and killed and their beaver skins seized.

But here again, fate decided Frank Corland's destination. The men with him rebelled against his leadership and flatly told him that they were going back to New Orleans and would sell the skins there themselves. They would, they told him, give him his fair share, but they would go no farther.

With the remembrance of his thwarted love affair still rankling, Frank defiantly replied, "Leave me two burros, and I'll go on by myself. You can sell the rest and pocket it among yourselves, and be damned to you. Only, when I get back, I'll start another company and you won't work for me, not ever again."

He had an old musket, plenty of balls and powder, and a hunting knife as his only weapons. His companions had left him enough jerky and hardtack for a week. Frank was intuitively suspicious of the rider and his warning about the Comanche war party, so he made the decision to veer far to the northwest, and by so doing he avoided the ambush.

Like most trappers and traders, he had heard of the annual fair at Taos. And so now, alone with his two burros and his pinto, he decided to disguise himself as a Mexican, sell his beaver skins at a fine profit, and then go back to Louisiana where he would form a new enterprise.

He was slim, not quite six feet tall, with long, black hair and beard. It was an easy matter to stain his face and hands with the juice of pressed walnuts and to let the intense sun deepen this improvised dye. Moreover, his mother, herself the daughter of a Pensacola beauty and a French sea captain, had taught him enough Spanish to be conversant with it. Frank believed that he could pass himself off as a Spaniard.

He arrived at Taos on August 14. He tethered his burros to a tree near the edge of the fair, unpacked his saddlebags, and calmly carried the piles of beaver skins to an empty place between a Pawnee chief and a burly Mexican trader from Chihuahua. The Mexican glared at him and growled, *"¿Que hace usted, donde viene usted, hombre?"*

"Vengo de Nuevo Laredo," Frank declared, and added, still in Spanish, "There was sickness in my family, and that is why I'm late. If this place is not taken, it would be an honor to be beside you, *compadre."*

The mustachioed Mexican shrugged and grunted. "The fair is nearly over, *hombre.* But I have not seen beaver skins from Nuevo Laredo before."

"I have brothers," Frank improvised, "who trap in Louisiana, along the great Mississippi. When I sell these here at Taos, I shall divide the profits with them for their good work."

"Ah, *sí, hermanos*—that is very good. I have only one, and he is a lazy, good-for-nothing," the Mexican confided.

Frank exhaled a breath of relief and, to solidify his story, offered the Mexican one of the best beaver skins as a gift of friendship.

By midday, the imaginative young Louisianan had sold more than half of his wares, and he was hoping that his good fortune would continue. If by the end of the day all of the beaver skins were gone, he could make his way back to New Orleans with no one the wiser.

At about four o'clock that afternoon, a sergeant and two

privates from Santa Fe rode along the winding mountain road, their orders being to inspect the last days of the fair and to make certain that there were no Americans present. Governor Manrique was reacting to an angry letter from the viceroy in Mexico City which ordered him to take sterner measures against the possibility of what he termed "*gringo* spies and adventurers who, under pretense of trade, would learn of our military fortifications and try to cause rancor between New Spain and the lawless government of *los Estados Unidos*." Smarting under this official rebuke, the governor had ordered the patrol to check credentials and to arrest anyone who could not give a reasonable account of his presence there.

John Cooper arrived at the fair sohrtly before the contingent of soldiers. He moved lazily along the stalls, on the lookout for gifts for his family. He observed that the Comanche chief, Sarpento, had long since finished the bartering for the goods he wanted for his people and left the fair, and that the Ute leader, Ortimwoy, had obviously also headed back for his distant village.

John Cooper paused at a stall where a short, burly, nearly bald Mexican from Chihuahua and his buxom wife offered gewgaws of ribbons and other decorative figures, as well as woven eyes of God (strands of varicolored wool shaped in triangles between polished sticks with a central round "eye" in blue or red or green that caught the eye of the beholder, no matter what part of the room he was in), and elegantly woven serapes. He decided to buy a serape for his father-in-law and also one for Carlos, and ribbon bows for Catarina, Weesayo, and Doña Inez. Impulsively he added another ribbon for the cook, Tía Margarita.

As he glanced over to his left, while the voluble Mexican thanked him for his purchases and the wife neatly folded the serapes and placed the ribbons into a little buckskin sack, he noticed Frank Corland stooping to reassemble the rest of his beaver skins. Thanking the Mexican woman and collecting his purchases, he moved over to the stall and scrutinized the skins with great interest. "That's some of the best beaver I've seen since I lived wtih the Ayuhwa," he pleasantly commented in Spanish.

Frank straightened, his eyes widening, and John Cooper's eyes widened in turn: the sight of the Louisianan's blue eyes was startling indeed. Then, as he glanced up at the road, he saw the trio of mounted soldiers from Santa Fe, and quickly murmured in English, "You're no more Spanish than I am, *hombre*. What are you doing here? See those soldiers? They don't want American traders, and you'll be in great trouble if they come down and start asking for your credentials."

Frank gasped, turning his head to stare where John Cooper was looking. "You're right, *amigo*," he murmured back. "I'd best get out of here."

"I've a better idea than that. Come along with me. My father-in-law, Don Diego de Escobar, is the *intendente* of Taos. You'll be safe under his protection. If those soldiers arrest you, you'll be sent on to the governor in Santa Fe and, like as not, wind up in some dirty, dark prison back in Chihuahua or Mexico City. Hurry up."

"But my burros—" Frank began.

"Let them be, *hombre!*" John Cooper fiercely interrupted, taking the trader by the arm. "And leave the beaver skins, too. I can see that your Mexican neighbor has an eye for them—"

"I know. I gave him one as a present so he wouldn't get the wind up. Who are you, anyway?" he asked the figure in buckskins.

"There's time enough for introductions once I get you safely to Don Diego's *hacienda*," he curtly replied. "Now, put your arm around my shoulders and pretend to be a good friend. Hurry, the soldiers are getting closer."

"I'm obliged to you, whoever you are. I guess maybe I took an awful chance coming all the way to Taos," Frank breathed as they made their way through the crowd.

"There now, we're safe enough. You see, that Mexican friend of yours is taking over the skins, and now the soldiers are riding up to him to find out what he's doing with them. Let's go down the road apace so they won't see us," John Cooper urged.

Swinging the serapes over his shoulder and holding the sack, he began to run and Frank Corland followed him, until they reached a dip in the valley which took them out of sight. "That's better," John Cooper grinned. "My name's John Cooper Baines."

"Judging by the way you talked, Mr. Baines, I'd say you

were a long ways from your original home." Frank grinned
back and extended his hand. "My name's Frank Corland. I'm
from Louisiana."

"We can slow down a bit, Frank. The *hacienda* isn't far,
and there's no danger." John Cooper paused to catch his
breath. "I see you tried to darken your skin. That was a right
smart idea, only it's starting to wear thin, and those blue eyes
of yours wouldn't fool any Mexican soldier, depend on it."

"I guess I was taking an awful gamble," Frank candidly
confessed.

"Well, we'll talk about what happened to you once I get
you back to the *hacienda*. I'll have you talk to Don Diego.
He's a fair man, and he wouldn't want to turn you over to the
authorities in Santa Fe and have you sweat out a couple of
years in a prison in Chihuahua or Mexico City."

"I'm very grateful to you, John Cooper. I wouldn't want
to stay in a Mexican jail, either. I guess I had more gumption
than sense when I headed for Taos. Thanks to you, maybe I
can stay out of trouble."

When they arrived, John Cooper led Frank to Don
Diego's study. The middle-aged nobleman rose from his desk,
for he had been busy writing a report of the activities of the
fair thus far to be forwarded to Governor Manrique. He
greeted his son-in-law warmly, then gave a cordial nod to
Frank who hesitantly lagged behind.

"Don Diego, I've a favor to ask of you," John Cooper
began. "This is Frank Corland, and he tells me that he started
out with some beaver skins, he and his partners, only they
had an argument and left him stranded in Texas. He took a
chance and came on here to Taos, and, as you see, stained his
face to look like a Mexican."

"It is not too bad a disguise," Don Diego chuckled,
pulling at his beard, "but *los ojos* give him away. I cannot
recall a Spaniard with eyes so blue."

"Sort of like mine, Don Diego. Yes, I saw that right off,"
John Cooper said, smiling. "Well, I know how Governor
Manrique feels about *gringos* who try to get into our fair, and
that's why I brought him right to you. I was thinking maybe
we could hide him here."

"That was very wise, *mi hijo*," Don Diego agreed. "First,
señor," addressing himself to Frank, "you will be my guest.
John Cooper will take you to a room and you shall have a

bath, and then perhaps you would do me the honor of joining us at dinner, where we can discuss the matter."

"That's kind of you, Don Diego. I'm beholden."

"The Spanish authorities—with the exception of myself —do not take kindly to *gringo* traders, for reasons I am sure John Cooper has told you. But I, as you can see, am not one who turns away *gringos*, for otherwise I should have turned away the very fine young man who is now my beloved son-in-law. You are welcome. Until tonight, then." Don Diego made him a courtly bow from the waist.

After he was settled in his room, Frank Corland had washed off the stain, and Carlos, who had taken an immediate liking to the young American, had lent him the costume of a *caballero*. At the dinner table that evening, Carlos plied the young adventurer with excited questions on his method of trapping beaver and the harrowing journey which had left Frank alone and on his own resources in southeastern Texas. Then he turned to his father and exclaimed, *"Mi padre,* you're *intendente* here, which means you can judge a prisoner of Taos. Can't you hold court here and now and let the Señor Corland go free? Must you report it to the *gubernador?"*

"I am convinced, *mi hijo,*" Don Diego smiled, "that the Señor Corland had no plan to threaten the safety of our royal government under the viceroy. And I agree with you, there is no need to bother Governor Manrique with the news of his presence here." Then, turning to the delighted young Louisianan, he declared, "Señor Corland, I fine you two *pesos* for selling beaver skins at the fair of Taos without a proper license. Once you have paid this levy, you are free to go where you wish. And I do not intend to report to Governor Manrique that any *gringo* appeared at the fair."

"That's very kind of you, Don Diego. I'm very much obliged. You've all been wonderfully friendly to me—you and John Cooper here. I'm a lucky man."

"Luck's usually on the side of those who deserve it, I've found," John Cooper chuckled. Then, more seriously, he asked, "Do you have any plans about going back and what you'll do?"

Frank shrugged. "Well, my dad was a trapper before me, and that's about all I know. I can sell my beaver skins, I've found that out already—even if it was against your law here. I'd certainly be grateful for any suggestion. Now that my parents are gone, and the fellows I was working with turned out to be unreliable, I really don't have any ties that bind me to Louisiana, to tell you the truth," Frank candidly avowed.

"I have a friend," Don Diego interposed, "a man in his late fifties, a widower by the name of Don José de Bernados. He owns a very attractive shop, just off the plaza, where dress goods are sold. His health has been failing the last six months, and last week he told me that he was seriously considering giving up the shop unless he could find a young assistant to run it for him. He lost his wife and his only son some years ago, and he is a lonely man. I think he would like you, and he for one is often impatient—as I myself am—with the stringent regulations laid down by our authorities as to what trading we may do."

"I hadn't thought about working in a store, Don Diego," Frank said slowly. "But it's certainly a good idea. Do you think I'd be safe staying here in Taos, though?"

"Of course. I would vouch for you, and so would Don José. And so long as you do not do any trading at Taos from now on, *hombre*, the authorities will not bother with you, leave that to me." Don Diego gave him a broad wink.

At the end of dinner, the middle-aged nobleman invited Frank Corland as well as John Cooper and Carlos to enjoy some fine French brandy in his study. Half an hour later, as Frank was making his way to his room, he turned in the hallway only to be jostled by Amy Prentice, who had just left Catarina's chamber.

"Oh, I'm sorry, excuse me," Frank blurted, his face reddening as he grasped the young girl by the shoulders to steady her.

"Oh, my goodness—it—it's all my fault, sir—I was hurrying back to my room—"

"Did I hurt you?"

"Oh, no!" Now it was Amy's turn to blush, and she demurely lowered her eyes.

"You're sure now?"

"Oh, yes—it—it's very nice of you to concern yourself, s—sir," Amy quavered.

"Well, then—I—my name's Frank Corland. I came here to Taos to sell beaver skins, and John Cooper was kind enough to take me away before the soldiers arrested me—you see, Americans aren't supposed to trade here."

"Oh, I didn't know that!" Amy looked up, wide-eyed.

Seeing that the black-haired young man's eyes were fixed on her pretty face, she blushed even more hotly than before. "I—I guess I'd better say good night. My—my name's Amy Prentice."

"You're not Spanish, either, Amy, any more than I am. How did you get to Taos?" he inquired with a smile.

"Well, my—my brother Tom and I—we came in a wagon to live with my uncle at a trading post in Wyoming country, and the—the Indians attacked us and—well, the Indian chief who captured Tom and me brought us here to sell us. And Mr. Baines was nice enough to buy us and rescue us, that's how."

"You poor girl—you certainly had a rougher time of it than I ever did. I'm sorry if I hurt you, Amy."

"But you didn't, really, Mr. Corland—I—I better go now. It's getting awfully late."

"Of course. Maybe I'll see you tomorrow. Good night, Amy."

She gave him a quick smile and hurried back down the hallway. But before she went back to her room, she turned around for a covert glance at him, and discovering that he was still standing there looking after her, she turned a fiery red and quickly went into her room and closed the door. "Oh, my goodness," she breathed softly to herself. "What a nice man he is!"

Miguel Sandarbal was reluctant to tell Bess Callendar that it was he who had arranged for the building of the little cottage which was to be her private dwelling. Troubled by feelings of guilt and unworthiness, he hesitantly approached Don Diego as the cottage was nearing completion and asked if he might speak to him in private. "But of course, *mi compañero*," Don Diego reassured him. "By now, Miguel, you should surely know that we are more old friends than *hacendado* and *capataz*. Come along with me into the study, Miguel, and we'll share a bottle of the finest Madeira I have been saving."

The two men went into the study, and as they sat, Miguel said, "I have no wish to offend you, Don Diego—"

"*¡Por todos los santos,* Miguel!" Don Diego fiercely exclaimed, "you have never done that, and you never will. Now stop acting like a timid schoolboy. As I recall, when we used to practice with rapiers, you were the one who always attacked me and drove me back. And if, as I know you to be, you are truly your father's son, you will not hold your tongue back now when I give you leave to say whatever is in your heart. Besides which," this with a humorous twinkle in his eyes, "I think I can guess what it is you find so hard to say to me. It is this *rubia linda,* the Señora Callendar, is it not, Miguel?"

Miguel gulped, and his weatherbeaten face reddened as he sheepishly nodded.

"I knew as much!" Don Diego declared. "And I am not surprised in the least. Besides, it is high time you were taking a wife for yourself, Miguel. A man is happiest when he has a sweet wife to share his hopes and dreams with. Yes," he added, stroking his goatee, "when my angel Dolores was taken from me, I was bereft of all my senses. But, thank *el Señor Dios,* though I took an unconscionable time to discover it, my grief was to be assuaged by my wonderful Inez. But here you, Miguel, all these years slaving on my behalf and so loyally devoted to my family, never once have you thought of yourself. Yes, indeed, it is high time!"

"That is all very well for you to say, Don Diego." Miguel's words came hesitantly. "But you are forgetting that I'm much older than she."

"What difference does that make? Let me tell you something, Miguel Sandarbal." Don Diego leaned forward across the desk. "When I proposed that she would work with you on the accounts of the household, she said it would be a great pleasure because she has seen how efficient you are and how well liked you are by the *trabajadores.*"

"She—she said that, *patrón?*" Miguel gasped, a wan smile creasing his lips.

"She did indeed, Miguel! So I am sure that, within a reasonable time, once you pay court to her, you will certainly find her willing to hear you out."

"But, *patrón,*" Miguel doggedly protested, "even if that is so, I can't offer her very much. Why, you saw yourself at the fair I did not have the *dinero* to bid her away from that old fool of a *hacendado.* It was you who bought her, *patrón.*"

Don Diego smilingly shook his head. "Once again, you are forgetting that we are much more than *patrón* and *trabajador, amigo.* We are old friends, and your father was my friend as well. Now what I really want is for you to court the Señora Callendar. In my opinion, she is very fortunate to have a suitor like you. So take my advice and don't delay."

"I will never be able to repay you as I truly wish, Don Diego," Miguel said gravely. "But I'll say this only, I'd gladly lay down my life for you and Doña Inez and Carlos and Catarina. This I swear."

Greatly moved, Don Diego did not speak. He came to Miguel and put a comradely arm around the *capataz*'s shoulders, and there the two men stood staring at each other and clasping hands in a bond of enduring friendship and understanding.

While Miguel Sandarbal slowly and secretly began his self-doubting courtship of Bess Callendar, Frank Corland and Amy Prentice fell almost immediately in love. The very day after their accidental nocturnal meeting, the young Louisianan met Amy carrying bolts of cloth out of Catarina's room. Frank bowed to the pretty young girl, and then smilingly proffered, "Allow me to carry those for you, Miss Amy. Otherwise, I fear, you might bump into someone going down the hallway."

Amy crimsoned and could only gasp, "Oh, my gracious!" whereupon Frank gently appropriated the bolts and, instantly apologetic, declared, "I didn't mean to tease you, Miss Amy, truly I didn't. The fact is, I'm awfully glad I had this chance of seeing you again. I—I was thinking, if you're not too busy maybe later this afternoon, we might go for a horseback ride—that is, if you do ride?"

"Oh, yes, Mr. Corland, my pa got me a pony when I was ten—" she eagerly blurted out, and then looked away, her eyes suddenly filling with tears at the remembrance of her parents' death.

"Oh, Lord," Frank groaned. "I seem to have a consarned habit of saying the wrong thing to you, Miss Amy. I'm truly sorry, please believe me."

Amy Prentice drew a deep breath and composed herself, then turned back to him with a tremulous smile. "Oh, no, Mr. Corland, you mustn't down yourself like that, honestly you mustn't! When I said that about the pony, it was—well, you see, Mr. Corland, my pa and ma were killed by those Ute who took Tom and me as slaves. But I can ride, and I'd just love to go riding with you this afternoon, if you'd really like."

Within a week, the pretty orphan girl and the lonely young Louisiana trader had fallen deeply in love, and Frank, after going to Amy's brother Tom and telling him how things stood between them, had an interview with Don Diego in the nobleman's study.

"That's very welcome news, Señor Corland," Don Diego beamed. "From what I know about you both and what I've seen of you in my *hacienda,* it would be a happy solution. And your coming to me now to tell me of your intentions strengthens the idea I had when we first met. You'll recall I told you about Don José de Bernados who is seeking an assistant for his shop in Taos. The only difficulty about your settling here permanently, as I see it, is that at some point the authorities in Santa Fe may wonder how it is that an *americano* has come to live here against their strict edicts prohibiting *gringos* from taking part in commerce. Yet I think I know of a way to outwit them on that score. That is to say, if you would have no objection to being adopted?"

"Adopted, Don Diego?" Frank echoed.

Don Diego nodded and, with almost the impish look of a small boy about to trick his elders successfully, stroked his goatee. "I have already told you that Don José de Bernados is a widower and that he is without issue. So long as I have known him, he has always wished that he had a son—not only to take over his shop but also to stand by him in his infirmities and old age. I have a notion that, once he meets you and comes to like you as much as I do already, he might see in you the son he could never have. Then, you see, I, as *intendente,* could draw up a formal notice of adoption. And once you are the foster son of Don José de Bernados, even Governor Manrique could find no legal reason to oust you from Taos. With your permission, then, Señor Corland, I shall take the necessary steps by inviting Don José here tomorrow night to our evening *comida.*"

Exactly a week from that evening, Frank and the elderly, ailing Taos merchant stood side by side in Don Diego's study and signed the formal document which the benevolent *intendente* had drawn up to establish their future relationship. And ten days later, Padre Juan Moraga married Frank Corland and Amy Prentice in the little chapel of the *hacienda.*

Nine

In this first week of September, 1813, Taos was agog with the news that almost four weeks earlier, General Joaquín de Arrendondo, heading the royal army from Mexico City, had reached the Medina River just west of San Antonio, Texas, and massacred a rebel force of *yanqui* adventurers and die-hard Hidalgo rebels. A sergeant from that army, whom General de Arrendondo had dispatched, had ridden into Taos, exhausted from the long journey and suffering from a minor wound sustained during that battle. His horse was foundering and dying under him as he reached the plaza of the sleepy little town.

The news caused great surprise among the older *hacendados* of the province who believed that the revolutionary attempt to separate New Spain from Old Spain had ended for all time with the execution of Miguel Hidalgo y Costilla. This priest, who sought a separation from the mother country because of its tyranny and the unbridled power of the *ricos,* had issued his famous *grito de Dolores* on September 16, 1810, using as his standard the banner of Our Lady of Guadalupe. He had rallied 80,000 *peones* to form Mexico's first revolutionary army, and at first scored shattering successes over better-armed royalist troops. They pushed back the royal army through sheer weight of numbers, and by October of that year they were at the gates of Mexico City itself.

On the verge of victory, the gentle priest realized that his unmanageable rabble would bring anarchy rather than reform to the country. So, instead of seizing the capital, he ordered his people to retreat. The royal army started after them and inflicted a crushing defeat in Guadalajara. Hidalgo himself had fled into the frontier province of Coahila, where he was betrayed, captured, degraded, and humiliated by the Inquisition and then shot. His head was put on public display on the ramparts of the town of Guanajuato as an object lesson for all malcontents. Surely, the *hacendados* of Taos thought, there could be no more such foolhardy attempts to overthrow the imperial Spanish might.

And yet just one year ago, a motley horde of two thousand Hidalgo supporters and American soldiers of fortune joined forces and swept down on Texas, capturing La Bahia and San Antonio. The victory was theirs for only a year, however. The sergeant's news was that just four weeks ago, General de Arrendondo had waited in ambush for the rebel force of nearly a thousand men who had swarmed out of San Antonio and blundered straight into their trap. They broke ranks and were methodically slaughtered. There were, the sergeant reported, perhaps at most a hundred survivors. Under his general's orders, he declared that any Spanish citizen of Taos would be guilty of treason if he harbored or gave any aid to these rebels.

At about the time the exhausted noncommissioned officer reached Taos with this disturbing news, another rider was halfway to Mexico City to present his general's report to Viceroy Calleja. The report cited eighty-one officers for gallantry in the battle, and one of the heroes was a nineteen-year-old lieutenant who was destined to become a major figure in the future of Texas and to dominate Mexican politics for nearly fifty years—a lieutenant by the name of Antonio Lopez de Santa Anna Pérez de Lebrón. History would mark him as liar, thief, compulsive gambler, notorious womanizer, ruthless and corrupt self-seeker, a man who was universally feared by his countrymen because of his consummate villainy and exquisite cruelty. They would nickname him *Don Demonio*, Sir Devil.

But though the royalists had crushed this latest revolutionary attempt, the seeds of revolt that had been planted by the heroic priest, Hidalgo, were still taking root. And what was growing, though as yet not made manifest throughout Mexico, would change the destiny not only of New Spain, but of the young United States as well.

Don Diego de Escobar, whose family had been loyal to the Spanish crown for long generations, was now beginning to see that authority delegated from afar and with no knowledge of local conditions was necessarily doomed to incompetence and finally failure. Don Diego could see that the traditions of total power upheld by the top echelon of officials in Mexico City and though to a lesser extent, by the governor at Santa Fe who was his immediate superior, dictated a policy that ignored the gradual changes of the economy, the wishes of the common people, and their eagerness for information and communication and freer enterprise of trade. And that was why, after the weary, battle-worn sergeant had come to his office in the plaza and made a private report of the Battle of Medina, Don Diego consulted with Don Sancho de Pladero.

"It is as I thought, Don Sancho," he declared once the two men had closeted themselves in the *alcalde*'s study. "The revolution did not die at Guanajuato. I am certain, old friend, that if you and I were to visit the poorest provinces of Mexico, we would hear Hidalgo's cry, 'Mexico for the Mexicans!' and we would realize that even the viceroy does not know how far the *peones* have come to the point of wanting their independence."

"I cannot blame them in my heart, Don Diego," the *alcalde* solemnly replied. "They work for the meagerest of rewards, they are subject to the lash and prison for the slightest sign of argument against their *patrones*. Even here in our own Taos I have seen the poverty of the Pueblo Indians, of the common folk who work for *hacendados* not so generous as you and I are in rewarding their *trabajadores*."

"What most of the complacent *hacendados* of Taos do not realize," Don Diego reflected, "is that the revolution for independence from Spain is not solely in the hands of the *peones*. The *Criolo* elite—the native-born Mexican upper classes, including the military leaders, high clergymen, and landed aristocrats—have deep-seated reasons for rebelling against Spanish rule. For over three hundred years they have been disqualified from holding the top posts in government; they remain frustrated underlings to insolent and often incompetent royal officials sent from Madrid. And the onerous taxes and numerous restrictions lessen their loyalty—and mine—even more."

Don Sancho shrugged. "But what can we here in this little village high in the mountains do about equality for the poor, Mexico for the Mexicans, indeed?"

"Perhaps we can try to help those stragglers who may,

after that terrible slaughter, reach Taos and seek sanctuary," Don Diego guardedly replied.

"You speak thus because you are a humanitarian. You realize, to be sure, that because of your status as *intendente*, the slightest connection between you and these rebels would be reported to the *gubernador* and thence to the viceroy himself. You would be disgraced and relieved of your post at the very least. I should not like to see that happen to my dear friend. I tell you that out of sheer selfishness, Don Diego."

The middle-aged nobleman clasped the *alcalde*'s hand, put his other arm around Don Sancho's shoulders, and warmly embraced him. "As a man grows older," he said gruffly, "he becomes more tolerant—if he has learned anything at all from his past life. What I say now may be traitorous—and the punishment may be more severe than exile from my native land—but the present conditions in Nueva España are intolerable. If any of these survivors make their way here to Taos, I shall do my best to save their lives. I do not think the *yanquis* seek war with Spain. I begin to think, indeed, that our authorities are very much like ostriches who bury their heads in the sands so they may pretend that nothing has changed in the world."

"Yes, you are right, Don Diego. Yet how can the two of us help these poor wretches? We do not even know which way they will come, or if they will get through the patrols which I am sure General de Arrendondo must be sending out to catch them."

"I know one man who could help find out," Don Diego said softly. "My son-in-law has lived in the mountains and on the plains and can track as well as any *indio*. And besides, he is the blood brother of the *jefe* of the Jicarilla Apache, and they will surely know when strangers approach their stronghold. I shall talk with him when I return to the *hacienda*, Don Sancho, and he will know what to do."

That afternoon, Don Diego de Escobar related the news of the Battle of Medina to John Cooper, and said to him, "You are like a son to me, John Cooper. Indeed, what I have told you I do not even share with my own son, Carlos. I am very proud of my son—he is a good and honest young man—but he still has much to learn about the ways of the world.

"I know the bond that is between you and the Apache *jefe*. Perhaps if you would ride to his stronghold and tell him what I have heard, he will send scouts with you to search for these poor unfortunates. I grow weary of political intrigues, and I wish in my old age to enjoy the unexpected happiness the good God has given me with my dear Inez. But I cannot, as a magistrate, bow to the harsh laws which condemn all *gringos* as spies and warmongers."

"I'll ride to Descontarti's camp tonight, Don Diego," John Cooper at once answered, "and I'll ask him to let me have Kinotatay and his son. The three of us will go hunting for the survivors. By now, from what you've told me, some of them may have already crossed from Texas into New Mexico, and may be closer to Taos than we think."

"May God bless you, *mi hijo*," Don Diego said softly as he gripped John Cooper's hand and fervently shook it.

After his interview with his father-in-law, John Cooper went directly to his wife's chamber. Catarina was in her sixth mouth of pregnancy, and John Cooper knew she was frightened. Doña Inez had explained to him that most women feel blissful at this stage of pregnancy but that he must understand the situation of his young wife. Losing her mother at an early age, being torn from her homeland, Catarina was particularly vulnerable, and John Cooper felt deeply for his beloved wife, who was in so many ways his kindred spirit.

Catarina did indeed weep a good deal and protest when John Cooper hesitantly told her that he planned to ride to the Apache stronghold. He insisted that it was at her father's urging, out of the strongest humanitarian principles, and he even explained that Don Diego had asked him to enlist the aid of Indian scouts in tracking the possible survivors from the massacre at the Battle of Medina. Still, she reproached him for wanting to leave her when she was feeling utterly miserable.

"Oh, I didn't know that having a child could be like this!" she exclaimed between anger and tears. "Sometimes I can't eat anything, other times I'm so starved I can't get enough—and then I feel sick—and then I feel the baby moving in me—and then I'm afraid."

"Please be a good girl and don't worry so much," John Cooper said tenderly. "You just concentrate on the baby, so it'll be a strong, healthy boy."

"Oh, and I suppose if it were a girl, you would not want her!" Catarina flared.

John Cooper shook his head. "Come on now, Catarina,"

he remonstrated, "you ought to know me better than that. I'll
be just as happy with a girl, and what's more, I'll let you
choose her name." Then, seriously, he continued, "The only
thing I ask, *querida*, is that if it is a boy, you'll let me name
him after my father, Andrew. I sort of promised that to
myself, and to Pa when I said my prayers."

And again, instantly, she was contrite and yielding and
anguished at the thought that she had irked him on the eve of
this mission for her father. "Oh, my sweet, loving Coop, I am
a fine one, being so nasty to you, when I love you so terribly
much! But don't you see, my darling, it is just because I do
love you that I need you so, and that I hate to see you go
away, even for a little while. But I'll be good, I won't
complain at all, and I'll let that darling Amy make a new
dress for me—a dress I can wear after I have had the baby,
when I am not so clumsy and ungainly—you know."

"You'll never be that for me, Catarina. And now, I'd
better go. I'll think of you all the time, and I'll hurry back as
fast as I can, you have my promise." John Cooper kissed his
wife fervently, then took his leave of her, thinking ahead to
the time when he, Catarina, and their child would live in
peace and freedom.

Don Diego, over the past three years, had initiated a
unique system of rewards and incentives, which no other
hacendado in the area had ever put into effect on his own
property. Needless to say, when Miguel's *trabajadores* occasionally went into Taos to amuse themselves at the local
posada, they were loud in their praises of both their generous
patrón and *capataz*. Being honest and simple men, they
boasted in the presence of other *peones* who were not quite so
fortunate in having such benevolent masters, and the stories
of Don Diego's bounties inevitably reached the ears of the
other ranchers. One of these, indeed, sought out Don Diego
to remonstrate with him on the grounds that such munifi-
cence would spoil things for everyone. To this, Don Diego de
Escobar smilingly retorted, "Don Esteban, I do not ask
anyone to follow my lead. My workers are particularly loyal
and devoted to me. I do not look upon them as *peones*, but
rather as free men who have chosen to honor me by associat-
ing themselves with my needs for sturdy, industrious workers.
If I compensate them more than is customary, it is because,
in my opinion, they are worth every *centavo*. However, I will

ask my *capataz* to make them stop talking more than they should when they go to the *posada*. But that is all I propose to do, *mi amigo*."

As a consequence, there was considerable grumbling among the rival *hacendados*, and when they sometimes met in secret at one *hacienda* or another, the merchant Luis Saltareno was invariably present. Ever since Don Diego had ruled in favor of the crippled Pueblo Indian on the matter of just payment for a religious statue, Saltareno had been Don Diego's avowed enemy. On the very evening when John Cooper Baines had taken leave of his father-in-law and his wife to seek out the refugee Texans, Don Esteban de Rivarola, who owned a flock of 3500 sheep about three miles from Don Diego's ranch, entertained five *hacendados* and Luis Saltareno.

As they were drinking their brandy and puffing at their imported cigars, Don Esteban querulously declared, "I have long thought that all of us should lodge a protest with the *gubernador* at Santa Fe, *mis amigos*. This Don Diego de Escobar gives himself airs, and he tries to humiliate and mock us by paying his *peones* much more than they are worth. *Dios*, if all of us were to imitate him, we should be bankrupt by now. And that leads me to another suspicion. I know that he was appointed *intendente* in Madrid, and doubtless awarded a very fine salary. Yet in my opinion, he lives beyond his means, and perhaps this income of his is not entirely come by through his administrative efforts, nor even by the tending of sheep."

"Are you suggesting, Don Esteban, that he is cheating the authorities and holding back the tariff which must be sent to Santa Fe each month?" wizened old Don Jaime de Toldano piped up.

"I suggest nothing until it can be proved, Don Jaime. But all of us must be vigilant as never before, or before we know, this *intendente* will be so popular with the poor and the *indios* that he will become a sort of hero to them. What we must do is to have our *trabajadores* listen very carefully from now on whenever they go to the *posada*. If then the men who work for Don Diego tell tales, and all of us know how a little tequila or *aguardiente* will loosen tongues and set them wagging, we may learn something that will help us once and for all to discredit Don Diego in the eyes not only of Governor Manrique, but also Viceroy Calleja himself!"

"*Sí*, that is exactly what we want!" old Don Jaime cackled, pounding his fist on the table.

But if his enemies could have known how Don Diego de Escobar had already circumvented the harsh Spanish laws against *gringo* traders, they would have hoped to do more than merely discredit him. They would have undoubtedly traveled in a body to the *palacio* in Mexico City to demand that the viceroy remove the *intendente* of Taos from office and try him for treason.

Ten

There were six of them, six young Texans, the two youngest being John and Henry Ames, seventeen and nineteen. Their mother had been a light-haired Mexican girl from Nacogdoches, their father a yellow-haired English seaman who had journeyed to Corpus Christi on a merchant ship and, with only his seaman's pay and not a relative left in the world, impulsively decided to try his hand at farming near the Nueces River, just across the Mexican border. He had instilled in his young sons, John and Henry, a fierce love for this vast country of Texas. And his young wife, before her death, had told them stories of the Spanish oppression of impoverished Mexico and how her own father had been a runaway *peón* who had fled from a tyrannical master in Durango to cross the border and become a stableman in Nacogdoches. Thus it was that the two brothers had at once enlisted in the army composed of Mexican followers of the martyred Hidalgo and eager young Americans seeking to expand the frontier of their own growing country. By then, their father had died from a lingering illness, and they had no one except each other.

There were also Edward Molson and his cousin, Ben Forrester, from the little Texas village of Sonora, both in their mid-twenties and both with reasons of their own to hate the imperialist soldiers of Mexico City. Their young wives, each barely twenty, had been abducted by a platoon of royalist troops from the little farmhouses while their husbands were out hunting. The women had been brutally ravished and then bayoneted. For Edward Molson and Ben Forrester, their motive for joining the revolutionary army was passionately simple: vengeance.

105

In addition, there were Malcolm Pauley and Jack Williams, men in their mid-thirties who had been trappers along the wide Missouri River and had come to Texas to seek their fortunes, having neither kith nor kin. They had gone into partnership on a small ranch near San Antonio and had worked two years to corral the wild Texas longhorns into the semblance of a herd. They spoke Spanish fluently, and they had made friends with the Comanche, even sold beef to those marauding wanderers of the plains. But patrols of the royal army had seized the herd, threatened Pauley and Williams with death if they dared protest, and driven the prime cattle off to feed the imperialist troops. For these Texans, the motive for joining the rebels was one of anger over military high-handedness.

All six of them had come together and become fast friends. But then the initially successful rebel force which they had joined had been duped by the wily Mexican general into leaving San Antonio without advance patrols, and the royal troops had decimated hundreds of their comrades. These six men, Texans, unified by comradeship under fire, knowing the stupidity of their betrayed leaders, now had to try to survive so that one day they might avenge the slaughter of their companions.

They had hidden, feigning death, in the thick rushes which fringed the banks of the Medina River just west of San Antonio. At midnight, when there was only a cursory patrol, they crawled away toward the west. Once they had escaped the patrol, they made their way on foot to Uvalde, and there, in a little hamlet of some twenty Mexicans, they found sympathetic friends. In their tattered, motley uniforms, with only a few *pesos* among the six of them, they were able to buy four horses. John and Henry Ames rode one of these, Malcolm Pauley and Jack Williams shared another, and Edward Molson and Ben Forrester each rode singly. Their only weapons by this time were hunting knives and two muskets, with about a dozen balls and just enough powder for that scanty ammunition.

Certain that they would be pursued, they shared the villagers' tacos and chili, thanked them warmly, and then rode off toward the northwest. Edward Molson had learned from one of the Uvalde villagers that Nuevo Mexico, particularly Santa Fe, was forbidden territory to *gringos*. Yet, his informant urged, if he and his comrades could head for the mountains of the northern part of that Spanish-held territory, they would be safe—if, that is, *los indios* did not kill them for trespassing.

And so they rode on at midnight, heading for the tiny town of San Angelo, and thence into New Mexico by way of Hobbs and Lovington. They followed the eastern boundary of the Pecos, up to Santa Rosa and Tucumcari just westward of the rapidly flowing Canadian River.

In General de Arrendondo's army, besides the young lieutenant Santa Anna, there were other ambitious young officers eager for glory. One of these was Lieutenant Jaime Dondero, a tall man of twenty-four, excessively vain of his person, with waxed mustachios and pointed beard. He and Santa Anna had often shared the officers' brothel, and he was bitterly envious that his younger friend had already been cited in the general's glowing report to the viceroy. That was why, entering the general's tent on the night after the battle, he asked permission to take a patrol of six men to pursue the fleeing fugitives.

General de Arrendondo readily agreed, and so, the morning after that bloody battle, Lieutenant Jaime Dondero and six men rode off, bent on pursuing those who had escaped death near the banks of the Medina River, whose waters still ran red with blood.

Ambitious Lieutenant Dondero was, like his brother officer, Santa Anna, a vicious sadist. He had estimated that many of the survivors would have gone on by foot and could be easily tracked down, butchered on the spot; yet there were sure to be others, more resourceful, who would try any means at their disposal to put distance between themselves and the imperial troops. And these, who would require lengthier pursuit, were exactly the victims he intended to bring back as prisoners to General de Arrendondo. They would have fled toward the west, and he spurred his horse in that direction.

Three hours after starting out, he halted and trained his field glasses on a huge clump of mesquite a hundred yards to his right. Detecting an unnatural movement, he grinned and signaled to his men to surround it. Armed with a holstered pistol and a heavy saber in his right hand, he rode up toward the bush and commanded, "You are surrounded, and have no chance to escape. Surrender peacefully, and you will be given quarter."

He heard the murmur of voices and turned to wink at

his stout, thickly bearded sergeant, Jacinto Perez, who enjoyed killing as much as he did. The sergeant nodded, took a firmer grip on the haft of his lance, and controlled his restive horse by jerking cruelly on the reins in his left hand.

A moment later, two men emerged from the huge thicket, their hands in the air. One was a young Mexican *peón*, not yet twenty, who had run away from his *rico* master to join the rebellion. Another was a Texan in his early forties who, during the ambush, had fought back courageously and killed seven of the enemy until his rifle had jammed and he had found himself out of ammunition.

"Very good, *bueno*," Lieutenant Dondero smiled at the two prisoners. "*¡Adelante!* Come forward, here to me. Ah, you, *gringo*," he gestured toward the Texan with the tip of his saber, "you have been wounded. You must have fought very well. And I am sure that you've killed some of my comrades."

The Texan stiffened, trying to bring himself to attention like a soldier, grimacing at the pain in his left calf where a rifle ball had imbedded itself. He had cut the ball out with his knife, bandaged the wound, and he and the young Mexican had crawled away from the carnage. All that night his arm around the shoulder of the young *peón*, he had hobbled in this desperate flight to safety.

Lieutenant Dondero considered him a moment, his smile deepening in his full, sensual mouth. "*Amigo*," he said gently, "you were wise to surrender. You see, you cannot run. So I will shorten your discomfort—thus!" At the last word, he trotted his horse a few paces nearer to the Texan, swung up his saber, and brought it down with all his strength to cleave the skull of the prisoner. The Mexican *peón* uttered a shriek of terror and turned to flee, only to find the sergeant's lance tip pressed lightly against his belly. "*Cuidado, hombre,*" Sergeant Perez mocked.

"But you, traitorous Mexican dog who turns against his master," Lieutenant Dondero continued as he pointed the bloody saber toward the trembling *peón*, "you seem strong - and healthy to me. *¿Es verdad, hombre?*"

Paralyzed with terror, the young Mexican could only nod, and a strangled whimper escaped him as he saw the horsemen wheel their mounts and come toward him.

"*Bueno*. I will give you a chance for your life, more than

you deserve. Run! Run for your freedom!" Lieutenant Dondero barked. "If you do not, I'll cut you down the way I did your *gringo* friend, *¿comprende?*"

The young Mexican glanced around him and then took to his heels with all his strength.

"Give him a good chance, *mis compañeros*," Lieutenant Dondero drawled. "It will be good exercise for our *caballos*." He waited until the *peón* was about five hundred yards away, then nodded. Sergeant Perez and two others galloped after him, their lances extended, the pennants fluttering in the soft breeze which had blown in from the Rio Grande.

The tall Mexican officer trained his field glasses, baring his teeth in a smile of anticipation. He saw Sergeant Perez prick the back of the neck of the captive, making him stumble and fall to all fours. The three horsemen drew up beside the *peón*, who began to sob and plead for his life. Sergeant Perez prodded him again and ordered him to keep running. They let him go another twenty yards before the three of them thrust their lances into his back and then rode back to their officer with satisfied grins.

"Excellent, Sergeant Perez," Lieutenant Dondero applauded. "That is the way to make a lazy *peón* amuse us. And now, let us go on. There must be others who think they can outwit the royal army!"

John Cooper Baines rode his mustang into the Apache stronghold and dismounted in front of Descontarti's wickiup. The chief of the Jicarilla Apache emerged, giving the impression of great solemnity and strength.

"It is good to see you again, my blood brother," he said as he greeted the young mountain man.

"And it is good to see you, Descontarti. I bring you greetings from your daughter, Weesayo, and from Carlos. It will not be long before Weesayo bears her child. She has told me to tell you that it will be within two moons."

"I will pray to the Great Spirit that the child will be a strong son. And that he will have the courage of his father and the wisdom and compassion of his mother."

"That is my prayer also, Descontarti." John Cooper observed that the Apache chief's face seemed drawn and his eyes were lusterless. "But my blood brother is not well."

"It is nothing, *Halcón*. Sometimes the pain of an old

wound I had in battle when we raided the *mejicanos* reminds me of my days of youth. But it passes, as all things pass. Yet tell me, *Halcón*, what brings you to our home?"

Quickly, John Cooper told him of the Battle of Medina and Don Diego's fear that some of the Texas survivors, seeking refuge, might attempt the arduous journey toward the province of Taos.

"I have learned that there will always be wars," the chief intoned, "but that the most terrible of all is that war in which men of the same country take sides against one another. Yet the country from which you came, *los Estados Unidos,* permits its young men to fight against the *mejicanos?*"

"I am told, Descontarti, that the men of Texas believe in freedom, and wish one day for Texas to be a part of *los Estados Unidos*. And because they love freedom so—as I do myself—they are willing to help those who believed in the teachings of Padre Hidalgo," John Cooper responded.

"Yes, we of the Jicarilla Apache know what freedom means. Here in the mountains we look down upon those who would be at war, and we are safe because we are a tribe bound together in our love of peace. And the tall mountain helps defend us against those who would invade. Go, then, to the wickiup of him who taught you how to speak our tongue so well. This evening, you will share food with me, you will smoke the ceremonial pipe, and our shaman will invoke the blessing of the Great Spirit to help you and Kinotatay and his son, Pirontikay, to save the *gringos,*" Descontarti declared.

Lieutenant Jamie Dondero posted in his saddle, ahead of his men, his swarthy, cruelly handsome face aglow with the joy of the chase. Several hours after he had flushed the wounded Texan and the young *peón* out of the mesquite thicket, he had come across four Hidalgo rebels, stumbling over the sandy, desertlike terrain and making toward the west. He had made them draw straws to see in what order they would try to run from the lancers, and when it was the turn of the last man, he had borrowed Sergeant Perez's lance and amused himself by jabbing the shrieking survivor, goading him into a hopeless attempt at escape. When at last the man floundered and sprawled, belly down on the sand, the tall Mexican officer thrust the head of his lance into his left calf. "There, *hombre,*" his voice purred with deceptive gentleness, "I will spare you because you have run so well. But you must get up and keep running, *amigo*. Get up, *hombre*, run. You have my word I will not use my lance again."

Sobbing, half-crazed with his terror and the pain of the wound, the *peón* had stumbled to his feet; he looked back at Lieutenant Dondero in his saddle, the lance held upwards with its bloody point aimed at the sun-bright sky. "*Gracias, gracias*, I will pray to *el Señor Dios* for your long life, *mi teniente!*" he gasped. He got to his feet and began to hobble off.

Lieutenant Dondero turned back to his grinning men and put a finger to his lips. He watched the exhausted *peón* drag himself, staining the sand red from the wound in his calf, and he called out, "Faster, *hombre*, faster. I told you you must run if you wish to be free!"

And then, he drew his pistol out of its holster, took careful aim, and pulled the trigger. The *peón* uttered a strangled scream, stopped dead in his tracks, tried to turn back, and then fell lifeless.

"So with all dogs who revolt against the crown! *¡Adelante, soldados!* I have seen the tracks of men ahead in the sand. We shall go on."

By nightfall, he and his men reached the tiny hamlet where the six Texans had found shelter and obtained horses. They rode in, tethered their horses to the branches of scrub trees, and Lieutenant Dondero strode to the largest adobe hut, owned by the elderly Mexican who had been appointed *jefe* of the little village and who had himself volunteered to aid the Texans by selling them horses for a pittance.

"*Viejo*, have you seen *gringos* go by your village?" he demanded of the white-haired *peón*.

"Oh no, *excelencia*, we have seen no one. There are only a few of us here, we farm, we have just enough food for ourselves, we are very poor, *excelencia!*"

Sergeant Perez approached his superior officer, and muttered, "Private Gonzalez has just told me that there is a corral at the back of this dog's *jacal*, and there is only one horse there. But he's seen the hoof prints of others."

Lieutenant Dondero commended the sergeant and turned back to the old man. "Now then, *viejo*. What happened to the other horses in your corral, *hombre?*"

"But there are no other horses, *excelencia*. There is only the one which belongs to me."

"You lie, *veijo*. We'll see if we cannot get the truth out

of you. And if not out of you, then some of the others," the
lieutenant declared contemptuously. "I want all of your
people here before my soldiers. Go bring them here. And no
tricks, *viejo*, or we will kill them all and you first and burn
your *jacales* and take that one horse you say is the only one
you have."

Ten minutes later, twenty-two frightened Mexican men,
women, and children cowered in two lines in front of the
jacal of Ignacio Montañez.

Lieutenant Dondero walked slowly to and fro, inspecting
the frightened Mexicans. His dark eyes glittered with lust as
they rested for a moment on a comely, buxom young woman
in her mid-twenties who held a baby in her arms. The baby
was crying, and Lieutenant Dondero softly murmured, "*Muchacha*, you had best stop your *niño* from crying, or I will be
obliged to shoot him."

The young woman, bursting into tears, promptly clapped
her palm over the baby's mouth. Dondero's eyes narrowed as
they fixed on her sumptuous, round bosom, whose cleft was
visible in the rough smock-shift which was her only garment.
After a moment, clearing his throat, he addressed the villagers: "It is my suspicion that some of you, out of a misguided
compassion, may have given horses to rebellious *gringos* or
peones who ran from the battle at the Medina River like the
cowards they are. If you will confess this, I will spare all of
you. Otherwise, all of the men will be shot, and the women
will be taken prisoners, brought before my general, and sent
to a *casa de putas* in Chihauhua. Very well now. I will give
you two minutes to tell me what became of the other horses
in the corral of your *alcalde!*"

The woman with the child, tears running down her face,
turned her head to stare at her husband, a stocky, bearded
Mexican in his early thirties, and then toward the *alcalde*, old
Ignacio Montañez. The latter covertly shook his head ever so
slightly, his eyes lowering to the ground, and, clasping his
hands, began silently to pray.

"Your time is nearly up!" the lieutenant barked. "I warn
you, I mean to carry out the promise I have made you. You
have a minute more, and that is all." Then, in a wheedling,
insinuating voice, he said, "What loyalty do you owe to
traitors? Ask yourselves, *amigos!* Why should you die to help
cowardly scum whom we shall catch anyway, whether you
assist us or not with the truth? Save yourselves, and my men

and I will ride after these traitors and bring them to justice!"

The white-haired Mexican finally raised his head and, in a trembling voice, exclaimed, "You cannot mean surely, *mi teniente*, to kill us? We are *mejicanos* like yourself and your men. We have done no wrong. Yes, I will confess there were several *gringos* who came this way, and we gave them a little food and some water. But I swear before my Maker that is all we gave them."

Lieutenant Dondero grinned evilly and passed a caressing hand over his beard as he considered this avowal. Then, very calmly, he put the muzzle of his pistol to the breast of the white haired *alcalde* and pulled the trigger. A chorus cry of horror broke from the others as they saw Ignacio Montañez slump to the ground.

"It does not pay to lie to an officer of the imperial army, *mis amigos.*" He lifted the pistol and blew the smoke away from the muzzle, then thrust it back into its holster. "What he has told me convinces me that those other horses were given to the rebels as well as the food and water. Very well. Since he has told only half the truth, I will not kill you all. I shall kill only five of you, by lot. And your women will amuse my soldiers—I see only three who are capable of providing enjoyment for my vigorous men. The rest of you may count yourselves lucky that I do not demand more reprisal from such traitorous people!"

He turned to Sergeant Perez who instantly saluted, a broad grin on his face. "I count twelve men, three children, one *niño pekueño,* and six *mujeres,*" the lieutenant rasped. "You yourself, having an excellent eye, Sergeant Perez, can see at once which three I meant when I said they could provide amusement for you and your subordinates. Now then! You will give these twelve men straws. Five of them will be short, and you and your men will mix them up and have each of the twelve men draw. To be sure, we shall not kill the little children or the little *niño;* we are not murderers."

"Oh no, *excelencia,* have mercy on us!" the young woman with the child burst ont.

"*Muy guapa, mujer,*" Lieutenant Dondero drawled, "but you are one of the three I have spared, and, indeed, honored. To prove this to you, I shall take you for myself afer we have executed these five traitors by my verdict of martial law.

Ah, I see the way you look at the man beside you—your *esposo*, no doubt? Well, I am afraid, *señora*, he must take his chances. But perhaps, because I can see that you love him so, of which the *niño* in yours arms is living proof, the good God will grant him his miserable life. If that is so, let us hope that he profits from the lesson all of you are to learn tonight! Sergeant Perez, carry out my order!"

Amid the sobs and groans of the six Mexican women and the plaintive, unanswered questions of the children, Lieutenant Dondero's soldiers chose at random a middle-aged *peón* to march to the little creek and to pick reeds. These gathered, Sergeant Perez gripped them in his left hand and, turning his back on the terrified villagers, began to cut them with his knife, until he had five shorter than the other seven. Then, shuffling them about in his pudgy right hand, he turned and barked, "Each of you men, forward and pick one of the reeds in my hand! Quickly now, or all of you will be shot!"

One by one, some holding back with faces contorted in fear, others defiantly striding forward and seizing one of the reeds, the twelve Mexicans decided their fate.

"Now then, open your hands and let us see who have the shorter ones," Sergeant Perez ordered. The husband of the comely woman with her little baby still in her arms had drawn one of these five.

Lieutenant Dondero smiled with pleasure, then snapped, "Sergeant, march those men over to the creek and then prepare the firing squad!" And, to the five doomed men, he called, "I regret, *mis amigos*, there is no priest to shrive you. Say your prayers, then, before we shoot you. Perhaps they will be heard, though I do not think that the prayers of traitors will find their way to heaven."

"Have mercy, in the name of Him who died to save us from sin," the young woman begged, as she turned to watch her husband marching beside the other four condemned.

"But I do, *muchacha*," Lieutenant Dondero smirked. "Tonight, I will show you that I am a better man than your *esposo*. And, because I am merciful, the rest of you shall remain here, even the women. I spare you the *casa de putas*, *mujeres*, but so long as you live, remember the price that is paid for treason against Nueva España!"

Then, turning to watch, he nodded to the sergeant. The other soldiers, kneeling, had leveled their muskets on the five victims. Sergeant Perez lifted his officer's saber, then swept it down and cried out, "*¡Fuego!*"

There were shrieks and sobs from those who watched as the five *peones* toppled backward, and the splash of their dead bodies in the creek was the final grim punctuation of the firing squad.

Lieutenant Dondero seized the baby from the handsome young Mexican woman, sat it down outside one of the *jacales*, and then, with a brutal laugh, gripped her by the wrist. "Now there is work for the living, *linda!*"

He dragged her into the adobe hut, while his men, seizing the two other women who were the youngest and most attractive of the six in the village, forced them into another *jacal*.

Numb with horror, the younger men who had been spared, the old women, and the old men remained standing, motionless, their faces blank with the tragedy that had befallen their tiny hamlet. And the cries of the ravaged women rang out in the starry night.

The six fleeing Texans had crossed the Pecos River and had gained time on their pursuers, thanks to Lieutenant Dondero's vindictive interlude at the little hamlet. Also, very wisely, at Malcolm Pauley's suggestion, they had changed mounts in four-hour shifts, so that no one horse had overly long to bear the burden of two riders.

Although Edward Molson had proposed that they head toward El Paso, all of his companions had vetoed this idea. There were certain to be imperial troops in that area, and moreover, they would be dangerously close to the Mexican border, perhaps fifty miles from the northernmost boundary of the province of Chihuahua. Once taken prisoner there, they could hope for nothing better than a swift death by the firing squad.

That was why, reaching the little village of Midland, they began to skirt the border of Nuevo Mexico and move on toward Lovington and then Portales. They would at all costs avoid Santa Fe, and as Molson's cousin, Ben Forrester, proposed, "If worse comes to worst, we'll find fresh horses somewhere else, and we'll push on till we reach Colorado territory. There are friendly Indian tribes, there's good hunting, fishing, and trapping, and we could do worse than to settle down there. At least we'd be away from these damned Mexican royalists."

Kinotatay, who was the same age as Descontarti, was short and wiry. He had a stony-featured visage which once John Cooper had believed expressed hostility to him as a white-eyes but which he now understood was the result of the indomitable self-discipline of the Apache. He had eagerly agreed to help seek the survivors of the Battle of Medina. His son, Pirontikay, almost exactly John Cooper's age, was taller and much less reserved than his father. He admired John Cooper because of the latter's exceptional skill with "Long Girl," as well as for his respect for Apache law and customs. It was Pirontikay who, after John Cooper had proposed that they go in quest of the gringo fugitives from the disastrous battle, was first to urge his father.

John Cooper was delighted to receive Kinotatay's support, but something else was troubling the young man. "I do not like the look of Descontarti, who says that it is only his old wound that troubles him."

Kinotatay nodded. "I have seen how he grows weaker with each new moon. Though we are the same age, I am the stronger. He is our chief, and when he knows that he can no longer lead us, he will appoint the wisest and bravest of us to take his place. There are younger men, men of the age of my son, Pirontikay, who are restless because we do not go on raids anymore against the *mejicanos*. They say that we grow soft and weak here and that Descontarti is an old man who does nothing but dream about the past strength of the Apache. They want new glory, new adventure, and that, too, is why I ride with you, *Halcón*. We shall leave at dawn. Pirontikay, you will pack the food we shall need for our journey. We will have our bows and arrows, our lances, and you have the stick that thunders. The three of us can kill many *soldados* before they even know we are upon them."

Eleven

It was *soldado* Pablo Yarangui who pointed out to Sergeant Perez the tracks of horses heading westward, and whose eyes were sharp enough also to detect that some of the hoofprints seemed deeper than the others. "*Bueno,* Yarangui," the sergeant growled. "Maybe you will get back to be a *cabo* again. I'll tell the *teniente* what you have seen."

Pablo Yarangui grinned and nodded. He was a stocky, brutish man in his early forties, with surly face and thick black beard, and his wrestler's arms, legs, and chest were matted with coarse black hair. He had twice lost his corporal's stripes—that was what Sergeant Perez had alluded to—for drunkenness and insubordination. Ten years ago, his pretty seventeen-year-old wife, Felice, frightened by his sullen rages and the whippings he dealt out whenever he had drunk too much tequila, had run away with a young sheepherder from Chihuahua. Yarangui had spent a month trying to find his wife and her lover and then, failing in the effort, had joined the army. There he found an ideal outlet for his vindictive hatred. His bloodthirsty slaughter of a dozen unarmed prisoners taken in one of the decisive battles which had suppressed the Hidalgo rebels three years ago had earned him his second pair of corporal's stripes. On the night when Lieutenant Dondero had taken his reprisal against the tiny hamlet for having aided the fleeing Texans, he, along with his five companions, had brutally ravished the two young Mexican women. And he had persuaded Sergeant Perez that killing the women would remind the traitorous villagers of the cost of their treason. So he had strangled each in turn, lingeringly and gloatingly, for in his warped mind he was paying back his faithless wife, Felice, for having abandoned him.

117

When Sergeant Perez reported to his superior what Private Yarangui had discovered, Lieutenant Dondero excitedly declared, "That must mean the *gringos* are riding double on some of the horses those idiots gave them! So much the better. That will slow them down and give us plenty of time to catch them."

"But, *mi teniente*," Sergeant Perez returned, "might they not take to the mountains? It would be harder to track them there."

"I do not think so. That would wear out the horses much too quickly. And besides, there are *indios* in the mountains, *indios* as dangerous to us as they would surely be to those accursed *gringos*. No, Sergeant, we will follow the tracks and they will lead us to the prisoners I'll bring back to General de Arrendondo. *¡Adelante!*"

The tracks of the fugitives were clear and easy to follow. By late afternoon of the next day, aware that their provisions were almost exhausted, Lieutenant Dondero directed his men to a small group of adobe *jacales*, set off about a mile to the southeast. "We will stop here just long enough to get what food we can, Sergeant Perez," he directed his noncommissioned officer. "And there is a creek near that little village, where we can fill our canteens. The men may have a few hours of rest tonight, and then we'll ride on. Those accursed *yanquis* will surely think by now they have escaped us, and they will make camp and sleep. Then we will catch them. Understand me now, Sergeant Perez, they are not to be harmed. They will be prizes for our glorious general, and if this mission is successful, both of us will be mentioned in his dispatch to the viceroy. You might even become a *subteniente* —and I, I shall become at least a *capitán*."

"*¡Gracias, mi capitán!*" The sergeant grinned, aware that his superior officer was flattered by the new form of address.

There were perhaps fifteen inhabitants in this desolate little hamlet, a few of them Toboso Indians who had intermarried with Mexicans. Their sustenance came from a small field of maize, and they had also planted some vegetables and melons. There were no horses, only two spavined burros used to pull the ancient plow which cultivated the fields. Sergeant Perez, waving his pistol, ordered the crippled old man who was the leader to have the women bring as much dry corn as they could and fill the soldiers' saddlebags. Also, he commandeered some of the melons, a welcome treat to soldiers who had subsisted on the meagerest fare during the Battle of Medina. Lastly, he seized their store of *pulque,* the fermented juice of the maguey which, when aged, was even more potent than *aguardiente.*

But of greater importance to Lieutenant Dondero than the provisions was the avowal of the elderly *alcalde* that, about twenty-four hours earlier, he had heard the sounds of horses riding northward and beyond his village. His eyes blazing, the bearded lieutenant ordered Sergeant Perez, "Make certain that the men sleep no more than two hours. We can overtake them, and we are on the right track at last. Now I am sure that they will try to reach the mountains of Nuevo Mexico, and we must cut them off before they find shelter."

The horse on which John and Henry Ames had ridden was wet with foam, its sides heaving, and by noon of the next day, it suddenly sank down on its knees and rolled over, its riders just having time to leap off. Edward Molson reined in his horse, walked over to the exhausted animal, and mercifully put a bullet through its head. "Now we've got three horses left, and that means two riders on each one of them," he grimly declared. "I'm saying prayers we'll run into a herd of wild mustangs. It's the only chance we've got."

"Can't we go on foot and climb these mountains and hide there in the caves, Molson?" Jack Williams demanded.

Molson shook his head. "Back in Texas, as you well know, we were told there are Apache in the mountains. They don't ask questions—they kill first. And after the long way we've come, hoping to escape the *mejicanos,* I wouldn't want it to end this way. No, we'll go on the way we planned, skirting the range of mountains and moving into New Mexico territory. I'm sure there are horses, and we'll find them. But right now, let's find out what ammunition and weapons we've got in case we have to make a stand."

"All I've got, Ed," his cousin, Ben Forrester, volunteered, "is a jammed pistol, about ten balls and some powder for it, and my hunting knife."

"I've got a musket that's only good at close range, and enough balls and ammunition for maybe an hour's fighting," Malcolm Pauley sighed.

"We've got one musket between us," John Ames piped

up. "Maybe eight balls and just enough powder to make each one of them count. And Henry and I have got knives, and that's about it."

"If there are troops following us, and I'm sure there are, they'll have lances, muskets, pistols, and plenty of ammunition," Molson declared. "I figure we're about twenty-four hours ahead of them. And we've got to keep it that way, if we expect to live. Now let's go on, give the horses about half an hour's rest, and then we'll mount up again. It will be slow going, and I'm going to say plenty of prayers we run into a herd of horses, you can depend on that."

Edward Molson's fervent prayers were answered by the end of the following week. As he and the others moved from the Texas territory into Nuevo Mexico by the northeastern border, they came at dawn upon a vast mesa, fringed by a towering mountain range. There were scrubby, gnarled juniper trees standing out from the yellow-brown plains, and patches of mesquite, cacti, and dark-green knee-high grass in which the tiny flowers of bluebells swayed in the wind.

For the past two days, the six survivors of the Battle of Medina had eaten roots and herbs, though they had found water aplenty in springs and mountain lakes. Their three horses had been pushed to the utmost, and their eyes were glazed, their sides were heaving, and white foam had formed at their nostrils and mouths. The six intrepid Texans realized that if they were going to escape the *mejicanos*, they would have to cross the mesa on foot.

Suddenly Edward Molson alerted the others. "Wait! What's that over there? To the northeast of us? My God, it's a herd of mustangs, or else it's a mirage!"

"It's a herd, all right!" Malcolm Pauley shouted. "Now's our chance! We'll ride after them, and we'll try to catch a few replacements. I hope our horses won't founder under us. And I sure hope we can catch some."

Molson had already considered the possibilities. "See over there? There's a range of mountains, and they're not too high to scale. We could do them on foot, if we can't get any of those horses. And we can hole up there and wait for those damned *mejicanos*. Look how big the mesa is—if we have to die here, it's as good a place as any. Now let's go try to get those mustangs!"

The six Texans conferred a moment, and then Molson, Ben Forrester, and Malcolm Pauley mounted the three remaining horses and, lariats in hand, rode after the herd. The two young Ames brothers and Jack Williams stood watching, glancing back along the trail they had come.

The leader of the herd, a black stallion, tossed his head and whinnied, then raced toward the southwest. Molson, spurring his horse and muttering prayers under his breath, angled to cut off the stallion from the rest of the herd, while his cousin and Pauley rode directly into the herd of some thirty wild horses.

Looping his lariat, Molson cast it out and caught the black stallion round the neck. As he tightened the lariat, he quickly dismounted, stumbling forward, while the horse that had been under him whinnied feebly, then toppled onto its side. The sturdy Texan dragged on the lariat, forcing the stallion to rear on its hind legs and paw the air. Meanwhile, Pauley and Forrester had already lassoed two brown stallions and, dismounting quickly, dragged back on their lariats and halted their prizes.

The Ames brothers and Jack Williams, with a wild cheer, began to run with all their strength toward the three Texans. In a quarter of an hour, the duel between horses and men was won, and the stallions snorted and pawed the ground, their eyes wild and rolling, as Molson, Forrester, and Pauley leaped astride them.

The rest of the herd had galloped off and disappeared behind a rocky canyon. Sweating, cursing, the three older men rode their wild mounts, trying to gentle them. At last their frenzied rebellion ended.

"Well, at least we've got three strong new mounts, boys," Ben Forrester called to the Ames brothers and Jack Williams. "We'll still have to ride double, but these horses have strength and stamina. They'll do us better than what we had. Let the other two go. They're half-dead now, but maybe after they rest they'll join up with that herd. Then they'll have freedom, the kind we want and are ready to die for."

The three other men hastened to clamber astride the three wild stallions, and at the double weight, they grew less restive and more docile. "We'll head along the side of this range as far as we can. The tracks are all mixed up; maybe that'll puzzle the *mejicanos*," Molson declared.

They began to ride toward the south now, in the territory of Nuevo Mexico. There was a vast silence around them, and they could see the towering mountain tops and the wild foliage and flowers which garnished the long-forgotten Indian trail.

What provisions they had managed to glean from stopping at little villages, or from picking berries and edible roots, were carried in their heavy knapsacks, strapped to their backs. And these knapsacks were nearly empty now.

"When we get farther on, and there's nobody in sight, we'll take a spell to find us some vittles," Edward Molson proposed. "Thank God there's enough water for today and maybe tomorrow, even if we don't find a creek or a spring. There's plenty of rocky country ahead, but that's as good for us as it'll be bad for those damned greasers. Chances are, they're not trained to cavalry, not the way we were on the ranches and farms we grew up on as boys—isn't that right, Ben?"

"That's for certain," his cousin answered. "But what worries me, Ed, is where you think we're going to wind up heading."

"I'd like to get somewhere near Taos," Molson explained. "That summer fair of theirs is over by now, and the Indians in those parts are friendly enough. And we might run into a friendly *hacendado* who doesn't have too much use for the Mexican bigwigs."

"I sure hope so," Malcolm Pauley spoke up. And the men's spirits seemed to lift somewhat as they continued on their way through the silent wilderness.

John Cooper, Kinotatay, and Pirontikay had headed toward the southeast for the first day of their journey, and then the next two days directly south, crossing a shallow fork of the Canadian River to the east of Tucumcari. At night they made their camp in a cave high at the top of the canyon, where they could see without being seen. The wonderfully clear air and the cloudless blue sky contrasted with the grotesque rock formations of the canyons and the mesas through which they rode. On the first night, they cooked a rabbit which Pirontikay had shot, and John Cooper nostalgically recalled how he and Lije had often feasted on rabbit in those early days when he had begun his trek westward in search of a new life. He had persuaded the Apache brave and his son to take with them not only their bows and arrows, but also a pistol and rifle, with plenty of ammunition, in the event they ran into a large detachment of Mexican soldiers who might be trailing the Texas fugitives. Thus far, they had come upon no human being, and they rode many miles in silence, each with his own thoughts amid the vast splendor of this primitive land which seemed to be as untouched by man as it must have been long centuries ago.

"If the *gringos* come on foot, many suns will set before we find them. And before that, the *mejicanos* may have already captured or killed them," Kinotatay stolidly declared at the end of the second day.

"They might have found horses in some of the little villages along the border," John Cooper parried, "or they may have even found a wild herd. The latter's the more likely, I think. You and your people are taking your horses from the wild herds on the plains below the Jicarilla Mountains."

"Yes, that is so. Yet by tomorrow, we come into the land where the Mescalero live. They are enemies of ours from the days when I was a papoose and when my father was still a young man," Kinotatay observed. "I do not want to fight them unless we must to save ourselves, *Halcón*. There is already bad blood between us since last year when Matsinga, the Mescalero chief, and Descontarti had a disagreement. Our chief had invited Matsinga and his war chief to a parley, and Matsinga gave insult to us by refusing some of the food we had prepared to honor a tribal chief. It was only because he was our guest that none of our braves demanded satisfaction for the insult."

"I understand you, Kinotatay. I have no love for the Mescalero, either. It was they who attacked Catarina when she ran away from the *hacienda* last spring. Well," John Cooper grinned, "we'll try not to run into any Mescalero. On the other hand, if those Mexican soldiers are seen first, maybe the Mescalero will do our work for us and that way help the Texans get through safely."

"This is what I hope also, *Halcón*." Kinotatay frowned and was silent a moment. Then he added, "I will tell you what is in my heart. Descontarti does not have the strength of old days. His wound bothers him much more than he will admit. And perhaps he has a sickness in his belly. Often he goes to the peak of the mountain to talk to the Great Spirit and to dream the dream which only he may know and may not tell of to any other man."

"You mean he is ill and may die?"

"All men must, *Halcón*, and no one can tell when his

time is at hand. But I worry that Descontarti may die before this anger of our tribe against Matsinga cools. For surely if the Mescalero learn that we are to lose our chief, their war chief and the young braves who are eager to count coup over enemies will attack us."

"Kinotatay, what you say is sad for me to hear," John Cooper responded. "But if ever my blood brother and his tribe should be forced into war with the Mescalero, I would surely help you. It is a debt I owe my blood brother—and to you also, who taught me the language and the ways of the Jicarilla."

"I am proud to have been your teacher, *Halcón*. And you have taught me much in your turn, as you have my son, Pirontikay. I did not think I could ever be like a brother to a white-eyes, even if he showed the courage you have shown. Now, we think and speak as one, and it is good. If all *gringos* were like you, *Halcón*, there would be peace and life would be good."

John Cooper, slightly embarrassed at the Indian's praise, got to his feet. "Well," he said, "we'd best be riding on if we're ever going to find those Texans."

Lieutenant Jaime Dondero halted his horse and peered down at the fresh tracks along the sandy trail through the mesa. "We are not far behind them now, *soldados!*" he triumphantly exclaimed. "Sergeant Perez, you see that carcass over there? That's one of the horses which that old fool of a *peón* let them take. They must all be riding double by now, *ciertamente*."

"That is true, *mi capitán*," the burly sergeant agreed. "But these fresh tracks are not the same as those we followed. Somewhere they found fresh horses. Perhaps wild mustangs."

"*¡Diablo!*" the lieutenant spat, with a furious grimace. Then, as he peered down again at the marks of the hooves, an evil grin creased his lips. "But my eyes are better than yours, Sergeant Perez. Do you not see how deep they are? Now, *hombre*, it is plain that they are still riding double and that they did not manage to catch enough for all of them. That will slow them down, and they can't have had much food. We shall go forward. Besides, isn't there a small village south of here?"

"*Sí, mi capitán*. It is not far from Portales and there, too,

I'm sure we can find fresh horses. Our own are tiring badly."

"Very well. We'll head on south, following these tracks. I can't wait to get my hands on those traitors!" He gave the signal, and the troop rode on behind him.

Of the five privates in the contingent supervised by Sergeant Perez, only Pablo Yarangui was still as eager for this mission as his superior officer and the sergeant. If he helped capture the *yanquis*, he'd surely get back his corporal's stripes, and then there'd be a furlough. He'd go back to San Luis Potosi, where he knew of a fine *casa de putas*. The woman who ran it was a friend of his, and there were two *muchachas* there who were not unlike his unfaithful wife, Felice. His brutal face brightened with lecherous anticipation. For a few extra *pesos*, the woman would let him whip the *muchachas* just enough to make them cry, so that he could pretend that he was paying Felice back for deserting him. Yes, it was something to look forward to, though not quite so enjoyable as when he had killed those two in the village. He patted his horse's neck and muttered an endearment to it. A horse you could trust; a woman, never.

The other four privates did not share Yarangui's eagerness for the mission. They were saddlesore, and they were tired of *frijoles* and maize. They had ridden long days and even nights, and they were not even certain that their lieutenant would find the men he was seeking. Besides, how would it benefit them? They had heard their sergeant flatteringly promote the *teniente* to *capitán*, but those were the only two who would profit from this undertaking. They would not even get corporal's stripes out of the business. And what was worst of all, they were in Indian country, where the Mescalero and the Jicarilla knew the terrain far better than they and might even now be lying in wait for them.

That evening, they were somewhat heartened by the news that the sergeant had learned in the little village some thirty miles from Portales: some of the people had seen six *gringos* on three horses heading to the north. They had even waved to them, but the *gringos* had kept riding and pretended not to notice them. It was about eight hours ago.

But Lieutenant Dondero was disappointed to find only one horse, and that badly lamed, alongside four burros in the tiny corral of the village. As for food, the villagers could spare them only more maize, some *tortillas,* and some dried deer meat which was already beginning to turn and which the lieutenant brushed away with a gesture of disgust.

However, the news that there were six men caused him to make an impulsive decision. He commandeered two men from the village to join his troop. The two scared *peones* rode their own burros, and carried antique muskets.

The trail now wound through a narrow canyon, and the tracks shifted to a smooth, gradually inclining ledge to the east. Lieutenant Dondero gestured to his troop to follow, and went on ahead, impatient to catch up with these rebels who had led him on such an arduous chase. They camped along this easily passable trail till dawn and then resumed their pursuit. And the four privates, Paco Rios, Pancho Segura, Manual Bensadón, and Pedro Gonzalez, grew more disenchanted by the moment. Behind them rode the two *peones* on their burros, and from their muttered conversation, the four men ahead of them could hear that they were not eager volunteers; if anything, they hated the *soldados,* for they had come from a little village near Nuevo Laredo some years ago, not long after the viceroy's troops had suppressed a rebellion near their village. And they had seen the gory reprisals taken against old men and women, even children, for having aided the good Padre Hidalgo.

"I don't like it, *amigo,*" Paco Rios muttered to Manuel Bensadón. "Our new *compadres* have no love for us. I tell you, I have an itch between my shoulder blades, as if at any moment they'd take a notion to fire those muskets at us. And then there are the *indios,* whom one never sees till it's too late."

"Silence back there, you men!" Sergeant Perez bawled, turning his horse partway to glower at the dissidents.

Then suddenly, without warning, there was the whirr of an arrow, and Pablo Yarangui uttered a bellowing scream, dropping the reins of his horse, and lifting his left hand to his left eye where a Mescalero arrow was imbedded. He toppled off his horse, his body thudding against the edge of the trail and rolling down to lodge against a gnarled juniper tree in the shape of a cross which grew atop a huge boulder.

"*¡Los indios! ¡Guardase!*" Sergeant Perez cried, turning back to the other four privates and the two *peones* who brought up the rear on their burros.

Lieutenant Dondero spurred his faltering horse, reaching the end of the trail which descended into the mesa. He unholstered his pistol and fired at one of the rocks high above the trail behind which he could see the glimpse of a coppery-tinted face and the black headband that proclaimed the tribe of Mescalero. Another bowstring twanged, and an arrow whistled past him, narrowly missing his upraised arm. Now there came the sounds of hissing arrows and the thudding of their barbs into flesh, and the two *peones* on their burros slid down and sprawled lifeless on their bellies.

"*¡Adelante, pronto!*" he screamed, glancing frantically back at the jagged rocks which topped this winding trail. Sergeant Perez turned in his saddle, drew out one of his pistols, and fired. A short, squat Mescalero, in the act of rising from behind the boulder and notching his bowstring, jerked backwards, then fell and rolled over onto his side.

"Into the mesa, *pronto!*" the lieutenant ordered, almost hysterically, pointing with his sabre toward the center of a rocky stretch flanked by two broad stretches of jagged hills. Another arrow buried itself with a vicious *thuckkk* in Paco Rios's neck, and his plaintive cry was drowned out by the thundering of the horses' hooves. He rode lifeless for a moment, his hands slackening on the reins, then his head bowed and he toppled from the horse which raced on, wild-eyed, foam at its mouth. The three surviving privates, the sergeant, and the lieutenant continued to drive their steeds to the utmost in their desperate flight away from this Indian ambush.

Then there was silence in the Mesa, and the Mescalero disappeared from behind their boulder shelters, satisfied that they had wrought sufficient reprisal against the *mejicanos* who had for years slaughtered their women and their braves. Standing on the tallest of the boulders, there appeared a stocky, gray-haired Mescalero, wearing a Mexican serape, a red-dyed feather thrust through his head band: it was Matsinga, chief of the Mescalero Apache.

Lifting his bow, he made an abrupt gesture toward the north, and a dozen of his braves scrambled toward him, left the boulders, and hurried to their mustangs. Then they rode off with scarcely a glance at the fleeing Mexican soldiers.

"Look, *mi capitán!*" Sergeant Perez cried out, pointing with his empty pistol. Though the sun beat violently down to bake the rocky ground of the mesa, it was no mirage: about a mile ahead of them, he and Lieutenant Dondero could make out the tiny figures of men on horseback—the fugitives!

"They are delivered into our hands, Sergeant Perez!" Lieutenant Dondero gasped, his eyes narrowed and glowing with sadistic eagerness. "*Los indios* have taken a toll, but there are still five of us of the imperial army, and we are more than a match for those traitorous *yanquis!* Forward! Do not spare the horses now. We shall overtake them and make them our prisoners!"

At dawn of this same day, the six Texans had suffered a disastrous delay in their flight. The young brothers, John and Henry Ames, after a hasty breakfast, had mounted their mustang, only to have it unexpectedly rebel. It had bucked and twisted and swerved, till John had been flung from the rear. He clung to his brother but was unable to hold on because of the violent gyrations of the rebellious horse. He had fallen with one knee crumpled under him, suffering a sprained kneecap. Henry Ames had tried to enforce obedience, but in vain. With a burst of sudden speed, the horse had galloped forward, then suddenly come to a halt and reared high into the air, pitching Henry onto the rocky ground. Then the mustang had galloped off down the mesa till it was out of sight.

"Damn it, we can't ride three to a horse, that's for certain," Edward Molson swore. "Here. Ben and I'll give you our horse. There's no help for it." Molson turned to look at his cousin, then both men began to dismount.

"No, you can't do that," John Ames said, attempting to rise. "My brother and I lost the horse, so we'll walk as best we can. It can't be helped; it's just our bad luck. But we've come through so far, and maybe, if God wills, we'll make it to safety."

"John's knee hurts him some," Henry Ames said as he helped his brother to his feet. "We're going to go none too fast with this sprained knee of his, and we'd hold you back. We'd best stay here with our weapons and try to hold off the *soldados,* if they come."

But Molson wouldn't hear of leaving the two behind, and the others agreed. He and his cousin, and Malcolm Pauley and Jack Williams, mounted double on the other mustang, broke into a slow trot. Their mustangs were exhausted, their sides heaving, their eyes wild, and slaver a their mouths. "What we've got left won't last much longer anyway, I'm thinking," Williams grumbled, dolefully shaking his head.

"All we can do is pray and go on," Molson answered. A devout Catholic, he crossed himself and looked up at the blazing sky. Then, with a heartfelt sigh, he clucked at the mustang with his tongue, and slapped the reins against the stallion's neck.

John Cooper galloped ahead of Kinotatay and Pironti-kay, for he had made out the distant figures of the Texans on the rocky mesa. "We've found them, Kinotatay," he called. "We'll take them back to Taos with us. They'll be safe with Don Diego and Miguel Sandarbal!"

"But see, *Halcón,*" Kinotatay pointed with his bow, "behind them are the *mejicanos!* They look no bigger than ants, but they come quickly and the *gringos* have little strength left in their horses. We must reach them first!"

John Cooper drew out "Long Girl" from his saddle sling as he raced his mustang forward; the Apache scout and his son drew abreast of him, urging their mustangs to the utmost.

At the southern end of the mesa, Edward Molson cried out as he reined in his exhausted horse. "My God, I see Indians riding toward us! There are three of them!"

"I see them," his cousin agreed. "The rest of you, get your guns ready! If we have to die, we'll take a few of them with us! For sure, we're not going to be made prisoners, either by Injuns or those damned greasers!"

"For God's sake," Jack Williams suddenly cried, having turned back in his saddle, "the greasers have caught up with us! They're about half a mile behind us and coming up fast! We're lost!"

"Not yet," Molson cried. "I don't fancy an Injun torture stake any more than I do being a greaser prisoner! Get off your horses, pull them down on their sides. You, John and Henry Ames, use your guns against the soldiers. We'll handle these Indians from the other side!"

So saying, he and Ben Forrester dismounted and dragged the whinnying mustang down. Crouching behind its back, they leveled their weapons at John Cooper, Kinotatay, and Pirontikay; while Pauley and Williams, emulating them, dragged down the other mustang and, with the two Ames boys, aimed their weapons at the furiously galloping Mexican soldiers who came up in the opposite direction. Williams got off a snap shot with his old rifle, but the range was too far, and the ball fell harmlessly many yards ahead of Lieutenent Dondero.

John Cooper raced on ahead of his two Apache friends, brandishing "Long Girl" and crying out, "We're friends, don't fire!" as he rode toward the older Texans.

"He speaks American, Ben," Molson shouted. "Keep him in your sights and let's see if it's a trick. He's in buckskin, but he's white and blond as a Texas wheatfield, so help me!"

John Cooper dismounted, and ran, crouching low, toward the two Texans who faced him behind their still struggling mustang. "Don't be afraid of my friends, they've come to help you," he shouted as he flung himself down and steadied the Lancaster rifle over the side of the mustang.

Meanwhile, behind them, Lieutenant Dondero waved his sabre. "*¡Fuego!*" he shouted, his voice a savage bellow reverberating through the vast mesa. But the bark of John Cooper's Lancaster answered him, and Pancho Segura dropped his musket, sank backwards, and then toppled from his horse.

Sergeant Perez fired his pistol, nicking the shoulder of Henry Ames, who returned fire. The sergeant jerked in his saddle, then slowly fell to the left and lay sprawled on the ground as his horse raced on.

Kinotatay and his son had dismounted and notched their bowstrings and, drawing the arrows back to the very zenith of the arc, let them fly. Manuel Bensadón and Pedro Gonzalez slumped in their saddles, and as their horses galloped on, they slid off and sprawled lifeless on the mesa's rocky soil.

Almost hysterical with fury and frustration, Lieutenant Jaime Dondero rode his horse directly against the two Ames brothers, cleared them with a mighty leap, and then, leaping from his staggering horse, slashed with his saber at John Cooper.

The young mountain man, who had had no time to reload, parried the vicious cut with the metal-embossed butt of his father's rifle. As the saber was lowered to the ground, he swung upward with all his might. The heavy butt caught Lieutenant Dondero in the jaw, breaking his neck and flinging him backward where he lay sprawled, his teeth still bared in the final rictus of hate and agony.

John Cooper stood panting, drenched with sweat. Edward Molson staggered to his feet, tears streaming down his cheeks. "God bless you, whoever you are, and your Injun friends!" he gasped.

"We heard of the battle and we thought there'd be men like you trying to escape," John Cooper panted. "I'll take you back to Taos, and we'll get you rested up. It'll keep you away from the soldiers, at least for a time."

"I won't say no, I'll tell you that. God bless you again. But as you can see, we're short of horses. And John Ames there, he's the youngest, just a boy, he's hurt his knee."

"He can ride behind me. And the other one who is helping him, he can ride with Kinotatay. It's all right now. There won't be any more soldiers coming, I'm pretty sure of that."

Edward Molson held out his hand, and John Cooper eagerly shook it.

Twelve

By this time, Miguel Sandarbal and his *trabajadores* had managed to complete the construction of a little cottage intended for Bess Callendar. Meanwhile, Don Diego had had several meetings with the attractive young widow and learned that she would be more than willing to undertake the work of preparing the monthly accounts. These would include details of the growing sheep flock, the total weight of wool obtained from the last shearing, the cost of food supplies for the workers as well as for the members of the household, the expenditures which would include wages as well as the replacement of tools, saddles, lariats, and the like, as well as the ledger in which the name of every worker on the estate was inscribed, together with his wife and children.

Don Diego had also taken advantage of these meetings to do what he could to press Miguel Sandarbal's suit. Choosing his words very carefully, he had explained to Bess Callendar that it was his *capataz* who had tried so hard to buy her freedom, not to win her for himself but simply to set her free from bondage. Don Diego had gone on to say that he himself was eternally in debt to Miguel Sandarbal for his loyalty and service to the family, and that the *capataz* was his friend, not his servant. The young woman had been overwhelmed with gratitude, and all she had been able to say was, "Both you and Señor Sandarbal are very good men, Your Excellency."

On the night before Bess Callendar was to move into the cottage, Miguel Sandarbal had gone to the lower slopes of a nearby mountain and gathered wild flowers. These he had arranged in clay bowls and vases on the table, on the little stand beside the bed, and even in the kitchen, which he had

132

had his men construct with a stone oven so that the young widow could cook her own meals.

Miguel had also cajoled the amiable maids of the *hacienda* to put up some curtains on the small shuttered windows, so as to give the little cottage as cheerful and warm a look as possible. The floors had been made of hard wood, and he had acquired several large Navaho rugs to cover them. Yet, not content with all this, Don Diego's *capataz* had bought a pretty yellow finch and a cage from one of the Pueblo Indians who had a little shop near the plaza.

Don Diego had reminded him that his services would be required as a commissioned agent at the January fair in Chihuahua, and that he should take with him four or five trusted and well-armed *trabajadores,* the fastest horses, and several *carretas* to bring back the purchases. He planned to leave early in November, and another part of this assignment, as Don Diego explained, was to listen attentively to what was said by the people of Chihuahua at the fair on the subject of tariffs and trade and, particularly, whether the military authorities sent by the viceroy from Mexico City had tightened the severe trade regulations.

Meanwhile, during this fall season, the *trabajadores'* tasks were extremely light. The supervision of the grazing herd, the occasional repairs to the bunkhouse and the *hacienda,* and the procurement of supplies comprised their only duties and left the workers plenty of time to enjoy life with their own families. Miguel had eagerly volunteered to take on still another task, that of helping to train Lobo while John Cooper was away.

"What I'd really like to arrive at, Miguel," John Cooper had told the *capataz,* "is to be able to let Lobo stay out all night and guard the *hacienda* and the bunkhouse and the cottages. I can't quite trust him yet, but the more we work on it, the more chance there'll be that he'll be broken in just the way Lije was."

For the first few times, Miguel used the leash and collar to take Lobo out of the shed and go with him on these walks, as extensive as he could make them, depending on what duties he had back at the *hacienda* and the corral. Thus it was, about three days after Bess Callendar had moved into her cottage, that as he was striding off toward the woods with Lobo impatiently growling and pulling at the leash, he encountered the lovely young widow.

"Oh, good morning, Señor Sandarbal!" she called to him.

"And to you, señora." Miguel shortened the leash and warily glanced at Lobo whose hair had begun to bristle around his neck. Bending to the wolf-dog, he scolded, "No, no, this is a friend. Be good now, Lobo." And then, remembering what John Cooper had told him, he made a fist of his left hand and rubbed his knuckles back and forth over the top of Lobo's head. Lobo relaxed, and his yellow eyes seemed to half close. "That is better now. Don't be afraid, Señora Callendar. Only, since I have just started his training, maybe you shouldn't come too close," he called to the young woman.

"What a marvelous animal—so strong and big—he must be part wolf," Bess Callendar exclaimed. Lobo eyed her with an indolent wave of his tail, not yet deciding whether she was friend or foe. Yet all the same, his hair no longer bristled and he stood passively as Miguel held him in tow.

"That is true, señora," Miguel explained. "He belongs to the Señor John Cooper. But you see, señora, John Cooper had—how do you say it, a hunting dog that was Irish—"

"An Irish wolfhound," Bess supplied.

"That is it! My English is only passable, señora."

"On the contrary, you speak it very well. I understand you perfectly, Señor Sandarbal."

Miguel flushed hotly and lowered his eyes, keeping his sombrero in his left hand and tightly pressed against his breeches. He felt mingled admiration and the most atrocious embarrassment, almost like that of a child caught trying to act beyond his years. Her soft, sweet voice was the loveliest he had ever heard, and yet at the same time, in his rough costume of *capataz* with dirty breeches and dusty boots and wrinkled sombrero, he castigated himself as being a fool to think that so beautiful a *gringa* could ever have the slightest affection for a humble *trabajador* like himself.

"And you know, Señor Sandarbal," she added with an engaging little smile, "I speak Spanish understandably—at least my husband used to say I did." At this recollection, the smile vanished a moment, but was then quickly replaced as she continued. "I am told by Don Diego that you will bring the accounts to me and I shall write the figures down in the ledger that I am to show him."

"*Es verdad*, Señora Callendar," Miguel hastened to assure her. "I am at your disposal, whenever it is convenient for you."

"Perhaps late this afternoon, then, if you have no other tasks, Señor Sandarbal?"

"I shall be there promptly, Señora Callendar." Self-consciously, he glanced down at Lobo and then rubbed the wolf-dog's head with the brim of his sombrero and chuckled. "Lobo, you see, wants to go for his run. It is true that he has wolf in him, but he is also very loyal and very brave. He will defend us all if there are *bandidos* or unfriendly *indios.*"

"Do you think it would be all right if I petted him, Señor Sandarbal?"

Miguel scowled with worry. For nothing in the world did he wish this idyllic conversation to be interrupted, and yet the fear that Lobo might mistake the young widow's approach as inimical rather than friendly greatly concerned him. He glanced anxiously down at the wolf-dog, then squatted and muttered, "Now you be a good boy, Señor Lobo, *¿comprende?* This is a *mujer linda*, and she wants to be friends with you. I swear *por todos los santos* that if you do not be kind to her, I will punish you, even if Señor John Cooper punishes me in turn." Then, dropping the sombrero to the ground and rubbing his knuckles over the top of Lobo's head, he hesitantly proffered, "Well then, Señora Callendar, walk slowly, and smile, and put both your hands out with the palms up to the sky. And do not make any quick movements. I have him on leash, as you see, but I would not want him to bite you with those terribly sharp teeth."

"Nor would I, Señor Sandarbal." She tilted back her head and laughed delightfully, and Miguel glanced up at her with his soul in his eyes. Then, afraid that she might have seen his adoring look, he scowled at Lobo.

Bess slowly came forward, smiling as she stared down at the alert animal. He regarded her, his yellow eyes narrowing a moment, and then his tail gave a brief wag. She too squatted down, but very slowly, and rubbed her knuckles over Lobo's head just as Miguel had. The wolk-dog's tail wagged briskly now, and a hoarse purring sound emanated from his muzzle, while his yellow eyes half closed again.

"You have made a friend of him, Señora Callendar!" Miguel exclaimed. "Now there will never be any trouble. Ah, the rascal, how he likes to have his head scratched. But you see, I have known many dogs back in Spain where I came from that like that, too, and cats, as well."

"Yes, that's very true, Señor Sandarbal. If one gives love, one receives love in return," Bess murmured. And then, with an exquisite coloring to her cheeks, she moved away slowly and addressed him. "I understand I have you to thank for that wonderful cottage, Señor Sandarbal. And the flowers and the rugs—they're marvelously woven! And the charming finch in the cage—that was your doing, too?"

"It was not I alone, Señora Callendar," he protested as he got to his feet and slapped his sombrero at the legs of his breeches to brush away some imaginary dust. "We have done all our chores now because, you see, the shearing of the sheep is in the spring, and then we graze them. And there isn't much, and the men need work or they will grow very lazy when the time comes for them to be busy again. It was really their idea to build the cottage and—and all the other things," he lamely finished.

"All the same, I'm grateful to you, Señor Sandarbal. And I'll see you later this afternoon, as we agreed?"

"It will be my privilege to give you all the help I can with the ledgers, Señora Callendar." Miguel's voice was unsteady, and his heart was pounding wildly. He tried to hide this emotion by turning to Lobo and rubbing his head again, then slapping his flank. "And now, with your permission, Señora Callendar, I'll take him for his romp. I am very proud of him the way he passed the test today. I shall tell Señor John Cooper how well he behaved with you. ¡Hasta la vista!"

Bess Callendar stood watching after him for a long moment, then, with a little smile, she went back to her cottage. Once he was well beyond the grounds of the *hacienda* and heading toward the slope of the nearest mountain where Lobo loved to run, the middle-aged *capataz* flung his sombrero into the air with a joyous shout and deftly caught it as it descended. He clapped it upon his head, and released Lobo from the leash. "Yes, Lobo, I am very proud of the way you behaved just now. I swear to you my heart was in my mouth when that beautiful señora came toward you. Oh, I almost died inside thinking that perhaps you would forget your manners and sink those terrible sharp teeth into her soft flesh—I would have strangled you, Lobo, yes, believe me. But you did not, and Señor John Cooper will be very happy when I tell him how you distinguished yourself this day."

Four days later, John Cooper, Kinotatay, and Pirontikay rode into the estate of the *hacienda* with the six Texans they had rescued. Edward Molson and his cousin, Ben Forrester, rode double on one of the wild mustangs, with Malcolm Pauley and Jack Williams on the other. John Ames, whose sprained knee had been set with improvised splints and with medicinal bark which Kinotatay had taken from shrubs, rode with the scout, while his older brother, Henry, sat behind young Pirontikay. Miguel Sandarbal and several of the *trabajadores* hurried to the riders. "God be praised, you have come back to us safely, young master," Miguel joyously grinned. "And you brought the *gringos* back safely, too."

"They will make good *trabajadores* for your sheep for the time being, Miguel," the young man said as he dismounted. "And there aren't any soldiers left to track them down to our *hacienda*."

"That is a very good thing. I will be glad to work with these young Americans. Tom Prentice is proving himself to be an excellent horseman, and I am sure these Texans will work hard, as well. And I have much to tell you about Señor Lobo. He is becoming very tame. Why, yesterday, Esteban Morales and his little son, Bernardo, actually played with Lobo, and he did not once growl or show his teeth."

"That's just wonderful, Miguel! That means I won't lock him up in the shed anymore. I think by now he's learned to be our faithful friend and guardian. But now, let's get these men to the bunkhouse. John Ames there hurt his knee. It's patched up, but you'll take a look at it and get him well."

"Do you think we can stay here safely, John Cooper?" Edward Molson asked as Miguel helped the teenage Texan down from the horse.

"Of course. Don Diego is the *intendente* of Taos, and no one bothers him. He administers the law, and the authorities rarely come here. Besides, Miguel will see that you wear clothes like the other *trabajadores*. It won't matter that you're *gringos*. And when the time comes, we'll help you get back to Texas whenever you want, my word on it."

"I'll never forget what you've done for us, John Cooper," Molson solemnly declared as he clasped hands with John Cooper and stared admiringly into his face. "We'll try to earn our keep while we're here, you've got my word on it."

John Cooper returned the handshake and then headed eagerly for the *hacienda* to find Catarina.

Now two months away from her time, Catarina felt serene contentment and joyous anticipation at the child that would cement their union. She reached out to her husband when he entered the room, and they spent the night together locked in each other's arms, saying nothing about John Cooper's mission in Texas, but thinking ahead to the birth of their child and the time they would spend together in their new home, wherever that would be.

That evening, when the air from the Sangre de Cristo Mountains had become exhilaratingly cool, John Cooper brought supper in to Catarina. She had gone to sleep early, however, and he kissed her forehead and straightened the coverlet about her, then walked out of the room and murmured a young Leonora, "She's gone to sleep already, Leonora. I know she asked you to bring chocolate, but you needn't do it. Sleep's better for her. And by the way, thanks for being so nice to her all this time. Tía Margarita has told me how you waited on her practically hand and foot."

"But it is my duty, and besides, I'm so fond of her—and of you, too, Señor Baines!" The pretty young maid curtsied and blushed.

"I've heard that that rascal Teofilo Rosas is courting you now, Leonora," John Cooper teased her.

Leonora gasped and put a hand on her mouth, then nodded, her blushes deepening.

"He's a fine man, he'll be devoted to you. Tell me this, though, because it concerns a friend of mine. Is the fact that he's much older important to you?" John Cooper, of course, was referring to his friend Miguel Sandarbal—with whom he'd had a long conversation that very afternoon on the subject of Bess Callendar.

"Oh, no, Señor Baines—that is to say—I mean—he is good and he works hard, and maybe he isn't *romántico* like the *caballeros*—but I think he would be more faithful to me than any of them."

"I'm sure that's true, Leonora. Besides, you're quite a *muchacha linda,* and I'm pretty sure you'd keep him faithful to you all the time. With a girl like you, he'd have no time to look at anyone else."

Leonora uttered a stifled giggle, then turned and ran down the hall, scarlet with happy confusion.

John Cooper emerged from the *hacienda* and whistled twice. There was a low growl, and Lobo bounded out of the shadows, wagging his tail and rubbing his muzzle against his young master's leg. John Cooper bent to rub his knuckles over the wolf-dog's head. "You're doing just fine, Lobo, just fine. Lije would be proud of his son. And as an extra treat, I'm going to take you for a little walk—because you've behaved yourself so well today. And I brought along something from the kitchen, a big piece of mutton. You'd like that, wouldn't you, Lobo?"

The wolf-dog's yellow eyes gleamed, and he gave an excited little yip. John Cooper laughed heartily, well-pleased with the results of the training. Then he strode off beyond the bunkhouse and toward Bess Callendar's cottage, where he could see the light of an oil lamp in the window.

At his knock, the door was opened after a moment, and Bess wonderingly exclaimed, "Mr. Baines, is something wrong?"

"Oh, no, Mrs. Callendar. Excuse me if I bothered you this late in the evening—I hope you weren't ready to go to bed—"

"In a little while. I was working on the ledger for Don Diego. Oh, it's Lobo. You know, he's very nice. We're friends already."

"I know. Miguel told me. I was thinking, it's so nice out, the air's cool and all, maybe you'd like to take a walk with Lobo and me. I want to say something to you, anyhow."

"Of course. Just let me get my serape. There now. As a matter of fact, I've been working on the ledger for hours, and a little exercise would help me sleep better, to tell you the truth."

They walked about the *hacienda* grounds for a time until John Cooper finally broke the silence. "Well, now, is everything going well with you? Work and all, and you have everything you need in the cottage?"

"Oh, yes And such flowers—I declare, I don't know who brings them, but whenever I come back from seeing Don Diego at the *hacienda*, there are always fresh flowers."

"I can tell you who brings them. It's Miguel Sandarbal, Mrs. Callendar."

"I—I suspected as much—" She lowered her eyes and blushed.

John Cooper winked at Lobo and then said gently, "I hope you'll excuse me if I'm rude, but I wanted to say something about Miguel. I like him a lot. He's a fine, brave man, and he's meant a lot to Don Diego and his family. And to me, too."

"I'm sure that's true. Yes, he *is* a fine man."

"And he happens to be in love with you—I mean, he wants to marry you. He wants that more than anything else in the world, Mrs. Callendar. But you see, he's afraid that you'd laugh at him if he came to you and said that."

"Oh, goodness! I never dreamed—I knew he was very gracious to me—but—"

"Oh, my gosh—did I put my foot into it?" John Cooper said boyishly, shaking his head to reprove himself. "Well, the cat's out of the bag, anyway, so I might just as well go on and say what I really wanted to say to you, Mrs. Callendar. He's never been married, and he's worked hard, and when he bid for you at the fair, it wasn't because he wanted to buy you. It was—well, darn it all, he just couldn't stand seeing you treated like dirt by an Indian, and still less being sold as a *criatura* to that nasty old *hacendado*."

Bess turned her face away from John Cooper as she walked along, pretending to stare at the trees. "I—I know. Don Diego told me about that. That was very good of him. Very kind and very decent, indeed."

"Well, that's what I was getting at, Mrs. Callendar. I mean, he figures that, because he's so much older than you are, you'd never think about him being your husband or anything like that. You know what I mean. I know I'm speaking out of turn, but he's too bashful ever to come and tell you straight out what he really feels for you. He doesn't think he has anything to offer you. He's the *capataz* here, and Don Diego trusts him like a friend, not just a worker."

"I know that, too, Mr. Baines. My goodness—I didn't think—"

"You're not offended by what I said? Gosh, I sure hope not. I mean, I like him so much as a friend, I think he'd make you happy. He'd be a good husband, and I happen to know he worships you. He'd do anything for you, Mrs. Callendar."

"Oh, dear—I—I didn't think he really felt that fo

me—truly I didn't." Her voice faltered and was faint in the
darkness.

"You see, what he's afraid of," he continued, "is that if
he came to you and told you right off he wanted to marry
you, you'd maybe laugh at him—"

"Oh, no, I wouldn't ever! Oh, no, I couldn't. He—he's so
kind, and he goes out of his way to make sure that I'm
comfortable—I can understand things better now. Mr.
Baines, you didn't speak out of turn. I think—I know I still
miss my husband, Edward, but I'm alone, and I don't know
about going back to Texas. Besides, I've nobody to go back
to. And he *is* kind, and I've seen how he treats the others, and
how he works with the animals. That means a lot to me.
Edward was the same way—about people and animals, you
see. That's why I married him."

"Good. Well, anyway, I'll apologize again if I offended
you. But I just wanted you to know."

"If—if it's as you say, Mr. Baines," her voice trembled
and was still faint, "I—I'd like to hear it from him. I mean,
then I could know how I feel about him."

"Sure. I remember my ma used to tell me the story about
Priscilla Alden and Miles Standish and Captain John Smith,
and how Miles Standish went to Priscilla and tried to talk her
into marrying the captain, and so she said to him, 'Why don't
you speak for yourself, John?' and—well, I guess this sort of
reminded me of that story. Anyhow, I just wanted you to
know how things were, really."

"I—I'm very glad you did, Mr. Baines. Thank you. I
hope your Catarina knows what a fine, good man you are,
too. And I hope she'll have her baby without any trouble and
he'll grow up to be a man just like you, Mr. Baines."

He stared at her, and he saw the glint of tears in her eyes
as she half-turned from him. Embarrassed, he coughed and
then gruffly said to Lobo, "All right, Lobo, you've had
enough. Let's head back. We mustn't keep this nice lady up
too late."

Early the next morning after breakfast, John Cooper
accosted Miguel Sandarbal as the *capataz* was giving his
orders for the day to the *trabajadores*. "A word with you,
amigo," the young man called out.

"*Ciertamente, mi compañero.* Now then, Señor Molson,
I would be obliged if you'd take two hundred of those sheep

up to the northeastern range, because there's thicker grass there, and we want them to get fat by next spring for the shearing. *Gracias.*" Miguel grinned and waved at the tall young Texan, then turned back to John Cooper. "And now, *amigo,* I am at your service."

"Let's walk up this way where no one can disturb us, Miguel."

The *capataz*'s earnest, homely face tensed with anxiety. "What is wrong, *mi compañero?*"

"You, *hombre,*" John Cooper chuckled and nudged Miguel in the ribs. "All you have to do is go tell Mrs. Callendar exactly what you feel for her and ask her to marry you."

"*¡Mi Dios!*" Miguel gasped. "How do you know this?"

"Because, and because I'm your *amigo* and your *compañero,* I talked to her last night, and I told her that you were in love with her and wanted to marry her."

"Heaven protect me! And of course she laughed and told you I was an old fool who should know his place, and not forget it," Miguel groaned.

John Cooper shook his head. "She did no such thing. You know what she really said?"

"*Amigo, amigo,*" Miguel breathed, "do not torture a man!"

"I don't intend to. She said she wanted to hear it from you yourself. And she said that you're kind and gentle to the *trabajadores* and to the animals, and that your kindness reminded her of her husband's. And the fact that you're twice her age, as you keep complaining, doesn't mean a tinker's darn. So now the rest is up to you, Miguel. I remember how you were that day you fought Santomaro and his men. So don't be a scaredy-cat, now. Go tell her."

"You really think—you mean—there is hope—oh, *Dios!*" Miguel sighed deeply, his eyes rolling heavenward.

"There's a better chance for you with Bess Callendar, *mi compañero,* then there was for me the first time I met my Catarina. So the rest is up to you. And by tomorrow, I want to hear some positive news from you. Because if you don't tell her, then I won't be your *compañero* any more. Good day to you, Miguel Sandarbal."

Miguel had given his workers orders to keep them busy that afternoon, anxiously trying to arrange a moment alone with Bess Callendar. The moment came after the noontime meal, when, by custom, the *trabajadores* had their *siesta*. And this time, he went boldly to the shed to get Lobo's leash and collar, whistled to the wolf-dog, then leashed him. Lobo emitted a soft growl to indicate that he was not too happy with the leash, now that he had proved himself worthy of total freedom, and Miguel playfully cuffed him. "This is necessary, *amigo*," he muttered. "You will help me get back my courage. After all, if she wishes to slap my face for being so bold in what I am about to say to her, you will be there to save me, won't you, Lobo?" And then, with a deep sigh worthy of the most romantic *caballero* in either Madrid or Taos, he said, half-aloud, "I swear to you, *Señor Dios*, that if she says 'yes' to me, I will make her the best husband there ever was in all this world. And I will burn candles to You in the church of Padre Moraga. And I will do much, much more."

Pretending nonchalance, he led the wolf-dog out on his leash to within yards of Bess Callendar's cottage. He stopped there, coughed, looked around, and ascertaining that no one was watching him, he addressed Lobo in a louder voice than necessary, "I know, I know, you are always wanting a walk. I tell you, Lobo, you are becoming spoiled. And it is only out of friendship for your master, Señor John Cooper, that I give in to your wishes, understand that, *amigo*."

The door of the cottage suddenly opened and Bess emerged, in a long white cotton dress, a shawl about her shoulders. Seeing him, she gasped and colored, then stammered, "Oh, I—I thought I heard voices—"

"It was I, Señora Callendar, forgive me. I did not mean to disturb you, *ciertamente*. Lobo here was arguing with me that he wanted a longer walk than I usually give him. Forgive me for disturbing you, Señora Callendar."

"But you didn't disturb me at all. In fact, there's something about the report that I need your help on with the ledger for Don Diego. It's the inventory of firearms and ammunition. I wasn't sure of the figures that you wrote down the other day."

"Oh, yes—I remember—well, perhaps when you are free."

"But I'm free now, if you wish. And you know that Lobo and I are friends. Do you remember what those figures were, or do you have to get them from your quarters, Señor Sandarbal?"

She avoided his eyes and studiedly smoothed the train of her skirt. Miguel stared at her, his heart in his eyes, seeing how her soft, yellow hair tumbled below her shoulder blades in a thick sheaf. Then hoarsely he declared, "As it happens, Señora Callendar, I—I do not remember them, either. But—but there is something I have to say to you—now, when no one else is around to hear us. And if you become angry with me, I shall beg your forgiveness in advance."

"But there's no reason why you should, Señor Sandarbal. You've never done anything to offend me. Oh, I'm the one who must ask your forgiveness—I never properly thanked you for that delightful little bird in the cage that you got for me. It's such a joy, and sometimes, would you believe it, it actually sings! It's so pleasant to hear a bird singing in the morning."

"I—I am overjoyed that you should find it a pleasant companion for you, Señora Callendar," he blurted. Then, hearing a soft growl from Lobo, he scowled and tightened the leash and muttered, "Stay still, don't you interfere now, if you know what is good for you, Señor Lobo!"

"You've been very thoughtful, Señor Sandarbal. I can't tell you how much it means to me. You've helped me forget all the misfortunes—well, perhaps not quite all—but it's given me a different feeling entirely, being here."

"I am very glad, Señora Callendar."

"My name is Bess to my friends, Miguel," she softly interposed and eyed him candidly for the first time.

He turned scarlet with confusion. He gulped and put his sombrero behind his back, crushing and twisting it in his embarrassment. And then, beside himself with anguished desire, he exclaimed, "I am an old fool, Señora—I—I mean, Bess—but I would ask for no greater happiness in all this world than if you would consent to be my wife."

"Do you mean that, truly, Miguel?"

"*Por todos los santos,*" he swore, his voice taut with the furious emotions swelling in him. "I have never meant anything more in all my life, I swear this to you, as I would before Padre Moraga in the confessional booth."

"You're very sweet. You've made me feel at home here, and I know of the many other things you've done for me. I think—yes, I know—I could try very hard to make you a good wife, Miguel."

With a cry of ecstasy, Miguel Sandarbal flung his sombrero into the air and, dropping Lobo's leash, took her into his arms. Tears glistened in his eyes as he stammered, "And I swear to you, *mi linda, mi corazón,* that I will spend every hour of my life making you happy, and never making you regret being my wife."

"If you do that, dear Miguel," she whispered to him, "you'll make me happier than I ever thought I could be again. How very dear you are, how very good and kind!"

She put her arms around his neck and offered him her mouth, and Miguel, as he kissed her, felt tears of rapture trickling down his cheeks. He closed his eyes and murmured a silent prayer of gratitude to the eternal God who grants paradise to mortals.

Thirteen

On November 9, 1813, Weesayo was delivered of a sturdy, black-haired boy, to the delight of both the young Apache girl and her devoted husband, Carlos. It had been a somewhat premature birth, but an easy one, and Carlos marveled at his young wife's courage and joy. When the soft-spoken midwife, Juana Cortado, who had attended the wives of the *hacendados* of Taos for more than a generation, came out of Weesayo's room to tell the anxious husband that he had a fine, strong son, Carlos crossed himself and thanked the woman. Then he went to the chapel and, kneeling down, prayed to the Holy Virgin to bless their son and to watch over his life. Weesayo would have the right to name the child, since Carlos had acceded to the ancient Apache custom whereby the mother was responsible for the child, for naming it, for shaping its life, and deciding what path it would walk. But Carlos also prayed that the child would symbolize the coming together of two different races, the amalgamation of *gringo* and red man in the ties of blood and the peaceful understanding of each other's way of life.

And by the irony of fate, on this same day when the son of Carlos de Escobar and Weesayo first saw the light of day, General Andrew Jackson inflicted a crushing defeat upon the warriors of the Creek nation at Talladega, Alabama. And it was to be the destiny of this intrepid Tennessean that, when he was president, the Indian nations of the southeastern part of the United States would be driven far to the west, to wander far from their hunting grounds and to be treated like wild dogs which one drives from one's campfire.

The afternoon the baby was born, Carlos entered his young wife's bedchamber, and her dark eyes shone with joy as she turned to smile at her infant son suckling at her breast.

"You are pleased, *mi esposo?*"

"They are not the words I would use, my Light of the Mountains, to describe the love I have for you and the joy of seeing our son."

Her gentle face flushed, and she held out a hand to him, and he kissed it reverently. Then, looking at her and whispering, "May I?" he took the infant from her and held it against him. Kissing its forehead, he murmured, *"Mi hijo,* I have prayed that my God and your Great Spirit will look down upon you and give you long life and health and strength and the wisdom to live in the new world that your mother and I will help build for you."

He gently gave her back the child, in its swaddling clothes, and Weesayo touched his cheek. "And now it is for you to name our son," Carlos said. "I promised you this."

"Mi Carlos," she whispered, her eyes filling with tears. Then, with a sweet smile, she turned to the little baby and fondly watched the child nurse. After a moment, she turned back to Carlos and murmured, "Would it please you if I were to name him after your father, *mi esposo?*"

"Very much. But do not do this only because you think it will please me, Weesayo. I swore before the shaman who made us one that I would follow in the ways of your people. And because I respect and love you, I respect your ways equally to my own."

"Then I have chosen. Because it pleases me to name our son Diego. I love your father almost as much as I love my own, *mi* Carlos." She paused for a moment, then added, "But I am worried about my father, for he is ill. He says it is from his old wound, but I think it is more than that. I fear he will soon be called to the land of the Great Spirit."

"I am sure it is not as serious as you think, my darling one. He is strong and still young. And he is still the leader of the tribe."

"That is true, for so long as he lives. But I know that, even before I met you, *mi esposo,* there were young braves who grumbled at his wish for peace and who desired to do great deeds and count their coups against their enemies, not only the Mescalero who have always hated us, but against your own people, especially the *soldados.* If he were to die, there would be discontent, and I fear that one of the younger braves might become chief and drive our people into battle."

"I will pray that does not happen, Weesayo. But do not think that your father will die. This is a time for us to think of life, my darling one. I see our little son, and he has your dark eyes and the gentleness of your mouth. I think of life and the years ahead of us, Weesayo."

He could not hold back his tears, nor did he think them unmanly as he bent to her and took her in his arms. And after their long embrace, he kissed their son, and then he rose and said in a tone he strove to make bantering, "You will tell me when you are strong enough to ride to your father's stronghold with me. We will visit him and show him our son that carries your blood and mine in his veins. And we will bring him presents, and I will give you something more to give your mother."

Weesayo smiled and settled back on her pillow. Her eyes danced with merriment as she murmured, "I should not tell you this, but she was very pleased with the gift I brought her. And I know that she understood from whom it really came, even though you might not look at her or speak to her. She said to me, 'Daughter, this man of yours has a good heart and his tongue is straight, and though we may not recognize each other, I should not be displeased if you let him understand that it is a joy to me to know that he is your mate.' "

"Now I can see from whom your wisdom and sweetness came, my dearest Weesayo," Carlos laughed. "I shall be back to bring you the evening meal and to visit with our son again."

He stood at the door for a moment, looking back at his wife and child, and then went out. Weesayo settled back again with a happy sigh and hugged her child to her breast. "Diego, Diego," she whispered, "we are greatly loved. There is such joy in me that it will make the milk I give you rich and strong so that you will be as brave and as good and kind as is your father, whom I love as much as life itself."

Four days later, Weesayo pronounced herself ready to visit her father, despite Carlos's great concern that the journey of at least three days and nights might be hazardous for her health. She had straightened her shoulders, her head high, and sweetly rebuked him: "I should not be worthy to be your *esposa, mi* Carlos, if I could not ride beside you to see my father. Do you not know that Apache women are strong, and that often, even a few hours after the child is born, they take an axe and cut firewood for their man's wickiup? See, little Diego is warm in his sling at my back, and I am as strong as ever, and I am eager to ride my father's mustang beside you."

She was dressed in her beaded buckskin, and he stared adoringly at her, but all the same, with a young husband's intense solicitude, he insisted that she wear a coat thickly lined and covered with beaver fur which he had bought at the fair. Then, having bidden his family *adios,* and having taken John Cooper aside for a moment to tell him that he had said a prayer this very morning in the chapel that Catarina's child would be as strong and sound as Weesayo's, he mounted the white stallion and rode off with Weesayo beside him.

They had packed ample provisions, and the mountain trail was not yet too difficult. Snows had fallen along the top of the Sangre de Cristo range, but the wind was not yet strong, though it was brisk and invigorating. Weesayo's eyes sparkled as she took long, deep breaths, and she exclaimed to her husband, "Already I feel I am back with my people, but that is not because I tire of this life here with you at the *hacienda, mi esposo.*"

On the morning of the second day of their journey, as they rode along a narrowing canyon trail, there was a sudden angry cawing, and a large raven swooped down to perch upon the gnarled branch of a juniper tree some ten feet above them. Weesayo looked up, and her face was shadowed. She turned to Carlos and murmured. "It is not a good sign, *mi esposo*. It speaks of dark things to come."

"But I thought that the buzzard was the omen of death, Weesayo. And you see it was not that," he tried to reassure her, glancing back up at the raven, which stood looking after them.

"That much is true. Yet because I think my father will not tell anyone of his sickness, I am greatly worried because of that sign."

"Weesayo, when I prayed in the chapel yesterday morning before we set out on our journey, I asked my God to keep your father well and to let him have long years as the wise *jefe* of the Jicarilla Apache."

"I, too, prayed to the Great Spirit for him, Carlos."

"Then surely our prayers will be stronger than the sign of the raven, Weesayo. But it may be, from what you have told me, that the young Apache warriors who prefer war to your father's way of peace may try to go their own way. What would happen then, Weesayo?"

She shook her head, biting her lip as she pondered the question. Then she said slowly, "Among my people, the elders hold council, and the fathers of these impatient young braves speak what is in their hearts. Then they decide—but till now the elders have always upheld the wishes of my father, Descontarti."

"Then I am sure that the elders will continue to side with your father, Weesayo. They see, over these years, how well he has led them and how they prosper, have food and trade goods, and are not bothered by the soldiers. Come now, smile at me, my beloved, and when we reach the stronghold, you will see that you have no reason for these fears. Are you warm enough, Weesayo?"

"Oh, yes! And so is little Diego. We are warm with your love, *mi* Carlos." She gave him a dazzling smile as she glanced back at the infant in the warm sling attached to her back.

When they rode into the stronghold on the morning of the fourth day, Descontarti stood with Kinotatay and Pironti-kay at the largest wickiup to welcome them. Carlos observed, with some concern, that Descontarti's face was drawn, and that he seemed leaner. But the alacrity with which the Apache chief hurried toward his daughter, and the joy in his face when she dismounted and gently drew the infant from its warm sling, somewhat reassured him.

"Mi padre," Weesayo exclaimed in her sweet, clear voice, "I have brought you your grandson, and I have named him Diego, after the father of my man who is my life and my very blood."

"My daughter, be welcome! I am well now, seeing the child. And that you, my blood brother and my son, love him also. Truly I see now that the Great Spirit chose you both to share a life together, that you might give life in turn."

"I have brought presents for you, Descontarti," Carlos gravely answered, "and Weesayo has remembered her mother, too."

Descontarti's face was impassive, but the crinkling of his eyes indicated his amusement at the young Spaniard's ingenious deviousness. "She is a dutiful daughter, as I knew she would be," he remarked.

Then, offering Carlos his hand, he led him toward the wickiup. "In my old age, I am content to let my daughter follow the ways of the *gringo*, because the *gringo* is bound to me by the sacred ritual of blood as by the union which our shaman performed. I ask only that as I grow older—if the Great Spirit is generous to give me time beyond what I think is allotted to me—he will let me see my grandson and my daughter from time to time."

"I swear to you by the bond of our blood brotherhood, Descontarti, that this will always be done," Carlos at once responded. "And you will not have to ask it of me, for I love your people, and I love this mountain stronghold where first I met Weesayo. My life is as much here as it will ever be in a *hacienda*."

Descontarti, putting his left hand against Carlos's heart, extended his right and held the young Spaniard's in a fervent grip. "Then I am content."

The next day, Carlos sought out Kinotatay and said, "You are John Cooper's good friend, and one of the elders. Tell me with a straight tongue—how ill is Descontarti?"

Kinotatay's face was grave. "He says it is his old wound which he took years ago on a raid against the *mejicanos*. But that is only a part of it, this I think in secret. I would not say this to anyone but you and to *El Halcón*: for if some of our angry young braves—who call us elders cowards, and sleepy old men—were to hear me, they would raise their voices to defy the will of our chief. But I tell you, Señor Carlos, that there are times when he goes to the highest peak of the mountain to be alone with the Great Spirit. And sometimes, when he comes back and he does not think that I have seen him, I see him spit, and sometimes there is blood in it."

"But then I should bring a *médico* to the stronghold to cure him, Kinotatay!" Carlos exclaimed.

Kinotatay shook his head. "This you will not do, I ask it of you as a friend. First, Descontarti would not allow this. Our shaman, Gonordonotay, knows the herbs and the bark and the *medicina* to heal those who have sickness. This he learned from his father who was shaman also before him. Besides, there are many days when Descontarti seems stronger, and it is the will of the Great Spirit, beyond all the shaman can do, which will say whether Descontarti lives or dies. No, Señor Carlos, you must give me your word that you will not speak of this again, nor bring a *médico*."

"I understand. I shall do as you wish, Kinotatay. But when I return to the *hacienda*, I will pray to my God, who is like your Great Spirit, to give long years to the chief of your people. And you must know, Kinotatay, that if ever your people need help, John Cooper, whom you call *El Halcón*, and I will come to fight beside you. Send your fastest horseman to our *hacienda*, and we will bring the loyal men of my father's ranch to help keep the peace between the Jicarilla Apache and Taos."

The day after Carlos, Weesayo, and their infant son, Diego, returned from the Jicarilla stronghold, Carlos sought out his brother-in-law and asked if he might go along with him on Lobo's daily run. "Perhaps, too, *amigo*," he pleasantly suggested, "we can try our skill with the rifles. I confess I have much to learn before I can even equal you."

"That sounds fine, Carlos," the young mountain man said. "I'd like you to come along with me because there's something I want to ask you about. I also think you've something to say to me that you don't want others to hear."

"*¡Mi Dios!*" Carlos pretended to be shocked. "Now you have a new skill, that of reading my mind." And then, looking quickly around, he added under his breath, "*Pero es verdad, amigo*. Yes, I have something to tell you, which I don't want anyone else to hear. So let us get our rifles, you and I, and take Lobo, and see what game we can have him bring back."

"He'll like that. I'm sure Catarina won't mind. She says she's only about a month away from having our baby. I still can't get over how strong your Weesayo is, to have taken little Diego along that mountain trail with the snow and the cold wind."

"That is because," Carlos boasted with a twinkle in his eye, "you did not marry an Apache girl. Now wait a minute for me; I'll get my Belgian rifle and load it and bring some extra ammunition."

"Oh, no, I begin to feel that this is a kind of duel between us," John Cooper exclaimed with a broad grin. "Very well. I'll even give you odds, but the fact is, Carlos, 'Long Girl' has a longer barrel than yours, and that's why I can be more accurate with it."

"We will see," said Carlos, grinning as he sauntered off to get his rifle. John Cooper shrugged, and then whistled for

Lobo. By now, the wolf-dog had the run of the *hacienda*. The training had been completed, and even those *trabajadores* who had been afraid of him at the very outset no longer eyed him with apprehension.

Carlos and John Cooper set off together toward the Sangre de Cristo range, Lobo racing eagerly ahead of them, wagging his tail and glancing back every now and again to make certain they were keeping up with him.

They were beyond the boundaries of the ranch, and Carlos turned and said in a worried tone, "You were right, John Cooper, there is something I want to discuss with you. I do not like the way Descontarti looks. Kinotatay says that he has seen Descontarti spit blood. I asked Kinotatay if I might not bring a *médico,* and he told me I must not even think of such a thing. If Descontarti were to die, there would be trouble with the young braves who are eager to go on the warpath against the Mescalero."

"I have thought of that a good deal, Carlos. You remember that I saw Descontarti before I went out to look for those Texans, and I, too, saw that he was growing weak and older, though he tried hard not to show it. As it is now, the Jicarilla Apache are allies to us here in Taos. If ever the soldiers from Santa Fe or Mexico City were to try to oust Don Diego because he has become too tolerant or has begun to question their authority, I know that Descontarti would send his braves to help us. But if anything happens to him, his braves might become unruly, might even decide to raid our village."

"Ah, the future is so uncertain. You know me well, John Cooper, and you know that I do not want to spend my life raising sheep. But if anything were to happen to my father's ranch, I don't know what we'd all do."

"I've been thinking about that just as much as about Descontarti's being sick. But what would you say, for instance, if I told you that we might look for a new *hacienda,* far away from the authority of Santa Fe? Perhaps somewhere in Texas, where there are no settlers, but where we could be sure of freedom and a chance to raise horses and cattle?"

"If you are serious, I would say yes at once!" Carlos exclaimed. "Perhaps in Texas there is a good life waiting for all of us. Do you know when we might go, John Cooper?"

"I don't. Right now we've got to concern ourselves with those six Texans we've got staying at the *hacienda*. If anybody finds out I brought them back, there's sure to be trouble from Santa Fe. They plan to stay here another few weeks, and then we'll give them some horses and provisions and let them go back to Texas, if they want. Descontarti promised that he would send a scout here to tell us if there were any more of the Mexican troops looking for those who escaped from that battle at the Medina River."

"That's good. They are good men. I have talked with them many times, and they want freedom."

"So do all of us, when it comes down to that, Carlos. Wait now, I thought I saw a deer there in the thicket near that tall spruce tree. Let's see you shoot at it with your Belgian rifle."

"I will!" Carlos quickly shouldered the slender stock of his short-barreled rifle and, holding his breath, waited for the deer to emerge. John Cooper uttered a low whistle, and Lobo pricked up his ears and stiffened, waiting to retrieve.

It was a young buck, with short antlers, and suddenly it bounded out of the thicket and swerved upward along the mountain slope. Carlos squinted along the sight and pulled the trigger. Then he shook his head and uttered in a forlorn tone, *"Caramba,* already I show myself to be a very bad shot. It is a poor start for today's sport, *amigo."*

"Don't reproach yourself, Carlos. It's because of the short barrel of your rifle."

"That is what affected my shot?"

"Sure. Look, when I was a kid, Pa told me how 'Long Girl' would give a man greater accuracy at a greater distance. And here's why. When you hit a mark, everything depends on your being able to hold the front and the rear of your gun barrel in line with the target. Well, now, if your gun barrel is short, it's hard for you to see a slight change of angle, and that would send the bullet away from a target as much as a hundred or more yards away."

Suddenly Lobo barked, and the young men turned to see that the buck had reappeared along the mountain slope. John Cooper carefully adjusted the long Lancaster rifle to his shoulder, squinted along the sight, then pulled off a snap shot. The buck leaped into the air, spun around, then fell onto its side, kicked convulsively for a moment, and then lay still.

As the two young men watched Lobo run off to the slope where the deer had fallen, Carlos remembered that his friend, too, had something he wanted to discuss. "You said you had something to ask me, *mi amigo*," Carlos said.

John Cooper thought for a moment, then spoke quietly. "Well, Carlos, it so happens that I've acquired some—ah—money. In fact, I've got enough so that I can buy some really topnotch horses to begin breeding with, for whenever we get that ranch we talked about. Since you know a lot about good horses, I thought you could tell me if there's any rancher in these parts who might be willing to sell me some."

Aside from Padre Moraga, John Cooper had told no one about the silver he had found, but he knew he could trust Carlos like his own brother. What was more, the young Spaniard was the model of tact and discretion, and John Cooper was certain he would not ask any questions about where the money came from or how much he had.

Carlos had considered a moment, then exclaimed with a smile on his face, "But of course! There is Don Ramón de Costilla. He has a big ranch south of Santa Fe. I have heard from Miguel, who went past there when he went down to the Chihuahua fair last January, that he has Arabian palominos."

"Hey, now, those are real horses! I'd give a lot to get a few, say like a stallion and two or three mares. You could help me breed them. And then if we ever did move to Texas, we could raise them, along with cattle. We could have all the beef we wanted for the *hacienda,* all the workers, and we could even sell some. It'd be a lot more rewarding than just raising sheep."

"I tell you, John Cooper," Carlos said with a sigh, "I am all for it. Even not knowing where or when we'll move, I'd say yes right now. Horse raising! Now that is something I'd like to do!" Then noticing that the wolf-dog was returning, he exclaimed, "Well, you've really trained Lobo. He's coming back to tell you that the deer is dead. I could tell as much from the way it took that shot. I wish I could get a rifle like 'Long Girl.'"

"There will be better rifles than this one, one of these days, you watch and see. And don't think I'm not keeping my eyes open when I run across one. Mine still takes too long to load. Someday, somebody's going to invent a rifle that you can load with two or three shots a minute, maybe. Then you could really defend yourself against bandits or hostiles. All right, let's each carry our share of the deer back. Tía

Margarita has a way with venison that makes my mouth water!"

Miguel Sandarbal, with two of his sturdiest and most dependable workers, all three well-armed and with plenty of provisions, had already departed for the Chihuahua January fair. Before he left, the *capataz* had said his farewells to Bess Callendar and, to his great joy, had obtained her promise that they would be married as soon as he returned. She had, indeed, visited Padre Moraga to ask him to proclaim the banns. "I will hurry back to you, *querida* Bess," he promised. "What a wonderful new year it will be, thanks to you! And every day that I am away from the *hacienda,* I will dream of you, and I will say prayers to the good God, pledging that I shall make you the most devoted and loving of husbands. Thinking of you that way will make the journey shorter."

She smiled and, without a word, kissed him and pressed him close.

But John Cooper's leave-taking from Catarina was not so serene. He knew it was not going to be easy to explain to his wife that he wanted to go off to Don Ramón's ranch near Santa Fe and buy the horses. With the baby due in a month's time, Catarina more than ever alternated between moods of contentment and irritation. To John Cooper's way of thinking, this would be a good time to go off—it seemed he could do little for Catarina except irritate her, and what was more, it seemed more important than ever to purchase the horses and to start preparing for the new life the whole family was going to lead.

"Now you're not to worry in the least, my dearest," he reassured her as he sat on the edge of the bed and told her his plans. "It's not much more than eighty miles to Santa Fe, and a few more beyond to Don Ramón's ranch. I'll certainly be back before the end of November. And one of the Arabian mares, Catarina, will be a present for you. I know how much you love Marquita, but the one I'll choose for you will please you very much."

"Oh, John Cooper," Catarina whimpered, "don't look at me, I am so terribly huge. Oh, I want you with me when our son is born—I just know it will be a son—how he kicks inside of me, wanting to be as free as you are."

"When we have our new horses, Catarina, the stallion will breed with the mares and there'll be ponies for our little son to ride. Yes, all three of us will go riding, just you and I and little Andrew. We'll be together all the time, and we'll have many adventures together."

"I am so afraid I'll have the baby before you come back. I don't care what the midwife says, I just know he is going to be born ahead of time. He is as stubborn and obstinate and willful as you are!"

"I wouldn't say that, Catarina," John Cooper chuckled. "I'd say he's inheriting some of that from you. It seems to me I can remember when you wouldn't look at me for dirt."

"And now you are being mean, when I am lying here helpless! Oh, I feel so useless, and you are just wicked to tease me like that—I know you can't possibly love me anymore, not when I am so big. I think you must hate me looking like a milk cow right now! I know I am ugly, I am sweating, and I am so big—oh, John Cooper, but I do love you, I need you—"

"Hush, Catarina darling," he stroked her flushed cheek and then her hair. "I don't have words to tell you how much I love you. Words don't mean anything between us anymore. We'll have our son. He'll bind us together as nothing ever could. Don't you see, darling, I've been without a family until now. And now it'll be a new life for the three of us."

"I wish it were all over. I say prayers that our son will come quickly. I just can't do anything, do you understand? And the way the midwife keeps after me—you would think I was made of precious china and would break if I want to take a little walk, even around the room here," she complained.

"It'll be over soon. Please don't fret so."

"How can you go away again when you know it is going to be so soon? Oh, how could you?"

"Sweetheart, truly, this is something I have to do— something for the whole family and the new life we're going to have. But I promise I'll be here when the baby's born. I mean it, Catarina, darling. I want to see you hold our son in your arms. I want to kiss you and tell you how wonderful you are, and how much you mean to me."

"But I want you here now!" she sobbed.

"But, Catarina," John Cooper said, becoming more and more impatient. "What difference does it make if I'm here? I just seem to make you angry when I'm around. I can't seem to do anything right. I might as well be away."

Catarina said nothing. She rolled over in the bed and

turned her back to him. John Cooper decided anything else he could say would be in vain, so he got up from the bed and left with a sigh. It seemed there were more problems in this life than he had ever anticipated.

Fourteen

The ranch of Don Ramón de Costilla was about fifteen miles southwest of Santa Fe, not far from the little town of Bernalillo. In the afternoon of the third day after he had left Taos, John Cooper rode his mustang up to the broad rail gate of the *hacienda,* dismounted, and tethered his weary horse to a tall hitching post nearby. In his saddlebags were the two ingots of silver which he had taken from the abandoned mine and buried in Lobo's shed. Clad in buckskin, he wore a leather belt which holstered two of the new pistols Miguel had purchased at the Chihuahua fair last year, and his father's long rifle was in its saddle sling. Around his neck, he wore his Spanish dagger. He could not explain why he wore it on this journey, except that it seemed to him like a kind of talisman. The truth was, he had a presentiment of danger on this mission, and that indeed was what had induced him to wear it about his neck.

He had been told that this nobly born Mexican rancher had been the son of a grandee from Granada, and that his mother had been the daughter of a *hidalgo* from Barcelona. More to the point, he had learned that Don Ramón was arrogant, opinionated, treated his *peones* like slaves, and had several powerful friends in the capital of New Spain who were inclined to overlook his occasional selling of weapons and strong drink to the Indians. Such a man, John Cooper reasoned, would be greedy for profit: the silver ingots would more likely lead him to part with some of his magnificent horses than mere silver or gold coins. Yet at the same time, the young man had ingeniously devised a story that would explain such an unusual form of payment.

The *hacienda* itself was ostentatious, larger than Don

Diego's or Don Sancho's, and there was even a projection of roof to form shade for a long bench where three men sat. Their arms were folded, pistols were thrust through the florid sashes wound round their waists, and the rims of their broad sombreros were decorated with colored Navaho beads. The one in the middle, fat and squat, a jagged purplish scar on his right cheek, rose and ambled toward the gate. "What do you want, *gringo?*" he called in a gruff voice, his eyes squinting with suspicion.

"To see your master, Don Ramón de Costilla. Tell him I wish to buy some of his palominos and that I have *mucho dinero* to pay for them," John Cooper called.

The fat *vaquero*, who was the *capataz* of the ranch, sneered and, turning to his cronies, said something rapidly in Spanish which John Cooper could only partly overhear. It had something to do with the presumption of this *gringo* dressed like an *indio* who dared bother their master with so vainglorious a boast.

"Go away, I will not disturb the *patrón* for such as you," he turned back to declare with another sneer. "Don Ramón is at his ease now. He is punishing a *criada* for breaking a dish."

"He will be able to buy many dishes of the finest china from across the seas with the *dinero* I bring for his horses," John Cooper retorted. Just then, faintly to his ears, came the strangled cry of a young girl. His face momentarily shadowed with the remembrance of the cruel José Ramírez, who had delighted in giving the whip to the helpless maids of Don Sancho's household. Then, in a propitiating tone, he added, "It is not a great crime to break a dish, *amigo*. Besides, if you interrupt the *patrón* now, it will save the poor girl from a worse beating. Then she will be grateful to you and, who knows, you may enjoy her favors."

The fat *capataz* burst into ribald laughter. "Now that is an idea, hombre," he guffawed. "Manuela is a *muchachita* I have wanted to feel my *cojones* for many a night. Perhaps you are right. Very well, I will chance it." He turned back, just as another cry, louder this time, reached John Cooper's ears. "But I warn you, if he is angry with me, my friends, Pedro and Jorge, and I will give you a sound beating and send you back where you came from, *gringo*. Wait here; do not open the gate until you are told to. Don Ramón receives only those guests he approves of, *¿comprende?*"

With this, he went into the house, and after about five minutes returned with his master. Don Ramón de Costilla was a man in his mid-forties, with angular, insolent features, a hawklike nose, high-arching forehead, and a thick goatee. He was dressed in ruffled silk shirt, red velvet breeches, and soft leather *zapatillas*. In his right hand, he carried a flexible black leather riding crop, the flap of which was stained with blood. John Cooper forced himself to smile amiably at this pompous tyrant.

"My *capataz*, Ignacio, tells me that you wish to buy some of my horses and that you have much money. By the bones of Saint Sebastian, I assure you that you will need more than you think! I will have you know that my horses are true Arabians, palominos, bred by a *morisco* in Granada, who brought them from their native land." He swished the riding crop in the air to punctuate his declaration, and stared almost contemptuously at the buckskin-clad man. "I do not believe you have any such sum of money that would interest me in selling even one old mare to you, *gringo*."

"What sum, Don Ramón, would you say we should discuss?" John Cooper riposted.

"Certainly no less than a thousand silver *pesos*," Don Ramón averred.

"I have that and much more, and I should like to buy a stallion and three mares."

"Assuming I would even sell to you from my prize herd, that would mean at least five or six thousand *pesos*. You cannot possibly come prepared with such a sum."

"But I have, and I ask the favor of entering your *hacienda* and showing you that I can pay what you ask, Don Ramón."

"*¡Caramba!*" the foppish rancher swore, impressed despite himself. "In that case, Ignacio, open the gate for the *gringo*. And you, Jorge, go inform *mi cocinera* that I shall have a guest for dinner today. What is your name, *gringo*?"

As the *capataz*, now as fawning as he had been insolent a few moments before, opened the gate, John Cooper came forward and introduced himself. "I'm John Cooper Baines."

"Ah, that explains it!" Don Ramón de Costilla chuckled knowingly. "Yes, I have heard from my friends in Santa Fe that you are the *yerno*, the son-in-law of the *intendente* of Taos."

"Yes, that's true, Don Ramón."

"Well now, why didn't you tell my *capataz* who you were? Do you know, I very nearly gave him a thrashing—I was occupied in chastising a lazy *criada* who is much too clumsy for her own good. But she has had only half her punishment, and I will attend to her after we have finished our business. Now come in, come in, Señor Baines. My *hacienda* is yours."

"*Muchas gracias,* Don Ramón. But as a favor, I'd ask you to spare her." John Cooper glanced with a grimace at the bloody riding crop. "I'd say she's had plenty already for only breaking a dish."

Don Ramón's face hardened, and he drew himself up haughtily. "It is plain that, though you may be the son-in-law of the *intendente,* you are not used to servants. I assure you, Señor Baines, that in this country, so far from my beloved Spain, it is important to maintain discipline as one would in Madrid or Granada or Barcelona. Otherwise, the servants take liberties and forget themselves, you understand."

"Well," John Cooper dryly obsrved, "my father used to say that you could get more out of a mule by cozening it than whipping it. I've sort of leaned to that method myself."

"So you say. But I'm sure Manuela will not soon forget the lesson I began to give her this afternoon. But now, you will want to freshen up, and then join me at the table. I have some superb wine, and my *cocinera* Carmen is a veritable artist. One of my friends in Mexico City, who is returning to Madrid, was kind enough to send her to me two years ago. Out here in this wilderness, she cooks dishes that bring back the happy memories of my days in Granada."

Pedro and Jorge had taken John Cooper's mustang to the stable and quartered it in a comfortable stall with plenty of hay and oats. Before he had entered Don Ramón's *hacienda,* John Cooper had insisted on making sure that his mustang would be properly sheltered, and he had taken his rifle out of the sling; but he had feigned indifference toward the contents of the saddlebags. Thus the two *vaqueros* had paid scant attention to these and the precious contents within.

After a sumptuous dinner, Don Ramón led the way to the stables. John Cooper had never seen such magnificent horses. Some of them were pure white, with flowing manes, long tails, and proud heads, sturdy and sleek. Others were brown and some gray, but all with the same splendid bearing and the indomitable breeding which for generations had made the Arabian palomino coveted. Don Ramón's stable was huge, and there were fully thirty of the breed, each in its spacious, separate stall, with special breeding pens for the stallions and mares. There were also smaller enclosures for the colts, of which there were a dozen.

"Now it's time for business, Señor Baines," Don Ramón said with a smile. "You have seen my palominos, and you tell me that you want a stallion and three mares. And I said five thousand *pesos,* and that is what I demand. Silver *pesos,* mind you. I do not want *reales.*"

"That's satisfactory to me, Don Ramón."

"You say that without even arguing over the price, do you? Well now, you must have untold wealth at your disposal. I should like to see some of it, so that I know that my time has not been wasted."

"Of course. I've brought it along in my saddlebags, Don Ramón."

"In your saddlebags? *¿Verdad?* And now you interest me. Let us go then, to where your mustang is quartered, and see if you really have five thousand *pesos.*"

John Cooper led the way to the stall in which his mustang was quartered. Calmly opening one of the saddlebags, he drew out the two ingots and handed them to Don Ramón.

"*¡Por todos los santos!*" the Mexican rancher ejaculated, his eyes widening with incredulity. "That is pure silver! Where in the world did you find it?"

"It happens that Don Diego's *capataz* dug up the ground of an old shed," John Cooper explained, "and he found these I suppose they must have been hidden years ago, maybe by a *peón* or someone who had found a silver mine and stolen them. All I know is that the *capataz* gave them to me when I told him that I wanted to buy horses."

"*¡Mi Dios!* But this is unbelievable!" Don Ramón hefted each of the ingots and shook his head. "By weight, I should say that each of these is worth about—well, let us be generous, since I have no assayer in this province—three thousand *pesos.*"

"I'd say rather more than that, Don Ramón. But, since I don't want to argue about price and I came by them quite by luck, as I've just told you, will you take them both for the stallion and the three mares?"

"Of course I will! Now, Señor Baines, perhaps, when

you go back to your esteemed father-in-law, you might ask this diligent *capataz* of yours if he thinks he might find more of these. Perhaps we can do more business, you and I? Pure silver—I have never seen such fine quality." Don Ramón hugged the two bars to his chest, his eyes moist and shining with greed.

"I'll ask, but it's a chance in a thousand. I myself didn't believe it when he showed them to me."

"Well, then, in any case, you may have your stallion and your three mares. I'll have Jorge and Pedro tether them, and you can lead them back to Taos. They are docile enough, because they have been well trained. And this stallion has already studded and given me four colts. I shan't cheat you, you see, Señor Baines."

"Nor have I any wish to cheat you, Don Ramón," John Cooper smilingly parried.

Excusing himself, Don Ramón de Costilla hurried back into the *hacienda* to put away the two ingots. When he returned, he was courtesy itself, clapping his hands and ordering Jorge and Pedro to assist this estimable Señor Baines to take back the palominos. The young man watched carefully, rifle in hand, as the two *vaqueros* led out the three mares and the stallion, expertly tethered them, and handed John Cooper the lead rope so that he could attach it to the saddlehorn of his mustang. "Thanks for your hospitality, Don Ramón," he said. "I'm obliged to you for these great horses. I'm going to breed them, and maybe one day my strain can race against yours."

"That indeed would be an honor, Señor Baines. You would be welcome anytime at my *hacienda*. It has been a great pleasure for me to meet you and to do business with you. Remember what I told you—send word to me if your *capataz* has such good fortune again in his digging."

"I'll do just that. Well, now I'll say *adios* and *gracias*." John Cooper climbed into his saddle, clucked his tongue, and started his mustang back to Taos. Glancing back, he saw that his four palominos followed docilely, and he turned back with a contented smile. He only hoped he had outfoxed Don Ramón. He was glad he was leaving early. He didn't have much stomach for a man who had to take a riding crop to a servant girl because she'd dropped a dish—a man who would force his servant girl to submit to his carnal demands. And he didn't like the way Don Ramón had shown such eagerness in wanting to get more of those silver bars. It just might be a good idea to go back sometime soon to the mine and make sure that everything was the way he'd left it.

Don Ramón stood watching him until he had disappeared from sight. Then he turned to address his men. "That *gringo* is a liar. But what is important, *amigos*, is to find out if there is any more of that silver. Ignacio, I showed you what he paid me with, didn't I?"

"*¡Pero sí, patrón!*" the foreman eagerly assented.

"Yes. So his *capataz* dug them up in an old shed? I think I should like to know more about this Señor Baines. Jorge, Pedro, saddle your horses. You will follow, but at a safe distance. See what he does when he gets back to his *hacienda*. You have done errands for me like this before, and you know what to do. If you have to hide near the *hacienda* of the esteemed *intendente* of Taos for a time, do so. I have a feeling that Señor Baines may lead the way to many more of those silver bars. It is something a good friend of mine would like to know about. It is something that will make us all very rich, if we are discreet and careful, *¿comprende?*"

John Cooper took an extra day returning to Taos. He did not want to tire the magnificent horses, but, suspecting that Don Ramón might have him followed, he took a different trail back, doubling on it and going off onto side paths. He was well aware that his story of how he had found the two silver ingots might not be wholly accepted. Moreover, he had taken an instant dislike to Don Ramón and his three *vaqueros*. In fact, during the last few hours of his return to Taos, John Cooper had the uncanny sensation that he was being followed. He had lagged behind on his mustang, halting the Arabians, and pretending to tighten the cinch of his saddle. He saw nothing, and yet the instinct for potential danger, sharpened by his years with the Indians of the plains and the mountains, persisted.

Pedro and Jorge, following their master's orders, had guessed that the young mountain man would not make too speedy a return to Taos, and so they meandered well behind him, allowing him to gain at least a full day on them.

When he reached the *hacienda* at noon of the fourth day on the return journey from Don Ramón's ranch, John Cooper led the palominos into the stable. Miguel Sandarbal and three of his workers had built a special stable near the corral, with Catarina's mare, Marquita, occupying the place of honor.

He saw to it himself that all of the horses were given oats, hay, and water, and then, going into the kitchen, much to Tía Margarita's delight, wheedled her out of a dozen pieces of lump sugar. These he took back to the stable, and fed his own mustang first, then Marquita and Valor, saving the other pieces for the stallion and the three mares. The palomino nuzzled at him, tried to nip him, and John Cooper playfully cuffed him. "You're full of fire. I'll call you Fuego, my friend. And I'll ride you, too, one of these days, just to show you that we're going to be good friends. As for your duties, they'll begin in due time. Be patient now and enjoy your new home. I'm sure I can treat you better than Don Ramón and his unfriendly *vaqueros*."

He returned to the *hacienda* and went directly to Catarina's bedroom. He was back just as he had said he would be, but still he didn't know what kind of reception he would receive.

His worst fears were realized. Catarina would not see him. Amy Prentice, now Amy Corland, came to the *hacienda* daily to visit Catarina while Frank was at work in the shop in Taos. She had just stepped out of Catarina's chamber when John Cooper came down the hall.

"She is resting," Amy said, her eyes lowered. "She does not want to be disturbed."

"Does she know I'm back?" John Cooper exclaimed, his temper rising.

"Yes, she knows," Amy said, trying to control herself. Then she suddenly burst out, "Oh, Mr. Baines—I mean, John Cooper—please don't be mad at me. I'm just telling you what she told me to. I wouldn't want to hurt you, not after all you did for me and my brother."

"Don't trouble yourself about it," John Cooper said gently, realizing that the young girl was getting more than her share of Catarina's bad temper. "We've had a little disagreement, and I guess it's made a bit worse when a woman's having her first baby. Everything'll be all right."

"I'm sorry, John Cooper."

"It's nothing," he said, trying not to show his distress. Then, as he turned to go, he said, "Be sure to give my best to Frank."

As he walked down the hall he made up his mind. Unable to do anything for Catarina, he would make a brief journey to the abandoned silver mine to see that everything was in order. First, however, he hesitantly approached Doña Inez to ask if she might consult with the midwife to determine when Catarina's child was expected. Nothing would prevent his being there when their baby was born. He only hoped that, after the child arrived, Catarina would become less irritable and more understanding.

When he learned that the baby was expected sometime about the second week of December—not for at least two weeks—he headed for the kitchen and packed a sack of provisions. When he had finished, he turned to the cook and said gently, "Tía Margarita, I'm going to ask you a great favor. If Carlos or Don Diego or anyone else asks about me, tell them I've gone to the stronghold to see Descontarti."

Six months ago, Miguel and Esteban Morales had caught two wild mustangs not far from the mountain range where the sheep grazed. They had broken them in and quartered them in the corral. John Cooper did not want to demand another taxing journey of his faithful mustang, so he saddled one of those mustangs. He left the pistols in their holster and put "Long Girl" back in the sling, primed and loaded for immediate use. Then he touched the Spanish dagger in the sheath that hung around his neck, and his eyes narrowed as he remembered Don Ramón's greedy excitement over the silver ingots. Now, more than ever, he was sure that the rancher had sent some of his *vaqueros* to track him down, to see what he was going to do. And if that was true, it was best to meet the challenge at once. Besides, even if he was wrong, it was just as well to make certain that no one else had found the mine. He owed that to Padre Moraga. And he owed that to his plans for the future. Soon, he hoped, he would find a new home where they could all be free of the tyrannical rule of the governor in Santa Fe and the corrupt officials of New Spain. It was his hope, too, that in the new land men would be stronger and would forget the hatreds and prejudices of the Old World.

He was interrupted from his thoughts by the sudden happy bark of Lobo, and a moment later the wolf-dog rubbed his muzzle against John Cooper's leg. "You're just the fellow I'm looking for, Lobo!" he exclaimed. "Come on now, we're going for a long ride to the mountains. Let's go!"

He swung himself astride the mustang, flicked the reins, kicked his heels against the horse's belly, and rode off. Lobo loped along beside him, his yellow eyes bright with eagerness for the adventure ahead of them.

Pedro Rojas and Jorge Tordonas sat attentively in their saddles and watched from a narrow trail high above the range where Don Diego's sheep grazed. Satisfied that they had tracked their quarry, they waited to see what he would do next. Jorge turned to Pedro now and demanded, "What if nothing happens? What if he stays where he is? We'll have had this long ride for nothing!"

"Patience, *amigo*. We'll do what the *patrón* says, and that is all. Even if we have to wait here until dark. If nothing happens, then maybe the story he told the *patrón* is true—but I for one don't believe it. But he just might ride off to the place where he really found those silver bars. And that is what Don Ramón wants to know."

"He talked to you, not to me. Did he tell you what to do if the *gringo* does take us to the place where the silver bars might be hidden?"

"Of course, *mi compañero*," Pedro grinned, showing uneven, decaying teeth. He patted the musket strapped to the saddle of his horse. "We let him take us there, we kill him, we take some of the silver if there is any there, and bring it back to Don Ramón. He has powerful friends; they'll know what to do."

"Perhaps we might take a bar or two for ourselves?" Jorge wheedled.

"*¡Estúpido!*" Pedro exclaimed. "I'll pretend I didn't hear you say that, *amigo*. If I were to tell Don Ramón you even had such an idea—" He did not finish, but drew a stubby forefinger across his throat.

"I meant no harm; it was only a joke." Jorge managed a sickly grin.

"Attend to what the *patrón* wishes, not to your jokes. Wait—do you see what I see?" Pedro suddenly pointed down toward the north. John Cooper on his mustang, with Lobo racing along, had taken the broader trail far below them, the trail that led to the *Montaña de las Pumas*.

"I see him, I see him," Jorge excitedly exclaimed. "The *patrón* knew what he was talking about, *¿no es verdad?* He is going to lead us to the silver, *por todos los santos!*"

"Gently, *compañero*. We will let him get well ahead of us. He must not know that anyone is following him," Pedro explained, and Jorge nodded his comprehension.

John Cooper stopped at sundown only long enough to share some of his provisions with Lobo, and then, having fed and watered his horse, continued at a slackening pace. The two *vaqueros* were at least seven or eight miles behind him, and they made a longer camp, satisfying their hunger with some tortillas made of cornmeal and a little dried mutton, together with a flask of wine.

"The devil take that *gringo*, he is going to travel at night," Jorge complained. "My bones begin to ache."

"We can find his trail. He is well below us, and it goes along the side of the Sangre de Cristo Mountains. Now I begin to see what he plans. The snow will help us find the hoofprints of that *gringo* and lead us to him. Now enough of your talk, *amigo*. I am as tired as you. Let's get into our sleeping blankets. The wind is rising."

Before dawn of the third morning, John Cooper and Lobo reached the plateau leading into the valley beyond which rose the towering peak of the *Montaña de las Pumas*. He could see that the mountain peak was already covered with snow, but only patches here and there showed along the valley.

His provisions had been supplemented by two jackrabbits which Lobo had proudly caught and which he had cooked. He reined in the mustang and looked back, but he saw nothing. Yet the uneasy feeling persisted, and he could not shake it. He remembered how he had slept before attempting to climb that mountain; this time, he would rest only an hour and then begin the ascent with Lobo. If Don Ramón had sent any of his *vaqueros* to follow him, they would soon have to declare themselves. If he was wrong, so much the better: he would return to Catarina a day or two before the time he had allotted to this mission. He meant to take back one of the silver ingots to give to Padre Moraga; next month was Christmas, and the food and clothing the silver would buy would make a fine Christmas present for the poor.

He did not think that those who had come to the Taos fair would have gone back by this obscure trail or even tried to scale that mountain to see what secrets it might hide. From what Descontarti had told him of the habits of the Mescalero, he was equally sure that they would not explore this forbidding peak.

So he contented himself with a brief hour of sleep, sure that, if there should be pursuers on his trail, Lobo would alert him with a bark or growl. Then, mounting his mustang again, he rode quickly over the plateau to reach the lower slope of the mountain and to take the narrow, twisting trail that led to one even more difficult to find—the trail that wound up the mountain to the plateau where he had found the skeletons of the monks and the soldiers and the narrow passageway of that mine inhabited by the guardian dead.

He tied the mustang to the branch of the same oak tree, and then he whistled to Lobo after having taken "Long Girl" out of the saddle sling. Carrying the rifle in his right hand, he drew out each pistol in turn from its holster, assured himself that it was primed and loaded, and then began to climb.

Night had begun to fall, and by the time he reached the plateau that seemed to circle the mountain about four hundred feet from its snowy peak, the stars twinkled in a cloudless sky. The wind tugged at him, and he was grateful for the warmth of the old bear coat.

Another hour of sleep would do no harm. If there were really pursuers after him, they would have to imitate him: leave their horses well below and make the climb on foot. And Lobo would hear the sounds of their ascent and warn him in good time. His heart was pounding quickly now, not only from the rarified air of the mountain and the exhausting climb, but again with the same keen anticipation of danger.

Pedro and Jorge had seen him reach the end of the valley and go up the slope of the distant mountain. Pedro swore under his breath, "The accursed *gringo* will make mountain goats of us. But it can't be helped. It was worth all this time, all this hardship. Don Ramón will reward us. And you, stupid one, you let me do the talking. I know how to flatter the *patrón*. I'll praise him for having guessed exactly what this *diablo yanqui* would do. You will see, he may even turn over Manuela to me."

"*Caramba,* what I wouldn't give to have that *puta* under me right now!" Jorge swore. "It is cold; I can feel it in all my bones."

"There is time enough to be warm, once we have killed the *gringo* and taken back some of that silver to show the *patrón,*" Pedro assured him. "Now it is sure that he is bound to sleep through the night. He has not seen us; he thinks he is safe. So we're going to go up that mountain and find him. It will be easy. We don't have to wait till he leads us right to where the silver is, because he wouldn't have gone up there unless that is where it was, *¿comprende?*"

"*Sí, es verdad,*" Jorge grudgingly agreed. "All the same, to climb that mountain at night—"

"Do you want me to tell Don Ramón that you are a coward and lazy as well? If we don't succeed, it will be your fault. Now, let's go," Pedro grumbled as he spurred his horse forward.

The two *vaqueros* left their horses at the slope of the mountain and groped their way on foot through shrubs and over small boulders until, by chance, they found the winding, narrow trail that John Cooper had taken. The sky was bright with stars, and the night seemed velvety soft. A dozen times or more, Pedro had to clap his hands over Jorge's mouth, for his companion swore and grumbled when he stumbled or fell. But by dawn, they had neared the plateau.

John Cooper had gone toward the northeasternmost edge and, just as the sun broke above the horizon, climbed up to the rocky ledge framed by the two giant fir trees. There lay the skeletons of the soldiers just as before, with their rusted morions, arquebuses, and muskets. The two rusted tripods still stood planted in the ground.

Below the young mountain man and Lobo, and some fifty feet behind them, Pedro Rojas and Jorge Tordonas, crouching low to keep out of sight, perceived their quarry. Pedro, his face damp with sweat, his eyes blazing with gloating joy, slowly raised his musket and cocked it. At that sound upon the silent mountain air, Lobo uttered an angry growl and turned, baring his powerful fangs.

John Cooper had heard the sound also. Whirling, then lunging to one side, he knelt down, leveled the long rifle, and pulled the trigger. Pedro staggered back, his finger tightening on the trigger of the musket, and there was the explosion of a shot as the ball whistled high over John Cooper's head. The *vaquero* lay sprawled on his back, his arms spread in a cross, his sightless eyes staring up at the snowy peak of the *Montaña de las Pumas.*

Paralyzed by the sudden and successful counterattack of their supposedly ambushed quarry, Jorge Tordonas gaped a

moment and then, too late, lifted his musket in shaking hands
and tried to cock it.

With a low growl, Lobo sprang from the ledge down on
the *vaquero*, who—seeing the shaggy, yellow-eyed animal
hurtling toward him—screamed and dropped his musket,
then turned to flee. With a vicious snarl, Lobo sprang at the
vaquero, sinking his sharp fangs into the man's left thigh.

"*¡Madre de Dios!* No, no, help me, señor!" Jorge
screamed, turning and trying futilely with his trembling hands
to grasp Lobo's neck and free himself. Lobo released his prey
only to spring at the *vaquero*'s throat. With a wild shriek of
agony and pain, Jorge Tordonas stumbled back.

"No, Lobo, stop! Enough, stop it, I said!" John Cooper
cried.

Lobo shook the almost unconscious *vaquero* as he might
a rag doll, then he relinquished his grip and sank down to all
fours. Jorge Tordonas staggered to the side, one hand pressed
against the jagged wounds left by Lobo's fangs.

John Cooper drew out the Spanish dagger, balanced it,
and sent it thudding into the *vaquero*'s heart. Without a
sound, Jorge Tordonas sank down on his knees, his eyes
rolling to the whites, then fell over onto his side and lay
still.

"I was right in thinking Don Ramón would have me
followed," he muttered to himself, shaken by the sudden
violence of this cool dawn on the silent mountain. "Lobo, you
saved my life. I'm glad I've tamed you, but not so you can't
fight when we have to keep alive. Good dog, good boy. And
now, I'm going to bury these *vaqueros* so there won't be any
trace."

He slid the two dead bodies off the rocky ledge down
onto the plateau. Then, scrambling down, with Lobo following him and barking in excitement, John Cooper covered
them with rocks and soil until they could not be seen. It was a
kind of funeral cairn. Now the *Montaña de las Pumas* would
have new secrets of the dead.

This done, he ascended to the ledge again and entered
the mine. He took a single ingot of silver, the one he intended
as a gift to the poor of Taos. And then man and dog made
their way back down to find his mustang and, placidly
grazing, the two horses of the dead *vaqueros* of Don Ramón
de Costilla. Tethering them behind his mustang, John Cooper
rode back to Catarina. He would be there in plenty of time to

see his child born. And now, more than ever, he knew that the peace of the *hacienda* would surely be threatened. Perhaps his own as well. For a greedy, arrogant man like Don Ramón de Costilla would not be likely to forget that two of his *vaqueros* sent out to learn about the silver had not returned. One day, John Cooper was sure, he would take other means to learn what had happened to them, as well as to the treasure they had sought for his own coffers.

Fifteen

❖―――――――――――――――――――――――❖

John Cooper rode back to the *hacienda* early in the evening of December 8, 1813, and was greeted by Edward Molson and his cousin, Ben Forrester, who were coming out of the bunkhouse with some of the Mexican *trabajadores*.

"Welcome back, Mr. Baines," Molson called to the young mountain man. "You've got two fine horses there with you."

"Yes, I found them riderless in the mountains and thought it would be a waste of good horseflesh to leave them there with the winter coming on the way it is," John Cooper replied. Then, an idea suddenly struck him. "Have you and your cousin and your four friends decided what you're going to do, I mean about going back to Texas?"

"We'd sure like to, Mr. Baines," Forrester earnestly spoke up. "Only, all of us have been talking it over the last week or so, and we've just about come to the conclusion that so long as the Spaniards are in control, there could be another invasion by their troops at any time."

"Well, if you wouldn't go back to Texas, then where might you go?" John Cooper pursued.

"Maybe to Missouri," Molson replied. "There's plenty of hunting and fishing and trapping, and there's good farm land, and we could raise horses and cattle there, I'm thinking. Maybe all six of us, if we had any kind of a grubstake, might want to try our luck back there. At least, we'd be far enough away from those damned soldiers who come from across the Rio Grande and act as if they own part of this country."

"I'm going to talk to Don Diego about you men," John Cooper answered. "I think maybe we can raise that grubstake you mentioned. To start you off with on your future plans, why don't I make you a present of these horses? They're good, sturdy mounts; they'll ride you a long ways without tiring. Put them in the corral, and maybe you can even brand them with the marks you used to use back in Texas."

"That's mighty decent of you, Mr. Baines. We won't forget what you did for us, not ever," Edward Molson said as they shook hands.

Now seeing Teofilo Rosas, John Cooper turned to him and called out, "*Holá*, Teofilo. What's the news of my wife?"

"Tía Margarita was just saying at the *almuerzo* that the midwife is here and thinks the child will be born in a few days' time, Señor John Cooper!"

"Wonderful! That's just wonderful!" John Cooper was beaming. "I have to go on an errand now, but I'll be back in an hour. Would you look after Lobo?"

"My pleasure, Señor John Cooper!" Teofilo grinned from ear to ear.

"You look like a happy man. I'm guessing that Leonora has said 'yes' to you, Teofilo," John Cooper said with a sly grin.

"*¡Es verdad, sí!* Ah, I tell you, Señor John Cooper, there is nothing like a *muchacha linda* to make an old man feel young again. Next week, would you believe it, Padre Moraga is going to marry us, and in Don Diego's own chapel. Truly, I am a happy man! Well, we'll watch Lobo for you until you come back. And I know that your lovely señora will be very glad to see you!"

"*Gracias*, Teofilo," John Cooper said, lowering his eyes, wondering if the older man knew that Catarina had, in fact, refused to see him. Then he untied the two horses which had belonged to Don Ramón's *vaqueros*, and Edward Molson took the lead rope and led them to the corral.

Mounting his mustang, John Cooper rode toward Taos and tethered his horse at a hitching post to one side of the church, glanced round to make sure that no one was watching, and then took out the silver ingot which he had packed in his saddlebag. Tucking it under his buckskin jacket, he went into the church and found the white-haired priest kneeling before the altar, head bowed and hands clasped in silent devotions.

John Cooper knelt down, crossing himself, and prayed silently. A few moments later, Padre Moraga rose and turned, a look of joyous surprise on his face. "My son, it is good to see you again!"

"And you, too, Father. Might we go into the rectory? I've brought you something—something for the poor this Christmas."

The priest nodded with a benign smile, and John Cooper followed him into the rectory. He drew out the silver ingot and placed it upon a small table near the door. "I have been to the mine again, Padre Moraga, and I took this one bar because I wanted to give it to you for your poor. Is there anyone you can trust to melt it down and maybe to arrange to turn it into food and clothes and the things some of the Pueblo Indians and the *peones* will need, Father?"

"Yes, I know a man, a widower who comes to church every day to pray for his wife's soul in heaven. He is a man of my age, and he is also one of us, the Penitentes. He is Heitor Nuñez, and, as you know, he repairs weapons. He also makes religious articles for the poor, and he charges them very little. Rosaries, reliquaries, and such—"

"Yes, I know him. He's a good, kind man."

"Indeed. His health is not good, and he will soon be among the saints, as I know his wife is already. I think that, if I were to give him this silver bar, he would be able to melt it down and to use it in his work, and in return he would buy food and clothes which I could distribute to the poor of Taos on the blessed day of the birth of our dear Lord."

"Good. That's what I want to do, then, Padre Moraga. And Padre—" John Cooper hesitated, then went on to explain about the two men he was forced to kill in self-defense.

The priest studied him for a moment, and said, "I have told you before, my son, that your heart is good and that, wherever you have gone and wherever you will go, God blesses you because of your honesty and your truthfulness. You did this in self-defense. God knows that."

"Would you say a prayer for me now, Padre Moraga, because Catarina's going to have her baby anytime now, and I'm hoping it'll be a son. I want to name him after my father, Andrew."

"We shall pray together, my son. And it will be a joy to me, if you will allow it, for me to baptize your child when the time is ready."

"Yes, Catarina and I'd want you to do that, Padre Moraga. Thanks."

The little priest opened the drawer of a table and hid the silver bar at the back, covering it with a cloth which a Navaho had woven. Then, his face serene, his lips moving silently, he took John Cooper by the hand, and the two of them went before the altar and knelt together in prayer.

Two days later, Doña Inez came up to John Cooper and solicitously told him that Catarina had just begun her labor and that the midwife was with her. She told John Cooper that it would not be wise for him to see her now, and then she added, "As I told you before, John Cooper, the last two months have been very hard for Catarina. And she's been angry with you for leaving her, when she was so near her time. She said to me yesterday that, if the baby came and you were not here to see it, she would never forgive you." Doña Inez put a hand on the young man's shoulder and added, "Of course you know she doesn't mean it, because this is all so new for her. You see, John Cooper, she has turned from spoiled child to willful girl and then to wife, and now she enters the most wonderful, but demanding, stage of life there could be for a woman—being a mother. You must put up with her scoldings, and there is something more—you must learn that now you won't take the central and only place in her life, John Cooper."

"You've been wonderfully good to me, Doña Inez. You know, if it hadn't been for your advice that time, we might not have even gotten married." He grinned. Then, his face sobering, he added, "I understand what you've told me. Since I've known Catarina, I've learned more about human nature than in all the time I spent by myself and among the Indians. I've learned that human relationships are very complicated and very demanding, and I've had to adjust a lot to my new way of life. After I met Catarina, everything changed for me."

"Yes," Doña Inez mused, "a woman can do that for a man. And if she is worth it, he adjusts himself." Then she, in her turn, smiled reflectively and went on, "For me, John Cooper, it was a question of patience, and of hiding my love for the man I so much admire and respect. And I told myself that, if it ever did happen—and I wasn't sure it could or would—I would be ever so willing to adapt myself to make him happy, even if it meant a drastic change in my own habits. But that is because I am a woman, you see. And you are a strong young man. You have had a lot to endure, terrible hardships and sorrows, too, and now you are your own man and master. And still so young—"

"I'd almost forgotten—tomorrow's my twenty-first birthday, Doña Inez," John Cooper said.

She sighed and shook her head. "How many long and happy years await the two of you! But when you are older, just as I am, John Cooper, you will learn to appreciate each new day for what it can bring you. When you reach my age, you will know that your days are numbered, and because of that you will find that you are deeply grateful for each new day of life which the good God grants you. In a way, it makes one humble and also more perceptive of the important things: the love and trust between two people, the integrity and the honor of family ties, the strength that creates a bulwark against hate and envy." Then she gave a nervous laugh and shook her head again. "Listen to me, talking like an old woman!"

"You're certainly not that. You're very beautiful—you're more beautiful now than when I first saw you, Doña Inez. And I know that's because Don Diego loves you and you love him. And that's the way I hope it'll be always for Catarina and me," John Cooper told her.

She took out her handkerchief and blew her nose, turning away from him to hide her tears. Then, in an airy tone, she bantered, "Now see what you have done! This is a time for happiness, not for dwelling on the past by giving you a sermon on old age, John Cooper! Let us both go into the chapel and pray for Catarina." She took his hand and led him to the chapel.

For some reason he could not explain even to himself, John Cooper had decided to sleep outdoors, beside the *hacienda,* in his bearskin coat and buckskin costume. The cool air was invigorating, and it helped clear his thoughts, tempered his anxiety over Catarina's imminent ordeal, and made him think also of all that Doña Inez had said to him.

He thought to himself, too, that there was a kind of justice in sleeping on the hard ground outside, under the stars, with the snowy mountains beyond, to remind him of the hardships he had endured in order to survive, to come this far to find a new life and love and—something he had never dreamed might happen—his first child. It was right—assuming it would be a boy, and he'd prayed for that, both with Padre Moraga and with Doña Inez—to name it after his father. That way, his father's name would go on after him. And if little Andrew grew up to be a man only half as good and kind as his grandfather had been, then he'd be a son a man could really be proud of.

And besides, out here on the hard ground, though he was warm in the old bearskin coat and his buckskins, he was punishing himself a little for having neglected Catarina. She was going through an awful ordeal, and he was also just a little scared about it. Now he was remembering something he'd overheard his mother once say to his father. He hadn't known what it meant at the time, but now it came back to him and that was what scared him. Virginia, his older sister, had been sixteen; she'd been the first child. And he'd heard his mother say, "Virginia was a hard birth for me, but the others were easy, Andrew."

Suddenly he stiffened, for he had just heard a faint cry from inside the *hacienda*. He rolled over onto his back and looked up at the starry sky, and he said aloud, "Please, dear God, don't let it be hard for her. She's just a girl, she's never had any real suffering or worries. She can't be used to a lot of pain. Please make it easy on her, God. You know I love her. I'm going to take care of her and the baby, see if I don't. Don't take it out on her because I had to kill those two *vaqueros*, God. You know I didn't want to. I had to. And maybe they weren't to blame, because they were only taking orders from their *patrón*. Yet they had to die, or they'd have killed me first."

There was another cry, shriller this time, and he ground his teeth and rolled over onto his side and closed his eyes.

He felt himself drowsing off and tried to fight it, wanting even in this isolated way to share Catarina's ordeal. But the events of the last weeks had taken a greater physical toll from him than he guessed, and before he knew it, he was fast asleep.

It was Tía Margarita who found him shortly after dawn, as she left the *hacienda* to go to the well to draw water for the morning meal. Dropping her bucket, she clasped her hands and cried out, "May the saints protect us all! Señor

Baines, are you *loco?* You will catch your death of cold like
this—oh, to sleep outside all night long—what a calamity!
Wake up, wake up, Señor Baines, the Señora Catarina has a
son, born just a few minutes ago! He is so strong and healthy
—oh, Señor Baines, come into the *hacienda,* you must be
chilled to the bone! *Pobrecito,* why did you do such a thing?
You have a son, Señor Baines!"

She had reached down to shake him, and he sprang to his
feet, still groggy with deep sleep. And then he understood,
and he uttered a whoop of joy. "Eeeyyaahh! A son, you said,
Tía Margarita? I love you, and for news like that, I promise
you I'll buy you the prettiest dress in all Taos!"

Again, he uttered a joyous whoop, seized her by the
hands, and danced a jig with her until she was out of breath.
Then, half-laughing, half-ready to cry, he strode into the
hacienda and went toward Catarina's bed chamber. The
midwife, Juana Cortado, was just emerging. "Is she all right?
And the baby?" he anxiously demanded.

"It was a beautiful birth, *señor.* Your lovely wife was
very brave, and it really did not take too long for a first one.
Ah, you can be proud of him; he's strong and he has his
mother's black hair and your blue eyes, Señor Baines."

"That's wonderful!"

"And she says she wants to see you. She kept saying
your name all night long. So go to her, but only for a
moment. You understand, she is still very weak. But she is so
happy—ah, it is like a blessed miracle to see her with the
child at her breast. And she is already calling him Andrew—
is that the name you wished for your son, Señor Baines?"

"Oh, yes, yes, it was my father's name. God bless you,
señora. And thank you for being with my wife and caring for
her and—and for my son." Those last two words came
hesitantly, but his eyes shone with joy and pride. He took her
hands and squeezed them and added, "I know where you live,
señora. This afternoon I'll bring you fifty *pesos."*

"Oh, no, Señor Baines!" the midwife gasped, shaking her
head. "That is too much, I wouldn't think of asking for such
a sum!"

"But it's my first son, and my wife and child are well,
and I'm grateful to you. I shall see you this afternoon. And
God bless you again, señora." He opened the door and went
in. The midwife smiled after him, shook her head, and sighed.

He stood staring at Catarina, unable to speak for the

emotions that welled up in him. She did not see him yet, for she had turned her head to look down on her infant son, whom she cradled against her breast. When he saw the look of devotion and love on her face, drawn and pale from the ordeal of birth, he looked up at the ceiling and his lips moved in a silent prayer of thanks to Him who had answered his heartfelt prayer. And then he said softly, "Dearest Catarina, may I see our son?"

"Oh, Coop, *querido* Coop! You are here with me—yes, I prayed you would be. I was so afraid when you were gone that you wouldn't be back in time. Look, isn't he adorable? He has your eyes, *mi corazón*."

He came over to the other side of the bed, knelt down, and reverently stared at the child in its swaddling clothes. Tentatively, he put out his forefinger and touched the baby's forehead and mouth, and the baby gurgled, and he uttered a nervous, yet happy laugh. "He—he likes it—"

"I'm sure he has recognized his father already. Oh, it's so good to have you with me and with little Andrew. Now we're really a family, *mi amor*."

"Yes, a family, Catarina. It's the most wonderful birthday present anybody could ever have in all his life. I love you, Catarina. I love our son. I swear I'll make you both very happy, and all three of us will share things together. When he grows up, I'll take him hunting and fishing and trapping and—"

"My goodness, Coop, he's only such a tiny little baby yet—give him time to be a little child and to learn to know you and to talk first," Catarina gently teased. She saw the concern and the love in her husband's face, and tears began to run down her cheeks as she lifted her head from the pillows, inviting him to kiss her.

"Catarina, my beautiful, darling Catarina, my wife, my love, the mother of my son," he said slowly, as if he could not believe the wonder of this moment. And when he kissed her, there was a soft little sound from the baby, as if it, too, rejoiced in this deeper pledge of fervent love and devotion.

"Oh, Coop," Catarina said looking up at him, her eyes now mournful. "I am so sorry I have been so bad to you, so awful. I really didn't want to behave that way—I don't really want to be so spoiled and temperamental anymore—but I was afraid, Coop. This is all so new to me."

"I understand, my dearest one, *mi corazón*. And it is all

so new for me, too. I just want what's best for you, for us, for our family. I want to plan for our future; I want to keep you safe, protect you. And I want to share with you the things I like, the things I do."

"Do you know what, Coop?" she said as he caressed her hair. "I'd like to ride with you and go back to the Apache stronghold. You remember how we watched those two get married by the medicine man, and how they rode off to their secret wickiup? Well, I'd love to go back there, and maybe they would let me build you our own little place, and we could have a sort of second honeymoon. Would you like that, my dearest?"

"It's a beautiful idea, Catarina, my darling. Of course we'd have to ask Descontarti to look the other way since it's not exactly according to Apache law," he added with a chuckle.

"Oh, he will, I know it. And I know I will be everything you want me to be."

"And I will be everything you want, too. And—I almost forgot. I got you a present. A beautiful mare."

"Oh, Coop, I can't wait to see it."

"And there will be a colt for little Andrew here," he said, and they both laughed when the little child raised his arms and sneezed.

John Cooper bent down and kissed his son and then his wife. For a moment, there was in his mind the sudden piercing sorrow of remembrance of the past, of having once been orphaned. Yet here, at the other end of this vast young country, with his wife and his son beside him, John Cooper Baines realized that the eternal cycle of life has ways of compensating for tragic loss.

Sixteen

Even in this new year of 1814, the news had still not yet reached Taos that, in the middle of last October, the allies had scored a decisive victory over Napoleon in the battle of Leipzig, also called the Battle of the Nations. Austria had joined the coalition of Russia, Prussia, England, and Sweden. And in this battle, most of the Corsican's German auxiliary forces had deserted to the allies. Now for the first time, it could be seen that his power was broken—there were 120,000 casualties in the four-day battle—and now the allies would pursue him into France. His days were numbered, and when they were at an end, a rightful king would once again ascend the throne of Spain.

Nor did the isolated citizens of Taos learn that, in the last month of the old year—although Fort Niagara had been taken by the British under General Gordon Drummond, who had, scarcely two weeks later, burned Buffalo and Black Rock with his combined British and Indian troops—the British schooner *Bramble* had arrived at Annapolis under a flag of truce, bearing dispatches offering peace terms in the war between the Americans and the British.

It was of far greater concern to the people of Taos that, in the first month of the new year of 1814, Lieutenant Santa Anna had taken a band of soldiers and slaughtered fifty rebels who operated as a robbery band, claiming that they were the heirs of the Hidalgo revolution. It was ominous news. It suggested that the struggle for power in New Spain could be won by a few ruthless men who had ambition and daring enough to defy the laws, even as they proclaimed that they served the country best by their brutal tactics. And the young, ambitious, amoral Santa Anna was already planning to become Mexico's despot. He claimed, "A hundred years to come, my people will still not be fit for liberty. A despotism is the proper government for them."

Although Lieutenant Jaime Dondero had been a good friend of Santa Anna's, the latter shed no tears for him when it was reported that he and six of his men were missing in action. General Arrendondo read their names in Mexico City and awarded them posthumous medals for valor. They had died, he sententiously announced, in the great cause of crushing traitors, and their names would long be remembered.

But in the household of Don Diego de Escobar this January, there was peace and love and happiness, and much hope for the future, if not in Taos, then in some new land of opportunity and freedom. Carlos and Weesayo delighted in seeing their infant son grow sturdier each day. And, greatly to Catarina's joy, John Cooper spent long hours with her almost every day, playing with their little son, Andrew, and showing her, in many ways, how greatly he cherished her and the child.

By the middle of the month, Catarina had so thoroughly recovered that she began to urge John Cooper to keep his promise to her: they must have a kind of second honeymoon in the Jicarilla Mountains. "I mean it, Coop darling," she earnestly declared one sunny afternoon, as he was holding Andrew in his arms and making faces at the baby, who gurgled and waved his tiny arms. "I want to go there, and I want to build a wickiup, just for the two of us, darling. I want to pretend that we are being married for the first time, because it was so beautiful, that ceremony we saw there. And that way, too, don't you see, I'll be sharing things with you, I'll be going along with you."

"I'd like that very much, *mi corazón*. But there's just one thing—Andrew's far too tiny to take along that mountain trail in winter."

"I've already thought of that," she said, her face bright and happy. "I've decided we will leave him with Concepción." Concepción, the wife of Esteban Morales, had recently given birth and was the wet nurse for little Andrew.

"That would be wonderful. But you'll have to ask her if she's willing."

"Yes, I will, this very day! Oh, it will be so wonderful. I shall ride the new mare you got for me, and we will ride together and we will camp till we get there, and then I'll build you your wickiup while you talk to your friends there and to the chief, Descontarti. You will have to tell him how wonderfully Weesayo's baby is doing, too, Coop."

"Of course I will," he laughed, amused by her burst of enthusiasm and secretly welcoming it. Having been cloistered in the *hacienda,* he was again beginning to long for the outdoor life which once had been his greatest solace.

"Here, then, Coop, you keep Andrew, and I'll go find Concepción," Catarina exclaimed. She leaned over to kiss him, then hurried to the door, blew him another kiss, and disappeared. He grinned sheepishly, sat down on a chair, and began to rock little Andrew in his arms. It was fascinating how already the tiny baby could look like the people who brought it to life, he thought. It certainly did have his blue eyes, and there was no doubt about Catarina's black hair. Gingerly, he put his forefinger out and touched the baby's cheek. At once, Andrew burst into a radiant smile.

"My gosh, you're quite some feller," John Cooper said huskily. "You're going to be a big, strong man when you grow up. I shouldn't wonder you'll be able to thrash me not many years off from now, if you don't like my telling you to do something. Seems to me, Andrew, you're going to be able to decide things for yourself and go ahead and do them. Well now, that's the way I was brought up, I guess. And by and large, it's not a bad way. You make some mistakes, but you pay for them right off, and you learn not to do the same fool thing a second time, if you want to keep alive. Yes, maybe experience is the best teacher, as Pa used to say to me."

As Catarina hurried toward the Morales's cottage, she came upon Doña Inez stooping to pet Lobo.

"Good afternoon to you, Tía Inez!" Catarina called. Then, with a little teasing moue, she added, "I am so used to calling you that, when I should call you *mi madre.*"

"I like Tía Inez just as much, to be truthful, dear Catarina." Doña Inez straightened and came smilingly toward her stepdaughter. "How lovely you look today, how radiant! One would never suspect, you minx, that you are already a mother and a very beautiful wife. And I'll wager John Cooper doesn't quite know what to make of you."

"Oh, is that so?" Catarina giggled, quite forgetting the dignified status of which Doña Inez had just reminded her. "I'll have you know that he has agreed to take me to the mountains, and there I am going to build a wickiup, and we are going on a sort of second honeymoon, just as if we were Apache. You know, the way Carlos and Weesayo were first married before Padre Moraga married them here in the chapel."

"I think that is a splendid idea. But your baby, darling—"

"Oh, I was just going to see Concepción. She will certainly be willing to take care of little Andrew."

"Yes, you are right. And, Catarina, I have some news to share with you. Can you guess what it is?"

"I can't guess. What do you mean, Tía Inez?" Catarina's curiosity was aroused, and she stared wide-eyed at her aunt.

"I—I am going to have a child myself, my dearest Catarina," Doña Inez said softly, and her cheeks turned crimson. "My prayers have been answered. I am the happiest, luckiest woman in all the world."

"Oh, Tía Inez, I am so glad for you—oh, that is wonderful news—and here I am thinking selfishly of going off on a honeymoon when you are going to have a baby—"

"Now, now," Doña Inez laughed heartily as she hugged John Cooper's beautiful wife, "you mustn't carry on as if it were such a momentous thing. After all, having a baby is quite natural and quite to be desired when one is married and in love. You have already proved that, and so did Weesayo. So why shouldn't I have my turn, too?"

"Oh, I know, but I am so happy for you, Tía Inez! When is it going to be?" Catarina whispered.

"I think sometime in August, *querida*."

"Oh, my! I shall have to visit Amy Corland and have her make a specially pretty dress for you. I want it to be my present. I love you so, Tía Inez!" Again she flung herself into her aunt's arms, and then questioningly whispered, "Have you told Father yet?"

"No, *mi corazón*. I wanted to be very sure of it. But I am now. I shall tell him tonight, when we are alone. It is something very precious when a woman has something like that to tell the man she loves. I want it to be just at the right moment. You understand."

"Of course I do! Oh, it is so wonderful! God bless you, Tía Inez, and thank you for really having been a mother to me—and I mean that with all my heart!"

With a happy little laugh, she hurried off to the Morales cottage, and Doña Inez stood staring fondly after her, then stooped again to rub Lobo's head and to murmur, "Indeed, Lobo, every day that I see you running about free and friendly with all of us, I am reminded how greatly your master changed the lives of everyone in this *hacienda*—yes, and for the better. May God bless him and dear Catarina and their adorable *niño!*"

Concepción Morales had told Catarina that she considered it a great honor to be privileged to take care of little Andrew. And so, two days later, John Cooper and Catarina set out for the Jicarilla Mountains. The day before, John Cooper had saddled the gentle palomino mare and let Catarina ride her so that horse and mistress would be accustomed to each other when the long journey began. For himself, he selected a sturdy young gelding, since his usual mount was a mustang stallion which might easily make overtures to the mare and delay the journey.

Their journey was a picturesque one, for snow covered the upper slopes and the peaks of the majestic Sangre de Cristo, the air was clear and cold, and the sky marvelously blue with only a few drifting clouds. Somewhat to John Cooper's surprise, Catarina had insisted that Lobo accompany them. "I want him to come along with us this time, dear Coop," she had told him. "Now that I know and love you so dearly, and know that he is your close friend and companion, I want us all to share in this honeymoon of ours."

Lobo welcomed the decision, and raced ahead of them, often stopping to look back, his yellow eyes bright with the joy of freedom. On their first night, he caught a rabbit and brought it into the little cave where they made their shelter for the night. And this time it was Catarina who built the fire and cooked the rabbit while John Cooper skinned it and cut it into equal pieces. This time, too, she ate ravenously and made friends with Lobo by offering him tidbits from her own share. The wolf-dog wagged his tail and nuzzled against her, and John Cooper laughed joyously and rubbed his knuckles over Lobo's head to make him emit that curiously catlike purr that was his sign of pleasure and contentment.

Then, after the cooking fire had been extinguished, Lobo moved outside the cave at John Cooper's order and lay vigilantly watching. The young mountain man took Catarina in his arms and kissed her gently, and she whispered endearments to him as she cupped his face with her soft hands and returned his kisses. They talked as lovers talk, reminding each other of their first moments together, and then how each had known, in turn, the love that now bound them. And they were chaste with each other, both moved by an exquisite tenderness which contented itself with communication, with kisses, with long silent looks, and the knowledge that each was there to protect the other while the wind howled outside and, from afar, the night birds called.

They rode into the stronghold on the morning of the fourth day, and Descontarti was there to welcome them. Again, John Cooper observed with great concern that the Apache chief's face seemed drawn with the pain he refused to show, but Descontarti's voice and bearing still retained the vibrant strength of a chief.

"*El Halcón* and his *Paloma* do us honor by coming here," he declared with a warm smile, as he clasped hands with the young man and then turned to Catarina to greet her. "You are happy with your man, señora?"

"Much more than that, Descontarti," Catarina replied. "We have a son. And we have named it after the father of *El Halcón*."

"That is a good thing," Descontarti gravely nodded. "I know this is a thing white-eyes do out of respect and love. With our people, once the Great Spirit takes a brave into the sky, we do not again speak his name. But this is not to say that we do not honor and respect him as much, though we keep it silent. And now, I will have one of the squaws prepare a wickiup for you while you stay with us."

At this, Catarina turned to John Cooper and sent him a pleading look. He smiled and nodded for her to say what she wished.

"I do not wish to offend you, Descontarti," Catarina falteringly began. "I have great respect for your laws and for your people. And love for them, too, for you gave my *esposo* friendship and comfort while he lived with you before I met him."

"I hear you, my daughter," Descontarti said. "Say to me

what is in your heart. For the Apache, those who speak with a straight tongue do not give offense."

"Thank you. It—well, I would like to pretend that *El Halcón* and I came to the stronghold to be united. You remember, how you let us watch when your shaman performed the ceremony with those young people?"

"Yes, I remember, my daughter." Descontarti regarded her with solemn interest, yet John Cooper could see the hint of a smile of secret amusement on the Apache chief's lips.

Heartened by his encouraging attitude, Catarina pursued, "It is my wish, Descontarti, to learn how to build a wickiup for my *esposo*, El Halcón. And to spend time with him alone in our secret place. I ask you to permit this, if it does not break your law."

Now Descontarti smiled outright, casting a glance at John Cooper to show his amusement at so unusual a request. Finally, he answered, "My daughter, I feel that you speak with a straight tongue, and from a warm, loving heart. *El Halcón* has, I see, told you of our customs. By Apache law, once a man and a woman have been united and spent their time of secret oneness in the wickiup she has constructed for her man, they may never go back to the place. Yet, though *El Halcón* is my blood brother, he was united to you by white-eyes law, and thus the law of our tribe does not rule here. Since I believe that you are sincere in this wish and that, in this sincerity, you pay tribute to our ancient laws, I will grant you this wish, my daughter."

"I am very grateful, Descontarti. You are very kind," Catarina impulsively exclaimed, tears sparkling in her green eyes. Only a warning sign from John Cooper prevented her from so forgetting herself as to embrace the Apache chief: that would have been to profane him. John Cooper interposed, "Weesayo has sent with me a message, Descontarti, that she and the child are strong and well and that she wishes to be remembered to her beloved father. And Carlos, her *esposo*, sends also his greetings and his pledge that he will always regard the Light of the Mountains as his beloved woman, and that he will teach the child the good Apache ways."

"That is pleasing to my ears, *Halcón*," Descontarti replied.

"Near Santa Fe, I was able to purchase three palomino

mares and a great stallion," John Cooper continued. "I shall
use these to breed fine horses. And I have promised the first
colt to your son, Pastinari."

Descontarti's dark eyes brightened. "I will tell my son.
Then he will not be so envious of my Lanza. I thank you in
his name. And now," he turned to Catarina, "I will send for
a squaw who is wise in such things. She will help you build
this wickiup of love so that you and your man may take shelter in the peacefulness of our mountains."

The Apache chief had the squaw summoned, and Catarina was introduced to her. Kitomani, first wife of the warrior,
Cochinda, an elder in the council, said she would be pleased
to be of assistance, and for the next three days the two young
woman spent long, happy hours near the far end of a
southern canyon. It was perhaps half a mile from the place
where Weesayo and Carlos had pledged their eternal troth
under the starry skies and known their ten days and nights of
primal joy in union.

The squaw instructed Catarina how to make the frame
of the wickiup, and what foods to bring. And she had brought
a string of silver bells which Catarina tied to the sides of the
door. Caterina had also cut pine boughs and bittersweet
and strewn some inside the wickiup, putting others in clay
bowls to brighten the interior and to convey a sweet perfume.

On the morning of the fourth day, when she and the
squaw returned to the stronghold, she went to John Cooper
and, taking him by the hands, whispered, "Everything is in
readiness for my love, for my *esposo*. Put me on your horse
and ride me to our secret wickiup, *mi corazón*."

And when he dismounted and lifted her down, he
walked hand in hand with her toward this hymeneal dwelling.
He halted her before it, and taking her by the shoulders, he
kissed her lingeringly on the mouth and murmured, "My
Catarina, now truly you are the mate of *El Halcón*. I see what
you have done, how industrious you have been, how eager you
have been to learn the customs of these kind people who gave
me life and shelter. It is as if we are beginning again,
Catarina. Yes, it's a good, a wonderful thing. I love you,
querida. I shall always love you. And now you know, here
under this vast sky with the pure air and the peacefulness of
being alone together, what brings me back to the mountains,
what takes me from you. But now you are a part of this, and

you will no longer be jealous if I must leave you. You'll understand why—in taking my freedom, Catarina, I take you with me in spirit always."

Then he lifted her up and entered the wickiup, and the silver bells tinkled as he brushed against them. She sighed raptly, tightening her hold round his neck, closing her eyes and surrendering herself to this exquisite magic. "Can we spend ten days and nights here, Coop?" she whispered.

"Yes, but no longer, my dearest one. If we did, that would be too selfish, and Descontarti would think that perhaps after all we did not respect the customs of his people. It was a great favor he did us by allowing this. We must not take advantage of his kindness."

"I almost wish it were forever, *querido!*" she confided as he lay her down upon the bed of blankets, under which she had placed sweet-smelling herbs. "Yes, now I understand what draws you here, Coop. Only this time, I am with you, and I can share all that you feel and love so much."

"We will learn more about each other, my darling, now that we're here in the mountains with no one around us," he murmured.

And when the ten days and nights were done, he lifted her onto his mustang and then rode back with her to the wickiup of Descontarti. There they both thanked the Apache chief, and Catarina regained her palomino mare which had been quartered in the camp corral. Lobo, all these days and nights, had guarded the wickiup of his beloved master and new young mistress.

When it was time to depart for the *hacienda*, John Cooper said to Descontarti, "I will pray to my Great Spirit, my blood brother, to give you strength and long years to guide these people and to keep their peace here in these beautiful mountains. And never forget, Descontarti, that if ever you need me, you've only to send a rider to the *hacienda*. I thank my blood brother for his hospitality and for his kindness to my mate."

"May the Great Spirit guide you both safely back and grant you both long life and the love I see you bear so deeply for each other," Descontarti solemnly answered. He stood watching as they rode down along the trail back to Taos, and he lifted his right hand just as they turned the bend and disappeared from view.

He stood a long moment after they had disappeared, and

on his impassive face there was suddenly a grimace of pain. Mastering it and stiffening, he took a deep breath, turned, and went back to his wickiup.

To Catarina's surprise, John Cooper detoured their return journey by riding to the isolated mountain where he had discovered the abandoned silver mine. When his young wife asked him why he had come so far out of his way and what there could possibly be on that mountain to attract his interest, he had evasively replied, "*Querida,* a long time ago, I found some old holy relics which I gave to Padre Moraga. I want to go see if I can find any more because I'd like to give them to him for the church. I'll ask him to hold a *novena* for our little son, Andrew." Catarina, devout Catholic that she was, was satisfied at this answer, though by now the lengthy excursion in the mountains in this cold winter had dampened her enthusiasm for the outdoor life, and she was anxious to return to the comfort of the *hacienda.*

He induced her to tether her palomino mare beside his mustang at the slope of the mountain and then took her up the winding trail. Halfway up, however, she protested against this arduous ascent. He then sent Lobo to hunt, and the wolf-dog came back with a mountain quail, which, when roasted over the fire, made tasty eating. Then, having found a dry cave nearby, he made a bed out of blankets and bade his wife sleep while she could until he returned with the relics. He posted Lobo to guard her, although the wolf-dog showed eager signs of wanting to accompany him.

As he picked up his saddlebags, he turned back to look at Catarina, and he was troubled by a sudden thought. Dropping the bags, he went back to her, knelt down, and took one of her slim, soft hands in his. "Catarina, I have to tell you something," he began.

She tried to rise, but he shook his head and stroked her forehead as he murmured, "No, no, *querida,* lie still and get your rest. Besides, I just want you to listen—it's true I'm going to the top of the mountain to find some old holy relics that were hidden in a secret cave. But—there's more, much more. A treasure, Catarina—no, don't speak, let me say what I must—a treasure that can give its finder great power for good or for evil."

Her eyes searched his face, and she waited for him to go on, touching his cheek in assent.

"I found it some time ago, *mi corazón*, quite by accident. Till now, I've told only Padre Moraga, because I knew his advice about what to do with the treasure would be good."

"*Comprendo, mi querido,*" she whispered back. "But you did not need to tell me."

"Yes. It's because I love you, because you're my life now and I trust you with it. But you must promise that this secret will be shared with no one else—I don't want to tell your father yet, unless there's a real need. If anybody asks any questions, I will have to make up a story."

"I will not betray our secret, my beloved Coop." She gave him a radiant smile. "And your telling me truly shows that at last I am worthy of your love, as I shall always try to be."

"I know that for certain, *querida.*" He bent to kiss her, and her arms wound around him to hold him to that tender communion. "I'll not keep you waiting too long, and you'll be safe here. Now I must go—and I love you more than ever, sweet Catarina."

Swinging his saddlebags over his shoulder, John Cooper ascended to the plateau and entered the silver mine. There, he took one of the silver ingots, then entered the workroom where he found the magnificent crosses and rosaries. He packed the ingot in the saddlebag and put a few of the relics into the pocket of his buckskin jacket. As he took a last look around the dark, tomblike cave with its grisly scene of the dead and preserved Indians in their final communion, he felt great relief to know that the person on earth who was his life shared his secret with him.

In the morning, after breakfasting on a little maize and jerky, they mounted and rode back to the *hacienda*. Catarina was in high spirits, feeling closer than ever to her husband who had shared his great discovery with her. Along the way, she lovingly referred to the wonderful second honeymoon they had known and the hope that someday again they might revisit the spot. John Cooper was also blissfully happy about this closeness with his wife, and he realized that she would need from time to time his reassurance that he was still as much in love with her and as devoted to her as at the very outset of their union.

Tía Margarita welcomed the young couple, and John Cooper confided Catarina to the cook's tender care, for the latter insisted on preparing a very special *comida* for John Cooper's young wife. Excusing himself, he took the horses to the stable, and then went to the bunkhouse to seek out the six Texans.

Edward Molson was playing cards with his cousin while Malcolm Pauley and Jack Williams watched and joked about their playing. The young brothers, John and Henry Ames, were busy repairing saddles, replacing worn cinch straps, and polishing the pummels till they shone.

"Mr. Molson, I'd like a word with you in private when you've finished your game," John Cooper drawled.

"I finished it right now, consarn it," the Texan chuckled as he flung down his hand. "Ben's too sharp for me. You know, Ben, I've been thinking, the way you play faro, you could open up a house in St. Louis or New Orleans and make us a fortune."

"Not hardly, I couldn't," his cousin countered, "because you forget we're not playing for *dinero* now. In a house, it's for hard cash on the barrelhead and that's something none of us has any to spare."

Molson affably nodded toward the others, then strolled over to John Cooper. "Well now, Mr. Baines, I'm at your service."

"I'd a sight prefer John Cooper to Mr. Baines," the young mountain man muttered with a grin. Then he added, "Come along with me. I want to show you something that might help you set up that gambling house you were just telling your cousin about. Leastways, it'll get you all to Missouri—I've heard you say many a time that's where you wanted to start up again."

"True enough," Molson answered.

"Well then, I think maybe I've found the way for you. And you'll want to leave right away. You've all been lucky so far that the *gubernador* at Santa Fe hasn't sent in any meddlesome officers to see if we have any *americanos* in Taos. But with spring not too far off, there's a good likelihood he might. Don't forget, he's under orders from Mexico City, and they're not very happy with *gringos*."

"Don't I know it!" Edward Molson grimaced, and his face darkened with a sudden look of hatred. "Mark my words, John Cooper, there may be war between the Texans and the Spaniards one of these days."

"I hope not. Anyway, let me show you some palominos, and also another horse that maybe isn't so distinguished in its breeding, but it's got richer prospects for you," John Cooper cryptically declared.

Once inside the stable, John Cooper led Edward Molson to his gelding, unfastened the saddlebag, and lifted it out of the stall. "There. This is for you, for you and your friends."

"My God—it's pure silver!" Molson gaped at the sight of the ingot.

"Go see Padre Moraga. He'll tell you where you can find a trustworthy old man who'll melt it down and give you trade goods and enough money to buy provisions to get you and your friends to Missouri."

"I—I don't know what to say—John Cooper. My God, you've saved our lives, and now you're giving us a stake for a new start!" Edward Molson avowed.

"You've earned it. And don't worry, I came by it honestly. The people who found this silver have been dead for a long, long time. I want to use it to do some good. And the first thing I can think of is to help you fellows get out of Taos before any of the authorities decide to inspect Don Diego's ranch and wonder why it is you *gringos* are living here. It won't be too good for Don Diego himself, you see."

"I understand that. God bless you, you and your sweet wife and baby!" Molson gripped John Cooper's hand and fervently wrung it. "I don't know how I can repay you—"

"You've earned your keep here, working the way you and your friends have. Don't think about paying me back. Just put distance between yourself and Taos. You've got those two horses I gave you some time back, and I can round up four others for the rest of your party."

"We'll leave tomorrow, then. I want to say good-bye to Don Diego and to thank him for keeping us here in safety."

"Sure. You'd best hide that bar. Let's see now—here, I've got an idea. I'll just put an empty saddlebag on your horse here, and I'll put the bar in there. Tomorrow morning you take that mustang and ride it out of here. Remember what I said, go see Padre Moraga first and ask him to take you to that old man. You can trust them both. Neither of them would say a word to anybody about that silver."

"I'll do that. I can't thank you enough, for my cousin

and the others. I wish you and yours all the best in the world, John Cooper. God bless you again and never stop blessing you, that's my wish."

"I couldn't ask for a better one. I'll say amen to it, and I'll wish you all Godspeed and a good life in Missouri, whatever you choose to do."

Seventeen

The six young Texans had come and gone through Taos undetected, thanks to the secrecy that was maintained by all the loyal workers of the *hacienda*. But Don Diego's enemies —the rival *hacendado*, Don Esteban de Rivarola, and the aggrieved merchant, Luis Saltareno—had not lost all opportunity to triumph over the noble *intendente*.

Early in October of the previous year, after the Battle of Medina, a St. Louis trader named Jackson Cromartie had determined to try his hand at gaining an entrance into the affluent though forbidden markets of Taos and Santa Fe. He had prospered during the preceding two years, and was willing to gamble some twenty thousand dollars worth of trade goods, estimating that he could earn at least five times that much, if the goods could be sold in New Mexico.

Accordingly, he had discussed with eight of his most trustworthy men the possibility of hunting on the upper Arkansas River and conveying the trade goods along in camouflaged wagons which would seem to contain nothing more than provisions and supplies for the expedition. Then, circling the known areas where Spanish patrols might be encountered, he and his men would make their way to Taos and Santa Fe, dispose of their goods quickly, and return with enormous profits.

Two of these men were Matthew Robisard and Ernest Henson. Robisard, a tall, wiry, bearded blond man of twenty-five, and his friend Ernest Henson, two years older, sturdy and black-haired, had both courted the same St. Louis girl. She had kept both of them dangling for eighteen months, pitting one against the other, selfishly enjoying their mutual attentions, even though she had no intention of wedding either one of them. Greedy and opportunistic by nature, Isabelle Durand—a willowy, coppery-haired belle of nineteen —detested her complacent, gentle father, and constantly sided with her ambitious mother. She had already determined to marry an elderly shopkeeper. He was widowed and extremely rich, and Isabelle enjoyed the prospect of being a widow in only a few years and having his fortune at her disposal.

Both Robisard and Henson were aggressive, vigorous, essentially honest young men who had had little experience with women. Their parents had come from the Eastern Seaboard a decade before, settled in St. Louis, and idolized their only sons. Indeed, being of extremely modest means, they had given both young men a considerable part of their savings in order to further them in the venture of trading, trapping, and hunting. Understandably, they hoped that their sons would marry and give them grandchildren. And it grieved them when they learned that both men sought the favors of Isabelle Durand, for they had heard of her reputation.

A week before Jackson Cromartie had decided to make an attempt to enter the market of Taos, Matthew Robisard and Ernest Henson had each sought a rendezvous with the capricious belle, only to learn that she had accompanied the wealthy widower to a ball. It dawned on them simultaneously that she had made fools of them both and had undermined their friendship for each other. And so, when Cromartie proposed this venture, both Robisard and Henson at once volunteered to take part in the expedition.

Jackson Cromartie and his eight volunteers traveled to the upper Arkansas. Almost two months later, an attack by hostile Comanche scattered the men and allowed the marauding Indians to steal half a dozen horses and most of the provisions.

Robisard and Henson had escaped the Comanche attack, in which three of their friends were killed. Under the cover of night, before the Comanche returned to renew the attack, they ingeniously managed to take over two of the wagons filled with trade goods, attach two of the sturdiest horses to each wagon, and head toward Taos. Cromartie and the other survivors, meanwhile, had abandoned the rest of the wagons and ridden off back to St. Louis to obtain more horses and provisions.

The only weapons that the two young men brought with them were two muskets, a brace of pistols, and several hunting knives, but with very little powder and balls for the muskets and pistols. Fortune favored them as they left the Arkansas River and crossed the Cimmaron, making for the Rio Colorado, nearly two hundred miles away. They crossed this safely and arirved in Ocate by the middle of January. By then, their horses were foundering, but again luck favored them. Both Robisard and Henson had long worked with horses. They came across a herd of wild mustangs and were able to lasso four of them and break them in after a day of arduous saddling and riding. Then, hitching the new mounts to the wagons, they continued their journey.

They came at last within the Sangre de Cristo range by the first week of February, and they could see the pueblos of Taos in the distance. They saw also the sheep quartered for the winter in shelters along the slope of the range, and, beyond, the *haciendas* of Don Sancho de Pladero and Don Diego de Escobar.

In those two wagons, they carried coarse and fine cambrics, calicos, shawls, handkerchiefs, various articles of cutlery, and mirrors. They had lived off the land like pioneers, eating herbs and roots, sometimes fruit, and occasionally, when they dared spare one of their precious balls and some of their gunpowder, killed and cooked a deer or a fat jackrabbit.

They turned off the mountain trail and headed toward the lower road which led to the *hacienda* of Don Diego de Escobar. Lobo was out for his daily run with John Cooper, who first spied the two thickly bearded Americans driving their wagons toward the ranch.

"Look there, Ernest," Matthew Robisard gasped, as he pointed toward the young man in buckskins with Lobo beside him. "That looks like an Injun and a wolf, for fair!"

"I'd say the same, Matt. Now that's a funny thing. But he's a white man, no Injun. And he's just as blond as you are!" Ernest Henson wonderingly exclaimed.

John Cooper held up his right hand in greeting and shouted, "Are you Texans?"

"No, from St. Louis, *amigo!*" Henson called, as he climbed down from the wagon. Lobo's ears flattened, his hackles rose, and he bared his fangs, but John Cooper rapped him on the snout with a brusk, "No, he's a friend, Lobo boy."

Then, he called out to Henson, "St. Louis, is it? That's a long way in the dead of winter. If you started for the fair last July, you're way late, and, anyway, there are restrictions against American traders."

"You speak our lingo, but you're living here in Taos and you're dressed like an Injun," Henson exclaimed. "How did that come about?"

"I'll be happy to tell you, but first tell me who you are and what brings you here."

"I'm Ernest Henson and this is my friend, Matthew Robisard." The latter had left his wagon and come to join Henson as they confronted the young man.

"Glad to know you both. I'm John Cooper Baines. This here's Lobo. He's friendly, but don't make any quick moves or he might take a notion to take a nip at you both," John Cooper warned. The men shook hands as Lobo eyed them with great interest, his head slightly cocked.

"We started out in October; there were nine of us, Mr. Baines," Henson continued. "Our boss was telling us about the trading here in Taos and Santa Fe, and he allowed that he'd have a shot at it."

"Well, that wasn't too brainy. I can tell you right off that the Spaniards don't much care for *gringos*. And still less for trade goods. They've got a monopoly, all the way from Chihuahua into Santa Fe and here to Taos and back. And it's all controlled out of Mexico City."

"Thanks for the warning. Well," Henson shrugged, as he glanced at his friend, "we're here, and that's the long and short of it. Are you suggesting we turn back?"

"Not so fast now. Did you see any Mexican soldiers along the way you came?" John Cooper demanded.

When both men shook their heads, he resumed. "Well, that's lucky for you both. You could have been clapped right into jail and taken to Santa Fe, and then maybe sent to Chihuahua or Mexico City to stand trial. It could still happen, but so long as you didn't meet anybody that's likely to get word to the governor at Santa Fe, you're safe for the time being. I'll call some of the *trabajadores* to put your wagons and your horses into the stable. Then I'll see about getting you some grub, and I'd bet you'd like a bath."

"That sounds like heaven." Robisard grinned.

Both men followed John Cooper back to the *hacienda*, and on the way he told them the story of how he ended up in

Taos. There they were shown to the guest quarters, and after bathing and putting on clean clothes, the two men joined the de Escobars at their evening meal.

"It's good of you to take us in, Don Diego," Matthew Robisard exclaimed as, lifting his wineglass, he toasted the *intendente* of Taos. Then, glancing at his friend Ernest Henson, he added, "We'll try to take as little advantage of your hospitality as we can. John Cooper here has told us how your authorities feel about *americanos*."

"Alas, gentlemen, it is quite true and may be even more serious than my son-in-law portrays it." Don Diego carefully chose his words while Tía Margarita and Leonora, now the wife of Teofilo Rosas, served the guests. Leonora filled the cut-glass goblets with El Paso wine and, when coffee was served, brought in special glasses for the excellent French brandy which Miguel Sandarbal had bought the year before at the Chihuahua fair.

"We don't want you to get into any trouble on our account, Don Diego," Matthew Robisard earnestly pursued. "We'd hoped we might be able to sell the goods we brought in those wagons to people like yourself, who are much more tolerant than your Spanish authorities."

"Well, gentlemen," Don Diego smiled, "I have inspected the merchandise you've brought, and I may tell you that I would like to buy quite a few of your wares for our household. There are some beautiful shawls and some dress goods which I am sure would delight my beloved wife." With this, he turned to Doña Inez and lifted his brandy glass to salute her. She lowered her eyes demurely, but her handsome face colored with pleasure at his public tribute to her.

"In that case, Don Diego," Ernest Henson spoke up, "we'll take only a very modest profit, because we certainly don't want to outrage your hospitality by putting high prices on the goods we've brought."

"Gentlemen, gentlemen," Don Diego beamed as he sipped his brandy, "you are my guests, and as such there is no need to speak of money—certainly not at the dinner table."

"Well then, I must thank you for a wonderful dinner, Don Diego." Henson rose and lifted his brandy goblet in a toast. "It's been a long time since Matt and I had such a feed—excuse me, I mean, dinner. What I'm trying to say, Don Diego, is that when you've come through a wilderness and escaped Indians and soldiers, and lived off the land as we've had to, to sit down at a table with silverware and fine linen cloth and napkins like this, and to eat such vittles, well, it makes us feel sort of civilized again, if you take my meaning."

"I do, indeed, and I thank you for so gracious and sincere a compliment, Señor Henson." The *intendente* smiled his appreciation.

"And here's to the beautiful *señora* who graced our table this evening." Robisard was not to be outdone on gallantry, as he rose in his turn and lifted his brandy goblet. His eyes dwelt for a moment on Catarina, who feigned an excess of shyness and looked down at her plate. John Cooper saw out of the corner of his eye that his wife was coloring with pleasure. Well, it wasn't a bad lesson these two *gringos* were teaching him: maybe if he'd honor Catarina with compliments every now and then, she might flirt with him the same way she was doing with them this evening.

"Tomorrow then, after the *siesta*," Don Diego resumed, "if you will permit me to inspect again the trade goods you have brought this long way, I shall be able to relieve you of a good part of them."

"That's mighty generous of you, Don Diego," Henson answered. "And we'll make the prices right, don't worry about that."

"Tomorrow, then," Don Diego concluded, "we shall talk about getting you back safely before the authorities can suspect your presence here."

The Comanche chief, Sarpento, who had come to the Taos fair to sell Bess Callendar as a slave, had left the fair with many silver pesos. On his return to his stronghold in the southeastern part of Texas, he had met two Comancheros, renegade white men, who—accepted by the Indians and hated by their own people—had for the past several years earned an excellent livelihood by selling the Comanche guns and ammunition, whiskey and stolen horses. Often, dressing themselves like Comanche, these renegades rode out to raid a small settlement, killing the settlers and stealing their possessions and livestock. Not only did they paint themselves like Comanche on the warpath, but they used bows and arrows and lances to kill their victims, much as the Comanche themselves might have done.

Sarpento had met with Caleb Harkins and Enos Davis

not far from the Colorado River, some twenty miles north of the little village of San Marcos. He was eager to trade, particularly for guns and ammunition; he had been able to buy only two old muskets at the Taos fair, and one of these was defective. Moreover, he had been advised by his war chief, Dumasito, that a raiding party of Kiowa Apache had attacked and, though the enemy had been driven off with heavy losses, six braves, three old men, and two squaws had been killed, as well as the two-year-old son of the war chief himself. It was in Sarpento's mind to induce Harkins and Davis to sell him guns that would shoot straight and enough ammunition to retaliate against the treacherous Kiowa Apache.

Plying him with cheap, raw whiskey, the two Comancheros soon parted Sarpento from all his silver *pesos,* and in return handed over four old Belgian rifles, a Lancaster (similar to John Cooper's) which had a not visibly broken trigger, and four old Spanish pistols. The pistols were fired by flintlock, but unless the wielder knew exactly how much powder to prime wtih, there was the danger that they would explode in his hand. In additon, the two Comancheros sold him six geldings which they had taken from a ranch after killing the husband, wife, and two young sons ten days earlier.

When Sarpento returned to the stronghold with his acquisitions, his war chief inspected the weapons and angrily declared that he had been badly tricked. Now thoroughly sobered, Sarpento himself examined the long rifle and the pistols, and in firing one of the latter blew off his right forefinger.

Sarpento vowed a savage oath of vengeance against Harkins and Davis and told his braves that, if ever these white jackals should be seen on Comanche terrain, they were to be hunted down and brought to the torture stake to atone for their deceit. But now Sarpento faced a crisis in his own village. It was he who had purchased these defective weapons. Moreover, two of the horses were spavined. He had lost face, and to lose face as a chief was to endanger his status.

Ingeniously, he thought of a way to regain both his authority as chief and the lost *pesos.* Some of his braves had told him that they had seen Texans and other *gringos* attempting the trail that led toward Taos and Santa Fe. Some of them, his braves insisted, came on wagons which must surely contain trade goods. And since everyone knew that the *mejicanos* forbade any *gringo* to bring trade goods into Nuevo Mexico, perhaps the *jefe* at Santa Fe would pay many *pesos* to learn of their whereabouts.

In this same reflective and regretful mood, the Comanche chief recalled lovely Bess Callendar and how he had sold her to a rich *hacendado* who, he had been told, was the *intendente* of Taos. If this *intendente* had taken that *mujer yanqui* into his household, was it not possible that he would give shelter to *yanqui* traders? It was certainly an idea worth exploring. Perhaps the *jefe* at Santa Fe would want to know about this so he could send soldiers to search the *hacienda* of this *intendente* to see if he was helping the hated *gringos*. And perhaps the *jefe* would offer the Indian chief some silver *pesos* for this information.

Sarpento held council with his elders and with his war chief. Haranguing them and boasting that he would not only see that the Comanchero traitors were punished as they deserved, but also bring back even more silver *pesos* than he had garnered at the Taos fair, he rode off on his mission.

Sarpento's plan was to go first to the ranch of Don Esteban de Rivarola in Taos. At the fair last summer, Sarpento had learned much listening to the conversations of the *trabajadores,* and one of the things he had learned was that Don Esteban had no love for his rival *hacendados.* True, he had no great love for *los indios,* either, but when he heard what Sarpento had to say—that one of the *hacendados* was harboring Yankee traders—he might be willing to work with Sarpento, knowing that the Indian would do all the dirty work to get the rival rancher in trouble.

Sarpento had not been wrong. Don Esteban greeted him happily when he learned that it might be Don Diego de Escobar who was harboring the Yankee traders. Now his desire to discredit his rival—who made all the other *hacendados* look stingy and mean—had a successful plan. Don Diego would not only be discredited; he would be condemned as a traitor. Don Esteban gave Sarpento some liquor and silver *pesos,* then sent one of his workers to fetch Luis Saltareno, the merchant, who would also be delighted at this chance to denounce Don Diego. Finally he sent one of his *trabajadores* to the ranch of Don Diego de Escobar to see what he could learn.

They didn't have long to wait. Luis Saltareno was already present—drinking brandy and smoking a cigar with Don Esteban and Sarpento—when the *trabajador* returned with the news that there were indeed two American trading wagons hidden in a stable on Don Diego's ranch. Sarpento was sent immediately on his way to Santa Fe to inform the *jefe*, while Don Esteban and Luis Saltareno celebrated their victory with another glass of brandy. Don Diego was as good as court-martialed!

So it was that on the morning after Don Diego had promised Matthew Robisard and Ernest Henson that he would buy what goods he could and help them return safely to St. Louis, Sarpento, clad in all his tribal finery, with full headdress and on the finest mustang in his corral, rode up to the *palacio* of Governor Josef Manrique. As two indolent soldiers snapped to attention and barred his way with bayonetted rifles, he said to them in his broken Spanish, "I wish to see *el gubernador*. Tell him that it is Sarpento, chief of the Wanderers. I am Comanche. I am a friend to *su excelencia*."

One of the privates roughly bade him to stay there, while his companion went in quest of the officer of the day. About an hour later, Sarpento was ushered into the office of Josef Manrique, a fussy, thickly bearded, nearly bald little man with the thin, compressed lips of an ascetic.

"You may speak, chief of the Comanche." Governor Manrique made a brusque gesture with his hand as he rose from his desk.

Inclining his head, summoning the best Spanish he could recall, Sarpento boasted that he and his braves had seen an army of *yanquis* who had crossed the Arkansas River and established fortifications near it. Also, that several of the advanced guard of this army had come into Taos and could even now be found at the *hacienda of* the *intendente*.

Governor Manrique scowled and stared at the tall Comanche. "Are you sure of this, Sarpento?"

"*¡Sí, excelencia!*" Sarpento exclaimed. "You will give Sarpento *pesos* for the news I bring you? I know well that you do not wish *gringos* to come to Nuevo Mexico with trade goods. I myeslf was at the great fair at Taos last summer. The trading was good. But if the *yanquis* come here, it will hurt the trade. This is what I am told."

"You have been told correctly, chief of the Comanche," Governor Manrique retorted. He clenched his fist and brought it down hard on the sheaf of papers on his desk. "If what you say is true, I will see that you shall have many *pesos*. You will be my guest at the *palacio*. And I will send *soldados* to the *hacienda* of this *intendente*. I know his name. It is Don Diego de Escobar. I have already had several complaints from other *hacendados* in Taos about how indulgent he is to his *peones*. Yes, Sarpento, it may be that you have done Nueva España a great service."

On this Friday of February, 1814, a mounted troop of a hundred Mexican soldiers, commanded by insolent, twenty-eight-year-old Capitán Joaquín Marduro, rode into the plaza of Taos. This captain—tall, stiff of bearing, and with a cropped, pointed black beard—dismounted and arrogantly pushed his way into the office of the *alcalde*, Don Sancho de Pladero.

"Are you the *alcalde* of Taos, señor?" Captain Marduro broke in on Don Sancho's work.

"Yes, *señor capitán*. I ask your indulgence for a moment till I conclude this affair with one of our Pueblo *indios*," Don Sancho replied.

"This is a matter of treason, *señor alcalde*," the captain insisted. "This stupid *indio* can wait his turn. I bring you a message from *el gubernador* himself. It takes precedence over any of these stupid curs in your dusty little village."

Don Sancho flushed hotly at this denigrating remark and, in a low voice, asked the old Indian to wait a moment until he could deal with this important *soldado*. Then, drawing himself up to his full height, he demanded, "I must confess, *señor capitán*, I did not quite comprehend you. You say this is a matter of great importance and from *Gubernador* Manrique?"

"Yes, by his orders. I have them here in my pocket." Captain Marduro touched the pocket of his shiny new uniform. "I am here to search for *yanquis*, at the *hacienda* of the *intendente* Don Diego de Escobar."

"But I assure you there are none—" Don Sancho began.

"I shall find that out for myself, as shall my men. I'll tell you this, *señor alcalde*. His Excellency suspects that Don Diego de Escobar may be guilty of treason in harboring *gringos* who are already setting up a fort and have brought many soldiers to the foot of the Arkansas River to prepare for war against Nueva España."

"But that is absolutely absurd!" Don Sancho protested, shaking his head with disbelief. "My friend Don Diego de Escobar is a man of the utmost honor and integrity. He came to us nearly six years ago, and he and I have administered the laws of Nueva España in the true way of the monarchy to which all loyal citizens of Spain are dedicated."

"I do not ask you to make a patriotic speech, *señor alcalde*," Captain Marduro sneered. "The *gubernador* has sent a scouting party toward the fork of the Arkansas River. If they should find guns and soldiers of *los Estados Unidos* preparing to launch an attack, it will go very badly for your friend the *intendente*. And now, if you will direct me to his *hacienda*, I shall be grateful to you. Understand, you are not named in this order to me, but I warn you that I shall not shirk my duty. If you yourself are guilty of harboring *yanquis*, you must be prepared to face *Gubernador* Manrique, as certainly the *intendente* will face him if my men find *gringos* on his estate."

"His *hacienda* is near mine, and it is easy to find." Don Sancho, with an inward prayer that this insolent young officer would have his journey for nothing, directed the captain to the *hacienda* of Don Diego of Escobar.

Outside the office of the *alcade*, Captain Murduro stationed most of his troops in the plaza, then himself rode to the *hacienda* of Don Diego de Escobar with only twenty of them. Appraised by the servants, who had heard the mounted soldiers ride into the courtyard of the *hacienda*, Don Diego himself came out to meet them. Without doing the *intendente* the honor of dismounting from his horse and conversing with him, the officer demanded, "Are you Don Diego de Escobar, *intendente* of Taos?"

"I have that honor, *capitán*."

"I am here on a mission from Governor Manrique. News has been brought to him that there are *gringo* traitors here in Taos, and it is said that you are quartering them here in your *hacienda*. I call upon you to surrender them in the name of the viceroy, as well as that of *el gubernador* himself!"

Don Diego flushed at this peremptory command. But with all his dignity, he fixed the officer with a disarmingly calm regard and replied. "It is true that there are two *americanos* here. They were abandoned by their comrades on the Arkansas, afraid of hostile *indios*, and were courageous enough to come to Taos in the hope of finding refuge and compassion for their hardships."

"So you say, Don Diego," Captain Joaquín Marduro sneered. "You will deliver these *gringos* to me this moment, do you understand, Don Diego? Doubtless they brought trade goods with them?"

"It is true they had two wagons," Don Diego began, trying to placate the officer, "but they had no choice. Did you expect them to abandon their wares, which perhaps represent a capital that took a year or more to acquire?"

"I expect only that you will obey my order, Don Diego," Captain Marduro countered. "We shall confiscate the wagons. Sergeant Duriago, take four of your men and search that stable over there. Doubtless that is where the wagons of these accursed *yanquis* are hidden. And now, Don Diego, bring out these *gringos*. I have orders to take them to Santa Fe. And I have no doubt that very soon you will be called upon to explain your part in this affair to *el gubernador* himself!"

Don Diego uttered a sigh. There was no help for it. "Give me a moment, *capitán*," he replied; and then, with a brief inclination of the head to show that he respected the authority of this officer who, after all, was acting on the order of Don Diego's superior, he went back into the *hacienda*. He quickly explained to Matthew Robisard and Ernest Henson that they would have to go with the soldiers. "But do not lose courage, *amigos*," he urged. "I myself will speak on your behalf. You did not come with any warlike motives, nor as spies, but in simple good faith as merchants. I cannot believe that to be a heinous crime."

"Thanks, Don Diego. It's not your fault. It's just a shame we didn't take off before this. Well, Ernest," Robisard shrugged, "best we go out and face these soldiers."

Don Diego accompanied them, and as the young Missourians came out of the *hacienda*, the captain barked, "Bind their hands, Corporal Sanchez, and tie the end of the rope to the tail of your horse. We shall take them back to Santa Fe in a manner befitting *yanqui* spies who would stir up war against Nueva España!"

"*Señor capitán*, I vigorously protest against such brutal treatment! Do you propose to march those two men behind a horse's tail from here to Santa Fe?" Don Diego demanded.

"I do, *señor intendente*," the officer mockingly drawled. "They are no longer your concern. They are prisoners in my keeping and by order of *el gubernador*. And let me give you another piece of information. His Excellency has sent another detachment of *soldados* to the upper fork of the Arkansas. It was told to him that these *gringos* here may well be leaders of an army of many thousands of men, with cannons and ammunition, and that these two came here to Taos not to sell trade goods—that was a very clever ruse, I will grant—but to spy on our military fortifications."

"But that is manifestly absurd, *capitán!*" Don Diego was nearly beside himself at the flagrant charge. "Their only weapons were hunting knives and old muskets with which they killed game along the trail to Taos. They have been here nearly a week, and I have had many conversations with them, and I assure you they are not the advance guard of any army sent against Nueva España!"

"You will have ample opportunity to present your own defense when you are summoned by His Excellency to Santa Fe. Ah, Sergeant, I see you found the wagons." He turned back to Don Diego again. "I shall take two of your horses to pull these wagons. Have no fear—they will be returned to you in Santa Fe, if His Excellency decides that you are not culpable in this matter."

"I have been a loyal subject of the king since my birth, and my father before me," Don Diego replied, his voice trembling with suppressed anger and indignation. "My loyalty has never been questioned. I do not take it kindly that you, knowing nothing of me or my work here in Taos, should so insinuate."

"I will make a note of your annoyance at what I have had to say to you, *señor intendente*. And now, our business here is finished. I'll bid you good day. *¡Adelante!*"

John Cooper was just returning from his run with Lobo when he saw the mounted soldiers in front of the *hacienda*. He gasped when he saw the captain give the signal for the soldiers to ride off, with Matthew Robisard and Ernest Henson forced to stumble along at the gait of the corporal's mount. Don Diego, shaking his head, tears in his eyes, stood staring after them.

When they had disappeared, John Cooper approached his father-in-law and said, "That's a fine way to treat decent men like that."

"Yes, *mi hijo*, and that insolent puppy of a captain intends to march them just like that all the way to Santa Fe. I pray God they will not die on such a journey!" Don Diego crossed himself.

"It'll mean trouble for you, won't it, Don Diego?" John Cooper asked.

"I'm afraid it will, *mi hijo*." Don Diego put his arm around the young man's shoulders. "But, although I'm an old dog now, I have finally learned that nothing in life is worth having unless one earns it. You have helped to teach me that, *mi hijo*. And so has my beloved Inez. Well now, like your Lobo here, I may have become tamed and gentled through all these long years—but I still know how to fight when my honor and my creed of life itself are to be fought for. And fight for these I shall, because those two *americanos* are very much like you, John Cooper. And, like you, they represent the world that will be, once we of the Old World have learned at last to set aside intolerance and fear and welcome them as our brothers. May God grant I shall live to see that day!"

It took three days for Captain Marduro and his men to return to Santa Fe, and for young Matthew Robisard and Ernest Henson—tied to the horse's tail, stumbling behind it, often jostling each other and sometimes falling and being dragged—they were three unending days of near exhaustion.

At night, when the troop made camp, the young Missourians were tied with their hands behind their backs and their ankles and knees constricted with rawhide thongs. They were given only a little water during the day, and only a little stew and a few stale *tortillas* at night. Yet they endured this without complaint, each determined not to betray the humanitarian kindness which Don Diego de Escobar had shown them. They understood that their very presence in his household might discredit him and could even lead to his removal and possible arraignment on a charge of high treason.

Since Governor Manrique was indisposed on the afternoon that the party reached Santa Fe, the two prisoners were at once thrown into the squalid dungeon at the back of the *palacio*. There was almost no air. For rations that night, they received only a jug of tepid water and some coarse bread.

And then at about eleven the next morning, they were brought before the governor himself in his audience chamber, each escorted by two privates on either side. Captain Marduro stood at one side of the governor's desk and openly sneered at them as he waited for Governor Manrique to read his formal report of the arrest at the *hacienda* of Don Diego de Escobar.

There was a long silence until at last Governor Manrique decided to regard the haggard, exhausted prisoners who were forced to stand at attention with bound wrists before him. "Do you speak Spanish?" he quickly demanded in that tongue.

"Not too well, *excelencia*," Matthew Robisard responded.

"So be it. I will speak in your *gringo* tongue, with which I have some passing acquaintance. I have it on credible authority that the two of you are members of an army of *americanos* who have drawn up at the fork of the Arkansas River and plan to make war upon us."

"That's not true, *excelencia*," Robisard courageously spoke up.

"I expect very shortly to have a report from my own patrol, which had ridden ahead at full speed to determine whether there is actually a fort or army at that point near the territory of Nueva España," Governor Manrique continued. "I would be within my rights if I were to have you put before a firing squad and shot as spies. Captain Marduro says that you represent yourself as traders."

"That's true, *excelencia*. We started from St. Louis, and the rest of our party went back for more supplies. We pushed on, thinking that we might be able to sell our goods to some friendly people in this area," Ernest Henson now spoke up.

"Yet surely all of you who are traders in *los Estados Unidos* must know that it is against our law for any *gringo* to come to Santa Fe or to Taos and to compete with our merchants. Our royal government prohibits it by the strictest edict, enforced by the viceroy himself, to whom I am an immediate subordinate. As I say, I could have you shot now, and there would be no possibility of appeal."

"But that would be to kill men who haven't committed any crime, *excelencia*," Robisard protested. "There wasn't any army, and there's no fort. There were about half a dozen of us, and the others went back to St. Louis to get supplies, as I just said. Your captain found that we had only two old muskets and hunting knives—I wouldn't call them the kind of weapons handed out to soldiers in any army going to war."

"You will not improve your position, señor, by levity." Governor Manrique scowled at him as he turned to study the captain's report. "However, until I hear from the patrol, I will be merciful and spare your lives. Meanwhile, you will remain in the dungeon as prisoners, in shackles and under the strictest guard. When I have all of the facts, I shall summon you forth before a court-martial. That is all I have to say to you at this moment. *Soldados*, take them back whence they came!"

"Your Excellency," Ernest Henson protested as the two privates seized him by the elbows and began to turn him to march him out of the audience room, "we Americans wouldn't treat you this way if you'd come into our territory. It's hard to breathe in that dungeon of yours, and the water is hardly drinkable and—"

Before he could finish, one of the soldiers guarding him viciously struck him a backhanded blow across the mouth, mashing his lip against his teeth and drawing blood. "*¡Silencio, gringo!*" he snarled. "When you are back in your kennel, you can bark all you like. *¡Adelante pronto!*"

The two Americans were rudely shoved out of the audience chamber and taken back to the dungeon. Before they were pushed into it by their guards, two corporals appeared, each carrying a pair of wrist and ankle shackles. Swiftly slashing the rawhide thongs which bound their wrists, the two soldiers deftly applied the manacles to their wrists, then stooped to lock the heavy irons round their ankles. Their guards opened the dungeon door and then brutally shoved them into it and locked it. They could hear the mocking laughter of the soldiers and footsteps that died away.

Matthew Robisard eyed his friend. "I really thought they were going to stand us up against the wall."

"They might yet, Matt. Well, not much we can do about it. Except pray, of course. And when we go in front of that court-martial His Excellency promised us, you and I had better say some good things about Don Diego. Otherwise, he might wind up in this stinking place along with us."

"You know, Ernest," Robisard observed with a flash of dry humor, "I'm not surprised His Excellency was worried about our being the scouts for an American army. If this is the way they treat Yankees, it might just be we'll have to go to war with them to teach them a lesson to keep the frontiers open."

"You might just be right, Matt. Well, let's save our strength. I'm going to get some shuteye. I'm plumb frazzled by that little excursion tour we took from Taos to Santa Fe behind the horse. All I've got to say is, I'd just like to get my hands on that captain. Just for about five minutes, no holds barred."

"You said it! And if you left anything of him after your time was up, I'd take over next. Well, let's both of us get some sleep. God knows we need it."

Eighteen

It was the morning of April 12, 1814. It would not be known in Mexico City, nor in Sante Fe, nor in Taos for many months yet, but on this very day, Napoleon Bonaparte, emperor of the French, who signed his decrees, "Napoleon I," this time signed his declaration of abdication. He would be exiled to Elba, where he would live with his megalomaniacal dreams of world domination. What concerned the people of Taos on this sunny spring day was that their *intendente*, Don Diego de Escobar, accompanied by his wife, Inez, whose pregnancy was visibly advancing, was to testify in the *palacio* at Santa Fe before the court-martial of the *americanos*. These two, until this very morning, had languished in their foul dungeon, in shackles, half-starved, but not broken yet in spirit.

Three days ago, a courier from Governor Manrique had ridden up to the *hacienda* and handed Don Diego the governor's summons, demanding his appearance before the court-martial and, with an ominous postscript, implying that he might himself be called upon to explain conduct unworthy of his high office and, indeed, potentially treasonable.

Miguel Sandarbal, having returned from the Chihuahua fair just the week before, had insisted on accompanying his master. He had hitched two of the strongest mustangs to the carriage in which Don Diego and Doña Inez would ride, and he had acted as coachman, clucking at the horses, urging them on along the road, dexterously guiding them past the treacherous wagon furrows and the holes which might shake the carriage and give discomfort to his mistress. John Cooper, leaving Lobo behind, had ridden his palomino stallion. He was as concerned with the ordeal that his father-in-law faced as he was with the fate of the two young Americans whom he had befriended.

Carlos, too, had accompanied his father and stepmother. Although Weesayo had asked if she might go with her husband and bring their child, he had gently dissuaded her.

At the *palacio*, before entering the audience chamber where the court-martial was to be held, Governor Josef Manrique emerged and stiffly greeted the *intendente* of Taos. Seeing Doña Inez beside him, the governor bowed and kissed her hand, and proffered a compliment which Doña Inez coolly acknowledged. As for John Cooper and Carlos, the governor acknowledged their presence only with a brief nod after Don Diego had presented his young son and his son-in-law.

The tribunal of the court-martial comprised Governor Manrique himself, a dour white-haired major from Mexico City, a fat, nearly bald colonel who commanded troops in the province of Chihuahua, and the same arrogant captain who had arrested the Americans. Don Diego was summoned into the audience chamber, but his wife, Carlos, and John Cooper were courteously but firmly informed that they might not be present. As a concession to Doña Inez, however, Governor Manrique provided a comfortable bench with cushions for her and the two young men just outside the chamber. There was a friendly sergeant standing guard in the hallway who, recognizing Doña Inez, slyly drew the door ajar so that she might be able to hear the testimony.

Governor Manrique opened the court-martial by admitting that a report from his special patrol indicated that there had been no trace of an army or any military fortifications at the fork of the Arkansas River, and therefore, the two prisoners were to be tried on the charge of attempting illegally to sell their goods on foreign soil.

He then had Matthew Robisard and Ernest Henson, in turn, narrate the story of their trek from St. Louis, sternly reminding them that they were under oath and that any fabrications or lies on their part would render them liable to severe punishment.

Each told a simple, direct story, and then it was Don Diego's turn to appear before the tribunal.

The elderly major adjusted his spectacles and peered at the *intendente*. "Don Diego de Escobar," he began in a reedy voice, "what prompted you to give shelter to these *gringos*, when you must have been aware that they could have been either spies or, at best, traders with contraband goods?"

"Major Bastagna," Don Diego courteously inclined his head to salute the officer's rank, "I consider them honest trappers and traders who found themselves deserted by their leader. When they came along the mountain range and toward my *hacienda,* I saw in them only two exhausted young men who had endured a grueling journey with many hardships. Out of humanity I gave them shelter, and I fed them, and in conversations with them, I was satisfied that they had no malicious intentions whatsoever toward our government."

"I see. I am told by Captain Marduro that you or other members of your household purchased some of these prisoners' goods. Is that true?"

"It is true, Major Bastagna." Don Diego permitted himself a smile. "Señores Robisard and Henson had brought along many things pleasing to the women of my household, and their prices were extremely reasonable. More so, I may add, than what I found merchants from Chihuahua to be offering of even lesser quality at their annual fair in January, as well as here in Taos last summer."

The governor brought his fist down with a sonorous thud on the cherrywood table before which he sat. Mastering his fury, he at last rejoined, "I wish to hear no more of your views on this subject, Don Diego. As *intendente,* it is your duty to adhere to royal law. I think, in this instance, you have overstepped your authority, although I will not charge these prisoners with further crimes because of your supposedly benevolent intervention."

"I acted in friendship and in humanity, Your Excellency, and I may say, also, that I dissuaded them from attempting to sell the rest of their goods in Taos. I wished to spare them the ordeal of incarceration in your palace dungeon—and still more the inhuman method by which they were conveyed to that dungeon."

"I shall let that remark pass. The court will now consider its verdict. You may be seated, Don Diego."

The three officers conferred, and the old major at last rose and whispered into the governor's ear. Governor Josef Manrique rose, drew himself up to his full height, and addressed the two young Missourians. "You have been found guilty, both of you, of the charge of entering Spanish territory with forbidden goods and attempting to trade. You *ameri-*

canos must be taught a lesson. Fortunately for you, no proof exists that you were the advance leaders of military forces seeking to overthrow our royal government—I say fortunately, because if that had been proved against you, you would have been summarily shot. Now, for the verdict." He glanced at the three officers of the tribunal, who simultaneously nodded. Matthew Robisard and Ernest Henson—still in shackles, dirty, unkempt, thickly bearded, the marks of their exhaustion and near starvation all too visible—stood silently before him.

"All of your possessions are to be confiscated. Each of you will be given a horse with which to return home to relieve us of your undesirable presence. You may count yourselves fortunate that we are inclined to clemency."

Robisard and Henson looked at each other and then shrugged. The experience of nearly six weeks in that dark, stinking dungeon, with its almost unendurable solitude and with total lack of communication from the outside, had led them, these last few days, to dread a sentence of long years in a prison in Chihuahua or Mexico City.

Governor Manrique resumed. "Major Bastagna has written out the sentence which I have just read to you. You will now kneel, and he himself will read it to you. Then you will kiss the paper on which it is written and sign it to indicate that you acecpt the verdict of this honorable and merciful court."

The two Americans eyed each other, and then again shrugged. Ignominious though this was, it was infinitely better than a long spell in a Mexican prison. "All right, we'll do it," Henson muttered.

"I am glad that you *gringos* are reasonable," Governor Manrique averred. "Major Bastagna, read the sentence and then see that the prisoners acknowledge it as you and your associates have decreed."

It was done, and Don Diego ground his teeth and clenched his fists in indignation to see the humiliation imposed upon these two sturdy, industrious young men whose only real crime had been the desire to extend the frontier and to bring trade goods at fair prices to the people of Taos.

When it was done, Governor Manrique addressed the *intendente*. "Don Diego, the court and I have decided to take no official action against you for your meddling—I cannot find a more appropriate term to describe your participation in this deplorable business. These men actually are little better than treasonable outlaws."

"Have I Your Excellency's permission to speak?" Don Diego rose to his feet, his eyes keen with indignation. When the governor reluctantly nodded, he declared, "For much too long, Taos and Santa Fe have been closed to honest, competitive trade. We know nothing of the world, save what we hear from Mexico City and Chihuahua. And what is happening in Europe has made all of us begin to believe that these restrictive monopolies, these high tariffs posed by the Spain we once knew, have no longer any realistic bearing on our way of life."

"I must warn you, Don Diego, that your words come perilously close to treason!" the governor fumed.

"And that I shall protest also, Governor Manrique. My forebears were among the most courageous of the nobility that upheld the Spanish crown. They go back, indeed, to His Most Catholic Majesty Philip II, who very nearly became the master of the world that was then known. Even though His Majesty Charles IV sent me from Madrid to rule as *intendente* of Taos, I have been faithful to royal laws and tenets. I pray that once again Spain will have a ruler to whom we may pay the full allegiance that all loyal Spanish subjects pay their king. Yet even when that comes about—and no man yearns for it any more sincerely than myself—I say that there will be changes in this new world. The officials of Madrid, yes, and even of Mexico City, do not mingle with the *peones* or with the *indios,* and consequently they do not comprehend the vast difference in the way of life between the *ricos* and the poor. Trading is our life's blood in Taos. We depend on the supplies from Mexico City and from Chihuahua, and perhaps twice a year we have caravans sent to us. We are forbidden to fabricate many of these goods which we could readily do, and we obey this law. We ourselves are made poor by the very monopolies which seek to protect our trade. I ask you, Governor Manrique, to think of this, and I am sure that you will not consider it treasonable when you know the facts as they truly are."

"This court-martial, Don Diego, is at an end. I have no wish to extend it, nor to tax the patience of these three gallant officers by listening to your improvisational remarks. I disagree with you violently. The law is the law, just as *el Rey* is *el Rey.*"

"I have no desire to quarrel with Your Excellency. May I ask to have a word with the prisoners?"

"If you like. We shall see that they have horses, and we shall escort them back to Taos, where they will then take the trail whence they came," the governor curtly declared, as he turned to the two officers of the tribunal, thus insultingly ignoring Don Diego.

The *intendente* approached the two prisoners and quickly whispered to Matthew Robisard, "I am sure the escorting soldiers will permit you to stop at my *hacienda* to take along some provisions. At any rate, do your best to persuade them. We will ride on ahead, and I shall see to it that you have some money to get you back safely to your homes."

"God bless you, Don Diego. We won't forget how you stood up for us in court today. Or your kindness, either." Robisard flexed his fingers to get the circulation back into his hands. The guards had removed the shackles to permit both prisoners to sign the paper on which the sentence had been written.

"I won't ever forget what you've done for us, Don Diego," Ernest Henson spoke up. "There's only one thing— when I was staying at your *hacienda,* one of your maids was awfully nice to me. I think—well, she seemed to like me some. Maybe I could get a chance to talk to her?"

"I shall venture to say it was Carmelita," Don Diego chuckled. "Of course, you will have a chance to talk to her. I only hope the man commanding your escort will be sympathetic."

"*¡Vámanos, gringos!*" one of the guards now roughly ordered, as he took Robisard by the elbow and shoved him out of the audience chamber, the other guard doing the same with Henson.

Don Diego followed them, and turned to the bench where Doña Inez, Carlos, and John Cooper sat. "You heard?" he asked with a resigned sigh.

Doña Inez rose and put her hands on her husband's shoulders. Her eyes were misty with tears. "I am so proud of you, Diego," she murmured.

"My adored Inez! God has been very good to me. Well now, we had best get to our carriage. I would like to ride ahead of the soldiers who will take our young *gringo* guests back to Taos, because I want to give them some food and some money."

Outside in the courtyard of the palace, the guard had made Matthew Robisard and Ernest Henson stand at attention while one of them went to the stable behind the palace to bring out two mustangs, harnessed only with reins and no saddles. Meanwhile, the sergeant in the hallway now emerged from the palace with two privates behind him. Observing Don Diego about to enter the carriage, he hurried up to him and, saluting, said in a low voice, "If you'd like to have these men stop at your *hacienda*, Don Diego, I can arrange for it. I am in no hurry to end this detail."

"*¡Gracias, sargento!* It is kind of you. Yes, indeed I should like to have some time with them."

"Your wife was very kind to me last year, Don Diego. My name is Sargento Luis Regado, at your service, *excelencia*."

"You have a good heart, Sargento Regado, and God will bless you for it. We shall go ahead now. You have only to follow our carriage back to the *hacienda*."

As they neared the village of Taos, Ernest Henson clicked his heels against his horse's belly to ride up alongside the compassionate sergeant and exchanged a few words with him in Spanish. When the sergeant nodded, the young Missourian rode up to Don Diego's carriage and, doffing his ragged hat, stammered, "Don Diego, I asked you before if I could talk to Carmelita when we returned to the *hacienda*. Well, the truth is, the few days Matt and I spent at your *hacienda*, Carmelita and I sort of had an understanding. I know it sounds crazy, but I—I'd like to take her back to St. Louis with me as my wife. Is there—could we—do you know a priest who maybe could marry us right away?"

Don Diego burst into joyous laughter in which Doña Inez joined. "To be sure, *amigo*," he assented. "We shall simply have Miguel stop the carriage by Padre Moraga's church. Once I explain to the good priest what you have in mind, he will come with us, and you and your *bonita* Carmelita can be married in our very own chapel."

"That's mighty decent of you, Don Diego. I'll make her a good husband, I promise! Thanks again, and God bless you!" Henson, his face colored with excitement, halted his horse and waited for the soldiers and Matthew Robisard to catch up with him.

"I know that *americanos* are quick to act," Don Diego

quipped, "because, after all, my own son-in-law John Cooper took very little time to win a place in all our hearts—especially that of my dear daughter, Catarina. But after only a few days, for this Señor Henson to induce our newest maid to leave our service and go off with a gringo to a part of *los Estados Unidos* she has never even heard of, well, that is a very swift accomplishment indeed!" He referred to the fact that Carmelita Lasarga, not quite seventeen, and orphan girl sponsored by the benevolent Padre Moraga, had come to work at the *hacienda* only a few months before.

So Miguel Sandarbal, in rare good humor over his master's courageous defiance of the *gubernador* himself, halted the carriage at the church in the plaza, and Don Diego dismounted, beckoning to Ernest Henson to follow him. They found Padra Moraga kneeling before the altar in prayer, and when he had finished and turned to them, Don Diego swiftly explained his mission. Padre Moraga declared, "Of course, I can quickly perform the ceremony in your chapel, Don Diego." Then, turning to Henson, he said gravely, "I am the moral and spiritual guardian of Carmelita Lasarga and since you propose to take her far from here, I must ask you to make an oath. Will you swear before our Lord whose blessed Son is shown in His supreme martyrdom above our altar that you will be true to her and stand beside her throughout the days of your lives together?"

"That I surely will, Father." Ernest Henson crossed himself.

"Then I willingly and eargerly go with you, Don Diego, to unite this good young *americano* with the sweet orphan girl."

When they reached the *hacienda,* Ernest Henson and Matthew Robisard were escorted to their former chambers, where they hastily tidied up and put on fresh clothes they had left behind. After he had dressed, Henson hurried to his companion's room and said, "Matt, I didn't expect a thing like this to happen, believe me. But, you remember how both of us were head over heels over that St. Louis flirt, and how she kept both of us dangling. Well now, I'll be out of the running for good, once I get hitched to Carmelita. So you'll have to find your own girl, but at least you'll know I won't be a rival any more. Shake hands and wish me well."

"God knows I do, Ernest. I'd like to be your best man, if you'll let me."

"I wouldn't want anybody else, Matt. Now let's go find Carmelita and tell her the good news," Henson exclaimed.

The pretty little maid, wearing a cotton skirt and apron and blouse, was overcome with surprise when she saw Padre Moraga come into the kitchen. She crossed herself, went down on one knee, and kissed his hand, then glanced shyly at Ernest Henson, who waited impatiently beside the white-haired old priest.

"Carmelita, my child," Padre Moraga gently said, "the Señor Henson has brought me here to join you both as *esposa* and *esposo*. Is it your wish, my daughter?"

"Oh, *sí, sí!*" Carmelita cried out, and then flung herself into the American's arms, sobbing joyously, "Ernesto, *mi amor, mi corazón,* I did not think you would ever want a poor orphan—but I swear before the Virgin I will make you a good wife, I will make you happy!"

They were married in the little chapel, with Matthew Robisard beside his friend as best man. Doña Inez tightly held Don Diego's hand, glancing at him with fervent love.

John Cooper hurried to the corral to choose a gentle horse for Carmelita to ride with her husband back to St. Louis, while Miguel and his *trabajadores* packed provisions. And Don Diego gave each of the Missourians two hundred silver *pesos,* and to Carmelita another hundred as a wedding gift.

The sergeant and his two subordinates waved farewell, and then turned their mounts and rode back to Santa Fe, while Don Diego, John Cooper, Carlos, Doña Inez, and Miguel watched the trio take the trail along the range of the Sangre de Cristo on their way back to St. Louis and to their new lives.

And Don Esteban de Rivarola and Luis Saltareno, who had been congratulating themselves a week earlier on their victory over the *intendente,* this day sat in gloomy silence at Don Esteban's ranch. It seemed their hated rival was born under a lucky star.

Nineteen

———————❖———————

Taos drowsed peacefully in the warm May weather which nurtured the brilliant hues of the wildflowers, trees, and bushes along the lower slopes of the Sangre de Cristo. Doña Inez gave thanks to the blessed Virgin in the *hacienda* chapel for her approaching motherhood, as well as for the extraordinarily good health which she still enjoyed in this middle stage of her pregnancy, at an age when many women were already grandmothers. To her, it was a divine manifestation that her love for Don Diego de Escobar had not been merely a selfish hope. And, seeing how he grew daily more devoted to her, more tender, and how their companionship was strengthened through his seeking her opinion on even the routine matters of his administration as *intendente,* she rejoiced that he had granted her so full a sharing of his life.

This warm spring, thus, seemed a benevolent augury for the future: she could perceive the happiness of Catarina and Carlos. What was more, her husband had been cleared of any charges of wrongdoing and was now, Doña Inez fervently hoped, once and for all free from the clutches of venal, shortsighted men. That was why, on this mid-May afternoon, she had Miguel Sandarbal drive her in the carriage to the church of Padre Moraga. She went to the confessional, and when he had shrived her, she had audience with him in the rectory.

"I bring you this gift of mine for the poor of your parish, Padre Moraga," she told him, as she handed him a little leather pouch filled with silver *pesos.* "I beg of you, when next you give a *Te Deum* in this beautiful church, to include my humble prayers unto Him who has granted me

223

such joy and happiness as I did not think I should ever know."

"I will do that with gladness, my daughter. God smiles on you, Doña Inez, because you have learned His lesson of wishing to give, rather than to take. I would that all the children of God knew that lesson and followed it in their lives." He made the sign of the cross over her, then helped her rise. "And may the Holy Mother of our Lord be with you at the hour of your deliverance; I shall pray for that, as for the privilege of baptizing your firstborn."

"Thank you, Padre Moraga. Your words greatly comfort me. If He wills it, you shall baptize the child late this summer."

He smiled benignly, as he again made the sign of the cross, then touched her forehead with the tip of his forefinger to convey the blessing upon her. "May God bestow His blessings upon all the members of your household. And thank you in His name for these alms to our poor."

She nodded, her eyes filled with tears, and suddenly kissed his hand. On the way back to the *hacienda*, Doña Inez looked up through the carriage window at the sky, crossed herself, and silently prayed to her dead sister, Dolores, to look down upon her and share in her own humble gratitude.

Isolated as they were under Spanish rule, the people of Taos had only the meagerest news of the continuing war between the *americanos* and the British. They had finally learned of the Creek massacre of over five hundred whites at Fort Mims, Alabama, and how General Andrew Jackson took the field against the warring *indios* of the South.

But if they had been concerned about such news at all, it would have been only with the vague fear that, if the *gringos* won their battle, the latter might be ambitious enough to force the frontier into their own quiet country and oust them from the complacency of their *haciendas*. At least, the rich *hacendados* dreaded this possibility, and discussed it often during this warm May which foretold a halcyon summer.

At the ranches of both Don Sancho de Pladero and Don Diego de Escobar, the sheepshearing had begun, and the wool was carefully baled for burro trains to be taken to Chihuahua and thence to Mexico City. Young Tomás, idyllically happy in his marriage to Conchita Seragos, had reason to be well content with his new life: his mother had, at last, begun to treat the former servant girl with the respect due the wife of her only son.

At the de Escobar *hacienda,* there was also a period of serenity after the frightening turn of events of last month, when Don Diego de Escobar had been tried for treason. Teofilo Rosas, happily married to his young Leonora, boasted that he would be a father by the year's end. Carlos and Weesayo rejoiced in the sturdy health of their little Diego, and John Cooper, though at times to Catarina's almost scandalized protests, often gathered up Andrew in his swaddling clothes and cradled the baby in his left arm as he rode on his palomino along with Lobo for their daily romp. Yet the infant seemed to thrive on this and happily pulled his father's beard. And sometimes, when the young mountain man dismounted, Lobo would stand on his hind legs and, to John Cooper's delighted amusement, run his pink raspy tongue over Andrew's cheek. Best of all was that the baby laughed and gurgled and reached out his tiny hand to touch the snout of the powerful wolf-dog.

During the last week of May, Carlos decided to spend the day hunting, and saddled Valor, put his Belgian rifle in the sling, and, after bidding Weesayo a tender farewell, rode off along the slope of the Sangre de Cristo. There would be quail and perhaps rabbit. The sky was a brilliant blue, and the sun bathed Taos with a warm, luminous mountain light.

Carlos had half a notion to ride to the stronghold of Descontarti, for, as he had explained to John Cooper, he did not like the looks of his wife's father when they had gone there to show Descontarti their child.

Valor was in high spirits today, prancing, snorting, turning his head back to regard his master affectionately, and Carlos chuckled and patted the stallion's head.

He breathed in the pure, rarified air, his eyes shining with joy. This was the life that he had foreseen when he had boarded *La Paloma* at Cadiz—*Dios,* it seemed a lifetime ago! And yet now he had never been happier, never known life to have a richer purpose and meaning. He had a son, by an *esposa* who was the most beautiful woman, the tenderest and the most loyal and wise and gentle, he had ever known. And now there was the possibility of a new life in Texas, where there would be even more open spaces, and also the chance to own a great ranch—not just for sheep, but for cattle and horses, as well. He looked up at the sky and his lips moved in a prayer of thanksgiving to *el Señor Dios*.

Suddenly Valor started, tossing his head, for there was a plaintive calling to the right where the trail wound around massive, grotesquely shaped boulders. He saw a movement, a fluttering, a black object moving. Suddenly curious, he halted Valor and dismounted.

The crying was shrill, and as he approached the nearest boulder, he saw the black shape flutter jerkily, trying to rise, then falling back to the branch of a juniper. It was a raven, and its right wing was broken. Its yellow eyes fixed him, its beak chattered, and there was terror in it; he felt a sudden pity for the helpless bird. "*¡Pobrecito!*" he murmured. "Don't be afraid. Ah, you have broken your wing."

Suddenly Carlos remembered how, when Weesayo and he had ridden to the Apache stronghold, a raven had swooped down upon them and had perched upon a branch and cawed at them, and how Weesayo had interpreted this as a sign of misfortune. And, indeed, now there was misfortune in the stronghold of Descontarti. But the young Spaniard could not believe the helpless bird in front of him was a bad omen, and he said aloud, "I think you are a good sign. You do not swoop, you need my help, and so the dark tidings do not exist. Now that is what I think, little raven."

He put out both hands to cup the frantic black bird, whose sharp beak nipped at him as it reiterated its shrill cawing. Soothing it with soft words, he finally cupped it in his hands and, opening his saddlebag, gently lowered it into the bag and tied it. He left it loose enough so the crippled raven might breathe.

Then, out of an inexplicable and mystic impulse, he turned Valor back toward the *hacienda*.

When he rode back, he encountered Miguel Sandarbal standing outside the entrance of the bunkhouse. Miguel was radiant these days. He had been married a week after his return from Chihuahua, and he lived in the cottage with Bess Callendar, who was now Señora Sandarbal. If he had had any misgivings, these had been banished by her tender and gentle acceptance of him as both lover and husband. And that, in turn, reflected in his face, for he smiled with a warmth and a joy which made him look at least twenty years younger. He joked with the *trabajadores* as he had never done before and was even more solicitous about their welfare and that of their families.

"I did not expect you back, young master, until sunset. Have you bagged the game you set out after?" he said to Carlos.

"No, Miguel, but I found a young raven with a broken wing."

"But you surely don't mean to eat that, young master?" the *capataz* quipped.

"Of course not, *estúpido*," Carlos bantered. "But I am going to make a splint for his wing and see if I can't train him as a pet. Do you know, my lovely Weesayo told me that a raven is a sign of bad luck. But I found this one lying on the branch of a juniper as I rode up the trail of the Sangre de Cristo. And perhaps, if I make him well again, the bad luck will turn away from us. There will be no more trouble for us—just happiness."

Carlos carefully opened the saddlebag, put both hands down, and gently drew out the still-cawing black bird. Its beak pecked fiercely at him, and he winced, but murmured, "Don't be afraid, *pobrecito!* We are going to be friends, you and I. And maybe you will make a friend of Lobo."

"But how can that be, young master?" Miguel gaped.

"When I was going to school in Madrid, Miguel, we studied the mythology of the Norsemen. The ruler of all the Norse gods, Odin, kept two wolves always at his side, Geri and Freki. They accompanied him in battle together with his two ravens, and they tore the corpses of the dead."

"I did not know that, young master."

"But it is true, Miguel. And there are German names which come from both wolf and raven, like Wolfram, which is taken from the German word *Wolf-braben*. It is the name of a great warrior, and in that mythology it says that, if one sees a wolf and a raven on the way to battle, it is a sign of victory."

"And you really think that Lobo will like your crippled raven?"

"When his wing is healed and he can fly and play games with Lobo, yes, I am sure of it. And in this way, I will have changed the sign which Weesayo feared," Carlos declared. "Come now, *amigo*, hold the bird very gently, and I will apply this little twig and tie it to the broken wing with some threads which I'll get from Leonora. Don't let it escape you now, Miguel."

The *capataz* awkwardly held the young black raven in his hands, and grimaced as its sharp beak pecked at his fingers. He crooned to it in Spanish, and the bird seemed to understand, for it ceased its struggles and lay, its heart beating wildly, in the cup of his hands.

Carlos returned and, instructing Miguel how to hold the raven, gently drew out the broken wing, affixed the twig, and tied threads carefully around it. The raven's beady eyes rolled wildly and it struggled again, but both Carlos and Miguel spoke soothingly, and once again it quieted.

"There now, it is done. Can you have Esteban Morales make a cage to keep it in?" Carlos asked.

¡Seguramente pronto!" the *capataz* asserted. "What will it eat, young master?"

"Mice, bits of meat from our own table. And of course it will need water. I shall have a little bowl filled with it. We'll keep the cage in the shed where John Cooper used to put Lobo. And when its wing heals, we'll take it out and introduce it to Lobo. But we must think of a name for it, Miguel."

"Since you said you wished to change the bad omen to good, young master, why not call it Fortuna?" the *capataz* suggested.

"That is exactly the right name, Miguel! I thank you. Yes, it will be good luck, and for all of us, you will see," Carlos exclaimed.

By the next day, Esteban Morales had improvised a little cage, and Carlos entered the shed, took the raven between his hands, and with the utmost gentleness, put it into the cage with its little bowl of water. One of the *trabajadores* had caught a field mouse, and Carlos tendered the mouse to the raven who, its beady eyes shining, began voraciously to peck at it.

"There, you see, Miguel, it is as I told you! Now we'll close the door of the shed, and, in time, the wing will be as good as new. Then Fortuna and Lobo will make each other's acquaintance," Carlos averred.

The next morning, Carlos told John Cooper about the raven he had found, and expressed his hope that perhaps Fortuna and Lobo might become friends.

Carlos had set the splint so expertly that, within a week,

the young raven was able to flap its wing and to essay a few tentative trials at flight. Meanwhile, John Cooper had put Lobo on a leash so that the wolf-dog might watch the raven. To his surprise, he saw that Lobo was wagging his tail and looking up at the bird with gleaming yellow eyes, his tongue lolling out of his mouth. "He seems to like Fortuna already, Carlos," he exclaimed.

"That is very good. In a few days more, Fortuna will be able to fly well. I hope he will decide to stay with us. But, of course, he has as much right to his freedom as you or Lobo."

By the end of the second week, the raven's wing no longer troubled it, and it tried several short flights from its cage in the shed to the roof of the *hacienda*. When Carlos clucked his tongue and made beckoning signs with his fingers, Fortuna returned, much as might a young falcon. "You see, John Cooper?" he exulted. "You are not the only one who can tame something wild. And soon we'll have Lobo and Fortuna become good friends. It will be a fortunate alliance, I am sure of it."

Lobo, for his part, watched the raven with growing interest. At times, seeing Fortuna hop about on the roof and then fly back to Carlos's outstretched hands, he wagged his tail and gave a soft bark. Several times, also, Fortuna perched in Carlos's palms and stared directly at Lobo with his beady little eyes. Then he gave a loud caw and seemed to ruffle his tail feathers, whereupon Lobo wagged his tail even more vigorously.

"What do you say to letting them go out on a romp together, while we both go hunting?" Carlos proposed the very next morning. John Cooper, always ready for an outing, eagerly agreed, and the two young men saddled their horses and rode out at dawn. Lobo ran beside John Cooper's palomino, while Carlos put the raven on his shoulder and soothingly ordered it to remain there, rubbing the top of its glossy black head with the tip of his forefinger. The raven closed its eyes and remained immobile. He bragged to John Cooper, "I wager that, if I really tried my hand at it, I could even tame a lion, John Cooper!"

To which the mountain man riposted, "Well, if you failed, I could always be there with 'Long Girl' as I was the first time we met."

They rode out to the slope of the Sangre de Cristo.

Carlos dismounted and, letting Fortuna perch on the back of his right hand, walked slowly over to Lobo. Putting his left hand out with the palm turned upward, he said, "Now, Lobo, here is a new *amigo* for you. This is Fortuna." Then, turning to regard the raven, he said gently, "Fortuna, you must meet Lobo. He will be your friend. Now, go perch on his back. You have no need to be afraid of him; you can fly away swiftly if he tries to snap at you, but I don't think he will."

Lobo uttered a soft purring growl, his tail wagging jerkily, as the young Spaniard, rubbing his head with two knuckles, extended his right hand to let Fortuna put its claws on the mane of the wolf-dog.

Lobo turned his head, his bright yellow eyes intent on the black raven. Fortuna cawed softly and then suddenly flew above Lobo. He came down to dart a circle over Lobo's head. Lobo nipped at him and held up a paw, as if to fend the raven off. With another louder caw, Fortuna swooped high into the air and then again descended, this time to dart at Lobo's tail. John Cooper and Carlos burst into laughter, highly amused at this game. "They are already good friends," Carlos exclaimed. "Didn't I tell you they would be?"

During the week that followed, both Carlos and John Cooper spent several hours each day developing and testing the friendship of Lobo and the raven. As they rode their horses toward the mountain trail, Lobo would bound ahead, glancing back over his shoulder, his yellow eyes gleaming with joy, his tail held stiffly out. Fortuna, cawing shrilly, flew ahead of him, sometimes pausing on the branch of a nearby tree to stare down at his new friend. Then, with a mischievous little cry, he would dart down and peck at Lobo's tail. At this, Lobo would stop dead in his tracks, whirl, and with a pretended growl of anger, lunge upward at the raven, which would then fly swiftly above to safety on the branch of a tree.

By the fifth day of this week, the two young men were fascinated to see how bold Fortuna had become. The raven flew down from its protective branch soon after they had arrived on the trail. Very quickly, it ran along the ground, glanced back, and then stood still. Lobo, slinking low to the ground, tail stiffly held above his head, began to stalk Fortuna. The wolf-dog came closer and closer, and John Cooper and Carlos held their breath, a little afraid that Lobo might catch the raven in his powerful jaws. But at the last moment, when Lobo was only about a foot away, Fortuna rose swiftly into the air with a taunting caw and flew about a hundred yards ahead, only to swoop down and run along the ground for a few feet before stopping. Again, Lobo stalked the raven, and once more this prank was repeated. Lobo wagged his tail and looked upward as he saw Fortuna fly to a branch of a tall spruce tree.

"Tomorrow, let us see if Fortuna will hunt along with Lobo," Carlos proposed. "We'll go up toward the top of the mountain, where I know there are fat jackrabbits. Let us see what the raven does once Lobo makes his kill."

And the next afternoon, about two hours before sunset, the two young men rode along the winding trail which led to one of the lower peaks of the majestic mountain range. The air was cool, and the peak itself was still capped with snow. Fortuna perched on Carlos's shoulder for most of the journey, but when he dismounted, the raven flapped its wings and flew off toward a fir tree, on the top of which it perched.

Lobo sniffed the air, eyes narrowing and fiercely glistening. "Go hunt, Lobo!" John Cooper called.

Then both young men watched as Lobo loped away from the trail up a straggling path broken by small boulders and gnarled shrubs. At the same moment, Fortuna flew down from his perch, cawing shrilly and flying ahead of Lobo until suddenly the raven darted down. It was as if his beak were pointing toward a quarry which he was marking out for his new friend.

Then John Cooper and Carlos heard a squeal and a low growl. As they hurried after the wolf-dog, they saw that Lobo had trapped a jackrabbit and killed it. Fortuna perched atop Lobo's head, then suddenly darted down and pecked at the bloody ground near where the rabbit lay, then flew back to take his perch again on Lobo's head.

"Good boy, good Lobo!" John Cooper praised the wolf-dog. Then Carlos stretched out his right hand, and Fortuna, with a plaintive caw, flew to him and found a secure footing on his wrist. From this perch, he peered down at Lobo, who had picked up the rabbit in his jaws and turned back to John Cooper, wagging his tail and looking up with anxious yellow eyes.

"I swear they are both human," Carlos breathed incredulously. "Fortuna actually wants to share Lobo's kill, and I'll wager he even led Lobo to that rabbit because, of course, being high above the ground, he could see it before Lobo could."

"I believe that's true, Carlos. Well now, the two of them will make a fine pair and Lobo won't be bored in the future, that's for certain," John Cooper chuckled. "Let go of the rabbit, Lobo. I'll put it in my saddlebag, and we'll have it tonight for supper. Tía Margarita will cook it with a wonderful wine sauce, and I promise I'll save you a share."

"And I promise that from now on there will be no more trouble for our family!" Carlos exclaimed. "Fortuna has showed us that bad tidings can be turned to good."

Twenty

Although Luis Saltareno and Don Esteban de Rivarola did not perhaps acquire the victory they had expected over Don Diego, there were other events, many of them not controlled by a single individual, which did not bode well for their rival. By the middle of July of this year of 1814, the news of Napoleon's abdication had at last reached New Spain, and it was learned also that Ferdinand VII had taken his place on the Spanish throne as the rightful king. But, as John Cooper had anticipated, conditions in the land did not improve. Instead, the government was becoming even more reactionary, and in Mexico City, the capital of New Spain, the viceroy was preparing to impose even stiffer prohibitions and restrictions on the residents of Taos.

In the palace of the viceroy in Mexico City, His Excellency, General Felix Maria Calleja del Rey, had hastily summoned his personal aide, Don Felipe de Aranguez, to discuss what steps must now be taken to ensure not only the loyalty of Nueva España, but also the vigilant collection of tithes from the subordinate provinces.

The viceroy, a tall, robust man whose soldierly bearing was quite in keeping with his military rank, gratefully dismissed the equerry who had brought him the tidings from abroad, and beckoned to his aide to seat himself opposite the teakwood desk in secret conference. Waiting until the equerry had closed the heavy doors behind him, Viceroy Calleja declared, "Don Felipe, I have a mission of the utmost importance for you. Our royal treasury is nearly empty. Now that our beloved monarch, Ferdinand VII, is back on the throne at the Escorial, we must do everything possible to

233

replenish it. This will mean that we can now afford strengthening our government, not only here in the capital, but also in the provinces."

"I am at Your Excellency's orders." Don Felipe de Aranguez inclined his head with an obsequious smile. He was thirty-eight years old, born in Barcelona to a minor nobleman who had married a beauty of great wealth. His parents, when he was only sixteen, had decided to take up residence in New Spain and had settled in a villa at the outskirts of Mexico City. Their tall, black-haired, insolent young son had been schooled by tutors, and then enrolled at a military academy restricted to children of aristocratic breeding. At twenty, Don Felipe had become a lieutenant; he now held the rank of colonel, and his parents had died about five years ago within about six months of each other.

At the time of their death, he had sailed back to Spain to settle the estate and had brought back the proceeds of that sale. Some of the money was employed in adding to the luxurious comforts of his parents' villa, and the rest was carefully hidden so that not even the viceroy himself was aware of Don Felipe's fortune.

Viceroy Calleja, impressed by the handsome officer's fluency in French, English, and Spanish, as well as his exemplary military record, had appointed him personal aide eighteen months ago. That record, to be sure, stressed administrative zeal, rather than courage in combat, for the fact was that the egotistic Don Felipe de Aranguez had no stomach for hand-to-hand fighting. His ambition was to become viceroy of New Spain, to establish a strong military force, and, if need be, to bring about a revolutionary coup and take over total power in Mexico City. He was not unlike a certain young lieutenant not much more than half his age, Santa Anna, except that he was more cunning and, to be sure, far wealthier. And it was with wealth that he planned to manipulate his way to the very chair that Viceroy Calleja now occupied across the desk from him.

What the viceroy did not know, and what Don Felipe had managed thus far to keep hidden from his superior, was that some of his wealth had already been expended to form a corps of some fifty crack troops accountable only to Don Felipe himself. Over the past few years, he had approached a number of noncommissioned officers and persuaded them to resign from the royalist army. In return, they would be paid far higher wages, they would sign an oath of allegiance to him as their commanding officer, and they would not wear the royalist uniforms. In effect, Don Felipe brought them together under the guise of a gentlemen's club, inviting them from time to time to his spacious and luxurious villa. There he entertained them with the finest food and wine, as well as with the favors of expensive courtesans.

He was not married and had no wish to be; for the past five years, ever since the death of his parents, he had contented himself with the pleasures that his beautiful thirty-year-old mistress, Isabella Valdez, provided. And because her perverse tastes matched his, she was able to recruit many attractive young women, many of them married to dull, dutiful, and unsuspecting husbands, to visit the villa to entertain her lover's private army enlistees. After he had plied these men with the luxuries of the villa and was assured of their loyalty, Don Felipe sent many of them to a ranch he owned hundreds of miles to the north. There, none of his superiors in Mexico City would notice the number of troops he was building up, and none would suspect that he was plotting a revolutionary coup.

"Don Felipe, it is imperative that you visit the provinces of Chihuahua and Durango," the viceroy declared. "The *intendentes* there have been remiss in sending their tithes. I suspect—mind you, I have no proof—that these officials may be diverting some of those tithes into their own coffers. I authorize you to demand all that money that is due to the throne of Spain for the maintenance and preservation of our royal government."

"I thank Your Excellency for his trust in me. I shall do my utmost to justify it," Don Felipe replied. Viceroy Calleja smiled at the younger man. Childless, he had often thought to himself that this handsome, neatly bearded, and articulate young man would have been exactly the sort of son he could have had if *el Señor Dios* had smiled upon him. Indeed, he was more solicitous toward Don Felipe than toward anyone else in the palace, and had often paternally remonstrated with Don Felipe on the latter's status as a bachelor. To this, Don Felipe had pleaded that he had not yet found the proper woman whom he wished to make the mother of his children, and that had sufficed the viceroy, who believed that this answer was only another indication of Don Felipe's admirable character.

"*Bueno*, Don Felipe," he now rejoined. "I wish you also to visit the provinces of Santa Fe and Taos. Of late, the revenues dispatched to us here have been meager. It may be that these villages are impoverished, but this you must ascertain for yourself. How long do you think it will be before you can reach Taos and Santa Fe?"

"Taos is over sixteen hundred miles away, Your Excellency. With relays of fresh horses throughout the provinces, and of course, allowing for the duties you expect of me in Durango and Chihuahua, I should say from six to eight weeks."

"I realize that I am sending you on a long, arduous journey, Don Felipe. But you are the only man I can trust for this work. And results are what I wish—you will bring back the tithes yourself; I shall dispense with the usual methods of collection. Besides, some of these *intendentes* wait until it serves their pleasure to send in their tithes by slow couriers."

"I follow Your Excellency's meaning. It might be wise," Don Felipe leaned forward and spoke in a confidential tone, "to write out not only an authorization that I represent you in these matters, but also a kind of *carte blanche* to provide against any unforeseen contingencies. By this, Your Excellency, I refer to insubordination or other such disloyal acts which I, as an officer and as your aide, would wish to take action against, but could not unless you gave me the power to act in your name."

"I see your point, Don Felipe. Here now," the viceroy scribbled his name on another sheet of parchment and then applied the royal seal of Nueva España, "is your *carte blanche*. Go with God, Don Felipe. I shall have to do my best to get along without your services until you return. I might tell you, Don Felipe," the viceroy added as an afterthought, "sometime ago, I sent couriers with dispatches to Governor Manrique and to the *intendente* of Taos, Don Diego de Escobar, to inform them that, in the event of just such glorious news as we have just been privileged to receive, they would do well to prepare for more satisfactory collection of revenues. So in a sense, I trust that I have paved the way for you."

"You have indeed, *excelencia*." Don Felipe bowed and then left the chamber. He glanced at the two rolled sheets of parchment in his right hand, and his sensual lips curved in a smile of gratification.

Three days before the viceroy's meeting with Don Felipe de Aranguez, the courier from Mexico City had galloped his exhausted horse to the *hacienda* of Don Diego de Escobar and asked to have an audience with the *intendente*. Don Diego had at once received him and learned that the courier had come from Santa Fe, where he had brought a dispatch for Governor Manrique. "Don Diego de Escobar, I am bidden by *su excelencia* the viceroy to deliver this edict which he has signed into your hands," the courier declared, as he drew from inside his tunic a sheet of parchment neatly rolled, tied with ribbons in the imperial colors of Spain and with the seal of the viceroy fixing the ribbons to the document.

"Convey my warmest regards to His Excellency, and tell him that I have received this from your hands and will at once absorb its directions, Captain."

The courier bowed and left the *hacienda*, mounted his horse, and turned back toward Santa Fe. Carlos approached his father, a wondering look on his face. "*Mi padre*, is this not unusual to have a courier come all this long way from Mexico City to bring you orders?"

"I fear, my son, it is the beginning of evil days for all of us here in Taos," Don Diego slowly replied, as he broke the seal, untied the ribbons, and unrolled the parchment. Scrutinizing it, he frowned and shook his head. "Yes, I was right. The viceroy has ordered that the collection of tithes for the royal treasury is to occur four times a year, instead of twice, as has always been the custom. Also, that for this immediate time, he plans to send his personal aide, a Don Felipe de Aranguez, with a military escort to collect the revenue due the throne."

"It is as if he does not trust you, *mi padre*." Carlos's voice throbbed with indignation.

"I ask myself why, for I too, *mi hijo*, have much the same feeling. When Miguel Sandarbal came back from Chihuahua this spring, he told me that he had heard many rumors of unrest throughout Nueva España."

John Cooper was just returning with Lobo from his afternoon run on the mountain slope. Fortuna, by now inseparable from his friend, perched atop Lobo's head and uttered a cheerful caw as Lobo stopped beside his master at the door of the *hacienda*. "No, stay outside, Lobo. I must go see Catarina and Andrew. You and Fortuna amuse yourselves. And be good, Lobo."

As John Cooper put out his hand to stroke Lobo's head, Fortuna, with a shrill caw of annoyance, swiftly soared up to the roof of the *hacienda*. Lobo looked up at the raven, his eyes eager and intent. With a laugh, John Cooper knuckled Lobo's head again, and then entered the *hacienda*.

He saw Carlos and Don Diego standing, their faces sober and dismayed. "Is it bad news? Can I be of help?" he at once proffered.

Eyeing his son, Don Diego uttered a deep sigh. "John Cooper, this is a matter which will concern you also, I fear. Let us go into my study and discuss the matter over a glass of good Madeira."

"Yes, of course, *mi suegro*."

The three men went into Don Diego's study and immediately the *intendente* began shaking his head. "John Cooper, the news from Mexico City is that the viceroy intends to collect our revenue to the crown four times a year, instead of twice. Also, he is sending an aide of his with an escort of soldiers to collect all that we can provide at the time of the aide's arrival. In all these years since I have been *intendente*, the collection has been a routine matter. And as to my report, all was forwarded in duplicate to the viceroy, as well as to the *gubernador* at Santa Fe, and it was never before questioned."

"Looks to me, *mi suegro*, that they're trying to take away your authority," John Cooper drawled.

"You see it, then, just as Carlos and I do," Don Diego quickly averred. He stroked his goatee and pondered a moment. "I was wrong, I was wrong," he said. "I thought that when the rightful king was back on the throne, equity and decency would be restored. But I was wrong. I had just told Carlos that, when Miguel came back from the January fair, he heard many evil rumors of trouble brewing throughout the provinces. One *capataz*, a very well educated man, Miguel told me, said that there were many *peones* who thought it was time to strike a blow for the independence of Mexico away from the mother country because they could not be sure that, even with the king back on the throne in Madrid, their lot would be any better. And they are right. The situation here is more oppressive and intolerable than ever, not only for the poor but for us, as well. And now I am being treated with suspicion and threats, as if I were a criminal."

"But no one's been more loyal to the crown than you," John Cooper protested.

"Of course that is true, *mi yerno*," Don Diego slowly replied, "and that is why it is an insult. At least if the viceroy had summoned me to Mexico to have audience with him and to explain this new procedure, my own honor would be satisfied. Instead, it is as if he were threatening me with an aide who surely does not know me, and who will come here with a troop of soldiers. It is high-handed, and it is intolerable!"

John Cooper, mulling over in his mind what he had been thinking for some time, looked hard at both Don Diego and then Carlos. He had decided that now, more than ever, it was imperative to keep the silver mine secret—Don Diego had enough on his mind, and to implicate him in any way with these secret riches might get him into more trouble with the authorities. For now, it would be enough to talk about immediate plans—the silver could wait until later to be put to good use. Finally he said, "Don Diego, we once talked of the possibility of finding a new ranch, a new way of life. Would it break your heart, Don Diego, to leave Taos now, if you could be free of all this governmental interference? Seems to me, a man would want his freedom so he could choose the way he'd act and the way he'd go, not be told from a long distance what was expected of him."

Don Diego frowned, regarding the young man with an expression of surprise. "What are you suggesting, *mi yerno?*"

"Well, Don Diego, you know that I bought those palominos and mean to breed them. I want to have a string of the finest horses any man could ever own. And, when those six Texans were here at the *hacienda*, I did a lot of talking with them about their country. It's big, big and untamed. Oh, sure, there are Comanche and Kiowa Apache and maybe other hostiles, too, but there's lots of room for everybody there. And even though Mexico's got a hold over Texas right now, it's too big for Mexican soldiers to patrol all of it. What would you think if I said I'd like to go find us a big, new *ranchero*, where we could breed not only horses, but also cattle. You know, settlers want meat and when towns begin to spring up with the settlers, they'll need lots of meat."

"John Cooper has already talked with me about this,

Father," Carlos said, his eyes bright. "I told him what you already well know: that I did not enjoy the prospect of becoming a sheep rancher. But I would be most eager to raise horses. And—in all due respect to you, *mi padre*—I believe we should make the move."

"With all respect, too, Don Diego," John Cooper said, "I can't say that I care much for the high-handed ways the Spanish government is treating not only fine, decent people like you, but also the poor *peones* and the *indios*. But suppose you could have your own ranch, Don Diego, where Carlos and I could make a good living, where you and Doña Inez wouldn't have to worry about what the governor in Santa Fe might think?"

"Well now, *mi yerno,*" Don Diego said slowly, "what is your idea?"

"With your permission, Don Diego," John Cooper replied, "I will go out to the southeast and find a good stretch of land that would be perfect for raising cattle and horses and sheep or whatever we want. Fruits and vegetables, too, enough to keep all the loyal *trabajadores* who want to come along with us busy and happy. A place where they can have their families, too, and go on living with us and working with us like a big family. And by settling on that land, we'd have it as ours when the time comes that the Mexicans might sell it to the United States."

"*¡Mi Dios!*" Don Diego blurted out. "You honestly think that Nueva España would give up its control of Texas territory?"

"One day it may have to. One day the Americans may decide that, if Mexico won't sell it, they'll occupy it and take it over."

"But that might mean war!" Carlos gasped.

"Maybe. Maybe not, too. At least for now, since everything's in such an unsettled state, it seems to me we could be a lot happier settling down somewhere else. I know that your position as *intendente* was given to you by the king and that you're paid for it. But I think you'd make at least as much money and even more if we had that land in Texas to settle on."

"It is a tempting idea, I will say that," Don Diego said as he stroked his goatee and looked at his son and his son-in-law. "It would be an exciting change—and it might well be for the better."

"What I'll do now, Don Diego, if it's all right with you, is to go looking for this land," John Cooper continued. "I've a pretty fair knowledge of where I'll find it, just beyond Eagle Pass. It's not too far from the Rio Grande, but it's not a part of Texas where there'd be many soldier patrols. And there's no fort of Spanish soldiers anywhere around there for miles —I found that out from the Texans who came here. Carlos, will you agree to stay and protect the *hacienda* while I'm gone?"

"I almost wish I were going with you, John Cooper," Carlos wistfully answered.

"I think it's better I go alone, and better if you stay here to watch over things. I'm hoping you and Weesayo'll keep Catarina company, though I'm sure she'll be angry with me for taking off again on a long journey."

"We'll both look after her, I promise, John Cooper." Carlos smiled as he shook hands with his brother-in-law.

Don Diego de Escobar put his arm around John Cooper's shoulders. "This time, my dear son-in-law, I am going to follow my instincts. I liked you when I first saw you, and you have already saved our *hacienda* from danger. Now I feel that what you plan to do might take us out of danger for good. *Vaya con Dios*—yes, John Cooper, find this land you speak of, and I for one will gladly journey with you, if it means freedom without oppression."

Viceroy Calleja in Mexico City, having sent his proclamation to all the *intendentes* and *alcaldes* of the provinces, informing them of the restoration of the monarchy and instructing them to strive for even greater allegiance, also wrote a letter to the *intendente* of the province of Chihuahua. In it he declared, "What is most essential now in this period of adjustment is the maintenance of discipline and order. The news of minor uprisings and of bandits marauding in several of the outlying provinces deeply concerns me; it strikes at the very heart of our government. I urge you to look to your borders, to the isolated little villages where notorious bandits are suspected of making their headquarters. Under the guise of seeking independence for Nueva España, these despicable hyenas plunder and rape and kill, whereas it is well known they do so only for their own profiteering."

Perhaps the viceroy's concern over bandit raids had been promoted by reports that a new outbreak of rapine had been taking place in the province of Sonora. It was the most far-flung area of Nueva España and, hence, virtually impossible to patrol with full military force from such a distance as Mexico City.

These outbreaks in the province of Sonora were the work of none other than the *bandido* Jorge Santomaro, in alliance with the former *capataz* of the de Pladero *hacienda*, José Ramirez. Since their meeting in that little *posada*, the two men had recruited a band of some fifty men, most of them *peones* who had run away from the tyranny of their *patrones*. Santomaro had eloquently preyed upon their yearning for freedom, boasting that, as their strength grew, they could in time overthrow the rule of the military and the clerics and make all Mexico free for the oppressed and the downtrodden. To men who had known long hours of work at paltry wages and punishments like flogging and cropping the ears, such a prospect represented paradise. And since most of them were men without families, uprooted and wandering outlaws with a price on their heads, the opportunity to ride into little towns and to plunder them and rape the attractive women whom Santomaro took as captives seemed only proper justice.

By the end of July, this wandering band had destroyed the town of Pitiquito about eighty miles south of Nogales. It had boasted some ninety inhabitants, and Santomaro and his men had killed all the old men and women, then offered the young and middle-aged men a choice: death or enlistment in his ranks. Thus, he had added twenty recruits, and executed another dozen who had courageously refused to become *bandidos*. The women, needless to say, fell as booty to the conquerors. The village was rebuilt, and it became the headquarters of this bandit band whose two leaders lived on that most powerful of all nutriments, the hope of vengeance.

A few days before the end of July 1814, he and fifteen of his men had chanced upon a lone military patrol of a dozen soldiers, attacked them from ambush, killed them all, and collected their weapons. Among these were four excellent Belgian rifles, several braces of *pistolas* with ample balls and powder, and a number of long, sharp-pointed lances. This addition to Santomaro's arsenal made him believe that he could best any force sent against him.

Jorge Santomaro and José Ramirez conferred this sultry,

rainy evening of the first week of August in the adobe *jacal* which had belonged to the murdered *alcalde* of Pitiquito. They sprawled at their ease on multicolored blankets, each with one of the younger women of the village at his side. Both Santomaro and Ramirez had imbibed nearly a full bottle of tequila, and as they pawed their naked consorts, Santomaro sniggered and declared, "I think, *amigo*, we should soon go and see how your *gringo* friend is doing?"

"*¡Caramba!* It is strange you should mention that, *mi jefe!* I had been giving some thought to that the last few days," José Ramirez replied. Brutally, he dug his stubby fingers into the ripe breast of his quiescent concubine, and he chuckled evilly when she cried and flung her arms around him, pressing herself against him in a feverish attempt to convince him of her total submission. "Oh, you like that, do you, Juana? And perhaps, if you are a very good *puta*, I'll give you a taste of my belt before I make you do to my *cojones* what I like best. You will be a good girl now, won't you?"

"*Seguramente, amorcito*," the frightened young woman gasped, shuddering with revulsion but forcing a smile to her lips.

"Well, *amigo*," Santomaro pursued, "I have not forgotten what you said about the *esposa guapa* of the *gringo*. I, for one, would like to see this marvel of beauty, this *aristocrata rica*. And do you know what I think? You and I and perhaps two or three of our best men should disguise ourselves as sheepherders or merchants. We'll go to Taos, we'll find out about this accursed *gringo* of yours. And, who knows, we may do more as spies than with all my *bandidos*."

"I do not quite follow you, *mi jefe*," Ramirez hoarsely answered, for the naked young woman beside him, doing her best to show her compliance, had opened his britches and was fondling his virile manhood.

"*¡Estúpido!* Now listen carefully. There is time enough for your *puta* when we have done talking, *¿comprende?* Now then, if you and I and a few good men come into Taos and make inquiries about this *gringo*, and perhaps he has gone off on some errand or other, or hunting, or who the devil cares—now, just suppose there will be nobody home except that *esposa guapa* of his. Why, *hombre*, we could have a little pleasure with her. And at the same time, we could see what it would take to destroy that accursed *alcalde*, Don Sancho de Pladero. I owe him a debt for my brother's sake. And in that way, we'll both be able to have our vengeance."

"By all the saints, I'll follow you to the fires of hell themselves if I could have an hour with that insolent bitch Catarina de Escobar!" Ramirez's face contorted with hate and lust. He glanced down at his complacent mistress and, twisting his fingers in her hair, forced her face down against him. "Homage me, *puta!* Do you see how *macho* you have made me? Satisfy me, or I'll strip the hide off your fat behind."

"Then we are agreed, *hombre*—we'll go to Taos soon. Until then we'll continue to lie low and enjoy ourselves here. Right now the viceroy's *soldados* are swarming all over the place, trying to maintain law and order. But from all I've heard, the viceroy is so busy planning new taxes to fill his treasury for the new king of Spain that he'll soon forget his campaign against *los bandidos*. And then we can go, and have our pleasure. You have seen, working for me, Ramirez, that I always get what I want, and no one can stop us."

"I see that, *mi jefe*. I shall never forget how kind you have been to me, and I shall serve you loyally."

"It is to your own advantage, *hombre*. I don't take kindly to traitors. And now enough of talk. My little Paquita here is eager for my arms." With a brutal laugh, Santomaro flung himself upon his naked young companion and savagely ravished her.

Twenty-one

Don Felipe de Aranguez had chosen only two soldiers from the garrison at the capital to ride with his escort. The eighteen others were drawn from what he liked to call his "private army" and were headed by a dour, burly man in his early forties, Luis Roblar. Roblar had resigned his post as sergeant with the viceroy's army to take secret employment with Don Felipe, who had promptly commissioned him as a lieutenant, and paid him higher wages than such a rank would have earned with the imperial troops.

The two regulars were a young private and a sergeant with florid mustache and haughty manner, not quite forty, named Juan Estigo. Six years ago, he had been a corporal who had ridden with Lieutenant Cortez in the escort which had conveyed Don Diego de Escobar, Doña Inez, Carlos, and Catarina from Mexico City to Taos. And Catarina had chanced to meet him in a lace shop of Matamoros where he was attempting to purchase a shawl from the old proprietress for three pesos fewer than she had asked. Catarina had recognized him as a soldier who used his spurs and whip on his horse far too often for her liking, and she had impulsively ordered Juan Estigo to pay the price the white-haired woman asked.

Estigo had not forgotten that lecture from a teenage girl, and, singularly enough, it had changed his nature for the better. Moreover, during the attack by the Toboso Indians on the escort and the carriage which was transporting the de Escobars, he had distinguished himself by his personal courage. He had received a promotion to sergeant shortly after returning to Mexico City with his commanding officer, had married a young widow with three children, and was hoping one day to save enough out of his pay to buy a little farm.

Don Felipe de Aranguez had selected Juan Estigo to ride with him because, after having investigated Estigo's service record, he had determined to lure the sergeant into his own ranks. Here was an uneducated man who had shown dogged determination and had risen probably as high as he ever would in the imperial army. With a wife and children and doubtless more to come, such a man could readily be tempted by the offer of higher wages and the title of *subteniente*.

The viceroy's ambitious aide took care not to dress his own men in the uniforms worn by the viceroy's troops. In their place, his soldiers wore red *calzonares*, black sombreros, and white blouses. Nor was their rank designated by epaulettes or any of the customary insignia. His lieutenant, Luis Roblar, for example, was designated as leader of this cavalry troop solely by the sign of a white star on the center brim of his sombrero. And if the viceroy had seen fit to ask Don Felipe how it was that so many non-uniformed men rode with him on a military mission, the latter would have glibly explained that these were his *trabajadores* from his own *hacienda*. Nor was that a lie: two years ago, he had acquired two thousand acres of land not far from the estate of his good friend Don Ramón de Costilla, who had formally purchased the land in his own name so that Don Felipe's motives could not be suspected. And it was on this ranch that some of his own troops often drilled and where, now, many of them lived and worked—at least maintaining the appearance of *trabajadores* in the event that any imperial patrols should ever stop to inspect the estate and to question them.

By the end of August, Don Felipe and his twenty men rode into the courtyard of Don Ramón de Costilla's *hacienda*. Thanks to the viceroy's documents of authorization, Don Felipe's task of collecting revenue for the crown had been greatly facilitated. The tithes, in silver, were carried in the saddlebags of three of his own men. There had been nearly six weeks of hard riding, with little time for amusement. This evening, however, he proposed to be completely at his ease with his old friend. Moreover, their meeting might cement a friendship that could be useful in furthering Don Felipe's ambitions. Don Ramón de Costilla, like so many of the arrogant *ricos* in the provinces far from the capital, was as eager to break away from the viceroy's regimen as was Don

Felipe himself. At their last meeting, the viceroy's aide had hinted that, if he were able to bring off a military coup, he would give Don Ramón an influential post in his cabinet.

Don Ramón came out to welcome the tall, black-haired officer, and the two men embraced. "It is good to see you, Felipe," the *hacendado* exclaimed. "I'll see that my *trabajadores* quarter your men and stable your horses. How long can you stay with me this time?"

"Not long, I'm afraid, Don Ramón." The viceroy's aide purposely flattered his friend by applying the title of nobility. "I have been ordered to Santa Fe and to Taos."

"*¡Caramba!* You surely must be saddle sore by this time, after that long ride north from Mexico City. But not too sore to ride in the saddle of one of my pretty *criadas*, I'll wager?"

"No, never that. I'd welcome it."

"I shall have four or five of the prettiest ones serve us dinner tonight, my good friend. And we shall talk."

Arm in arm, the two men walked into Don Ramón's study, where the *hacendado* poured out wine. They clinked glasses as Don Ramón toasted, "To our future, and to a new Mexico!"

After discussing the changes in the political situation, Don Ramón brought the conversation around to the subject of horses. "I shall be glad to sell you horses from my herd," he told his companion. "As a matter of fact, not long ago I made a sale to a young *gringo*. He is the son-in-law of Don Diego de Escobar, the *intendente* of Taos."

"Now that is interesting! Don Diego is on the list of officials I have been ordered to visit." Don Felipe straightened in his chair and set down his goblet on a little tabouret. "A *gringo*, you say, married into the de Escobar family? Most unusual."

"In itself, yes, but how this *gringo* paid me was still more so, Felipe. Do you know, he gave me two ingots of the finest silver I have seen in years. He told me that Don Diego's *capataz* had dug up the ground of an old shed and accidentally discovered where they had been buried for years."

"And you believed that?"

"Of course I didn't. Do you know, I sent two of my best *trabajadores* to follow that *gringo*. And the damnable thing about it is that they have not returned. I hardly think it wise to make inquiries that would be traced back to me. I can only conclude that they met with some misfortune, or perhaps found another *patrón* more generous than myself. Or else," Don Ramón's face darkened and his lips tightened, "that this *gringo* found them out and killed them. Naturally, I have no proof."

"Ingots of silver," Don Felipe de Aranguez repeated, relishing the words and leaning forward, his face taut with interest. "Perhaps there are more silver ingots buried in that same plot of ground? It would be very interesting, when my men and I arrive at the *hacienda* of Don Diego de Escobar, to make a search for that."

"It would be a service to me, Felipe. You might even learn, by diplomatic and very tactful questioning, whether my two men ever appeared around that accursed *hacienda*." Don Ramón de Costilla chuckled sardonically. "To be sure, two silver ingots are worth a good deal more than what I asked for the four horses I sold the *gringo*. And they are surely worth the lives of those two scoundrels. They were useful to me, but there were times when they took too many liberties. I do not mourn them, but of course you can understand that I should resent a *gringo*'s disposing of them."

"I promise you that I shall try to find out the secret of this mysterious silver, Don Ramón."

"*¡Bueno!* And now, dinner awaits us. And you shall make your choice of your companion for the night, my good friend."

On the very day when Don Felipe de Aranguez had paid a visit to his friend and secret ally Don Ramón de Costilla, Doña Inez gave birth to a daughter. Don Diego had prayed for long hours in the chapel that his handsome wife's labors would not be prolonged, since she was in her forties and was bearing her first child. Miraculously, his prayers were answered, for after only five hours of what the devoted midwife pronounced an unbelievably easy ordeal, Doña Inez rested with her baby at her bosom.

His face streaked with tears, trembling with emotion, Don Diego entered the room, knelt down, and kissed her hand. "My Inez, my brave, wonderful Inez! My prayers have been answered!" he said hoarsely.

"But it is not a son, Diego. How I wanted to give you a son, *querido!*" she murmured, her face drawn but her eyes soft with tenderness as she lifted the baby for him to see.

"You must not reproach yourself. God has been good to all of us, and to give you a daughter that will remind me of you—see, she has the same color of hair that you do, and yes, those same enchanting eyes!" he reassured her as he leaned over the bed to kiss her and then, very reverently, to touch the forehead of the child.

"I had thought we might name her Dolores, *mi corazón*," she whispered.

But Don Diego shook his head. "No, my darling, you must not efface yourself. I know that you wish in this way to pay tribute to your sister, who was my dear wife and companion. But it is you now, in this life of ours together, Inez, whom I love. No, my dearest one. Let us name her instead after your mother, Francesca."

"¡Oh, Diego, *mi esposo querido!*" Doña Inez could not restrain her tears. She drew him down to her to give him a kiss of unspoken gratitude and devotion.

The war between the British and the Americans was reaching its climax. Last month the Creeks had signed a peace treaty at Fort Jackson, Alabama, turning over to the United States most of their vast lands. The British assault on Fort Erie had been repulsed by American troops. And though the American peace commissioners, including John Quincy Adams and Henry Clay, had already met the British commissioners at Ghent, hostilities still raged. On August 24 British troops defeated American forces at Bladensburg, then entered Washington and burned the Capitol, the White House, and other public buildings. Now, as this first week of September came to an end, the British were preparing a land and naval attack upon Baltimore, an attack which was destined to be repulsed and to inspire Francis Scott Key to write the words of the "Star Spangled Banner" during the bombardment.

It was on the last day of this first week of September that Don Felipe de Aranguez and his twenty mounted soldiers rode up before the *hacienda* of Don Diego. Miguel Sandarbal and Esteban Morales, who were working in the corral, hurried out to meet the soldiers. Dismounting, Don Felipe insolently declared, "You there, *trabajador,* go fetch your master, Don Diego de Escobar. Tell him that I am the envoy from *su excelencia* the viceroy, and I order him to appear before me at once."

"I will tell the *patrón*, señor," Miguel said with studied politeness. "But he is not a *peón* who comes running to the order of a *soldado*, señor. He is *intendente* of Taos."

Don Felipe's face contorted with anger. He gestured to his men to dismount. "Teniente Roblar, you will put our horses in the corral there. Drive out the others. And you, *hombre*," gesturing toward Miguel, "come here to me."

Miguel calmly walked forward and faced the viceroy's aide. Don Felipe drew off his gloves and slashed the *capataz* across the mouth with them, drawing blood. "That will teach you, *trabajador*, not to insult the personal aide of His Excellency General Calleja! Now take me at once to your master!"

Miguel Sandarbal did not flinch under the unjust and humiliating blow. He put his hand to his mouth to wipe away the blood and stiffly inclined his head. "I shall inform Don Diego of your presence, señor," he said and entered the *hacienda*.

But Don Felipe, not satisfied with this, followed directly behind Miguel and pushed his way through the door which the *capataz* was about to close. At the same time, turning back, he signaled to his men to follow. Some fifteen of them entered the house. Down the left hallway, two pretty young maids, Frasquita Flores and Asunción Rodriguez, had just emerged from the little chapel where they had said their Sunday prayers and were preparing to go to the kitchen to bring the noon meal to the de Escobar family. Four of Don Felipe's men, with lewd gestures and lascivious praises, strode down the hallway after them. Frasquita uttered a cry and ran, pursued by a burly rogue who had been cashiered for theft in the viceroy's army and gone over at once to Don Felipe's retinue. Asunción stood her ground and, as two of the soldiers began to paw at her, slapped one of them viciously and made him stumble back.

At this moment, Don Diego emerged from his wife's chamber, having spent much of the morning with her and little Francesca.

His face congealed with anger as he quickly took in the situation. "Miguel, who are these men and how dare they profane the holy day of our Lord?" he demanded.

"I can explain that—I take it that you are Don Diego de Escobar, *intendente* of Taos?" Don Felipe de Aranguez stepped forward to confront Don Diego.

"I am, sir. But I do not understand why you and your men forced your way into my *hacienda*. Am I, then, under arrest?"

"No, Don Diego. I am Don Felipe de Aranguez, special envoy and personal aide to His Excellency General Calleja. I have here documents authorizing me to collect the revenues due from the province of Taos." He raised the rolled parchment documents.

"I see. Yes, I have had a letter from General Calleja indicating that you would be sent here to Taos. But may I remind you, Don Felipe, that I am master of my own *hacienda*. It was necessary only for you to announce your presence, and I should at once have invited you into my home."

"I do not need a lesson in protocol or manners from you, sir," was Don Felipe's sneering retort.

"And I shall ask you to order your men not to take liberties with any member of my household. I wish that understood." Don Diego was pale with anger and controlled himself only with a supreme effort.

"Ruiz, Portales, Corbacho, Santimar, let those *criadas* alone! Place yourselves on guard outside the door of this *hacienda* and see that our horses are kept in the corral," the viceroy's aide commanded. Then to Don Diego, he remarked, "You may wish to examine my credentials." With this, he unrolled both parchment documents. On the blank one, which he had ingeniously induced General Calleja to sign, he had written what amounted to an order of confiscation, using the phrase, "and shall have power to seize such goods and monies as are considered contraband or are of suspicious origin, though not pertaining to royal revenues due unto *el rey*." By this trickery, Don Felipe had already managed to fill one of the saddlebags with silver that he intended to keep for himself.

Don Diego, almost blind with anger, took the documents from Don Felipe's hand and stared at them for a full moment. At last, he read them, folded them back, and returned them to the viceroy's aide. "Your authority is plain, señor. I have prepared my report, and the tithes from Taos will be given to you. Although I find it unseemly that you should collect them on this holy day, nonetheless as a loyal subject of *el rey* I stand prepared to do my duty."

"How very obliging!" Don Felipe sneered. "But I suspect

that you have not included in these tithes a portion of the treasure which I am told your *capataz* found on the property of your estate—which I have no doubt was granted you by *el rey* to go with your post as *intendente*."

"I do not know to what treasure you refer, Don Felipe. But a just and accurate accounting of the tithes are in the report. It was prepared by Señora Sandarbal—the wife of my *capataz*, who is also my trusted and loyal friend."

At this moment, Carlos came out of Weesayo's room and, as he came down the hall, overheard the last interchanges between the viceroy's aide and his father. Meanwhile, Catarina and Weesayo, hearing the loud sound of voices and the cries of the two maids, had come out of their rooms with their babies in their arms.

"*Mi padre*, what is happening? I heard loud voices, angry voices, and the cries of women—who are these men?" Carlos demanded.

"My son, this is Don Felipe de Aranguez. He comes from the viceroy himself to ask for the tithes due from our province."

"Miguel—your mouth is bleeding—have any of these swine dared to strike you?" In his youthful indignation, Carlos pushed ahead of his father and put his hand on the basket guard-hilt of his rapier. "Sir, whoever you are, if you struck my good friend Miguel, I will challenge you to a duel."

"You young puppy, I do not duel with the likes of you! As for your famous Miguel, he treated me without the courtesy due my station, and so I taught him a lesson. Take care, I would not advise drawing that rapier. I should not like my men to disarm you—it might be painful in the process," Don Felipe mocked.

"Please, *mi corazón*." Weesayo came up to him and spoke with concern. "You must not fight him. Oh, how·I wish John Cooper were here."

"John Cooper," Don Felipe repeated, having overheard Weesayo's use of that name. "Is that not the *gringo* who married your daughter Catarina, Don Diego?"

"It is, señor."

"I should rather have you call me Don Felipe, since I too have a hidalgo's blood in my veins. I am also a colonel in the army of the viceroy."

"And I suppose, Don Felipe, that if I persist in calling

you 'señor,' you will strike me with those gloves—yes, I perceive now that is the weapon you used on Miguel," Don Diego countered.

"Surely you jest, Don Diego. I would not think of striking the *intendente* of Taos. However, I should like to know where this *gringo* son-in-law of yours is."

"He is out hunting, if you must know, señor," Catarina flashed, as she shouldered her way beside Don Diego, holding little Andrew in her arms, her green eyes bright with contempt. "Will you slap me with your gloves, too?"

Don Felipe had the good grace to flush and to lower his eyes before this rebuke from so beautiful a young woman. He tried to make amends by making a courtly bow, but Catarina sniffed and turned her back on him. "Forgive me, señora. And forgive me, Don Diego, for intruding on you during your holy day. I shall put off further business until tomorrow, and ask that you quarter my men here until then. I will take your accounting and the revenues at both our leisures."

Don Diego bit his lip and frowned. But, trying to make the best of a bad situation, he forced a smile to his face and graciously replied, "It will be my pleasure to entertain you and your officers at dinner this evening. There are guest rooms for them in my *hacienda*. But for the enlisted men, I fear I must ask you to quarter them in the bunkhouse. My *capataz* will take them there."

"That is gracious of you, Don Diego. And I shall accept your hospitality. We have many things to talk about, the treasure particularly. Very well—Teniente Roblar, you are my only officer. You will, therefore, march the others out to this bunkhouse, and see that the *capataz* arranges for their needs."

Luis Roblar briskly saluted. Carlos, fuming with indignation, his fingers gripping the hilt of the rapier, watched them go. Then he muttered under his breath so that only his father could hear, "Now I cannot wait for John Cooper to find us a home far from these greedy brutes!"

Namantay, Descontarti's first wife and the mother of Weesayo, longed for her daughter. It seemed many moons since Weesayo and her man had visited the stronghold to show Descontarti their firstborn. How clever the Spanish man who had mated with the Light of the Mountains was—to have Weesayo bring her gifts which she knew were truly from him. He thus showed great respect while, at the same time, not violating the strict Apache law that he must never speak to or look at the mother of his squaw!

But what concerned her most was the growing weakness of her own man. Descontarti would often leave the wickiup late at night and would go out to the tall peak, where he would commune with the Great Spirit. She would pretend to be asleep, but she would hear him cough. And sometimes she would find the trace of blood which he had tried to cover up with the sand just outside their lodging. He would not give in to his illness; he would still be *jefe* of the Jicarilla Apache. She had prayed that the Great Spirit would not be angry with her if she sent to the *hacienda* where Weesayo lived with her man. Perhaps they would have some magic medicine that would help Descontarti grow stronger again, or at least ease the pain she knew he hid from her, as from all the others.

And so on this Thursday evening when he had gone again, earlier than was his wont, to the mountain to commune, she hurriedly called to Manakonday, one of the young scouts who was always boasting that he could outrun and outride any brave. "Go you to the *hacienda* to the south, where Weesayo dwells," she told him. "Tell her and her man that I am eager to see her again. Tell her also that our *jefe* grows weaker and that I pray there may be a way to give him back his strength. Perhaps Weesayo will speak to her man, and he will know what can be done—this without making Descontarti grow smaller in the eyes of his people."

Manakonday set out on this mission at once. He took with him only the scantiest provisions, and he contented himself with only a few hours' sleep. When he rode into the courtyard of the *hacienda*, it was late Sunday afternoon. Some of the *trabajadores* who were standing outside gossiping and taking their ease, resentful of the soldiers who had forced them to share their quarters in the spacious bunkhouse, greeted the young scout as he dismounted and tethered the mustang to a hitching post near the corral.

A few moments later, the four men who had tried to assault Frasquita and Asunción came out of the bunkhouse and, seeing Manakonday, hurried toward the *hacienda*, one of them calling to him, "¡Alto, indio! What do you do here?"

Manakonday's only weapon was his hunting knife, and he saw two of the four soldiers draw *pistolas* from their holsters. In broken Spanish, he assured them that he meant no harm and that he had been sent by the *jefe* of his tribe to bring a message to the latter's daughter.

"You lying dog, you have come to beg or to steal! Go back to your mountain, or I'll shoot you," the man who had been slapped by Asunción snarled as he leveled his pistol at the young scout's chest. Then, seeing Manakonday stop and lift his hands in a sign of surrender, he grinned at his companions. "Let's teach this Indian dog a good lesson. Let's thrash him and send him back to his mountain."

Manakonday understood, but he foresaw the consequences if he tried to defend himself with his knife. Unflinchingly, using his arms only to fend off some of the blows, he sustained a severe beating and at last sank down on all fours. "There, that will teach you we mean what we say, Indian dog!" his chief tormenter mocked him, aiming a vicious kick at his buttocks. "Now get on your horse and ride back to your kennel and the rest of your mangy dogs of a tribe!"

The scout stumbled to his feet, untethered his mustang, and, wincing with pain from the beating, dragged himself into the saddle and rode off. The man who had threatened his life lifted the pistol and, for sheer spite, sent a ball whistling above his head. At this, the scout drummed his heels against the mustang's flanks to urge it into a gallop, and the soldier turned back to his fellows with a triumphant laugh. "A yellow dog, as well as a mangy one, eh, *mis compañeros?*"

Twenty-two

For John Cooper, these past seven weeks had been an unforgettable adventure. They had served to sharpen the skills of woodsmanship that he had learned from living among the Indians during his youth.

His decision to leave Lobo back at the *hacienda* to guard had been a wise one; when he had left Shawneetown, he had had to rely on Lije for his own survival. This time, he was dependent wholly upon himself. And his palomino, whom he had named Fuego because of its magnificent spirit and stamina, had responded to the young mountain man's guidance with rare intelligence. With Fuego, he had established the same kind of companionable communication that he had known with Lije and now with Lobo.

When he had left Taos, he had crossed into Texas territory by the Canadian River and journeyed southward over the Pecos. From there, he had headed southeast until he had come to the surging Frio River, near Uvalde. In this uninhabited region, he had seen a valley and rolling land and grazing grass. More than that, he had seen huge long-horned cattle meandering idly. There were no forts of Mexican soldiers in the area for many miles on either side. Here, then, would be an ideal site for his new home . . . a home in which Don Diego and Carlos could share with him the freedom from oppression by an intolerant government.

Satisfied with his discovery, he had headed back, intending to visit Descontarti in order to pledge the Jicarilla Apache chief to the protection of Don Diego's *hacienda* until the time came when they would move to this new home. But as he rode back and crossed the Canadian River, a sudden thought struck him. What would become of the silver mine once he and the others established their new home so far distant? Might not someone else come upon it and, drawn by the mystery of those skeletons outside the hidden opening to the mine, discover the real secret that those monks and soldiers had guarded for so many years? Perhaps, then, the best would be to dispose of the skeletons that had for so many years served as macabre sentinels of the secret mine.

Thus it was that he decided to ride Fuego to that isolated mountain. Tethering the palomino on the lower slope, he ascended to the plateau. He had no tools for burial, and so, first having knelt and said a prayer for the souls of the dead, he forced himself to gather up the dry bones and the ancient weapons and the rusty morions and to hurl them down from the edge of the plateau into the dense shrubbery and boulders hundreds of feet below. This done, he descended, mounted Fuego, and rode off for the stronghold.

Long days under the hot sun had tanned his face almost the color of an Apache's. He was leaner and wirier, and that was good after the much too comfortable life at the *hacienda*. There had been plenty of game, and his tinderbox had furnished the fire for cooking the antelope or the rabbit or, once, the delicious roasted meat of a *javelina*, which had charged Fuego out of a thicket of mesquite.

It was the second week in September when he rode into the stronghold and went to Descontarti's wickiup. The Apache chief greeted him warmly and declared that there would be a feast this evening in his honor. After it was done, John Cooper and Descontarti sat before the fire and watched the ceremonial dances. And the old shaman performed the ritual of union between a young brave and a maiden, reminding the young mountain man how Carlos and Weesayo had been joined under the starry sky and how his own Catarina had so delightfully induced him to spend their second honeymoon in this peaceful place.

Then he turned to Descontarti and spoke quickly of the journey he had made and the reason for having made it. "You have my word, my blood brother," Descontarti gravely avowed, "that my braves and I will guard your *hacienda* and see that no harm comes to your people or your dwelling until you have gone to your new home. I understand why you seek to leave Taos. What you tell me of this war across the seas and what it will do to change the ways of the *mejicanos* makes me fear for my people, also. I do not know if the soldiers, who have left us in peace for so long, will now wish to drive us out. But that is for the Great Spirit to say."

"There are no Spanish soldiers near the place I've found, Descontarti. It's a part of the Texas territory the Spanish government doesn't seem to have done much about, and that's one reason I picked it."

"Still, we remain blood brothers, and it will not be too far for either of us to send messengers when there are tidings of good or evil," Descontarti mused.

"I will always be your blood brother and you mine, Descontarti. But let me speak with a straight tongue now, as I've always done with you—the sickness still tears at you, doesn't it?"

Descontarti looked away from the fire and was silent for a long moment. Then he said, "It still consumes, *Halcón*. I pray to the Great Spirit to give me days enough to teach my restless young braves that the way of peace is best for all of us. They would still make war upon the Mescalero. Kinotatay has become my right hand in counseling them to wisdom. And, if it is the will of the Great Spirit that I may be taken to my ancestors, then let it be Kinotatay who is *jefe* in our stronghold. But you will say nothing of this to anyone, my brother?"

"I will say nothing," John Cooper promised.

Because he was deeply concerned over Descontarti's health, John Cooper allowed himself two days in the stronghold, rather than the one he had originally planned. As he was preparing to go to his wickiup to sleep on his last night before returning to Taos, there came a shout from one of the lookout scouts. "Manakonday comes!" he called.

A few minutes later, the young scout raced his exhausted mustang up to the wickiup of Descontarti and sank down on the ground on all fours.

"What are these marks on your face and your body, Manakonday?" Descontarti asked. "What evil news do you bring from Taos?"

"*Mi jefe,*" the young scout gasped as he staggered to his feet and wearily made obeisance to his chief, "there were *soldados* at the *hacienda* where *El Halcón* dwells. I wished to bring the message from Namantay to her daughter, Weesayo, but the soldiers would not let me. They threatened to kill me, and they beat me and called me a mangy dog and bade me go back to my kennel."

John Cooper had heard the lookout scout's cry, and hurried to join the chief. When Manakonday had finished, he exclaimed to Descontarti, "That's just what I was afraid of! Before I left to search for the new land, Don Diego had received a letter from the viceroy saying that soldiers would come to collect the *dinero* which Taos must pay to *el rey*. I must go back there at once. If those soldiers have dared hurt Catarina or Carlos or Don Diego or Doña Inez, or your Weesayo, they'll pay for it!"

"You cannot do this alone, *Halcón*. You will need my braves to ride with you. Manakonday," the Apache chief turned to the exhausted scout, "how many *soldados* were there at the *hacienda?*"

"I did not see all of them, *mi jefe*, only the four who beat me and held a *pistola* on me so that I did not fight back. But I saw their horses in the corral, the saddled horses of the *soldados*. I counted twenty."

"Then I will send forty of my braves with you, *Halcón*. Leave now. It will take you two suns and two moons to reach your *hacienda* if you ride now and do not stop too long for rest or food."

Don Felipe de Aranguez had collected the official revenues from the province of Taos, accompanied by Don Diego's formal report which Bess Sandarbal had painstakingly inscribed at his dictation. Yet he was reluctant to leave the *hacienda* without investigating the treasure about which Don Ramón de Costilla had spoken. After the heavy pouch with its silver *pesos* of tithes had been packed into his own saddlebag, he declared to Don Diego, "By this authority of the viceroy, I shall exact from you all the knowledge you possess of how your *capataz* came upon the ingots of silver which your *yerno gringo* used to buy horses from my friend, Don Ramón de Costilla."

"I have told you before, Don Felipe," Don Diego said, nettled by the harassment and by this untoward imposition on his hospitality, "that I have already spoken with my *capataz* and the *trabajadores*, and no one here knows anything about this buried treasure. You must have been misinformed. And your constant implication, Don Felipe, that I am trying to conceal revenue from the viceroy and from *el rey* himself is shamefully insulting. By now, even Governor Manrique knows that I am loyal and honest—perhaps to a fault."

"Take care how you choose your words to me, Don Diego," the viceroy's aide retorted. "I seem to detect in that last remark of yours the feeling that you begin to question the wisdom of fealty to our most glorious majesty, Ferdinand VII."

"I do not question that at all, señor. I question only your continued presence here. I ask you, since the tithes and the report concerning them are now in your possession, that you and your soldiers leave my *hacienda*. Surely your official business with me as *intendente* of Taos is at an end."

"It is at an end when I choose to say it is, and not before, Don Diego. I will have my men dig up all of this ground where I was told that your *capataz* found the silver. And I may have more questions for you then. We shall start tomorrow morning."

Don Diego's eyes rolled upward, and then, resignedly, he inclined his head and left the room.

On the following morning, Don Felipe himself summoned Miguel Sandarbal and asked him pointed questions about the exact location of the site where the silver ingots had been found. He had been told, Don Felipe said, that the silver was dug up in the floor of a shed. With a shrug, the *capataz* took the viceroy's aide to the hut which Lobo had formerly occupied.

Don Felipe's four soldiers spent all of Tuesday digging up the ground of the shed, finding nothing at all except a bone which Lobo himself had hidden after one of his forays.

Don Felipe was not entirely satisfied. He wished, however, to spend a few days with his good friend Don Ramón to indulge himself in the carnal pleasures which the rancher would offer him, and also to have a few days to himself so that he could alter some of the reports from the *intendentes* of the provinces whose taxes he had collected. A good many of the silver *pesos* in his saddlebags and those of his men would find their way into his own pocket.

As a consequence, he told Don Diego at supper that Tuesday evening that he would ride back to the viceroy with two of his men, but that he would leave the rest of his troop quartered in the bunkhouse until the *gringo* returned from what he now regarded as a suspiciously long hunting trip.

On the following morning, Don Felipe conferred with his lieutenant, Luis Roblar, and gave him strict instructions:

"You will remain as a guest in this *hacienda,* and keep the men in the bunkhouse—see that they don't disturb these sensitive little *criadas* of our worthy *intendente.* Have your men mingle among the *trabajadores,* listen to them. Often by chance, someone says something not meant for other ears, *¿comprende?* And do not leave until this *gringo,* John Cooper, returns, no matter how long it takes, do you understand me? You are to question him about the silver. When you have found out all you think you can, rejoin me at the *hacienda* of Don Ramón, where I shall be staying for a few days."

He had ridden off with the young private and Sergeant Juan Estigo. He had a particular purpose in choosing these regular soldiers of the royalist army: he intended to recruit them to his own private ranks and build his military force. He had admired the way the sergeant had conducted himself, firm and yet discreet, without giving offense. He also knew Juan Estigo's record and was impressed by it. And finally, since the sergeant had happened to mention that his wife was about to deliver his second and her fifth child, he was certain that Estigo would welcome the pay and the title of *subteniente* which he could offer.

Before they had arrived at the ranch of Don Ramón de Costilla, Estigo had reluctantly agreed to resign his noncommissioned post and accept employment with Don Felipe de Aranguez.

Leading the way on his great white palomino stallion, with "Long Girl" primed and loaded in his saddle sling, John Cooper left the mountain trail of the Sangre de Cristo and descended into the gentle valley which led to the *hacienda.* Forty of Descontarti's braves galloped behind him.

Hearing the thunder of the horses' hooves, Luis Roblar came out of the *hacienda,* belching and patting his belly, for he had eaten his supper early and imbibed a good deal of Don Diego's best wine from El Paso. He uttered a startled cry when he saw the Jicarilla Apache, naked to the waist, their bodies painted with the symbols of war, armed with lances, bows, and arrows, riding toward him with the *gringo rubio* at their head on a great white stallion. Cupping his hands to his mouth, he bawled, "*¡Soldados, aquí pronto!*"

At his call, the bunkhouse door was flung open and several of his men hurried out, as startled as he by the sight confronting them.

"Are you John Cooper Baines, señor?" Roblar hoarsely demanded, his hand at the holster of his pistol.

"I am, though I don't know who you are to have the right to ask it," John Cooper said levelly. "You'd best get your hand away from that *pistola, hombre,* because Kinotatay has an arrow aimed right at your heart."

"You cannot talk this way to soldiers of the viceroy," Roblar tried to bluster. "I am here to ask you about the bars of silver you claim the *capataz* found in the abandoned shed. The *capataz* has informed me that he knows nothing about the silver."

"That's true. I found the silver, and that's all there is. You're wasting your time if you think you're going to find any more anywhere around here. Well now, if you're in command, I'd advise you to ride your men out of here and back to the viceroy. You can see that my friends aren't exactly ready to smoke the pipe of peace with you."

Luis Roblar swore under his breath and drew his hand away from the holstered pistol. He had seen Kinotatay's arrow drawing back to the maximum of the bowstring, leveled at his chest. He saw also that the Apache far outnumbered his men, most of whom had not taken their sidearms with them to answer his call. Grudgingly, he conceded defeat. "Very well, Señor Baines. I do not intend to have my men massacred by your savages. But I shall report this to Don Felipe, you may be certain of it." Then, a scowl on his face, he gestured to his men. "Saddle your horses. We ride to the *hacienda* of Don Ramón de Costilla!"

In a short time, Don Felipe's men were on their way and Don Diego, trembling in the aftermath of first anger and then vast relief, strode forward to clasp John Cooper by the shoulders. "Surely *el Señor Dios* sent you to us at this moment, John Cooper!" he exclaimed. "I think that, if those ruffians had stayed another day, I should have led my *trabajadores* against them to drive them out."

"And I, John Cooper," Carlos vehemently declared, stepping beside his father and putting an arm around the latter's shoulders, "I very nearly bloodied my rapier for the first time since we came to Taos."

"These were the soldiers from the viceroy, to collect the taxes?" the young mountain man asked.

"That is true. Yet the curious thing is that they did not wear the uniforms like the *soldados* I saw in Mexico City and

Santa Fe," Don Diego mused. "Only two of them, and one was a sergeant. The man who commanded them, who called himself Don Felipe de Aranguez, showed documents with the viceroy's seal; that was clear enough. But they came on Sunday, and, not content with collecting the taxes with my full report, this Don Felipe insisted on searching for the silver."

John Cooper frowned and nodded, saying nothing. He realized that the silver he had found was creating greater problems for Don Diego. The sooner his father-in-law left Taos the better, and John Cooper was relieved to think that he had found a good site for the new ranch.

"Well, Don Diego, I think I've found the answer to all our troubles," he said aloud. Before sharing his news with his father-in-law, he thanked Kinotatay for his help and sent the troop of Indians back to their stronghold.

"Let's go into the house," John Cooper said. "I've ridden a long way, and after I've seen Catarina, I'll come to you and tell you about my trip." John Cooper realized, as he entered the house, that there would be questions about the silver and about his involvement with it. He would tell Don Diego what he could, and when the time was right—when they had moved to their new ranch—he would tell the whole story.

His reunion with Catarina was blissful indeed, as he had hoped it would be. No longer did she reproach him for having been away for so long, nor did she accuse him of having gone hunting in order to shirk his responsibilities to her and little Andrew. Now, more than ever before, there was sharing and understanding between them.

Don Diego had meanwhile assembled his entire family in the study. Don Diego had also asked that Miguel Sandarbal and his wife, Bess, be present to share the news that would affect them as well, since their lives were inextricably tied to those of the de Escobars. He poured a glass of his finest wine and, when John Cooper came in with his wife and child, toasted his son-in-law: "To him whom *los indios* call *El Halcón*, not only because he is brave, but because he has become so vital a part of this family and now proposes to give us greater life than ever!" They drank to this, and then Don Diego turned to the young man. "Tell us what you wish, and I shall listen with a very open mind, that I promise you."

"I rode off to find some land where we could settle in

Texas," John Cooper began. "Yes, it's true that it's still under Spanish rule. But there aren't many settlers. I found out from one of the Texans who stayed here that the largest city is San Antonio, but it has only about three thousand people. Some of them are merchants, others trade with the Indians, and some trade illegally with the French and the Americans. The Spanish there live off the land—there are a few large ranches and many small farms. And most of the soldiers of the viceroy would, if they went to Texas, be stationed only in the vicinity of San Antonio."

"Then where is this land you speak of, John Cooper?" Don Diego eagerly asked.

"It's west-southwest from San Antonio, I'd say. And there's a wonderful, cool river, not a sluggish one, and that will mean plenty of water for cattle and sheep. There are pecan trees, and I saw trees in which the bees were making great combs of wild honey. Think of how it'll taste on some of Tía Margarita's wonderful biscuits!" There was a ripple of laughter at these last words.

"But what about los indios? I have heard there are many savage tribes there—the Apache, the Comanche," Don Diego interposed.

"You forget that I have lived with Indians for about five years, Don Diego," John Cooper went on. "As blood brother to the Jicarilla Apache, I'd have a wampum belt which Descontarti would give me. It would show the other Apache tribes that I am a friend, and that I mean them no harm. Besides, these Indians in the Texas territory are wanderers, and they hunt the buffalo. We aren't interested in buffalo, we won't take away their food—if anything, by raising cattle, we might even manage to sell a good lot to the Indians, who always need meat for their campfires."

"Well, that is true enough," Don Diego agreed.

"The Comanche may try to steal our horses, but there again I'll have my Indian signs to show them that I'd rather be at peace with them than fight them. For that matter, if I can breed enough palominos from my stallion and the mares, there's no reason why I couldn't sell a few colts to the Comanche and at a pretty good price, too. From what the Texans tell me, the Comanche are the greatest horsemen they've ever seen, even better than the Apache. I'm not so sure that it's true, but it's not a bad thing to think about when we're raising horses and cattle. Sheep—well, it might be difficult to raise sheep as well as cattle and horses. Sheep eat grass down to the bare roots, as Miguel will tell you."

"That is true, *mi compañero*," the *capataz* put in.

"Now, we have to think about who should go first," John Cooper said. "Of course, it will have to be the *trabajadores*, with Miguel. They'll have to build a house for us and quarters for themselves and their families. I don't know if it would be such a good idea for the workers to take their wives and children with them—that's in case they should run into any trouble from the start."

"Father, I should like to go with Weesayo and Diego, and I can take charge of the building and the rounding up of the cattle—Miguel will help me with that, too, because he was born to work with animals." This was from Carlos, who had whispered to Weesayo and seen her nod her consent. She entwined one hand with his, as she held little Diego with the other.

"I should like to go with my son, if Doña Inez will come with me and bring Francesca. I for one am not afraid of danger. In my view, *los indios* will treat us more fairly than the men of this viceroy's aide—and there will be others like him, mark my words," Don Diego prophesied.

"I've got a feeling you're right about that, too, Don Diego," John Cooper assented. Then, turning to Miguel, he asked, "How soon can you and the *trabajadores* start for this new country? I've arranged with Descontarti to send along twenty of his braves to guard you while you're building the *hacienda* there. And they'll know the way, because I've told Descontarti exactly where it is."

Miguel approached the young man. "*Mi compañero*, I'll talk to the *trabajadores* this very night. I am sure they will all want to come with us. But we should certainly leave a few here, if you're going to stay on with Doña Catarina. What if soldiers come again?"

"We've about fifty workers in all, and don't forget the maids and the cook," John Cooper said, after thinking a moment. "Leave me fifteen good men who know how to use weapons. And that's another thing, Miguel. You bought some rifles, muskets, and *pistolas*, as well as powder and lead, in Chihuahua. Be sure to take along enough for your men. It may not be easy to get more ammunition quickly. I can get some in Taos, so you don't need to worry about how much you leave me with."

"I'll see to that, too, *amigo*," Miguel gruffly agreed. He put out his hand and John Cooper vigorously shook it. "I only hope it won't be too long before you come to join us. This is your idea, and it is a good one. Maybe I am speaking out of turn—I sometimes do, as my sweet *esposa*, Bess, never fails to tell me—but I am glad about this. For the sake of my *patrón* and all the rest of us, too. I have had my bellyful of soldiers and officers and their high-handed ways."

"Then it's settled?" John Cooper turned to look at Don Diego, then Carlos, and saw them both nod and glance fondly at each other. "Good!"

"But there is one thing you haven't really told us, my son," Don Diego suddenly burst out as they were about to leave the study. "What is all this about buried silver? I confess, it reads like a fairy story."

John Cooper and Catarina exchanged knowing glances, and then he said, "Well, I dug up the ground in the shed where I used to keep Lobo, and there it was, sticking right out. It came in handy for buying the palominos, and it was just luck. I don't think I'd have had that sort of *dinero* to buy those four beauties from Don Ramón de Costilla otherwise." John Cooper slyly put his right hand behind his back and crossed his fingers to fend off punishment for his fib. And he remembered, with a stab of nostalgia, how he had sometimes done that when he had told a lie to his mother or his father back in Shawneetown, so many years ago.

Twenty-three

Once a king of Spain said, "Ambitious men are certain to have enemies at court. But if they are ingenious enough and their loyalty is unquestioned, they can survive even this." In the case of Don Felipe de Aranguez, his enemy was Bautista Vergara. And though the viceroy's aide was ingenious enough, his loyalty was coming into question.

Bautista Vergara had been named by the viceroy as *protector partidario*, protector of the Indians. His function was that of defending the rights of Indians, in court, if necessary; to free them from all oppressors, and to make sure that they were receiving proper religious instruction. At one time, Vergara had taken monastic vows, but then left the church because Charles IV had appointed him to head a special commission investigating both the religious and the secular affairs of Nueva España.

He was an austere man, not quite fifty, lean, tall, with a pointed gray beard and cold, impersonal eyes. Vergara brought to his task a selfless devotion and objective appraisal of what he saw take place. And because Viceroy Calleja admired a man who could not be corrupted in an age of corruption, he gave great credence to Vergara's reports. He admired the relentless perfectionism which this lonely, self-disciplined ascetic—who had had neither mistress nor wife throughout his life—pursued as his code of living.

Bautista Vergara had taken umbrage at one of Don Felipe de Aranguez's cynical remarks. And he had thought to himself, "If this man mocks our governmental traditions of the monarchy and has so glib a belief that its laws may accommodate his own selfish desires, then here is a man to be watched." And from that day forth, a year ago, he had set as his personal mission the investigation of the true character and loyalty of the viceroy's favorite aide.

Among other things, it had been reported to him that, when Don Felipe set out from Mexico City to collect the revenues from the provinces, he had chosen only two soldiers from the regular troops, and selected men who were not enrolled in the lists at the garrison of Mexico City. This seemed strange to the *protector partidario*. In his official duties, he had occasion to employ a few men who, disguised as sometimes *peones* or again traders, passed through the provinces and learned, purely through casual conversation, many interesting facts which could not otherwise have been gleaned.

For some six months, Bautista Vergara had had a report on his desk that told of a deep friendship between the viceroy's aide and Don Ramón de Costilla. What distressed him particularly was that there had been an earlier report about Don Ramón's own somewhat suspicious activities. The debauched rancher was suspected of purchasing guns in Chihuahua and selling them to *los indios*. Throughout the provinces the last several months, there had been minor uprisings. Indian tribes like the Toboso had attacked military escorts as well as unarmed travelers going from one town to another. On three separate occasions, after these renegades had been driven off with heavy losses, it had been discovered that some of their weapons were of the latest models, available only in Chihuahua. And since it was against the law for *los indios* to have firearms, Vergara began to fix his attention on Don Ramón.

Because his pragmatic mind had been developed by the stern tenets of the Dominicans, in whose order he had taken his vows, Vergara firmly believed that where there was smoke, there must be fire. Don Ramón's excesses had become too great by now to ignore; and if Don Felipe, the viceroy's trusted personal aide, was known to be his closest friend, that would surely render Don Felipe suspect. To that end, therefore, the *protector partidario* sent two inquisitors, Brother Hermano Solar and Brother Gonsalvo Martinez, accompanied by ten mounted soldiers, to the ranch of Don Ramón de Costilla.

They arrived there three days before Don Felipe, on his way back to Mexico City from Taos, stopped to visit his good friend. When the two inquisitors in their black robes entered the *hacienda*, Don Ramón noticeably paled and began to stammer as he knelt and made the sign of the cross. Perhaps the Holy Inquisition was not so merciless in this New Spain as it had been in the land of Torquemada, but these stern-faced Dominicans cast terror into Don Ramón's heart.

Nor was he reassured when the elder of the two, Brother Hermano Solar, announced, "Don Ramón de Costilla, we are here to interrogate you on the matter of several forbidden acts which are contrary to the laws of both Holy Church and *el rey*. You are suspected on the charge of selling firearms to *los indios*. And these firearms have been used against *mejicano* troops. By this association, therefore, if proved, you could be charged with treason and mutinous rebellion against the crown."

Don Ramón knew better than to question the circumstances of how the inquisitors had garnered this news. The spiritual as well as temporal power of the inquisitors overruled all other considerations. And so, to save his own skin, he sank down on his knees, bowed his head, crossed himself, and admitted his guilt.

"That is a good beginning, my son," the older inquisitor commended him. "And now I am bound to ask you what association you have with the aide to the viceroy, Don Felipe de Aranguez. Is he associated with you in this deplorable enterprise?"

Trembling, his voice unsteady, sweat beading his temples, he betrayed Don Felipe's illicit distribution of province revenues and, worst of all, intimated that the viceroy's aide had formed his own military corps.

The two inquisitors exchanged a startled look. This was indeed better than they had hoped for.

Still on his knees, Don Ramón looked up at the stern face of the older inquisitor and stammered, "What do you mean to do with me, Brother Solar?"

"For the moment, nothing, Don Ramón. We shall report your confession as well as your contrition to the *protector partidario*. He will decide then what is to be done. I advise you to pray, my son, for the salvation of your soul, and to make good resolutions never again to violate the laws of God and man." The two black-robed priests then turned and left him kneeling there, damp with sweat and frightened as he had never been before.

When Don Felipe and his two recruits rode up to Don

Ramón's *hacienda,* the viceroy's aide was surprised to see the agitation and nervousness of his good friend. "What is wrong with you, Don Ramón? You look ill. Perhaps a touch of the sun?" he bantered.

"Oh, no, Don Felipe, much worse than that! A few days before you came, I was visited by two inquisitors sent by the *protector partidario, su excelencia* Bautista Vergara."

"That would be disturbing, I admit. Why did they come to you?"

"They—they found out—the devil alone knows how!—that I had sold weapons to the Toboso."

"That is a serious charge. I should have thought you'd have been more clever, knowing you as I do, Don Ramón."

"Yes, but—but that isn't all—" The *hacendado* stopped short, then paled and bit his lips, aware that he had said too much.

The viceroy's aide was quick to catch this. "What else did you tell the inquisitors?"

"Forgive me, Don Felipe—I had no other choice, you see! It is like this—they asked me about you and what my association was with you."

"That I am a friend, naturally. What else could you have told them? Or, did you tell them what should never have passed from your lips, Don Ramón?" Don Felipe's eyes narrowed, and he stepped forward, his hand at his pistol.

"By all the saints, Don Felipe, you know me better than that—I—I—"

"Well, *hombre?*" The question came like the hiss of a reptile about to strike. "Perhaps you told them about the silver?"

"Oh, no, I did not say a word about the silver, I swear it!" Don Ramón took out a bandanna and mopped his sweating face.

"Well then, something else is troubling you. You have nothing else to admit to, of course. Or can it be that you said more than you should have about my private business?"

"I had to—forgive me—they left me no choice—they might put me in an *auto-de-fé*—"

"Out with it, *hombre!*"

"I—I said that you had your own military corps—"

"You are not only a coward; you are a traitor, as well. You see, my dear Don Ramón, I can no longer trust you."

With this, Don Felipe de Aranguez drew out his pistol, put it to Don Ramón's temple, and pulled the trigger.

The two soldiers riding with him stifled a simultaneous cry of horror at this cold-blooded execution. But the viceroy's aide looked at his men with glowering eyes and curtly announced, "I am going to ride back to Mexico City. I am empowered to execute a traitor, which I have just done, and you men are witness to it. Roblar, you will be in charge here. Estigo, you will accompany me. Now, *Vamanos!*"

But the inquisitors and their military escort had reached the viceroy before Don Felipe. And when the latter was ushered into the audience chamber of the ruler of New Spain, he met with a frigid reception.

"Don Felipe de Aranguez," General Calleja sternly declared, "I herewith remove you from your office as my aide, and I strip you of your military rank of colonel. You have betrayed my trust and that of our king. The inquisitors have told me how your friend Don Ramón de Costilla accused you of irregularities in the collection of revenues from the provinces. Since I have not yet formally received these revenues nor your report concerning them, I do not pronounce this sentence upon you for that suspected offense. No, Don Felipe, I cannot permit an aide of mine to retain his own private army. It smacks of treason as well as revolt against my rule, which is entrusted to me by our rightful king."

"Your Excellency misjudges me," Don Felipe began, but was waved to silence by a peremptory gesture.

"Let me have the monies and the report. You will keep yourself in readiness in one of the guest rooms of the *palacio* until I send for you again. If I find that you have appropriated any of these monies for yourself, I shall demand a court-martial for you."

Realizing that he was caught, Don Felipe made the best of a bad situation by answering, "I ask Your Excellency's permission to bring the tithes and my report within the hour."

"Granted. An hour and no more, Don Felipe."

Once back in his room, the viceroy's aide feverishly restored the initial figures of the tithes which had been turned over to him by the provincial *intendentes*. To make the sum come out exactly right, it was necessary to turn over the single, heavy pouch that had been in his own saddlebag and

that had been intended for his own coffers. But the prospect
of a court-martial, its subsequent disgrace, and perhaps im-
prisonment, decided him.

Back in the audience chamber, he sat waiting while
General Calleja itemized the report and had his treasurer,
standing beside him at the desk, count out the monies. Then
at last he addressed Don Felipe. "For your sake, I am happy
to clear you of the charge of theft. But my verdict still stands.
You are dismissed from my service. You are henceforth no
longer a colonel in the Mexican army, but a private citizen.
And I warn you that your comings and goings will be
watched. The least irregularity, Don Felipe, may involve you
in far more serious consequences. I dismiss you, and I say
good day to you."

Broken and humiliated, Don Felipe de Aranguez bowed
in acknowledgment of this edict, turned his back, and walked
out of the audience chamber. He had gambled and lost. His
ambition to raise his own army and become the viceroy was
thwarted for the time being. But there was still a bright
prospect before him, humbled though he might seem. Now he
alone could pursue that elusive secret of the silver ingots;
certainly no one would suspect what he was up to since no
one but he and Don Ramón—and, of course, the *gringo*—
knew about the silver. And Don Ramón was dead. Perhaps
the *gringo*—who must assuredly know more than he had thus
far admitted—would have to die, too, if he didn't tell what he
knew about the silver. More than ever, Don Felipe de
Aranguez was convinced that John Cooper Baines had killed
the two *trabajadores* for the purpose of sealing their lips
forever over the true source of those gleaming silver bars.

The exodus of the household of Don Diego de Escobar,
intendente of Taos, began in October, 1814. Don Sancho de
Pladero was aghast when he learned that his good friend had
decided to resign his post and leave Nuevo Mexico. After
Don Diego explained the reasons for this drastic step, Don
Sancho proffered, "You know, old friend, permission to
venture outside of this territory is usually obtained from the
gubernador himself, but the right to travel within it can be
granted by myself as *alcalde*. Therefore, I shall not ask you
where you are going, but officially issue you the permission."

"You are truly a friend, Don Sancho. And so as not to
implicate you in the event that you are questioned, I shall not

tell you whither I am bound," Don Diego replied as the two men smiled and shook hands.

They spent the rest of the afternoon together, discussing old times. Don Diego also arranged to sell all but five hundred of his sheep to Don Sancho, and he invited the *alcalde* to a farewell dinner to be held at the *hacienda*.

Don Sancho de Pladero was distressed at the news his friend had shared with him. Perhaps for the first time since he had come to Taos so many years before, Don Sancho wondered if it was not time for him also to seek a new life away from the constricting regime which limited his powers and made him virtually a menial whose opinion was rarely sought on matters of state. Yet there was so much to be grateful for here in Taos. Young Tomás had just told his father that Conchita was going to bear his child, and Don Sancho had received the news with a bluff heartiness which concealed pride in his son's resurgent manhood. As for Doña Elena, she had singularly mellowed: even the servants had begun to sing her praises as a gracious, tolerant, and indulgent mistress. Not only was Doña Elena gracious toward the servants, but she and Don Sancho relished their evenings— and sometimes afternoons—of conjugal lovemaking. Well, perhaps it was not the passion of youth, but it was an unexpected and delightful bounty all the same. Thus Don Sancho was reluctant to do anything to disturb the peace and happiness of his household. Perhaps, they, too, would move, would seek a new life, but not just yet.

The farewell dinner at the de Escobar *hacienda* was tearful but joyous. The Baineses and the de Escobars were filled with great hope and excitement for the future, and the loyal friends who came to see them off, though saddened by the imminent departure, expressed their best wishes. The entire de Pladero family was there, and the greatly transformed Doña Elena continually dabbed at her eyes with a handkerchief. Amy and Frank Corland were also there, and Amy repeatedly hugged her young brother, Tom Prentice, who was accompanying the de Escobars to Texas. Finally, Padre Juan Moraga arrived to give his blessing to the Baineses and the de Escobars, as well as to the good people remaining in Taos.

On the next day, the de Escobars parted. John Cooper and Catarina, she holding little Andrew in her arms, said their farewells to Don Diego and his son, Carlos, to Doña

Inez and Weesayo, and to Miguel Sandarbal and his beloved Bess, as well as to the loyal *trabajadores* who set out that next morning on horses and burros, drawing the *carretas* of furnishings, cut timbers, tarpaulins, and the other supplies that would be needed to begin the construction of the new *hacienda* in the beautiful Texas valley that John Cooper had discovered. Descontarti, true to his promise, had sent the escort of armed braves to accompany this processional beyond the Sangre de Cristo Mountains and on to the luxuriant and fertile valley.

Twenty of the Jicarilla Apache would remain quartered in the bunkhouse until such time as John Cooper, Catarina, and little Andrew decided to follow their loved ones. Of these, Kinotatay and his son, Pirontikay, were the leaders: they spoke Spanish fluently and, at the very outset, convinced the somewhat frightened *trabajadores* who remained at the *hacienda* that they could be friends and companions in the tasks that remained to be done. Moreover, Kinotatay had reassured Don Diego that the braves who accompanied him and the others would be able to construct wickiups out of brush and wood and bark that would serve even more comfortably than the crude tents that Miguel had proposed they use. Until the new *hacienda* and bunkhouse were ready for their occupants, the emigrants from the province of Taos would be as comfortable as possible.

When that long processional had at last disappeared from view, Catarina turned to her husband and wistfully asked, "How long will it be before I can see Carlos and *mi padre* and *madre* Inez again, dearest Coop?"

"If all goes well, we should be able to leave here by January, my Catarina. Meanwhile, we've the *hacienda* all to ourselves. Tía Margarita, with Leonora to help her, will continue to cook all the dishes you love, and Teofilo Rosas, Leonora's husband, is one of the *trabajadores* who are staying here to guard us. So you see, my darling, we'll be quite comfortable. And I will be here to look after all of us."

"And to be with me and love me," Catarina whispered as she leaned forward to kiss him ardently on the mouth.

Twenty-four

Don Felipe de Aranguez had gone directly to his villa, ordering his beautiful, dissolute mistress to pack what clothes she needed and to be ready to accompany him at a moment's notice. Next, he had sent messages to the men of his private army to join him at the ranch of Don Ramón de Costilla. Finally, he had amassed his personal fortune of gold and silver *reales* and *pesos* and then, with his mistress, taken a carriage out of Mexico City well after midnight to avoid any imperial patrols, and headed for Don Ramón's ranch, hundreds of miles to the north.

His reasoning was that, by making his headquarters at the *hacienda* of the man he had killed, he would be far away from the scrutiny of the viceroy and, even more, from the *protector partidario*, Bautista Vergara. It would be an easy matter to compel the *trabajadores* who had worked for Don Ramón to come over to his side; the distribution of a little gold and silver would make them change allegiance without the slightest concern of scruples. Then, with this additional force, he could move against that mysterious *gringo* who had the key to the treasure of silver. With it, he could become master of all New Spain.

It was even easier than he had believed. His soldier, Luis Roblar, had kept good order at the ranch, and by November, Don Felipe returned and installed himself as head of Don Ramón's *hacienda*. The viceroy's former aide then summoned the *trabajadores* and promised them, in the most alluring terms, rewards beyond their wildest dreams if they would join his private army. He boasted that, because of his close association with the viceroy himself, he knew the workings of the government, and that because of the coming unrest, he

275

would be in a position to bring off a military coup which would bring all of Mexico under his control. Those who would be loyal to him in this shifting of power would be handsomely rewarded.

Not long after Don Felipe had established headquarters at Don Ramón's estate, a sturdy middle-aged *trabajador* named Paco Columbar had caught his eye. Columbar was well liked by his fellows, and like so many other *peones* in New Spain, he could recount the brutality of a *hacendado rico* against his parents. What interested Don Felipe the most was that Paco Columbar's father had worked in a silver mine near Hermosillo, in the province of Sonora. He had been unjustly accused of hiding pieces of raw ore in his clothes, sentenced to a public flogging, and after it had been administered, shown his bravado by spitting in the face of the mine owner. He had been dragged back to the whipping post and lashed to death. Paco Columbar had witnessed his father's martyrdom and had sworn to avenge it.

When he had grown to manhood, Columbar had run away from the *hacendado*'s estate; his mother had died the year before, and he was an only child. For a time, he had been an outlaw, and then he had gone to work for a sheepherder in Chihuahua. Disenchanted by the low wages and the offensive treatment he had received from his *patrón*, he had at last come to work for Don Ramón de Costilla. At the time that Don Felipe had killed the latter for his treachery, Columbar had held the rank of assistant *capataz*.

It was not out of sentimental compassion for Columbar's tragic boyhood that Don Felipe was interested in the man: it was his knowledge of how silver was mined and what it would look like in its refined form. When he described to Columbar the silver ingots that John Cooper had presented in payment for the palominos, the worker shrugged and retorted, *"Mi jefe,* I don't believe it was just dug out of the ground. There is certain to be more of it. To make bars like that, you have to take out the ore, melt it down, and shape it. And not just one man could do that—there must have been many. Whatever this *gringo* told you, he lied."

Don Felipe nodded, his face contorted with greed. Opening the drawer of Don Ramón's desk, he took out a small pouch filled with silver *pesos* and tossed it to Columbar. "You could be very helpful to me, *hombre.* I have other business to occupy me now. But tomorrow we'll talk again. I want you and some of your most trustworthy men to go to the *hacienda* of this *gringo* and find out what he is doing. And if you are able to learn where that treasure is really hidden, you can depend on my rewarding you as you deserve."

With this, dismissing the man, he went to the ornately decorated bedchamber of his former friend, where his mistress awaited him. Before he blew out the candle and clambered into the wide bed, he whispered to her, "*Mi corazón*, we are going to be very rich. And one day, if all goes well, you may become the wife of the new viceroy of Neuva España!"

The next day, he summoned Paco Columbar and bade him choose four of his best men who could be relied on for discretion and cunning. At Don Felipe's order, the quintet disguised themselves and rode off across the border into the province of Taos. Knowing the rule of restricted travel between the provinces, Don Felipe had ingeniously prepared a pass which he signed as aide to General Calleja. He counted on the fact that the viceroy would not yet have disseminated the news of his dismissal to all of the provinces and particularly to Santa Fe and Taos.

Six days later Columbar and his contingent of four men reported that the *hacienda* seemed deserted, and that the *intendente* had resigned his post and left Taos forever. More to the point, it appeared that the *gringo* had taken charge of the *hacienda* and might well be preparing to join Don Diego.

"You have done well, Paco." Don Felipe tossed him another pouch of silver *pesos*. "Now listen carefully. We shall ride to Taos in our full strength, all well armed. We shall capture this *gringo* and persuade him, forcibly if need be, to lead us to that cache of silver. We will ride tomorrow. Go tell the men you supervise, and have Subteniente Estigo report to me at once!"

A few minutes later, the former regular army sergeant reported to his new commander. Juan Estigo had begun to have serious doubts about his wisdom in resigning his noncommissioned post with the viceroy's troops and taking service with Don Felipe de Aranguez. First of all, he had been told that it was not yet time for him to move his family to his new quarters; he was needed at this ranch and Don Felipe had no wish to have women and children settle there. Besides, he had had many misgivings when he had witnessed the cold-blooded murder of Don Ramón de Costilla.

"It is good to see you, Estigo," Don Felipe genially greeted his latest recruit. "I will place you in charge of my *soldados*. Tomorrow, we ride back to Taos. We go after a rich treasure, and until now there is only one man who possesses the secret of where it is hidden—a *gringo* by the name of John Cooper Baines. Once we arrest him and force him to reveal its hiding place, I alone shall be in command of that secret. And with the wealth I hope to acquire, I shall one day become the ruler of all Mexico."

"*Comprendo, mi jefe.*" Juan Estigo nodded, but the lack of enthusiasm in his tone irked Don Felipe, and he lectured the man on the need for valor in the pursuit of glory and riches.

In all, a mounted force of eighty men, with Don Felipe at their head, rode toward Taos. All of them were dressed in the unique uniform that the former aide to the viceroy had devised to differentiate his private army from the royal troops. Yet, though he had been stripped of his rank, he wore his colonel's uniform, with two holstered pistols at his belt and a long knife with bone handle in the pocket of his tunic.

Directly behind him, commanding the men, was Subteniente Juan Estigo. They had bypassed Santa Fe, and taken an unused road which wound through tiny pueblos and hamlets. About five miles south of Taos, Don Felipe halted his little army as the sun was setting on this Saturday in November.

Turning in his saddle, he beckoned to Juan Estigo to draw abreast of him. "Take four men, Estigo, and go ahead of us to the *hacienda* of Don Diego de Escobar. See if they have guards posted. We want to take this *gringo* by surprise."

"*Sí, mi jefe,*" Estigo saluted his commander.

"Have you issued orders to prime all muskets, rifles, and *pistolas*?" Don Felipe demanded.

"I have, *mi jefe.*"

"*Bueno.*" Don Felipe's lips curved in a sadistic smile. "If there is no strength to protect that *hacienda*, Estigo, we shall take it at once. Your job will be to capture this accursed *gringo*. Do not hurt him, for we must find out where he has hidden that silver, you understand me? But then, I see no reason why your men should not enjoy the booty left behind by an *intendente* who has deserted his post. Yes, I hereby declare it forfeit. And, of course, there will be some pretty *criadas*—you may tell the men that to the victors belong the spoils of war."

"War, *mi jefe?*" Estigo anxiously asked.

"Of course, *hombre!*" Don Felipe barked. "Ask yourself if the prohibitions of the viceroy and the *gubernador* of Nuevo Mexico do not pertain to a *yanqui*. No *americanos* are allowed to come to Taos or Santa Fe to trade—well, this *gringo*, John Cooper Baines, without the *intendente* to protect him, is now fair game. And, for that matter, so is his wife, who is *muy linda, muy guapa*. Of course, she falls to me— that is understood."

Hearing this, Estigo involuntarily stiffened. He had seen Catarina when Don Felipe had made his first visit to the *hacienda* to collect the revenues of Taos. And he had well remembered how she had spiritedly taken that old woman's part and forced him to pay five *pesos* for the shawl he wanted. And now this Don Felipe was proposing, ever so callously, to torture her *esposo gringo* and to take her as his creature—no, it must not, it would not happen! If it hadn't been for her, he wouldn't have had the good fortune to meet his own *esposa*, to have a family, pride in his manhood. Now he knew that he had made a terrible mistake in leaving the army of the viceroy to take service with Don Felipe de Aranguez.

"Are you daydreaming, Estigo?" Don Felipe rebuked him. "*Hombre*, let me catch you again not paying attention to my orders, and I will demote you to a private in my ranks. You have your orders—pick your four men and scout that *hacienda* at once!" Estigo saluted mechanically. Wheeling his horse, he rode down along the double file of mounted men, choosing at random, hardly aware of what he did. When the four he had chosen rode out of the ranks to come behind him, he saluted Don Felipe and then, in an unsteady voice, ordered, "*¡Adelante, soldados!*"

It was a dark night; the moon was hidden behind clouds and there were few stars. Already a velvety blackness tinged the slopes of the Sangre de Cristo Mountains and seemed even to obscure the pueblos on the outskirts of Taos. Juan Estigo galloped his horse, the four men behind him keeping pace. Then suddenly he halted his horse and held up his hand. "I'll go on ahead, *amigos*," he called. "I want to see for myself—I was here before with Don Felipe when he came to collect the tithes."

The man nearest him, a swarthy, black-bearded former corporal of the viceroy's troops who had been cashiered for the brutal rape of an Indian woman, protested. "But *mi subteniente*, those were not Don Felipe's orders. We are to go in together, to see if there are any guards at the *hacienda* of this *gringo*."

"I am your officer; you will do what I tell you, Hernandez!" Estigo ordered. Then, in a sudden desperate impulse, he kicked his horse's belly and urged it on to a gallop ahead of his four soldiers. Santiago Hernandez scowled, then lifted his primed musket, squinted along the sight, and pulled the trigger. Estigo uttered a cry, clapping a hand to his left shoulder, swaying in his saddle; then he bent forward and urged his horse to its utmost gait.

"*¡Caramba!*" Hernandez swore, as Estigo disappeared in the darkness. "He has disobeyed the orders of our *jefe*—I'm going back to tell Don Felipe. You others wait here for me!" And wheeling his horse back along the trail, he galloped back.

"The idiot, the fool!" Don Felipe snarled when Hernandez told him what had happened. "I might have expected this. Yes, it is my fault. Estigo behaved with deference to that *gringo* and the *intendente* and his family. I think he has changed sides. You four, ride after him, kill him! You say you wounded him, Hernandez?"

"*¡Sí, mi jefe!* I saw him stagger, put a hand to his shoulder. He is hurt badly. Perhaps he won't reach the *hacienda*."

"We cannot take that chance. Damnation, if he is still alive, I shall put him in an anthill and let the ants strip the flesh from his filthy bones! There is no help for it, we must attack now!" Brandishing one of his pistols, Don Felipe called, "*¡Adelante, hombres, a toda velocidad!*"

The throbbing pain of the ball in his shoulder made Juan Estigo grind his teeth to supress his groans. He could hardly move his left arm, and he tightened his hold on the reins with his right hand as he repeatedly kicked his heels against his horse's belly to urge it on. Glancing back, he saw that he had thus far outdistanced his pursuers, and he prayed that he could reach the *hacienda* and give warning.

At last he reached the estate of Don Diego de Escobar, and the low structure of the *hacienda* was silhouetted in the darkness. His horse began to founder, and with a last shrill whinny stumbled and went down. Juan Estigo was thrown from the saddle, landing on all fours with a jolt that sent a wave of fiery agony through his shoulder. He staggered to his feet and stumbled toward the *hacienda*, hoarsely shouting, "*¡Guardese! ¡Guardese! ¡Los soldados de Don Felipe vienen!*"

John Cooper was lying beside Catarina in the wide bed, with little Andrew sleeping in his crib. He was naked but for his *calzoncillos*, and Catarina lay in the cradle of his left arm, as his right hand caressed her. Suddenly the hoarse shouts of Juan Estigo shattered their tender mood. John Cooper leaped out of bed, dressed hastily, reached for his Spanish dagger, and looped its thong round his neck. Then he retrieved "Long Girl" from the corner near the door. "Don't move, Catarina!" he exclaimed. "I don't know why Don Felipe's soldiers are coming—but there may be an attack on the *hacienda*. I hope Kinotatay heard the warning, too! Now you stay there, and keep Andrew close to you."

"Be careful, *mi corazón!*" she gasped. In her nightshift, she hurried out of bed to lift little Andrew into her arms and then to crouch down beside the crib, her heart wildly pounding, a prayer on her lips.

As John Cooper hurried out of the *hacienda*, Juan Estigo, his right hand pressed against the bleeding wound, staggered toward him. "*¡Guardese, por el amor de Dios, señor!* It is Don Felipe—he has brought his soldiers to make you tell him about the silver—he says he will take your woman and let his men have the *criadas*—I rode ahead to warn you, because of the Señora Catarina—" Then, with a choking gasp, he sank down on his knees and rolled unconscious onto his side.

"Kinotatay! *¡Aquí!*" John Cooper bawled. "*Trabajadores*, get your guns and *pistolas*, we're being attacked!"

The bunkhouse door was flung open and Kinotatay and his son, Pirontikay, hurried out, armed with their bows, the quivers of arrows slung over their shoulders. John Cooper bent down and dragged Estigo into the house, instructing one of the maids to minister to his wounds, then ran toward the two Apache. "It's the same men you helped drive off before, Kinotatay! I don't know how many there are, but we've got to fight them off!"

"My braves come now—and your *trabajadores* with them," Kinotatay shouted, turning to gesture back at the bunkhouse. The young braves, some with old muskets, some with lances, most with bows and arrows, quickly followed his order. And with them came the sheepherders, also armed with muskets and pistols.

"Don't stay out in the open to make targets for them," John Cooper exclaimed. "Kinotatay, have your braves climb onto the roof of the *hacienda*. Esteban, put some of your workers in the tool shed—they can shoot out of the windows and door. Have the others hidden near the stable and the corral. Fire when they're close, and don't waste your powder. Make every shot count!"

Ten of Kinotatay's warriors clambered up the adobe wall of one side of the *hacienda* to take their station on the roof. One of them called out, "They come, first four men ahead of the others!"

John Cooper moved like a cat to the other side of the *hacienda*, knelt down, and took careful aim. Santiago Hernandez, first among the patrol of four, saw the young mountain man and leveled his musket. John Cooper pulled the trigger of "Long Girl" and the Mexican dropped his musket, bowed forward, and fell to the ground, as his horse galloped wildly on. There was the whirring sound of arrows, then the dull *thuckkk* as they imbedded in human flesh, and finally the screams of the three men behind Hernandez. Two of them were flung back out of their saddles and sprawled on the ground; the third man, though lifeless, rode on a few more yards with an Apache arrow in his heart, then slowly slid from the saddle and rolled over and over in the dust.

Don Felipe, at the head of his column, saw the fatal rebuff of his first attack and, reining in his horse, held up a hand to halt his riders. "The treacherous Estigo betrayed us, *hombres!*" he cried. "But we are sure to outnumber whatever defenders they have. Break into three groups—you, Duarte," gesturing to a burly sergeant in his company, "ride back and divide the *soldados* into three equal groups, *¿comprende?* And you take one and choose a *jefe* for the second and for the third. Have one group make a frontal attack and have the other two each circle the back of the *hacienda* from opposite sides."

"Understood, *mi coronel*." José Duarte smartly saluted, wheeled his horse, and rode back to communicate Don Felipe's orders.

Don Felipe viciously yanked at the reins, forcing his exhausted horse to the side of the road, and waited to see the success of the frontal sweep against the *hacienda* of Don Diego de Escobor. As José Duarte, brandishing a saber, rode by him, Don Felipe cried out, "Don't hurt the *gringo!* Remember, I want him alive!"

Although Lobo was reasonably docile in the presence of the Apache, John Cooper had thought it best, with so many strangers now staying at the *hacienda*, to keep the wolf-dog in the shed. But now he released Lobo. Fortuna swooped high into the air, flapping his wings in great excitement. "Lobo, enemies are coming! When I tell you, go for them!" John Cooper exclaimed.

John Cooper beckoned to Lobo to follow him to the main tool shed, which was midway between the bunkhouse and the *hacienda* itself. He crouched down there, pulling the door partway open to act as a defending screen. Then with feverish speed he began to reload "Long Girl" and waited.

The attack was not long in coming. Paco Columbar, with a wild yell, led his troops in a galloping, circling dash around the front of the *hacienda*. But before they could complete the arc which brought them past the door, four of them had already been dropped by expertly aimed arrows from the roof above. Two of the men at the end of this column, observing their comrades' plight, leveled their muskets and pulled the triggers. There was a yowl of pain and one of the Apache fell back dead; the other dropped his bow and sank to his knees, dully staring at the gaping wound in his left thigh.

As Columbar neared the tool shed, John Cooper squinted along the sight of his father's rifle and pulled the trigger. The burly Mexican was flung back, as if by an invisible hand, and was dragged, one foot in the stirrup, as his horse galloped wildly on with its dead rider leaving a bloody furrow on the ground behind. Two of the foremost riders in the dead man's column were toppled from their saddles by accurate fire from the bunkhouse. A third man, seeing John

Cooper crouching beside the partly opened door of the tool shed, wheeled his horse and made for him. John Cooper had just finished priming and reloading "Long Girl" and, retaining the rifle in his right hand, reached for his holster with his left, drew out a pistol, and snapped off a shot that killed his assailant. Lobo, with an angry snarl, nipped at the horse's leg as the frightened beast dashed off.

Now the two other columns had begun their sidelong attack around the *hacienda* and the corral and the bunkhouse, and the darkness was filled with the explosions of muskets and old flintlock rifles, with the shrieks of the wounded and the dying, with the thundering of horses' hooves. The *trabajadores*, lying on their bellies near the corral, surprised the second column, which had made a galloping dash around from their left. In short order they killed eight of the soldiers of Don Felipe's private army, wounding six others. However, two of the workers were killed and one wounded by close-range pistol fire.

Don Felipe, his face a mask of hate and fury, watched the three depleted columns regroup and await new orders. They had drawn up their horses near a clump of tall fir and spruce trees, with wild hedges further obscuring the darkness of the wintry night.

During this respite, the defenders carried their wounded off to safety in the bunkhouse, reloaded their weapons, and prepared for a fresh assault. Inside the house, Tía Margarita and Leonora, kneeling in the kitchen, their hands clasped in prayer, were weeping with terror and begging the Holy Mother to protect them and all others in the *hacienda*. Catarina, holding Andrew to her bosom, likewise prayed with fervor, mostly for the safety of her young hubsand.

By this time, nearly a third of Don Felipe's force had been eliminated by death or serious wounds. He gave swift instructions to Hermano Ruiz, a tall, bearded ruffian who had killed his brother over a woman and fled to Mexico City, joining the army to save his neck from the rope. "Those accursed *indios* on the roof of the *hacienda* are picking us off like flies, Ruiz," he snarled. "Take ten of the best marksmen —you know who they are—and advance on them. Then you, Ignacio," designating the fat *capataz* of Don Ramón de Costilla who had all too willingly joined forces with him after his master's murder, "take twenty more men and charge from the east, toward the corral. From the sound of the gunfire there, I know they have a concentration of *trabajadores* or *indios*. Kill them, to a man! I will make you a *capitán* if you are successful. Now go on!"

Hermano Ruiz swiftly selected ten marksmen, who primed and loaded their muskets and pistols and old Belgian rifles, and then, at his signal, rode back toward the *hacienda*. As they neared the broad, square building, Kinotatay, whose keen sight could make out their figures in the darkness, uttered the call of a coyote. At once, six bowmen crawled to the southern edge of the roof and launched their arrows with deadly effect. Four of Ruiz's men died instantly, and two others took arrows in the neck and shoulders, one of them falling from his horse and dying before he hit the ground; the other man, trying vainly to pull out the arrow, slumped forward over his horse's neck as the animal galloped aimlessly beyond the *hacienda*.

But the other men in Ruiz's group had commenced firing as soon as they saw the Apache bowmen move on the edge of the roof, and three of the Indians were killed before the remaining braves could send off a new volley of arrows. Three more of Don Felipe's soldiers dropped lifeless to the ground.

Meanwhile, Ignacio Marquez, sweating with fear but not daring to show his cowardice before Don Felipe, led his forces in a flanking move toward the corral. By great good fortune, he escaped the withering fire from the *trabajadores* who had been expecting just such a maneuver, and his horse suddenly stumbled and halted, with a strident whinny of pain, near the tool shed where John Cooper crouched.

"*¡Matar, matar!* Kill!" the young mountain man cried. Lobo bared his fangs, gathered himself, and sprang at the fat *capataz*. Marquez dropped his musket and uttered a scream of terror as he saw the shaggy wolf-dog, its yellow eyes gleaming, spring at him. Lobo gripped the wrist of the *capataz* in his jaws and dragged him down from the saddle. He did not loosen his grip until John Cooper, drawing his other pistol from the holster, took careful aim and ended the agony of the *capataz* with a bullet through his forehead.

Once again, the enraged Don Felipe ordered an attack, this time against the back of the *hacienda* and the patio. Fifteen men rode into the connecting passageway which separated the *hacienda* into two rectangles ... the same strategy the bandit Jorge Santomaro had employed almost two years earlier. Some of the soldiers fired their muskets and pistols into shuttered windows. The Apache on the rooftop concentrated a volley of arrows down on the mounted men, who found themselves trapped at a dead end. In wheeling their horses round to retreat, they lost fully ten of their number, two being pierced by lances thrown by Kinotatay's young braves. Three of the horses ridden by those who escaped were struck by arrows. They threw their riders, who ran for their lives as if the devil himself were pursuing them.

By this time, Don Felipe had lost over half of his private army. He was livid with rage as he enjoined the survivors to regroup and to concentrate an overpowering attack. When one of the *peones* who had formerly worked for Don Ramón demurred at the order to take a dozen men and circle behind the corral to attack the *trabajadores*, Don Felipe drew one of his pistols and shot him down from the saddle. "He was a traitor, a coward! Now you, Vernaga," gesturing with the still-smoking pistol to a lean soldier who had risen no higher than corporal but had the witless courage of a beast of prey, "take the men and attack those *trabajadores* from the mountain side of the corral. Are you going to let stupid *indios* and *peones* drive you off? For shame, *hombres!*"

Juan Vernaga grinned and, brandishing an old saber, flourished it and called to his companions to follow him into battle. They made a wide circle around the *hacienda* and the bunkhouse, coming up from the north. But Esteban Morales, who had posted the *trabajadores* in front of the corral, anticipated such a maneuver—and John Cooper had called to him to be prepared for it—by having half of his force turn around and train their guns on that unguarded part of the corral. Hence, when Don Felipe's soldiers rode up, fire from three muskets and two pistols in the hands of the sheepherders dropped three of the men from their saddles. The horses, by now terrified from all the loud reports of gunfire and the cries of the wounded and the dying, reared and whinnied, fighting their riders. In the melee, John Cooper squinted down the sights on "Long Girl" and pulled the trigger: Juan Vernaga dropped his saber and slid off the saddle.

That was too much for the rest of the men who had

followed him in this furious charge. They wheeled their horses around and rode off toward the Sangre de Cristo mountain slopes, thinking only of surviving, their service to Don Felipe at an abrupt end.

When he heard the lull of battle, Don Felipe realized that this gamble, too, had failed. Gnashing his teeth, he reloaded the empty pistol and then called to his remaining men, who were now fewer than thirty, "I myself will lead you. This time, we will take the *gringo!*" Then, kicking at his horse's belly, he urged it forward against the back of the *hacienda*. As he rode, he wound the reins around his saddle horn, drew out both pistols and, seeing the shadowy figures of the Apache on the rooftop, fired both pistols simultaneously. A howl of pain was heard, and one of the bowmen stumbled, fell over the edge of the roof, and lay sprawled on his back on the ground below. An arrow whistled past Don Felipe as he rode off to a small clearing and hastily reloaded his pistols. His men charged on, galloping their horses around the back and toward the eastern side of the estate. Two of them were dropped by Apache arrows, one by a spear that pierced the man's back, the tip emerging from his chest. He seemed riveted to his saddle and rode on, eyes glazed and hugely widened, past the *hacienda* until at last his exhausted horse halted. Its front legs bent under it, and with an agonized exhalation, the horse rolled over onto its side, kicked feebly, and then was still like its rider.

But Don Felipe's other soldiers bore themselves with exemplary courage despite the now overwhelming odds and the fact that they offered all too vulnerable targets to the Apache on the rooftop, as well as to the *trabajadores* who lay in wait for them. The fire of their muskets and pistols killed two of the workers and three of the Apache. Pirontikay himself was wounded in the fleshy part of his left arm from a pistol ball. But his father sent an arrow through the neck of the man who had fired that pistol, and felled him.

Don Felipe had escaped without a scratch thus far. Leading a dozen men, he was attacked by one of the *trabajadores* who ran at him and tried to brain him with the butt of his musket. Wheeling his horse to one side, Don Felipe aimed one of his pistols and pulled the trigger. It misfired and the worker's musket thwacked viciously against his right kneecap. With his other hand, he fired the second pistol and killed the worker. Wincing with pain, he wheeled the horse around and rode toward the shed where John Cooper crouched with Lobo bristling beside him.

Two more of his men fell to the musket fire of the *trabajadores* and another to an arrow launched from the rooftop. The survivors, finding themselves in a trap on both sides, lost all heart for the battle, and thought only of salvation. Several of them turned their horses toward the Sangre de Cristo, and the others headed for the western side of the *hacienda*, hoping to flank it and go back to the trail whence they had come. As they did, three Apache leaped down from the rooftop, seizing the riders and wrestling them to the ground. They swiftly drew their hunting knives, and hoarse shrieks ended in gurgles of death. The *trabajadores* leveled their muskets and pistols and sent a last volley after the fleeing survivors, killing two of them.

Don Felipe was left alone, both pistols empty. Leaping from his horse, he swore as his injured knee buckled. But he dragged himself erect and, drawing his hunting knife, rushed at the young mountain man.

Lobo barred his path. With an angry growl, the wolf-dog lunged. Don Felipe feinted to one side, stepping back, and slashed at Lobo with a knife, nicking his haunch and drawing blood. Then, with a cry, he hurled himself on John Cooper.

There had been no time to reload either "Long Girl" or the pistols after that last foray. John Cooper leaped to one side to avoid Don Felipe's murderous lunge, and drew the Spanish dagger from the sheath round his neck.

"I will cut your tripes out, you *gringo* scum!" Don Felipe hissed, his face twisted with insane rage, the thought of the loss of the treasure driving all caution from him. "And before you die, you will tell me where you have hidden the rest of that silver!" With this, he made another lunge, but John Cooper parried the sidelong swipe with his dagger, and there was a clash of steel. Drawing away his blade, John Cooper darted catlike to one side and thrust upward at Don Felipe's belly. To parry it, the former aide to the viceroy had to step back, and his bruised knee made him stumble again.

Lobo sprang at him again, but John Cooper cried out, "No, no, leave him to me, Lobo, obey!" The wolf-dog halted, snarling, questioning John Cooper with blazing yellow eyes. But he obeyed—his rigorous training had taken effect.

John Cooper chivalrously waited until Don Felipe regaining his footing, but in that moment, the traitorous aide had scooped up a handful of dirt in his left hand, and now he flung it at John Cooper's face. Momentarily taken aback, the mountain man retreated, and at the same moment, Don Felipe lunged with his knife in a downsweeping arc aimed at the *gringo*'s heart.

It ripped the buckskin jacket, John Cooper's instinctive movement alone saving his life. But it also left Don Felipe totally vulnerable. And now John Cooper gripped Don Felipe's right wrist and thrust the Spanish dagger to the hilt into his adversary's heart.

He saw Don Felipe stiffen, then his head bow forward and his body slump. He drew out the dagger and let Don Felipe's body crumple before him. Lobo snarled and moved forward, but John Cooper again called him off: "No, no, Lobo! I don't need you anymore now. And he'll never need to know where the treasure is, either."

Exhaustion claimed him, and he closed his eyes and drew in deep gulps of cool mountain air. Then he called hoarsely to Esteban Morales and to Kinotatay, *"¡No puedo más!"*

Twenty-five

The long-drawn war between the British and the *yanquis*
continued without abatement. In this month of November,
1814, Fort Erie had been abandoned and blown up by
American troops who promptly retired from Canada. Two
days later, General Andrew Jackson conquered Pensacola,
clearing the East Florida territory of British troops. He would
then head for New Orleans to take command in what was
destined to be the final battle of a war in which there were no
victors. Yet it was a war that established the prestige and the
honor of a budding new country impatient to push through
the frontiers and expand, without interference from Europe.

In Texas, Don Diego de Escobar and his family, Miguel
and Bess, and the sturdy *trabajadores* who drove the sheep
from Taos, had reached the fertile valley which John Cooper
had so glowingly described. The Apache who rode with them
as their mounted guard had not once been called upon to
defend them.

For Doña Inez, it was an exciting adventure. She did not
miss the comforts of the *hacienda*, not even when she had to
share a rude tent with Don Diego and little Francesca.
Indeed, their very nearness and the crudity of their shelter
seemed to enhance the intimacy of communication between
them. Never had Don Diego talked so frankly of his boyhood, his hopes and dreams, his doubts when he had been
banished from Madrid. To Doña Inez, it was a kind of rebirth
to see her mature husband look forward with youthful zest to
the days ahead. And in turn, her reassurances and her pledges
of devotion greatly heartened him on this sudden upheaval.

For Carlos, with Weesayo and his little son, Diego, it
was the beginning of a new life, free from all the artificial

trappings of aristocratic society. Now he could be himself and do what he most liked: exploring his new land, raising horses, and being with his wife and child all the time. Here in Texas he truly believed he would find what he was looking for.

The *trabajadores*, expertly directed by Miguel, worked diligently. They built some adobe shelters for themselves, felled timber, used those cut pieces of wood which they had brought along in the *carretas*, and soon the frame of a new *hacienda* took shape on this serene and fertile stretch of land.

And for Miguel, the joy of an exhausting day's work and the contentment of his marriage with Bess fulfilled all the thwarted dreams he had had as a young man back in Madrid. He, like the rest of them, regretted nothing. And he could understand, perhaps better than the others, why it was that John Cooper preferred life under the sky and on the earth that gave back bounty for industry and did not betray those who toiled upon it.

It was mid-November now. The mares John Cooper had bought from Don Ramón de Costilla would have foals next year. It was a quiet time of waiting at the *hacienda* of Don Diego de Escobar, a time that gave the young man many hours to spend with Catarina and Andrew. Nor did he neglect Lobo, whose raven friend, Fortuna, greeted John Cooper whenever he came out of the *hacienda* to take the wolf-dog for his daily romp. Esteban Morales had begun to pack those household goods which should be taken when at last all of them left Taos. It had been agreed that one of the Apache who had ridden on to Texas would ride back to Taos to tell John Cooper when the *hacienda* was ready for them all. Meanwhile, now that peace had been restored to the Taos *hacienda* after the raid of Don Felipe and his men, Kinotatay, Pirontikay, and the other braves returned to the stronghold. Juan Estigo, who had risked his life to warn John Cooper about the attack of the *hacienda*, had recovered from his wounds and returned to Mexico City, hoping to be reconciled with his family and to reenlist in the viceroy's army.

One morning, after bringing Catarina breakfast on a tray decorated with a bowl of winter flowers from the mountain range, John Cooper went to take Lobo for his romp. Fortuna, having perched all night in a giant spruce tree not far from the corral, swooped high into the air, flapping his wings and cawing loudly in his joy at being reunited with his playmate. Lobo wagged his tail, looked upward, his eyes gleaming with pleasure. John Cooper laughed heartily, rubbing Lobo's head and then playfully cuffing him as he said, "You've been very good, Lobo. Today I'm going to let you make a kill by yourself, and we'll see if Fortuna helps you flush it and squabbles with you over tidbits."

John Cooper mounted Fuego, clucked his tongue, and jerked lightly at the reins. The palomino stallion tossed his head, glancing back at his master, and then began to trot ahead toward the mountain range. Lobo, pursued by Fortuna, kept pace.

The wintry air was cool and brisk, and John Cooper breathed it in deeply. In the valley he had chosen for their new *hacienda,* it would be much warmer during the winter. The land was vast, and it was isolated, and there would be all the time in the world to lead a life of freedom and to be far from the domination of the viceroy's government. And, of course, there would always be the wealth from the abandoned silver mine to be used against the future.

He turned Fuego's head to the left along the familiar, broad trail of the slope of the Sangre de Cristo, laughing at Lobo's playful snapping when the raven flew close to him. He suddenly halted Fuego, who snorted angrily at being checked in his loping gait, as he saw a lone rider approaching him from the bend in the trail about two hundred yards beyond to the north.

As the rider galloped toward him, he recognized Kinotatay's son, Pirontikay.

"Pirontikay, you ride like one who has a band of enemies behind him wanting to count coup on you!" he called to the sturdy young Apache.

But the smile died on his lips when he saw Pirontikay's grave face contort in exhaustion. "I am the bearer of black news, *Halcón.* Our chief has gone to the Great Spirit."

"Descontarti dead? But when? When I saw him last, he seemed stronger—" John Cooper exclaimed.

"He had gone to the top of the mountain to talk to the Great Spirit two nights ago, *Halcón.* Before dawn broke, my father said to me, 'I fear for our chief, you must go to find him. Do not let him see you, for it would hurt his pride. Yet I have had bad dreams, and they disturb me.' And so, *Halcón*, I rode to the peak, and I saw him who was our *jefe* lying on his belly, his arms outstretched toward the ledge which peers down into the canyon below. And I came to him, and I feared to touch him, but when I did, I saw that he had already been taken from us."

"I mourn my blood brother. I must go with you for the ceremony."

"But wait, *Halcón*, there is worse news than this. The chief of the Mescalero, Matsinga, who had already insulted our great chief—whose name I no longer speak—by refusing the food we offered him to honor his rank as chief, sent a messenger to the stronghold the day before the spirit of our *jefe* rose to the heavens. This messenger rode to the wickiup of our great chief, *Halcón*, and thrust a spear into the ground and then rode off without a word."

"A declaration of war—" John Cooper said aloud. "Your father told me that this might happen. Do you think that the Mescalero know that your chief is dead?"

"Not yet, *Halcón*, but they have learned that he had a great sickness upon him. And they know also that we have young braves in our stronghold who are eager for war."

"I will ride back with you. But first, I must tell my *esposa* why I have to leave her now. Tell me, Pirontikay, have you seen a scout from the valley in Texas pass by your stronghold?"

"Not yet, *Halcón*. My father says that we watch daily, so that we may send the news to you at once. I know that you long to join them."

"But I can't now, because I have to defend against your enemies. When I became blood brother to your chief, Pironti-kay, I swore that I would fight on his side against those who declared war upon him. This is my oath, and I shall keep it. Come with me now to the *hacienda*, and then we shall ride back to the stronghold together."

As they rode up to the *hacienda*, John Cooper dismounted and sought out Esteban Morales. "Esteban, I must go to help my friends, the Jicarilla Apache. Their chief is dead, and some of the young men who have been eager for war against their enemy the Mescalero are without a leader. I must see that they choose a chief who is as wise as Descontarti was. Things are quiet here now, and soon we'll be leaving for Texas, but while I'm gone, you and the *trabajadores* look after my wife and child. I'm going to take Lobo with me, for he's a fierce fighter."

"I will look after your family as if they were my own, Señor Baines," the young Mexican earnestly replied. "You once saved my son. I swear that when you return, your child will be as safe as mine now."

"*Gracias, hombre.*" John Cooper gripped Esteban's hand. Then he went to the *hacienda* and into the little interior courtyard where Catarina and one of the maids were watching with delight as Andrew fumbled with a toy Esteban Morales had made for him.

"I heard voices outside, *mi corazón!*" she exclaimed as she rushed toward her husband. "Oh, is it the scout who has come to tell us that we can join Carlos and my father and Doña Inez at last?"

"No, my sweet Catarina. Descontarti is dead."

"That strong, powerful chief? But how can it be—was he killed in battle?"

"No, Catarina, he had a wasting sickness. I knew it for some time, but he was too proud to let me bring a *médico*. But there will be a battle, between the Jicarilla Apache and the Mescalero—and you remember how the Mescalero captured you when you went riding Marquita."

"I shall never forget that! That was when you saved me, that was when I really knew I loved you—oh, I know—you want to go help Descontarti's people, don't you?"

"Dear, understanding Catarina, yes, I must. I was his blood brother, and I took a vow to fight against his enemies. Now his people have no real leadership. They must choose Kinotatay as his successor. Then I'll help them organize to fight the Mescalero."

"And you will leave me all alone?"

"No, my darling. Esteban Morales is the *capataz* now. He and the other men will guard this *hacienda*. But there's no danger." He took her hand and kissed it, then bent down to kiss his little son's forehead.

"But I am worried for you, my darling. If there will be war between those two tribes, you could be killed—"

"There's not that much danger." He laughed with the buoyant confidence of youth, as well as the knowledge of having already survived many hardships and dangers. He kissed her tenderly, and then again his son, and hurriedly made his final preparations.

From the weapons shed, John Cooper packed three pistols, four muskets, and two Belgian rifles, as well as a large pouch of gunpowder and several lead molds. Then, whistling for Lobo to follow, with "Long Girl" primed and loaded and firmly thrust into the saddle sling, he galloped off with the young brave toward the Apache stronghold.

It took two days and nights. When they arrived, they found the elders in the council. And the village was in an uproar, the young braves eager for war against the Mescalero and each of them advancing his own claims to the mantle of leadership.

Kinotatay came out of the council, which was held in the clearing before the dead chief's large wickiup. The elders could not agree, and some of the young braves who had already counted coup for deeds of valor had tried to influence them.

"They speak with many voices and so loudly that there is no wisdom here, *Halcón*." Kinotatay gravely shook his head. "Some of them are all for making a raid upon the Mescalero villages. But that is a great distance and would take many of our horses and supplies. I say it is better for them to try to attack us. Then the others say that I am a fool, an old woman."

"Have the Mescalero attacked yet since that messenger rode in and planted the war lance, Kinotatay?" John Cooper demanded.

"Some of their scouts have been seen on the trail below, and one of them killed Imanisay, who guarded the winding trail from the rock that is shaped like a wolf's head."

"Would you let me speak to the council and have those young braves who defy your wisdom listen to me also, Kinotatay?"

"I will ask the elders. We have not ever before allowed a white-eyes to take a place in the council. Still, you were blood brother to him who was our chief, and the elders know this. I will go back to them now and speak about it."

"I will ask them to make you chief, Kinotatay. There is no other man in this stronghold better able to replace him who was your leader," John Cooper said in the Apache tongue and made the sign of friendship. Kinotatay looked at him, drew a deep breath, and returned the sign, gripping John Cooper's left wrist with his right hand and putting his left palm over John Cooper's heart. Then he turned and went back to the elders.

A quarter of an hour later, he rose and went to where John Cooper stood looking out over the valley far below. "They will listen to you, *Halcón*."

John Cooper drew out his father's Lancaster rifle and strode toward the circle of the elders. Among them were several of the younger braves whom Kinotatay had pointed out as troublemakers.

A hush fell upon the circle as the young mountain man stepped into the circle. He waited a long moment until he knew he had their attention, and then, in the Apache tongue which he had never forgotten, he began, "You know me as *El Halcón*. You know also that I am blood brother to him who was your chief. We do not speak his name, but I remember his wisdom, his kindness, and how he kept the stronghold free from attack and at peace, even with the *soldados*. Now that he has gone to the Great Spirit, you have no leader. I have lived among you, I know your ways, I respect and honor them."

There was a murmur of assent, even from the suspicious younger men.

"The Mescalero are my enemy, too," he continued. "Before I married her whom you call *La Paloma*, the daughter of the *intendente* of Taos, she rode out on her mare and she was captured by Mescalero. They had her at the torture stake; they would have done great harm to her. I killed them. They were clever, but my skill with 'Long Girl' "—here he lifted his arm as high as he could to display the weapon and to make the symbolic gesture that besought the Great Spirit to look down with favor—"helped me outwit them and defeat them. I ask, as the blood brother of your great *jefe*, that you permit me to fight beside you against the Mescalero."

There was an astonished murmur, and even the rebellious young braves now turned to one another, startled by so bold a proposal.

"Hear me, men of the Jicarilla Apache," John Cooper vibrantly declared. "I have taken a vow that the stick which thunders and gives off fire shall fell Matsinga, the leader of the Mescalero. Once their leader is gone, you will know them as a band of cowardly curs who slink back to their campfires to be consoled by the old women who will throw them scraps." This brought laughter, and John Cooper could see grudging smiles on the faces of those who opposed Kinotatay and had rebelled against Descontarti. "But you must have a leader of your own blood. Though I am blood brother, I am not Apache. I speak for Kinotatay. He taught me your tongue, and I speak it well. He taught me your customs and your ways, and I walk in those ways and I do honor to the Apache nation. He is a brave warrior who himself has counted many a coup over an enemy. He has made a plan that will defeat the Mescalero and drive them back to their land, never to threaten you proud people of the Jicarilla again."

"What is this plan?" one of the wizened, white-haired elders of the council countered.

"It is the way the Comanche and the Sioux use, and which I am sure you elders know also. You will send a force down from the stronghold to lure the Mescalero toward us. But toward the southern end of the stronghold, there is a narrow trail. Horses cannot go by it, but Apache warriors can. We will come upon the Mescalero from the rear, and thus we will have them between us as two fires hold a prairie and destroy it. I will kill Matsinga with 'Long Girl'—and I ask that, in return for my help, you hear me speak the name of Kinotatay as *jefe* and that you name him now to lead the two forces that will destroy the Mescalero."

Now there were noisy voices, a babble of words, and even the elders seemed animated by the enthusiasm of the young mountain man. At last the old man who had first asked to know the plan of attack rose and said in a reedy voice that trembled with age, "I am oldest of the elders of the council, I, Somanito. And what this young white-eyes has said to us has been said with a straight tongue. I for one know how he has helped us and defended us, honored and respected us. I speak also for Kinotatay."

"And I!" "And I also!" Soon the circle of elders rang with shouts that acclaimed Kinotatay as *jefe*. And even the most dissident of the younger braves could not hold back the tide that dashed aside all their opposition.

John Cooper turned to Kinotatay and held out his hand and the two men stood staring at each other as the voices hushed. "I wish before we go into battle to be blood brother to Kinotatay now that he is *jefe*," John Cooper said, and the old shaman performed the mystic ritual.

When it was done, the young mountain man said, "As Pirontikay and I rode to the stronghold, I saw below in the valley and to the north the lights of the campfires of the Mescalero. Do they yet know that your great *jefe* has passed into the heavens?"

"I fear it is so, *Halcón*," Kinotatay solemnly answered. "Two braves whose names we shall never speak again, for they are dead to us, rode from the stronghold when they learned that he had gone from us. They had called us old women because we would not fight. And now I think, in truth, they have gone to the Mescalero and will join them to fight against us."

"That's good, Kinotatay. Because then it will mean that the Mescalero will be eager to attack, thinking that the stronghold can't defend itself because it has no chief. And they will attack at dawn, most likely. Well now, send thirty of your braves down the trail we always take to and from the stronghold. You and I will lead a hundred braves down the southern slope and wait there on the wide ledge—you know which place I mean?"

"Yes, *Halcón*. It was not far from there that you buried the great warrior wolf when you fought against the Sioux," Kinotatay answered.

"I have brought you *pistolas* and muskets and some rifles and much ammunition over the past few years, Kinotatay. In my saddlebag, I have brought more weapons for this fight. You will need these against the Mescalero. And your bowmen will finish what the weapons do not. Now let us go ahead so that before dawn we shall be ready for their attack."

Twenty-six

Jorge Santomaro, José Ramirez, and three of Santomaro's *bandidos* had decided it was time to strike, now that the ranks of the viceroy's soldiers patrolling the countryside had begun to thin out. Thus they left the little village in Sonora and headed for Taos, avoiding the main roads so that no remaining patrols could question them. Ramirez had suggested that they pose as poor sheepherders in search of employment. They had dressed themselves in the long robes of sheepherders, and Josef Manriago, one of the three *bandidos* who accompanied the *jefe* and the former *capataz*, carried a shepherd's crook for the sake of authenticity.

By nightfall on the third Tuesday of November, they reached the outskirts of Taos, and José Ramirez directed his companions to the shop of Barnaba Canepa.

The latter, a man in his late sixties, wizened, his hair sparse and white with wispy goatee and cataract-blurred eyes, had been a useful friend to Ramirez in the days when the latter had been *capataz* at the de Pladero *hacienda*. Thus far, the old man had escaped the attention of the authorities, although he dealt in stolen goods and secret potions, as well as poisons. Many of the lovelorn *peones* sought his counsel in devising spells and potions which would make certain diffident young females fall in love with them. And since, on occasion, he had had success in this regard, Barnaba Canepa prospered.

His shop was on the eastern end of Taos, near the pueblo where the Christianized Indians lived. Jorge Santomaro scowled and muttered to José Ramirez, "Are you sure this *viejo* can be trusted?"

"Like the grave, *mi jefe*. I know enough about him to

have him hanged, if I were to tell the authorities. And since he knows that, he is loyal."

The two confederates made their way to the back of the shop, while their three companions remained on guard outside. Ramirez reached for the little bell rope outside the door and jerked it vigorously. After a few moments, there was the sign of a lantern in the darkness, and a cackling voice demanded, *¿Quién es?"*

"*Soy* Ramirez." The former *capataz*, his hands cupped to his mouth, leaned to the crack of the door so that his voice would carry only to the old storekeeper.

"*¡Caramba!* Have you come back, then, from hell itself? *Un momento, por favor.*" There was the sound of a bolt being drawn, and then Barnaba Canepa, peering out with squinting eyes, held up his lantern. At the sight of José Ramirez's clean-shaved face and cropped, dyed hair, he crossed himself. "But you are not the Ramirez I knew—"

"Old fool, let us go inside before you wake all the *indios* in the pueblo!" Ramirez hissed. "I'll show you I am who I say I am plain enough. Enter first, *mi jefe.*" He deferentially stepped back so that Jorge Santomaro might precede him.

At the back of the shop, the glow from Barnaba Canepa's lantern cast an eerie glow on shadowy vases and jars, some of which contained dead toads, scorpions, rattlesnakes, and one an embalmed Gila monster. The bandit chief shivered despite himself and made a furtive sign of the cross to ward off evil spells.

"Who is this one with you, Ramirez, if you are truly he?" the old storekeeper querulously demanded.

"It is Santomaro, the famous *jefe* of *bandidos*," José Ramirez declared. At this, Santomaro sent him a ferocious glance and put a finger to his lips. "But you are to forget that name, Barnaba. Now, let us get down to business. We have come to you tonight because it is well known that you, of all men, know all that takes place in Taos. What can you tell us of this *gringo* John Cooper Baines?"

Barnaba Canepa set down the lantern on the table, and rubbed his bony hands, his wizened face twisting in a conspiratorial smile. "There have been many changes since you left Taos, Ramirez. To begin with, the son of your former master married that Conchita Seragos. It is said that she is with child by him, which is as it should be. Oh, yes, let me not forget about the *intendente*, who has left Taos with his family. This was told to me by one of the pretty *criadas* from the de Pladero *hacienda* who came to me some weeks ago in search of a love potion."

"The devil!" Jorge Santomaro swore. "Do you mean to say, old man, that the *intendente* resigned his post?"

"That is precisely who I mean, señor. Many of the *trabajadores* left also, and they took with them some of the sheep—the others were sold to Don Sancho, from what this little *criada* told me," Canepa affirmed.

"And that accursed *gringo?*" Santomaro eagerly demanded.

"He remains, señor, and he has had a child by the so charming Catarina de Escobar. A fine young son, I am told. I do not know where Don Diego has gone with the rest of his household and the *trabajadores,* but I believe that the *gringo* waits until he has word from them before he, too, will depart from Taos."

Santomaro grinned evilly and turned to Ramirez. "This grows better and better, eh, José? From what you told me about this *gringo,* he enjoys hunting with that murderous wolf he has made a pet of. Now, if we are fortunate in our mission and he is absent from the *hacienda,* I begin to see a way in which I can avenge myself on him. And you, too, shall have your chance for amusement." Then, turning back to Canepa, he queried, "Have you any other news that may be important to us, old man?"

"Of a certainty. But you are keeping me from sleep, and I make no profit on this business," the old shopkeeper grumbled.

With an oath, Santomaro reached into the pocket of his sheepherder's robe and tossed a golden coin to the old storekeeper. "There now. Perhaps it will loosen your tongue a little?"

"To be sure, señor. *Gracias.* By the same *criada,* I was told that an officer of the viceroy himself, with many soldiers, attacked the *hacienda* of Don Diego de Escobar. Also, that there were many *indios* who helped defend it. This girl, who prattles like a parrot, had overheard her master say that the viceroy had sent these troops to collect the taxes of Taos, but that the officer himself was greedy for hidden treasure—what that means, I have no way of knowing; I merely relate to you what was said to me."

"Treasure," Santomaro repeated, his eyes glistening with

avarice. "José, this *gringo* of ours interests me more and more. And an idea begins to take shape in my mind. Perhaps there is a way to have revenge on the *gringo* and to put our hands on this treasure at one and the same time." Then, turning to Canepa, he gruffly added, "If you value your life, *viejo*, you will say nothing about our little visit this evening to anyone, *¿comprende?* I will hear if you have betrayed me, and your life will then be worth not a single *centavo*. Be silent, and you may have more of these gold pieces."

"As to that, Señor Santomaro," the old man cackled, "I know how to be as silent as the grave itself in return for a very small profit from your enterprise. And now, if you have no further need of me, I am dying for sleep."

"*Bueno*. Only remember, take care that you do not earn from me the eternal sleep instead of more of these gold pieces. *Buenas noches*, Señor Canepa."

Only the pale crescent of a quarter-moon shone as John Cooper and Kinotatay carefully made their way down the narrow, tortuous path that led from the southwestern end of the stronghold. Meanwhile, Pirontikay and Dugaldo—a short, powerful Apache in his early thirties and one of the chief dissidents against the peaceful rule of Descontarti—led the decoy band of Jicarilla down along the usual trail to entice the Mescalero to attack in full force.

Jorge Santomaro and José Ramirez had, the night before, sent their three companions near the *hacienda* to scout. They had returned to tell the bandit chief that they had seen no sight of the *gringo rubio*, but that there were perhaps twenty *trabajadores* working in the corral and around the bunkhouse. Some of them were building *carretas*. There were no sheep in sight. Also, they had seen some of the young *criadas* come out into the courtyard and go to the well for water.

"Now here is my plan," Santomaro muttered to his companion. "This *esposa del gringo* has a son, we're told. We'll take him with us."

"*¡Diablo!*" Ramirez gasped. "But why not kill the brat?"

"Because, Ramirez, the thought amuses me. I will give it to an old woman I know who will bring it up like a *peón*. It will never see its father again, and that is even better vengeance for that *gringo*'s having killed so many of my good men than to smother it or cut its throat now. And he'll never

find it, ¿comprende? All his life, he will have the torment of
not knowing whether his brat is alive or dead, and only I shall
know."

"And the *esposa del gringo?*" Ramirez asked.

"As to that, *hombre,* you and I can enjoy her favors.
That, too, will be part of my revenge on that accused *yanqui.*
Then, in good time, my band will ride down on the *alcalde*
and settle that score. They will plunder and they will take the
gold of the *alcalde* and his women. But first, tonight, when we
are sure that everyone is asleep, we will get into the *hacienda.*
One of my men will take the child and ride back to our camp,
to give us a good head start. Are you agreed?"

"*Seguramente, mi jefe.*"

That night, the three bandits who had acted as scouts led
the way toward the kitchen door of the *hacienda.* Antonio
Larado, a slim, handsome, runaway *peón* who had knifed his
master in the province of Durango, tested the door and, his
eyes widening with delight, put a finger to his lips as he
turned to his two confederates. "This will be as easy as
shearing sheep, *mis compañeros.* They haven't bolted the
door. Now then, we all know what the *jefe* wants of us, it is
agreed?"

"There is no need to talk, *hombre.* Let's go in and do
our business," Sanchez Escanos, a burly, thickly bearded man
in his mid-thirties, softly growled.

"Get on with it, *amigo,*" Hermano Cordobar hoarsely
whispered. A swarthy, stocky *peón* from Chihuahua, he was
nearly forty and had a price on his head for the murder of his
hacendado master and the latter's wife and children.

Stealthily they opened the door and slipped inside the
kitchen. Ramirez and Santomaro, pressing themselves against
the adobe wall of the *hacienda,* waited a moment, looking
toward the dark, silent bunkhouse. Then they, too, followed
the trio into the *hacienda.*

Tía Margarita had been unable to remain asleep that
night. Her concern for John Cooper had made her have fearful
nightmares ever since he had left for the Jicarilla
Mountains. Now she woke suddenly out of a new nightmare
and found herself sweating with terror. She had seen in her
dream John Cooper in hand-to-hand combat with a half-
naked Mescalero warrior, hideously painted, brandishing a
tomahawk and trying to thrust his hunting knife into John
Cooper's heart. And the dream had been so vivid that she had

wakened with a fitful start. The loud beating of her heart seemed like a hammering, and yet—and yet—there was a noise outside in the hallway.

She crossed herself, put a robe on over her shift, lit a candle, and stealthily opened the door. Then her mouth gaped in a soundless cry, for she saw the scowling, bearded face of Antonio Larado, who at once pressed his pistol to her heart and lifted his knife above her. "A sound out of you, *mujer,* and you are dead. Get back to bed. Wait, I have a better idea. Lie on your belly, fat one. I shall tie and gag you, so consider yourself lucky that I don't do worse than that."

"*Sí, s—s—señor,*" Tía Margarita quavered. She walked back unsteadily to the bed and lay down on it on her stomach. Quickly, Larado tore one of the sheets and in a hoarse whisper ordered her to put her hands behind her back. Then he bound her wrists and ankles, and finally gagged her. With a soft chuckle, he dealt her a vigorous open-handed slap on her plump bottom. Tía Margarita was clammy with terror as she saw him leave the room and go down the hallway. *Catarina—oh, Dios, save her, save her!* she prayed, and wept at her own cowardice.

The three *peones* had found their way to Catarina's bedchamber, while Santomaro and Ramirez, holding their breath and hiding themselves against the wall of the hallway, waited. Sanchez Escanos tried the knob of the bedchamber and opened it. Catarina lay with her head turned toward the shuttered window. She wore her nightshift, and Andrew slept in the crib beside the bed.

The three men turned back to their *jefe.* Sanchez gestured toward the sleeping baby, and Santomaro nodded. On tiptoe, the *peón* moved toward the crib, bent down, and caught up the child. Andrew, startled out of sleep, began to cry.

"What is it, *niño querido?*" Catarina drowsily asked. Then she sat up, only to utter a cry of horror as she saw the shadowy figures of the men in her room. "Who are you? My child—no—"

"*¡Silencio, mujer!*" Jorge Santomaro whispered, leering at her and putting his pistol to her firm breast. "If you wish the child to live, you will not utter a word, *¿comprende?*"

"But why—who are you—my husband will be back with *los indios*—" Catarina began.

"Your *esposo gringo* is not here, and we shall be gone long before he returns, of that I am certain," Santomaro chuckled. "You have the *niño?*"

"¡*Sí, mi jefe!*" Sanchez Escanos whispered back.

"*Bueno.* You know what to do. Ride swiftly, and do not let yourself be caught. Tell my *compañeros* that I will be back directly. They will wait for my orders."

"It will be done as you wish, *mi jefe.* ¡*Adios!*" Escanos, his palm over little Andrew's mouth, hurried out of the bed chamber.

"My baby—why do you take him—I have done nothing to you—I don't even know you—" Catarina groaned. Upright in bed now, she clasped her hands in prayer and held them out to the bandit.

"I would like to see you, señora." Then to José he said, "You have a candle and a tinderbox in your robe; give us some light." He snapped to his two other confederates, "Go outside and stand on guard. If anyone challenges you, kill him quickly and do not let him make a sound. We shall be out presently, when we have done what we have come to do."

Antonio Larado and Hermano Cordobar nodded and left the bedchamber.

The light of the candle flared, and Catarina shrank back against the headboard of the wide bed, unable to believe what her eyes saw. She recognized neither one of them, but her eyes fixed on Santomaro's coarse-featured, fat-jowled face and she shuddered inwardly with revulsion. His mouth curved in a lustful smirk. "I had not known how truly *linda y guapa* you were, señora. Allow me to introduce myself. I am Santomaro," he drawled. "Now then, señora, if you cry out, it will be the last sound you make upon this earth, be advised of that. And I keep my promises. My enemies know this."

"But who are you, why do you do this, why have you taken my baby?" Catarina gasped, tears trickling down her flushed cheeks.

"Your husband, señora, killed many of my men. He and that accursed wolf of his—and then besides, you are the daughter of the *intendente* of Taos. I have no reason to love rich aristocrats who use their high office to hang innocent men—"

"But my father has hanged no one! In God's own name,

tell me why you do this—what are you going to do to poor
little Andrew? He has never harmed anyone—it is cowardly,
it is vile!"

"I do not need a sermon from you, señora," Santomaro
brutally interposed. "Personally, I have no hatred for you,
and it is true that you have done nothing to me. It is your
husband I hold responsible. But since he is not here, you will
have to suit my purposes." He sniggered and played with his
mustache as he eyed her. The night shift clung to her supple,
voluptuous young body, and it inflamed his lust to see her
shrink back in terror of him. "I'm sure your *esposo gringo*
loves you very much. Well then, if I enjoy you, and my
friend, as well, it will be a blow against his *macho* pride. And
that will be part of my revenge on him, señora."

"What—what do you mean, you cruel, vile man? You
have never had children, you don't know how horrible it is to
steal an innocent little baby—he will die—"

"He will not die, señora. I know an old *mejicana* who
will take good care of him. It is true that when he grows up
he will not have all the advantages that your father and your
esposo could give him. But then, señora, let me remind you
that there are many *peones* in all of Mexico who live like
dogs, like slaves. Yet they live. No, I say to you that I will not
have your child harmed. But now I have had enough of
talk."

Catarina understood his meaning. She began to tremble
violently, but she forced herself to remain as calm as she
could, and tried to reason with him. "If I cry out, the
trabajadores will come to help me! There are many of them,
and they all are armed—"

"You lie, señora. They are asleep. And if you cry out, I
will kill you. It is as simple as that. Now you are going to
accommodate me. *Hombre*," he said to José, "stand close to
the bed and keep your *pistola* on her."

"*¡Si, mi jefe!*" Ramirez breathed. His eyes devoured the
trembling, shuddering, black-haired young woman, and he
had already visually stripped her naked of her shift. At this
moment, he envied Jorge Santomaro for being the first with
her.

Swiftly, the bandit leader divested himself of his sheepherder's robe, and opened his short britches to expose his
turgid manhood. Then he flung himself down on the bed, his
hands gripping Catarina's shoulders, and he silenced her with

a brutal kiss. She writhed and tried to fight him, but his strength overcame her. With a laugh of triumphant lust, he ripped her nightshift from her body and then mounted her.

Catarina groaned in her shame and anguish, closing her eyes, turning her face from him so that, in no way, would she participate in his pleasure. Brutally, he violated her, and at last, slaking his lust with a stifled bellow of delight, rolled away from her. Then, staggering to his feet, he drew his own pistol and whispered to Ramirez, "Now it is your turn, but be quick! The sooner we are away from this *hacienda*, the better off we will be!"

"*¡Gracias, mi jefe!*" Ramirez panted. He handed Santomaro the guttering candle, cast off his robe, and then flung himself on the half-fainting young woman.

She ground her teeth and tried to hold back her tears as his pudgy fingers viciously pinched and mauled her. His rape was even more lustful, more demeaning to her, and his obscene endearment and vile praises almost made her vomit in her loathing.

And when it was done, he turned reluctantly to Santomaro and panted, "*Dios*, what I wouldn't give to take this *puto* with me, to be my *mujer!*"

"You would be a fool, *hombre*. Now you have had your fill, back to our camp!" Santomaro put on the robe and donned his sombrero. Then, as Catarina sprawled naked and wept hysterically, both hands over her mouth to muffle the sounds of her shame and disgust, he doffed his sombrero and made a mocking bow toward her. "I thank you Señora Catarina. Your *esposo gringo* is a fortunate man to have you in bed with him each night."

Half-fainting though she was, wretching with the revulsion that swept through her bruised, violated body, the young mountain man's wife sought a final time to propitiate her ravishers. "Look—if it is *dinero* you want, I will pay anything you wish—let me have my child—why should you have your revenge against an innocent baby? If you loved your mother, *hombre*, think of her and give me back my child."

"You plead very well, señora, but it is useless. Content yourself with my promise that your child won't die. And now, *adiós! ¡Vámanos, hombre!*"

Jorge Santomaro and José Ramirez hurried out of Catarina's bedchamber. After they had gone, she dragged herself to her feet, sought a robe with which to cover herself, and stumbled out into the hallway in the hope of crying out for help. But they had already vanished. In the distance, there was the sound of horses' hooves, gradually receding; and then there was only the dark silence, the faint light of the approaching dawn, and Catarina's convulsive sobbing.

Twenty-seven

The traitorous Jicarilla braves who had ridden to the Mescalero camp to tell them of the death of Descontarti had served their own tribe better than they could have known. The Mescalero chief, Matsinga—nearly as tall as John Cooper himself, his head shaven clean except for a scalp lock through which was thrust an eagle's feather dyed in red—had ordered an attack at dawn upon the stronghold. Nearly a hundred and fifty braves rode with him, as he led them on Daga, his magnificent black stallion. He was revered by his braves because, unlike many tribal chiefs who directed their warriors from a distance and transmitted orders by their war lieutenants, Matsinga fought beside the lowliest young brave. He had a Spanish dagger thrust into the red sash around his naked waist, and his upper body was painted with the red and purple and ochre symbols of warfare. Tied to his saddle was a Spanish musket with which he was extremely accurate, and thrust through the sash at his right side was a flintlock pistol.

"With Descontarti dead, the Jicarilla will be like women," he boasted to Nemalo, his war chief, a short, wiry, and laconic man in his late thirties, six months Matsinga's junior. "When we reach their sentry posts, we will ride like the wind and sweep all before us. It may be that we shall lose a few braves to those sentries, but we shall find their camp unprepared for our strength. Tonight we shall have a great feast. I have it in mind to post many Mescalero here and make that stronghold a fort for the mighty Mescalero!"

"It will be as you say, *mi jefe*," Nemalo agreed. "With your Daga leading us, we shall be invincible!" And he raised his lance to the heavens.

309

Halfway up the trail, Matsinga reined in his stallion with a startled and angry cry, "They are coming to attack us! How could they have known this? Nemalo, the Jicarilla traitors must have betrayed *us* now. Do they ride with our braves?"

"They do, *mi jefe*."

Matsinga drew his forefinger across his throat, his face hardening with anger as he saw the distant riders of the Jicarilla slowly approaching.

Nemalo saluted with his lance, rode back to the end of the line and, without a word, thrust his lance into the hearts of both of the traitor braves.

The Mescalero contingent had now ridden past the southwestern side of the mountain where Descontarti had maintained his stronghold. Far above them, cautiously, the Jicarilla braves, led by Kinotatay and John Cooper, threaded their way one by one down toward the broad ledge.

Pirontikay and his battle aide held up their hands to slacken the pace of the braves behind them. Kinotatay's young son turned to call back, "Engage them slowly, let them come to us! The attacker loses more men than the defender. Bowmen, draw your arrows and wait for the signal. You with muskets and pistols, pick your targets. To me, the chief, Matsinga—see him there, strutting ahead of his braves on his black stallion—he is mine before either *El Halcón* or my father can reach him. This is my vow this day!"

Now as the first rays of the sun began to bathe the mountains with daylight, the Mescalero charged. The black stallion, Daga, his long legs stretching out, surged forward in a galloping burst of speed. At his side raced Nemalo, his lance drawn back in his right hand, his face contorted with hate, his eyes gleaming with blood-lust. And behind them, the Mescalero riders, their horses' hooves thundering, raised a bloodcurdling whoop.

When the last of the Mescalero riders had gone past, John Cooper beckoned to Kinotatay to give the signal for his men to quicken their descent and to take their positions along the ledge.

Matsinga rode forward to meet Pirontikay, who lifted his lance in the sky, then leveled it toward the onrushing black stallion. Pirontikay chanted a prayer to the Great Spirit to let his aim be unerring. But the wily Mescalero chief twisted himself to one side and bent over his saddle as the point of Pirontikay's lance passed over his head. Wheeling the stallion in the same movement, he rode after the young Jicarilla. Seizing the dagger at the left side of his sash, he buried it with an exultant cry to the hilt between Pirontikay's shoulder blades.

The young brave stiffened, his eyes glazing as he tried vainly to lift the lance. It dropped from his hand, and he sank forward, his head against the neck of his mustang. The horse continued on through the opening ranks of the Mescalero warriors until Pirontikay at last slipped from the saddle and sprawled in the dust, the Spanish dagger still sticking in his back.

Now the sounds of muskets and pistols, the cries and the grunts of pain, the clash of steel and the shrill whinnying of horses filled the air of this bright morning. Seeing his friend die at Matsinga's hand, Dugaldo uttered a savage cry and, drawing a tomahawk, flung it at Nemalo, who was riding toward him, lance extended. Nemalo uttered a wild shriek of agony and reeled backward in the saddle; but with his last ounce of strength he sent the lance deep into Dugaldo's side. The Jicarilla lieutenant arched back in his saddle, baring his teeth in a rictus of agony, tried to drag out the spear, and then toppled from his saddle to the ground. The hooves of the Mescalero horses trampled him as they did the body of Nemalo.

Now John Cooper leveled "Long Girl," took careful aim, and fired. One of the Mescalero riders at the back of the attacking force fell from the saddle without a word or cry. At Kinotatay's signal, a dozen Jicarilla bowmen launched arrows, bringing down five of the Mescalero.

"On foot, to the trail, attack them!" Kinotatay cried, flourishing his bow and leaping down from the ledge to the winding trail.

His men advanced, notching arrows to their bowstrings and speeding them toward the rear ranks of the Mescalero.

Taken by surprise at this attack from the rear, the Mescalero braves wheeled their horses and tried to confront their adversaries. Matsinga had killed two Jicarilla warriors with his pistol and musket and now, momentarily weaponless, he seized a lance from one of his own wounded warriors. With a defiant yell, he rode into the thick of the fighting, thrusting and jabbing with the lance, killing three Jicarilla in short order.

"*Jefe, jefe*, the Jicarilla, behind us!" Nipartisay, a gaunt-faced, battle-scarred warrior in his early forties, shouted to Matsinga.

"We are tricked! But they are on foot—no match for our mounted warriors!" Matsinga cried. "Turn, ride back over them, crush them, kill them all! Those who face us are fewer in number than we, and fewer now that we have taken their measure! To the death, on to victory for the Mescalero!"

Brandishing his bloodied spear, he wheeled the great black stallion and rode on toward the Jicarilla who stood fast and waited his charge. His other warriors, turning at his order, gave free rein to their horses, and now a hundred Mescalero thundered down the trail against the men of Kinotatay and John Cooper.

At his master's order, Lobo had scrambled up to the wide ledge and waited for the signal to attack. But the rear-guard attack of the Jicarilla had been so unexpected and successful that there was no need for Lobo to use his deadly fangs against the enemy.

By now John Cooper had reloaded "Long Girl" and scrambled up to the broad ledge. He knelt down, adjusted the Lancaster rifle, and squinted at the sight until he had Matsinga fairly in it. Then he pulled the trigger.

The Mescalero chief seemed to shudder as if a galvanic current had passed through his body. The lance dipped toward the ground and he slipped backwards out of his saddle. Daga, with no hand at the reins, raced on, and the Jicarilla men opened their ranks to make way.

There was a cry of horror and alarm from the Mescalero who had seen their leader fall. Now Kinotatay gestured to the bowmen. The whirring of arrows filled the air, and then quickly there were the screams of the wounded and the dying. Meanwhile, the mounted Jicarilla riders, having regrouped after heavy losses, now charged from the rear of the Mescalero force, thus trapping them in a fatal pincer.

It was not long before the survivors surrendered, flinging down their weapons, their faces bleak with shame in their defeat and despair over the loss of their great leader.

Kinotatay rode up to the defeated survivors and proudly called, "I am chief of the Jicarilla. Who is now your chief, that Matsinga is no more?"

"We have no chief. We ask for quarter," said Dumarni, one of Matsinga's war lieutenants. There were tears on his cheeks, a rare sight among the Indians, but the humiliation of defeat and the loss of a legendary chief had overcome the stoicism of the Mescalero.

"Then you shall be the chief of the Mescalero. Speak your name!"

"It is Dumarni, Kinotatay. We have done with fighting. We have done our best, but our chief is dead, and too many of our braves. We cannot continue against you. We sue for peace."

"Let there then be peace between Mescalero and Jicarilla," Kinotatay intoned. "Go back to your land. Know this, Dumarni, new chief of the Mescalero: never again will you dare attack the Jicarilla so long as I am chief. For every man of the Jicarilla who falls to a Mescalero, I will exact ten Mescalero lives. I have spoken. Go you back now in peace."

"I hear you, and I obey, chief of the Jicarilla," Dumarni replied. Wheeling his mustang, he gestured to his men to follow him back to the valley where they had made their camp.

The Jicarilla men shouted, waving their weapons high in the air and taunting their defeated foe. Kinotatay rode up to John Cooper and held out his hand, saying, "Because of you and 'Long Girl,' we have defeated our old enemy. You, my blood brother, have kept your pledge to kill Matsinga. Once again, you have shown us that our peace can have strength that will give us victory when war is forced upon us."

"Your warriors were brave, Kinotatay. It was lucky the plan worked. But I'm glad I helped you. I promised I would. And now, I've got to go back to the *hacienda* and make sure that my wife and baby are safe and sound," John Cooper earnestly declared.

But now one of the Jicarilla riders had dismounted and come running toward Kinotatay. He saluted Kinotatay as he would have done Descontarti and, his voice flat and dull and his eyes downcast, said, "*Jefe* of the Jicarilla, you have brought us a great victory over our hated enemy. But you have lost your son, and many others."

"Oh, my God, I'm sorry—Kinotatay, I didn't want that to happen—" John Cooper groaned.

Kinotatay had closed his eyes for a moment, stiffening in his saddle, his head thrown back and his shoulders straight. After a long moment, he said in a toneless voice, "It is the will of the Great Spirit. There is no victory without loss. I have lost a son and one of our bravest warriors, as well. But we have defeated the Mescalero. I do not think that they will ever again attack our stronghold. It is a great price to pay for such a victory, but it is a price that will help make no more widows during the days while I am *jefe* of the Jicarilla."

John Cooper, turning to one side so that the Apache would not see him, brushed his buckskin sleeve over his eyes to hide the tears. Young Pirontikay, so exuberant, loving life with such a zest, his good friend, was gone. And he knew better than most how deeply Kinotatay had loved his only son.

But by now, Kinotatay had recovered himself, and he sat with stoic dignity astride his mustang. "*Halcón,* tonight you will be our honored guest at the feast of victory over the Mescalero. All the village shall know how you killed Matsinga."

"Forgive me, Kinotatay, but my work is done. I promised my *esposa* I'd hurry back to her and to my son."

"I understand you. Five of my braves and I will go back with you to the *hacienda* to make sure that all is well there. I owe you this, *Halcón.* And you can be sure, even when you are in Texas, we will remain friends and offer you our protection." His face impassive, Kinotatay chose five of the sturdiest Jicarilla warriors to accompany him. He and John Cooper rode side by side on the winding trail back to the valley along the slope of the Sangre de Cristo and toward the *hacienda* of Don Diego de Escobar.

When John Cooper, Kinotatay, and the five braves rode into the courtyard of the *hacienda,* Esteban Morales stood waiting for them. As the young man dismounted from Fuego and stooped to rub Lobo's head while the black raven flew to the top of the shed, the Mexican sheepherder sank down on his knees and began to weep.

"Esteban, for God's sake, what's got into you? You certainly didn't miss me that much!" John Cooper joked.

"It is not that, Señor John Cooper, it is that my soul is black with *vergüenza.* I have broken my oath to you, and *el Señor Dios* will hold this forever to my account. I ask of you, I beg of you to kill me, for it is I who failed you and thus brought dishonor upon you."

Thunderstruck, John Cooper approached the kneeling young man, bent down, and gripped his shoulders. "What are you trying to tell me, Esteban? Of course I won't kill you."

"But you should, you must! I have failed you. I, whose little son you saved, I whose son still lives while yours is gone—"

"Gone? What are you telling me—come out with it, Esteban! For God's sake, no speeches, tell me what's happened," he hoarsley exclaimed.

Esteban covered his face with his hands and rocked back and forth on his knees, sobbing convulsively. At last he lifted his stricken face and stammered, "We were asleep, Señor John Cooper. And the *criadas* in the *hacienda,* too. Tía Margarita had forgotten to bolt the door to the kitchen, and it was thus they entered, those villains, those monsters—"

"Go on, for God's sake, tell me quickly!"

"The men told her they would kill her if she cried out, and they gagged her and bound her. And then—oh, God have pity on my cowardice, my laziness for having slept when I should have been defending the *hacienda* as I promised you I would—"

"Tell me!" John Cooper cried, his fingernails digging savagely into Esteban's shoulders.

The young sheepherder closed his eyes and shuddered. "They took *el niño* from the Señora Catarina, and one of them rode off with him—and then—then—two of them—do not make me say it, for the love of God, do not make me say it!"

With an agonized cry, John Cooper rushed into the *hacienda.* At the door, he nearly collided with one of the young maids who had come out of the kitchen. Seeing him, she uttered a wailing cry and began to sob. He strode down the hallway to Catarina's bedchamber. As he put his hand to the door, he heard the soothing voices of Tía Margarita and young Leonora. Very pale, and seized with a sudden fit of trembling, he entered.

"Oh, señor, Señor John Cooper, how we prayed you would come back in time!" The cook turned to him, holding out her arms, tears running down her face. But his eyes were only for Catarina. She was sitting up, with several thick pillows behind her shoulders and back, and Leonora was on the other side of the bed holding out a cup of hot chocolate. His wife's face was haggard, her eyes red and swollen from tears.

"Catarina! My God, did they hurt you?" was his first agonized cry.

She did not seem to see him as he entered. Now she slowly turned her head, and then she burst into convulsive sobs and held out her arms to him. "Oh, Coop, *querido* Coop, they have taken Andrew!"

"Who did this? And how long ago, Catarina? Tell me, my sweet darling!"

"It was three nights ago, Señor John Cooper," Tía Margarita interposed. "Oh, may the Holy Virgin forgive my cowardice, but I didn't dare scream for help—the man who tied me would have killed me—"

"I know, I know, I'm not blaming you or anyone, Tía Margarita!" John Cooper said tersely as he went down on his knees beside the bed and reached out to cup Catarina's tear-wet cheeks with all the tenderness he could muster. "Catarina, do you know who the men were? Did they hurt you?"

"It does not matter—it does not matter what they did to me—oh, Coop, you have to find poor Andrew—he is only a baby, and those horrible men have him, and they said I would never see him again—it was to punish you for having killed so many of his men—"

"Whose men, Catarina? Don't cry, please, darling, I'm here now, but I must know all this so that I can get Andrew back!" His voice broke as a sudden, violent rage shook him.

"He—he said he was Santomaro, the *bandido*, Coop—and there was another man with him—but—but I didn't recognize him—"

"Jorge Santomaro," John Cooper repeated to himself, his eyes narrowing with anger. "But this other man—you didn't recognize him, you say?" He turned to Leonora, who still held the cup of chocolate. "Did they hurt her? Tell me the truth, Leonora!"

"Truly, n—no, s—señor," Leonora quavered through her tears. "But the Señora Catarina is much better now—the *médico* came the very next evening."

"The doctor—those two men—did they—Catarina—" He could not say the rest; he could only stare at her with agony in his gaze and black fury in his heart.

Catarina slowly nodded, and then reached for him, locking her arms around his shoulders and burying her face against his chest. "But it doesn't matter," she sobbed, "it's over now; all I want is Andrew—Coop, Coop, please find him

for me, bring him back—they said I would never see him
again—"

"There, there, *mi corazón,* cry it all out, it is good for
you. There now, there now, Catarina. Leonora, Tía Margarita, take Catarina to Don Sancho de Pladero's *hacienda.*
There you will be safe while I'm away. I'm going to find our
son." At last, reluctantly, she released him and sank back
against her pillows, still weeping.

Straightening, he dug his fingernails into his palms almost to the blood. And he said in a shaking, hoarse voice, "I
was the one responsible for this. It wasn't Esteban. I was the
one who said you'd be safe because the *trabajadores* would
look after you. If I hadn't gone to help Kinotatay fight the
Mescalero, this wouldn't have happened." He turned to the
two women attending his wife, who stared at him and could
not control their sobbing, and he said softly, "Take care of
her, both of you. You won't see me again until I've brought
Andrew back. But first, I've got to find out where Santomaro
and this other man went. By now they're probably in Mexico,
and there's no way to find them without help."

As he walked out of the bedchamber, Catarina uttered a
sobbing cry. "Oh, Coop, they didn't say a word about where
they had come from or where they were going—*Dios,* how
can you find them and find little Andrew? Mexico is so vast,
they could lose themselves forever in it!"

"There's only one thing I can do, darling Catarina. I can
ask for God's help. Adiós, *mi corazón.*"

In the courtyard Kinotatay sat astride his horse, the five
braves drawn up behind him. Esteban Morales stood waiting,
and when John Cooper appeared he put out his hand and
stammered, "Let me go with you, let me help you find your
son, Señor John Cooper. Let me make up to you for failing
you. I beg of you, I could never be happy with my Concepción or my children again if I did not do something to help
you get your *niño* back."

"Yes, Esteban, I'll need help. It was Jorge Santomaro,
the bandit. We fought him and his men off, and we thought
that had been the last of him. He came with another man,
and they must have had others who took the baby away while
those two—" The young man could not finish. He dug his
fingernails into his palms.

Kinotatay gravely intervened: "Each of us has lost a
son, *Halcón.* But yours might still be alive. And if you had

not come to help us against the Mescalero, I would not be chief and perhaps these warriors who came with me and many others would have died at the hands of the Mescalero. I will ride with you, and so will my braves. We will help you track down the men who did this to your wife and took your son."

"Santomaro would have many men. They will have weapons. And there will be only eight of us, counting Esteban," John Cooper slowly said. "But somehow, with God's help, we'll track down those men and we'll bring Andrew back to my Catarina. Yes, and we'll take Lobo with us, too. He's a good tracker and a good hunter. And he can frighten many a man with a weapon in his hand—he'll add to our strength, Kinotatay."

He walked slowly to his palomino stallion, mounted it, and called to Esteban Morales, "Saddle yourself the fastest horse in the corral, Esteban. Go to the supply shed and bring along some muskets and pistols—yes, and there's another Belgian rifle we can use for *los indios*. Bring all the powder and shot you can find. Then we'll ride to Padre Moraga's church."

John Cooper entered the church alone and found Padre Moraga absorbed in his prayers. When the priest at last rose from the altar, John Cooper came to him and, kneeling down and crossing himself, quickly told him what had happened at the *hacienda*.

"Padre Moraga, Catarina told me that it was Santomaro the bandit. There was another man with him, and they both—they both abused her. But she didn't recognize the other man, Padre Moraga."

"My son, my son, how often the innocent are made to suffer by those who live with hatred instead of love in their hearts!" The old priest sighed. "But let me think now. In order to have come unobserved across the border and learned that you were absent from the *hacienda*, these wicked men must have had an accomplice, someone in Taos who would know your comings and goings and who himself would be as evil as they to aid them in stealing your child and profaning your beautiful wife."

"I've thought that, too, Padre Moraga."

The priest's face grew stern. "I know such a man in

Taos. And I think that tonight *los Penitentes* will visit him and force from his lips the truth. Perhaps these evil men told him where they came from in Mexico. At least, it is worth trying."

"Whom do you suspect, Padre Moraga? Who in Taos would want to help others hurt Catarina and steal our baby?" John Cooper's voice was strained with torment.

"Barnaba Canepa, my son. Ten years ago, I declared him excommunicate from Holy Church because of his blasphemies and his trade in idolatrous potions and necromancy. He cares more for gold than for his soul. Yes, my son, tonight *los Penitentes* will pay a visit to the shop of this ungodly man."

At midnight, a dozen black-robed, cowled figures moved slowly in the shadows at the back of the shop of Barnaba Canepa. Beyond them, the six Apache warriors waited, while John Cooper stood with Lobo beside him, the black raven perched on the wolf-dog's back and uttering soft chirping sounds in the stillness of the night.

One of the black-robed figures approached the rear door of the shop, pounded upon it with his fist, and loudly intoned, "Barnaba Canepa, come forth to meet your judges!"

Twice more he repeated this cry, until at last the glimmer of a lantern appeared, and the cackling voice of the old shopkeeper responded. "Why do you wake me, an old man who needs his sleep? Go away, I do no business at such a time!"

"Our business is that of the blessed Lord who has turned His face away from you, Barnaba Canepa," was the monk's answer. "We are *los Penitentes*, and we have come with charges against you which must be cleared."

"*Los Penitentes?* A moment, I will open the door for you." The shopkeeper's voice quavered with fear. The door was opened, and he stood on the threshold, holding up the lantern. When he saw the black-robed figures approach him, he cried, "But I have done nothing! Why do you come for me? I am an old man, I haven't long to live, do not hurt me—not the *crucifijo* and the *látigo!*"

"Ah, you know our ways, though Mother Church cast you away as a sinner long ago," the monk solemnly responded. "It is true. With us is the *sangrador*. If you are guilty of the crimes with which we charge you, Barnaba Canepa, we will take you out to the mountains, tie you to the cross, and scourge you until you repent your sins!"

"No, no, it would kill me—please—I have done nothing —don't whip me—what do you want of me?" the man whined, as he sank down on his knees, shrinking from the monk who bent toward him.

"Then speak, and do not lie, for God is your judge this night and we are His instruments. Was it you to whom the *bandido* Jorge Santomaro came to make inquiries about the *hacienda* of Don Diego de Escobar? And of the *gringo* who married his daughter, Catarina? Answer, Barnaba Canepa!"

"Yes, yes, it was he! But I meant no harm—"

"But by helping this outlaw and his evil accomplice, you caused great harm, Barnaba Canepa. The Señora Catarina was violated by those two brutes, and her baby stolen from her. And this Santomaro swore to her that she would not see the child ever again, though it would not be killed. Now then, if you wish to escape the cross and the lash, answer truthfully —who was that other man?"

"I will tell you, let me be—it was—it was José Ramirez! I swear it on my life!"

"Black-hearted wretch that he is—and his life was spared when once we punished him for poisoning the sheep of Don Sancho de Pladero," the monk declared. "But how is it that the Señor Catarina did not recognize him? Surely she had seen him at the *hacienda* of the de Pladeros?"

"It was because he had shaved off his mustache and dyed his hair—please—the night air is cold, and my bones are old and weary—"

"Not yet, Barnaba Canepa. If this child is not found and brought back to its mother and father, you will be as guilty as Santomaro and Ramirez in the eyes of our blessed Lord. Therefore, I charge you to tell me if you heard either of them say where they had come from to do this foul deed! Speak, or I shall turn you over to the *sangrador!*"

"No, not the *sangrador!* Wait—I am trying to remember —yes, now I know—he said that if anyone came after him, he would lose himself in the wilds along the coast of the Gulf of California."

"That would be in the province of Sonora. Is there anything more that you remember, blasphemer and idolator that you are? If you lie to us or hold back the truth, Barnaba

Canepa, God will judge you far more sternly than we of the Penitentes ever could—remember that, evil one!"

"I—I can't think of anything more—except that, since I knew both Jorge Santomaro and his brother, Manuel, it would be his way as a *bandido* to recruit men who would serve his purpose and then take over some little village and make it his headquarters. But that is all I know, I swear it—please, let me go back to my bed now—"

His interrogator turned to the others and there was a brief consultation. Then he turned back to the frightened old man and said solemnly, "Very well. For now, you may go back to sleep, Barnaba Canepa. The *esposo* of the Señora Catarina and his Apache brothers will go in search of Santomaro and Ramirez. But if they find that you have lied, and if the child dies, you will have much to answer for. Let your treachery occupy what dreams you have this night."

Barnaba Canepa uttered a cry of terror, and quickly slammed the door and bolted it. Extinguishing the lantern, he sank down on his knees, sobbing out his terror of the Penitentes.

Padre Moraga went back to John Cooper and told him what he had learned. Kinotatay had listened intently and, when the priest had finished, said excitedly, "In the days of this Santomaro's brother, some braves and I raided a Mexican village in Sonora. It was not far from these wilds which the old man spoke of. It is a place where such as he and his followers could easily hide. Soldiers do not go there, and because it is so poor, even the Apache no longer raid it."

"Can you take me to that place, Kinotatay?"

"Yes, *Halcón*. But it will be a long journey there."

"How long?" the young man feverishly demanded.

"Perhaps eleven or twelve suns, *Halcón*."

"I can't ask you, as chief, to leave your stronghold for so long. This is my fight, Kinotatay."

"No, *Halcón*, I would not have been chief except for you, and we should not have beaten the Mescalero without your help. And in our doing of this, these men stole your son and shamed your woman. I would not be a worthy *jefe* of the Jicarilla if I let you go alone. Now that the Mescalero are beaten back and will not try soon again to war upon us, the young ones who would make trouble at the council fire are silent. They will wait for their *jefe* to return, and we shall return together with the child—this I vow to the Great Spirit."

John Cooper's eyes were wet with tears as he gripped Kinotatay's hand.

Twenty-eight

The air was warm and sultry, even for this first week of December, as they skirted Santa Fe to the southwest, took the trail to the base of the Continental Divide, picked up provisions near Magdalena, and continued their relentless journey toward the edge of Lordsburg and then on into Mexico near Canánea. For much of the time, the six Apache braves, Esteban Morales, and John Cooper had ridden in dogged silence. And when they paused briefly to make a campfire and to share the evening meal, or to rest for a few hours before pursuing the trail which Kinotatay remembered from his raiding days, they rarely spoke of what it was that drove them onward. Kinotatay, mourning Pirontikay, impassively held his own grief within him. True to Apache custom, he did not again speak the name of his dead son. But John Cooper saw him, many a time before they sought their sleeping blankets, walk a distance away from the little camp and stand staring out at the darkened sky.

One of the five braves who rode with Kinotatay was Menogoches. He had followed the marks left by the horses ridden by the outlaws, and had seen the marks left by a single rider who had galloped to the southwest—that had been the *peón* who had taken little Andrew and gone on ahead to Santomaro's secret headquarters.

Esteban Morales, brooding over his own self-imposed guilt in the abduction of John Cooper's infant son, had at the outset of their long journey reaffirmed his vow to make up for his failure to defend the *hacienda*. But John Cooper had shaken his head and made a peremptory gesture, bidding him be silent; from that day forth, the young Mexican sheepherder had become as silent as the six Apache warriors.

323

Lobo savored this outing with his young master. He easily kept pace with the galloping horses, and the black raven often flew ahead of all of them, perching upon a cactus or a clump of mesquite or a scrub tree, cawing impatiently, as if to urge them to catch up with him.

Just outside Canánea, they had unexpected good luck. Menogoches, who had ridden ahead of them to scout the trail, wheeled his mustang and galloped back to them, his face aglow with excitement. "The tracks of four horses, to the southwest, in the sand. And the droppings of horses—not older than six or seven suns!" he reported.

Kinotatay turned to John Cooper. "Now I think we have come the right way. When the braves and I rode into this province, we raided a town called Altar. It is on the edge of a narrow river which winds to the great water, and beyond it is Pitiquito which was too poor to raid—yes, it comes back to me now. And beyond Pitiquito is wilderness where many men might hide from the *soldados*."

"Then we go to Altar," John Cooper declared. He was leaner now, and darkened by the sun. Fuego had shown heroic stamina. The horses ridden by the Apache and by Esteban Morales, although their riders had rested, grazed, and watered them as much as possible during each day, were showing signs of exhaustion. They had come four hundred fifty miles, and it was the twelfth day of their journey.

Kinotatay wheeled his mustang in the direction of Altar and said to John Cooper, "If this Ramirez has cut off his mustache and shortened his hair and dyed it, how will you recognize him?"

"Lobo will know him. Lobo and I found him when the Penitentes had tied him to the cross and flogged him for poisoning Don Sancho's lambs. I'll know him, too, by his squinting eyes, by his features, by his size."

Kinotatay nodded. "And your heart will tell you when you find this enemy, as my heart has told me many a time when I have met a man who has evil in him, *Bueno*. We ride to Altar."

José Ramirez had left the bandit headquarters that had once been the impoverished town of Pitiquito to visit a little *posada* in Altar. He was in rare good humor, for Santomaro had praised the alliance that had enabled the bandit chief to exact such a terrible vengeance against the *gringo* who had defeated him. The bandit had praised him before all the men of the band and then and there promoted him to *capitán*, second only to Santomaro himself.

Two days hence, the entire band would return to Taos, this time to strike at the *hacienda* of Don Sancho de Pladero, and Jorge Santomaro would avenge the hanging of his brother, Manuel. He personally had promised to kill the *alcalde* and to ravish his wife. And he, José Ramirez, had sworn to kill Tomás and then—yes, at last, he would bring back with him that tasty little *puta*, Conchita. How he would pay her back for having flouted him, for having preferred that young milksop to a man of his own exceptional virility!

Tonight Ramirez rushed to reward himself and celebrate. There was a *muchacha linda*, Rosa, who worked at the *posada* at Altar. She was buxom, not yet twenty, and she had no *novio*. The owner of the *posada*, her uncle, had brought her up when her parents had died from fever. And the young men of the village were all poor, humble *peones* who worked from dawn to sunset and could not afford a *mujer*. Tonight, he, José Ramirez, would take her for a little walk out near the edge of the river and give her a few silver *pesos* and promise to marry her—it would be very simple. She was really a stupid girl, but her body was almost as delightful as the Señora Catarina's. He grinned wolfishly, remembering his pleasure with that one. *Ayudame*, how he had glutted himself on that fine aristocratic flesh of hers, pinching and gouging, mouthing the foulest obscenities, but the bitch had turned her face away and closed her eyes and pretended that nothing was happening. Oh, yes, but she'd known what a man he was when she felt his *cojones!*

There was no need to disguise himself any longer. He had washed away the last traces of the dye, and he would let his mustache grow back in time. Besides, mustache or no mustache, Rosa had shyly smiled at him the last time he'd been to the *posada*. Yes, tonight would be a true celebration.

He swaggered into the little *posada*, seated himself at one of the two tables in the shabby little saloon, and in a loud voice called, "A bottle of your best tequila, Señor Caranza!"

As he had hoped, Rosa came out of the back room and, receiving her uncle's whispered order, promptly brought him the bottle and set a glass before him. As she bent to him, he could see her deep cleavage beneath the coarse cotton blouse she wore, and his eyes glowed. He put his hand to the pocket of his breeches and, with a lordly gesture, flung down five silver *pesos*.

"But, señor, it is only two *pesos* for the bottle," she timidly murmured.

"I know, little dove. The others are for you. That is because you are *muy linda*, and you smile at me."

"*Gracias, señor.*"

"Tonight, if there are no other customers, perhaps you would take a walk with me near the river? I have something to say to you, Rosa. And my name is José—that is what my friends call me. I'd like you to be my friend, too," he grinned at her.

Rosa blushed, glanced quickly back at her uncle, then nodded. "I'll see, Señor José. There will not be many customers tonight. My uncle will go to bed, and perhaps by midnight I could walk with you—but you will be very good, won't you? My uncle says it is time I found a husband."

"Well, my little dove, although I do not wish to say so romantic a thing in a place like this, I had something like that in mind. We will talk about it when we meet. I'll wait for you then, near the river at midnight?" He could scarcely conceal his excitement.

"*Sí*, S—Señor José." She blushed deeply, and hurried back to the counter of the bar.

José Ramirez had turned in his chair to admire the way her skirt swirled about her calves and thighs. He licked his lips, and he felt his manhood swell with lust. Tonight, indeed, would be one to remember. And this one wouldn't turn her face away or pretend he wasn't having her. Oh, no, not this stupid little girl with the superb *tetas* and the soft rosebud of a mouth and the shy, dark eyes!

He turned back to the bottle and poured himself a liberal portion, downed it almost with a single gulp, set the glass back down with a clatter on the table, and smacked his lips. *Ayudame*, it was good to be alive, to have one's strength and manhood, and best of all, to have had one's revenge—and more yet to come. Tonight he would pretend that Rosa was Conchita. And if the little *puta* enjoyed a real man as he suspected she would, he might teach her the pleasures of the whip. Indeed, several of the maids back at the de Pladero *hacienda*, once they had been broken in, had come to find excitement in a few lash marks on their skins—it made them the better in bed.

Rosa's middle-aged uncle nodded pleasantly at his solitary customer. "Everything is to your satisfaction, señor?" he politely asked.

"It could not be better, *hombre*. Business is slow, *¿no es verdad?* Well now, perhaps things will change for the better."

"I fear not," the owner of the *posada* sighed. "The people of Altar are poor, they buy the cheapest *pulque* and *aguardiente*, and not too often at that. Yes, I have thought of leaving Altar. Perhaps I will one of these days. And for my niece, you understand, there is not much future here. I wouldn't want to see her married to one of these *peones* and live in a dirty *jacal*."

"Of course not. She is a fine girl and does you credit. Well now, I'll just sit here and enjoy my tequila."

"As you wish, señor. I have something to do at the back of the *posada*. You will excuse me?"

"*Sí, seguramente.*" Ramirez lifted his glass in genial salute as the man disappeared.

Then he reached for the bottle and was about to pour himself another glassful, when suddenly he heard the door of the *posada* swing open. He turned and the bottle fell from his hand. John Cooper stood there in the doorway. Lobo at his side. And the wolf-dog bared his fangs and uttered a low, menacing growl.

"*¡Santísima María!*" José Ramirez crossed himself, his voice faint and choking. "It—it is you, *gringo*—"

"Yes, it's I. And you're Ramirez. Lobo recognizes you, *hombre,* and so do I."

José Ramirez forced a weak smile to his trembling lips while his right hand edged down toward the heavy leather belt of his breeches. He had a knife hidden there, and if he could get it and fling it, this apparition would vanish forever.

But John Cooper had anticipated such a move, and he swiftly drew the Spanish dagger which hung from his neck. "I wouldn't try it, Ramirez. Come outside. We've got something to talk about, you and I."

"I—I don't know what you mean, s—señor. As you see, I am down here in Sonora, making a new life and—"

"Come outside. Or should I set Lobo on you? I only have to say a certain word to him, and he'll go for your throat, Ramirez," John Cooper said coldly.

"But why are you so unfriendly señor? You were kind to me, you—you cut me down from that cross and told me to go to Mexico. Well, as you see, that is what I have done—"

"You'd better get up and come outside. Lobo doesn't like you, *hombre*. But before I kill you, I want to hear you confess the reason why, from your own dirty mouth. Now get up!"

"K—Kill me? But why—I have done you no harm—"

"You filthy, damned liar! If you'd rather have Lobo tear your throat out, I'll be glad to oblige you. Now do you get up, or do I say the word to Lobo?" John Cooper's face was twisted with fury.

Slowly, the former *capataz* rose from his chair, his legs unsteady. He lifted his hands in the air and again tried to force a wheedling smile to his sweating face. "There now, señor, I am doing what you want. Let's be reasonable. We can talk outside, ¿*no es verdad*? And then you'll see you have picked the wrong man—I have worked as a sheepherder down here and—"

"Get outside!" John Cooper's voice was sibilant with a rage he struggled to suppress.

Ramirez drew back as he neared the wolf-dog and his eyes, now glazed with terror, hideously fixed the contorted face of his opponent. "He—he'll tear me to pieces, Señor John Cooper! For the sake of the merciful Father of us all, don't let him bite me!"

"He won't attack until I give that word, Ramirez. Out with you!" John Cooper bent to stroke Lobo's head, murmuring, "No, Lobo. No, stay!" And as the former *capataz* sidled quickly by the shaggy beast, John Cooper turned and kicked him in the behind so violently that Ramirez was sent lunging toward the door, landing on the ground outside, sprawled on all fours and groaning with pain.

When he lifted his terror-stricken face, he uttered a strangled cry of horror: before him stood Kinotatay and the five braves, and Esteban Morales.

"No, for the love of God! No, not *los indios*," he panted.

"On your feet, Ramirez!" John Cooper directed him.

"Will my blood brother punish this man himself, or will the wolf-dog tear him to pieces?" Kinotatay gravely asked.

"Something like that. First, I want to hear what he's got to say about what happened back at the *hacienda*. Move on, Ramirez!"

"Let me speak, *Halcón*. Let us punish him the Apache way once he has confessed his evil," Kinotatay declared.

John Cooper clenched his fists, his face hardening. After a moment, he said hoarsely, "I know what you mean. I had a more merciful way—he'd prefer Lobo, I'd think. But let's first hear him talk. Keep moving, Ramirez, and no tricks!"

As he spoke, he reached for the Mexican's belt and plucked out the knife concealed beneath it. Then he shoved the man, who once again sank down on his knees and began to babble hysterically for mercy.

Kinotatay made a sign, and Menogoches and one of the other braves seized José Ramirez and dragged him to his feet, then marched him several hundred yards to the south of the little *posada*. Then they turned him to face Kinotatay and John Cooper, who advanced with Lobo beside him and, in a voice that shook with anger, said, "Padre Moraga sent *los Penitentes* to the shop of Barnaba Canepa, Ramirez. The old man told them that it was you and Santomaro who got him the *hacienda* and stole my son and forced my wife."

"No, no—"

"Lies won't help you now, Ramirez. We know it was you and Santomaro."

José Ramirez bowed his head and began to sob hysterically. "He—he made me do it—he said he'd kill me if I didn't help him—you have to believe me, Señor John Cooper—for the love of God, don't kill me!"

"Then you admit it was you who forced my wife? You who arranged with Santomaro to take away my son? Before you die, Ramirez, and the Apache have ways of making death very slow and painful, as you probably know, tell me where my son is."

"If I do, will you spare my life? I'll tell you anything you want—I swear I will—oh, for God's sake, don't let them touch me—not *los indios!* If—if you are going to kill me, let it be with a gun—please, I cannot stand pain—"

"You dirty yellow coward! I'll make no bargains with you. But Kinotatay and his men will torture you until they find out anyway, so if you can't stand pain, you'd best tell me now—where is my son?"

"He—he is with Santomaro. There is an old woman who is tending the brat—I mean—your—your son—they are at the village of Pitiquito. Santomaro raided it and took it over, you see—there, I have told you what you want to know— now please, don't let them torture me, please!"

"You heard, Kinotatay?"

"Yes. And I claim this man by Apache law. He has done great evil to my blood brother, and thus he has done it to me."

"Take him, then," John Cooper said in a toneless voice.

José Ramirez began to shriek as Menogoches and his companion dragged him on toward a low anthill. The three other braves began to dig a deep hole in the sandy soil near the river. When they had finished, they thrust the former *capataz* down into it up to his neck. Kinotatay knelt down and took his knife, and deftly cut away each of Ramirez's eyelids.

"Oh, no—not that—oh, *Dios, santísima María, Jesus, Cristo*—save me—not this way!" Ramirez's voice rose in an agonized, inhuman scream. He had seen the anthill.

"Menogoches," Kinotatay ordered, "go back into the *posada* and ask for a comb of honey. They will have one. Then you will smear it on this evil man's face and we shall wait for the ants."

"Oh, no—for the love of God in heaven—Señor John Cooper, I beg of you, kill me, kill me quickly—I can't bear this—oh, God, I didn't mean to—Santomaro made me—"

"I can't stop the Apache now, Ramirez. And don't forget, you had your second chance. You'd have done better that time if you had turned yourself over to the soldiers when I cut you loose from that cross of the Penitentes. Say your prayers and make your peace with God, if you can, *hombre*."

"Please, Señor John Cooper—oh, no, not the honey— aiiiii!" For Kinotatay had taken the comb of honey and begun to smear it on Ramirez's face and scalp and the bloody rims of his bulging, glazed eyes.

The ants did not wait till dawn. Attracted by the honey, crumbs of which the Apache chief dropped near the anthill in a trail that led toward the former *capataz*, they ventured out. Within half an hour, José Ramirez's face was covered with the red ants, and his cries became faint and delirious. The black raven, Fortuna, swooped overhead, his curiosity piqued by the fearful sounds that rent the silent night. Then, opening his beak and uttering a plaintive caw, he flapped his wings and turned northwestward. Already the Apache, John Cooper, and Esteban Morales had mounted their horses and were riding toward the bandit camp of Pitiquito, some eighteen miles distant.

There were no sentries at the outskirts of this humble village. The eight riders tethered their horses to scrub trees about half a mile from the village and stealthily crept toward the small adobe *jacales*. Kinotatay was armed with the Belgian rifle, his five braves with pistols, muskets, and their bows and arrows, and John Cooper with "Long Girl." Lobo trotted beside his master, and again Fortuna was perched on the wolf-dog's head.

Crouching silently, they moved into the village, and John Cooper stood before the largest *jacal*, certain that it would have been the one chosen by the bandit chief. "Jorge Santomaro, come out!" he called. "It is I, John Cooper, the *gringo!* Come out, unless you are a *cobarde* as well as a stealer of children and an abuser of helpless women!" He spoke in Spanish, using the most insulting terms to inflame his enemy.

There was a cry from a *jacal* across the way, as one of the bandits emerged, drowsy with sleep, his arm around a half-naked young Mexican woman. At the sight of the eight men, the wolf-dog and Fortuna, he uttered an oath and turned back to go into the hut for a weapon. One of the Apache braves, who had already notched an arrow, released his bow, and the bandit stumbled forward and sprawled on his face dead, his female companion screaming in terror.

"Jorge Santomaro, coward, murderer, come out! Your friend José Ramirez has already paid for his crimes—now it's your turn!" John Cooper cried out again.

Out of the doorway of the *jacal*, Santomaro emerged, clad in only his britches. In one hand, he held a half-empty bottle of tequila, in the other a pistol. At the sight of John Cooper and the others, he uttered a blasphemous oath, "*¡Por los ojos del diablo!* Have you come all this way to die, *señor gringo?*" With this, he raised his pistol and cocked it. But before he could fire, John Cooper had muttered the word, "*matar*," and Lobo had sprung at the bandit chief. With a cry of alarm, Santomaro stumbled back, the pistol exploding and the ball whistling harmlessly into the air above the eight men who confronted him. Lobo had seized him by the lower left thigh; and the bandit leader, his face contorted in agony, tried to grip Lobo's neck and force those terrible fangs from his bleeding flesh.

"Hold, Lobo, no!" John Cooper shouted. Reluctantly, with an angry snarl, Lobo backed away, still baring his bloody fangs. When Lobo had sprung at Santomaro, Fortuna had cawed noisily and flown to the top of the *jacal* to watch the scene.

"The men with me will kill anyone who comes out with a weapon, Santomaro," John Cooper declared. "I could kill you now—I could have let Lobo tear you to pieces. And for what you've done to my wife and for the taking of my son, Andrew, you've earned death. But I want to kill you myself. I'll fight you, Santomaro."

"Yes, and if I should kill you, *señor gringo*, then your *indios* would kill me." Santomaro uttered a mocking laugh, his bravado undiminished by the pain of the wound in his thigh.

"No, it will be a fair fight. But you won't kill me. I'll fight you any way you want, pistols, knives, fists—take your choice. But if you do kill me, my friends will see that my son is returned safely to his mother. That's the only condition I've set for you, Santomaro."

"You have courage, *gringo*. Very well. It will be with knives. I will ask you one question only—how did you find me here in Sonora? I know that *los indios* are good trackers and scouts, but Mexico is vast."

"You're forgetting Ramirez's friend, Barnaba Canepa. He told us what we had to know."

"The meddling fool—I should have cut his throat," Santomaro muttered with an evil grin. "But what is done is done, *¿no es verdad, señor gringo?* I'll get my knife and be ready for you."

"See that that's all you bring out with you, Santomaro, or I'll tell Lobo to go for you again," John Cooper warned.

"Have no fear, *gringo*. In all Mexico, there is no better man with a knife than Jorge Santomaro. But then, I can understand you. And I may as well kill you so that you won't fret too much about how I enjoyed your *mujer linda*, the Señora Catarina."

"You bastard, get that knife and get out here fast!" John Cooper's voice was choked with rage.

"At your orders, *señor gringo*." The bandit chief gave him a mocking bow, then disappeared into the *jacal*. A moment later, he emerged with a sharp-bladed knife with a broad bone handle. It was longer than the Spanish dagger, with a wider blade and a curving point. "Do you see the notches on the handle of this knife, *señor gringo?*" Jorge Santomaro taunted. "There are twelve of them. You will be the thirteenth—an unlucky number, particularly for you. Well now, where shall we fight?"

Before John Cooper could answer, there was the sound of a pistol shot—one of the Apache, perceiving a bandit coming out of one of the smaller huts with a musket in his hand, had fired and killed the man. "You'd best tell your men to stay where they are, Santomaro," John Cooper advised. "For certain you outnumber us, but we've got the drop on you. And I've challenged you and called you a coward to your face—which you are. I don't want any interference, just the two of us to ourselves, settling this for once and for all. Let's go out into the clearing. There's a fair moon, and I want to see you. I want to see that ugly face of yours when I kill you for what you did to my wife and child."

"You will be sure to call off that wolf of yours, I trust, *señor gringo?* He has already given you a little advantage, you see, because of my leg. But it won't keep me from cutting out your tripes. And when I do, you can remember as you die that I had great pleasure with the Señora Catarina."

John Cooper ground his teeth and stiffened, his face dark with rage at this obscene taunt. Yet he knew its purpose: Santomaro wished to provoke him into such blind fury that he would be reckless in the duel. And so he only shrugged and said coldly, "My friends will stay here to keep your men safe and sound in their *jacales*. I've got no score to settle with them, only with you. Go ahead of me now. And I promise you, Lobo won't bite you again."

"In that case, I am entirely at your disposal, *señor gringo*." Santomaro grinned. With an insolent swagger, not altogether successful because his wounded leg was paining him, he walked to the clearing. Then he whirled, crouching, gripping the curved knife by the handle and pointing it upward as he bared his teeth. "Come then, *gringo*. First I kissed your woman, and now I will kiss you with my steel! Soon I will have to cut another notch on the handle of this knife. Come then, *gringo*, why do you wait? Are you suddenly afraid?"

John Cooper uttered a dry, humorless laugh and crouched, the Spanish dagger held out before him as he warily circled his adversary.

Esteban Morales had delegated himself as spokesman, and now moved down the rows of *jacales*, calling out to the bandits to stay inside if they did not wish to be shot down in their tracks the moment they showed their faces. Kinotatay and his five braves trained their bows and arrows, muskets and pistols on the openings of the huts. All the same, some of the bandits peered from the openings of their *jacales*, curious to see what would take place.

As John Cooper approached the bandit leader, Esteban Morales called to him, "Señor John Cooper, I'll turn loose the horses in their corral! I'll just keep some fresh ones for the Apache and myself—then they won't be able to come after us!"

"That's good thinking, Esteban. *Gracias, amigo.* Just you and my friends there make sure nobody interferes with what I've got to do," John Cooper called back. Then, he turned quickly to Lobo and commanded, "Stay, Lobo! Stay, be good!"

In that moment, Jorge Santomaro seized his chance and lunged at the young man with his knife thrust upward, seeking a fatal belly stab.

Instinct alone made John Cooper twist himself away to one side, and into his mind there flashed the remembrance of how he had nearly been gored by a wild boar soon after his flight from Shawneetown; how he had said aloud, "Pa, I had that coming, just being stupid and forgetting what you taught me about tracking."

Santomaro's lunge and John Cooper's instinctive evasion had made the bandit stumble forward, almost jostling Lobo, who snarled wickedly and bared his fangs. "No, stay!" John Cooper shouted. Then, in a voice that shook with his long-held anger, *"Hombre,* you'd best not try a trick like that again. Now fight, you yellow-livered skunk!"

His words stung Santomaro with fury, and again the

bandit chief lunged at him with a violent oath. Once more, John Cooper leaped out of the way and, with a short jab, drew blood from Santomaro's left shoulder, then leaped back as the outlaw tried to counter with a vicious sideways sweep.

Panting, snarling, Santomaro crouched low, pausing to gain his wind and to appraise his wily adversary. Suddenly his booted right foot shot out, scuffing up sandy dirt at John Cooper's face. At the same time, with a bellow of rage, he charged, jerking the knife upward toward John Cooper's belly. But once again, the young mountain man had anticipated, and his right foot flashed upward to kick the side of the blade and avert it from him; at the same instant, lunging from his left, he buried the Spanish dagger to the hilt in Jorge Santomaro's heart, then drew it out and leaped back.

The outlaw's face was a mask of horrified surprise. His eyes rolled to the whites, his lips opened as if to speak, and then he crumpled to the ground.

John Cooper bent and wiped the bloody dagger on the dead man's breeches, then sheathed it and walked slowly back to where Kinotatay, the five braves, and Esteban Morales waited. "He's done for. Now we've got to find Andrew. Ramirez said there was an old woman taking care of my son—we'll have to search the *jacales*."

"*¡Bueno!* I have turned loose all but ten horses, Señor John Cooper," Esteban told him. "When we leave, I'll take the saddles off the ones we rode in and then turn them loose, too, so the *bandidos* won't get them. Look—one of the *bandidos* is coming out of his hut with his hands in the air—come here, *hombre, pronto!*" he suddenly called.

A squat, middle-aged *peón*, one of the villagers of Pitiquito who had enlisted in Jorge Santomaro's villainous band to save his own life, approached the eight men, a pleading look on his bearded face, "Señores, is the *jefe* truly dead?"

"He is, *hombre*," Esteban assured him. "Where is the *niño gringo* whom the *jefe* had brought to this village?"

"*Sí, comprendo*—he is in the hut of Abuela Marta," the *peón* eagerly offered. "I will take you to her. You understand, *hombre*, I did not wish to be a *bandido*, but that one, that Santomaro, he put a knife to my throat and said that I must join or else die. What would you, señores? My wife is dead, and I have no children, but life is precious."

"Very precious," John Cooper echoed softly, as he felt

his eyes moisten with tears. "It's my son, *hombre*. Take me to my son. And you may ride back with us on one of the spare horses. I can use a good *trabajador* at my new *hacienda*."

"Oh, may the saints bless you señor!" the *peón* exclaimed. "The *jacal* is at the very end of our little village. There, I will waken her—"

He entered the *jacal* and called in a loud voice, "Abuela Marta, Abuela Marta, *¡venga usted aquí pronto!* Bring the *niño* with you, the *jefe* orders it!"

A few minutes later, a white-haired old woman, her face angry at being wakened from sound sleep, came out of the *jacal* with little Andrew in her arms. The *peón* swiftly explained to her in Spanish that this was the child of the *gringo,* stolen by the cruel *jefe,* Jorge Santomaro, who was dead.

The old woman stared in wonderment at the buckskin-clad young man, and then nodded and put the child into John Cooper's arms.

"Thank You, God, thank You!" John Cooper fervently murmured, as he looked up at the dark sky. "Andrew, it's time you got back home to your mother. It's time I did, too." Holding the baby to him in his left arm, he plunged his right hand into the pocket of his britches, drew out some silver *pesos,* and handed them to the old woman. "*Gracias,* Abuela Marta. *¡Adiós!*"

Then he said to the *peón,* "Ride with us, *hombre*. You'll go to Texas with us."

"My name is Pedro Arribas, *servidor de usted, señor!*" the *peón* proudly declared.

"And *gracias* again, Pedro Arribas." John Cooper stared tenderly down at Andrew and blinked his eyes to clear them of the tears. "Well, youngster, your daddy's going to have a birthday next week, and you're the best birthday present he could ever have. Now let's get back home quick as we can to your mama."

Twenty-nine

The sun was bright, and the air warm on the day before Christmas in the fertile Texas valley west-southwest from San Antonio. The *trabajadores* had almost completed the sprawling frame house which would quarter the de Escobars and, one day soon, John Cooper and his Catarina and little Andrew.

Miguel Sandarbal, devoted to his young wife, Bess, seemed to have a new lease on life. He had shown much alacrity and enthusiasm, working side by side with the younger men, hauling the hewn timbers and setting them into place, showing all his men by his own example how eager he was to build this new home for the de Escobars. He had done most of the work himself on the large adobe *jacal* which he shared with Bess.

And if, this Christmas eve, he seemed more radiant and jovial than ever before in his life, there was a good reason. As Bess had served him his breakfast early that morning, she had blushingly murmured, "Dearest Miguel, I want you to know how happy you've made me. At first, I'll confess, it was gratitude I felt for you—but now I know how much I love you—" She turned away for a moment to pour out his coffee, took a deep breath, and then hesitantly confided, "And—and —I—I'm going to have your child, Miguel."

He started back in his chair and then, with a boyish whoop, sprang up and clasped her in his arms. "Bess—oh, *querida*, I am beside myself with joy—what a Christmas present!" He took her hand and kissed it as ceremoniously as he would that of a queen. "Heart of my heart, joy of my soul, tonight you and I will pray in the chapel which will be finished in time—I shall see to it myself!—and there I will

337

thank the good *Señor Dios* for you and the little one and the wonderful life He has been kind enough to give ugly old stupid Miguel Sandarbal—"

"Hush, my husband," she murmured, putting her palm over his mouth. "You're none of those things. You're kind, good, gentle—and my love. And now, if you please, sit down and finish your breakfast."

And that evening, Don Diego and his wife, Carlos and Weesayo, and Miguel and Bess knelt side by side in the little chapel. There were *retablos* of the Holy Mother with Child, the wise men coming to the stable, and the angels telling the shepherds of the blessed birth of the Christ Child.

"To Thee, most merciful God, I give humble thanks for Thy manifold blessings," Don Diego said, his voice choked with emotion as he glanced toward Doña Inez and observed how his handsome son, Carlos, held Weesayo's hand in both of his. "Bless our new *hacienda,* and all of us who come before Thee to celebrate this holy day of the birth of Thine only Son. Bless our loyal *trabajadores* and their families who followed us without concern for the dangers of this new land. And the brave *indios* who guarded us from harm till we could reach this our new home."

"Amen," Carlos and Miguel murmured in unison, as did Weesayo, Doña Inez, and Bess.

"And I pray to Thee to bring my beloved daughter Catarina and her brave *esposo,* the Señor John Cooper Baines, and their son—my grandson, Andrew—safely to this new home, where, may it be Thy will, we shall begin our new lives in peace and in love." He crossed himself reverently.

On the day before Christmas, John Cooper rode into Taos with Esteban Morales and the six Apaches and Pedro Arribas following him. Even with the child, they made the return trip in good time, for Andrew seemed to thrive on the arduous journey.

John Cooper carefully dismounted from Fuego, and turned to his loyal companions. "I'll just be a minute, I want to see Padre Moraga."

Kinotatay nodded and watched the young mountain man enter the church. Then he said softly to Esteban Morales, "It was my prayer to the Great Spirit that, when *El Halcón* goes to his new *hacienda,* he will not forget his blood brother and his friends in the mountains. It will be a long journey, and he goes into land where the Jicarilla Apache have not ventured. But it is my hope that he will not forget us, and that one day he will come to visit us and tell us of the new *hacienda* and the freedom he will find there."

"He will not forget you, Kinotatay. He is the finest man I have ever known," Esteban Morales said in Spanish, and the new Jicarilla chief solemnly nodded agreement.

Inside the church, John Cooper, holding little Andrew against his heart, knelt to pray, his lips moving in silent thanksgiving to the just and merciful God who had restored the child to Catarina and to him. Padre Moraga came out of the rectory and uttered a joyous cry, "My son, my son, God has answered my prayers!"

"And mine, too, Padre Moraga. He's safe and sound, and the long trip back didn't seem to tire him one bit. Catarina's given me a wonderful boy, Padre Moraga."

"Yes, my son. And now you will leave with the others to go to your new *hacienda* in Texas?"

"I mean to, Padre. By now, the Apache who rode with Don Diego and Doña Inez and Carlos and the others must have returned to tell them that the new place is ready for us. But I wanted to see you before I left, to talk to you about the treasure."

"Yes. The secret is safe with me—what you have told me of it I keep in the strictest confidence, as is my duty as your priest, John Cooper."

"I know, Padre Moraga. There aren't any signs now of the people who used to guard that cave in the far off mountain. And the Indians won't go there, because of their superstitions. On my way to Texas, I'll take a little more silver, just to have on hand for supplies, to pay the *trabajadores*, and to make things comfortable for all the people I love and the workers and their families, too. But the rest of it will stay there. Maybe by next Christmas we will be able to do a lot to help the poor, to help your church, and maybe to buy the freedom of the *peones*."

"God will bless you for your intentions, my son. Such treasure in the hands of a greedy man could be a power for evil. You are not tempted by it. Yet you do well to guard the secret carefully so that others will not shed innocent blood to take it from you. I will give you my blessing, and I will bless Andrew. Before you leave Taos, John Cooper, bring your lovely Catarina to me. We shall pray together for the life I know He will see fit to bestow upon all of you."

"Yes, I want to do that, Padre Moraga." John Cooper bowed his head as the priest intoned a blessing and made the sign of the cross. He bent his frail body to trace that sign with his forefinger on the forehead of the mountain man's little son.

"Oh, Coop, my beloved Coop, *mi corazón*, what a wonderful Christmas this is to have you and Andrew safely back!" Catarina joyously exclaimed, as she cradled little Andrew in her arms. She, along with Tía Margarita and Leonora, had returned to the *hacienda* with her husband after staying at the de Pladeros for the past few weeks. Three days before, one of the Apache had ridden into Taos to bring the news that the *hacienda* was completed and waiting.

"And you're well, my dearest Catarina, my love?" he asked.

"Oh, yes. It is as if it never happened."

John Cooper looked quizzically at his young wife, and there was a determination—even a fierceness—in her eyes.

"You see," Catarina went on, "I prayed. I prayed when those wicked men assaulted me, and I continue to pray. As long as I am thinking of God, nothing bad can happen—and nothing can spoil our love. Only—" she blushed and turned shyly away, "you will not think less of me because—because it happened and I could not stop them?"

"My God, Catarina, I'd never think a thing like that," John Cooper exclaimed, his look also fierce and determined. "Those men paid for what they did. We'll forget them, we'll forget everything except that we're together again, and that we're going to start our new life very soon. After the celebration of the New Year, Catarina, now that Esteban tells me that the *trabajadores* have finished all the *carretas* and packed everything in readiness, we'll begin our journey to our new home."

"Our new home," she softly repeated, her green eyes shining with love as she leaned over to kiss him.

"Yes, a home where there'll be freedom for all. A home where the hawk need never be caged, because he'll be free. In Texas, Catarina, only your little Pepito will have his cage, but all the rest of us will be free to live and to do as we choose."

★ WAGONS WEST ★

A series of unforgettable books that trace the lives of a dauntless band of pioneering men, women, and children as they brave the hazards of an untamed land in their trek across America. This legendary caravan of people forge a new link in the wilderness. They are Americans from the North and the South, alongside immigrants, Blacks, and Indians, who wage fierce daily battles for survival on this uncompromising journey—each to their private destinies as they fulfill their greatest dreams.